...into locked rooms where politicians traded the Alaskan environment for a six-figure campaign contribution

...into the communes of the radical left, where extremists plot the pipeline's destruction

...into the Eskimo villages where the ravages of the white man's whiskey and the squalor of poverty take their toll

...into the yearning desires of the men and women who seek warmth and love amidst a frigid world of ruthless ambition

...PIPELINE...THE NOVEL THAT RIPS THE LID OFF THE GREAT "OIL SHORTAGE" HOAX!

ADVENTURE!
DRAMA!
PASSION!

Only once in a generation is there a novel like PIPE-LINE — or a scandal as enormous as the one it portrays.

Across Alaska the pipeline stretches—built with human greed, determination, and corruption—built by ruthless oil spectulators who will stop at nothing to rip the treasure of "black gold" from the rugged, beautiful Alaskan terrain.

PIPELINE is the explosive saga of building and destruction, of corruption and violence, that irresistibly sweeps the reader along with its stunning narrative power.

... into locked rooms where politicians trade the Alaskan environment for a six-figure campaign contribution

... into the communes of the radical left, where extremists plot the pipeline's destruction

... into the Eskimo villages where the ravages of the white man's whiskey and the squalor of poverty take their toll

... into the yearning desires of the men and women who seek warmth and love admidst a frigid world of ruthless ambition

THE NOVEL THAT RIPS THE LID OFF
THE GREAT "OIL SHORTAGE"
HOAX ...
PIPELINE

PIPE LINE

A Novel by MILT MACHLIN

PYRAMID BOOKS   ▲   NEW YORK

PIPELINE

A PYRAMID BOOK

Pyramid edition published November 1976

Library of Congress Catalog Card Number: 76-46183

Printed in the United States of America

Pyramid Books are published by Pyramid Publications (Harcourt
Brace Jovanovich, Inc.). Its trademarks, consisting of the word
"Pyramid" and the portrayal of a pyramid, are registered in the
United States Patent Office.

Pyramid Publications
(Harcourt Brace Jovanovich, Inc.)
757 Third Avenue, New York, N.Y. 10017

ACKNOWLEDGMENTS

The author wishes to thank the following publishers for permission to quote from the sources listed:

Audubon, The Magazine of the National Audubon Society, for "The Age of The Oil Berg" by Nöel Mostert, May 1975 issue Copyright © 1975. Reprinted by permission.

Harper's Magazine Press for *Dirty Business* by Ovid Demaris. Copyright © 1974 by Ovid Demaris. Reprinted by permission.

Alfred A. Knopf, Inc. for *Supership* by Nöel Mostert. Copyright © 1974 by Nöel Mostert. Reprinted by permission of Alfred A. Knopf, Inc.

New York Magazine for "War, the Ultimate Anti-Trust Action" by Andrew Tobias, October 14, 1974 issue. Copyright © 1974 by the NYM Corp. Reprinted with the permission of *New York* Magazine.

The New York Times for "Blood, Toil, Tears, and Oil" by Winthrop Griffith, July 27, 1975 issue. Copyright © 1975 by the New York Times Company. Reprinted by permission.

"To the Alaskan Native, the land is their life; to the State of Alaska, it is a commodity to be bought and sold. Alaskan Native families depend on the land and its waters for the food they eat—hunting and fishing as they have for thousands of years. Often a thousand acres are required to support one person. In some regions a village of two hundred people may require as much as six-hundred thousand acres."

—*Native Alaska: Deadline for Justice*

Chapter One

Prudhoe Bay, Alaska—March, 1968

Takolik, wearing his surplus National Guard parka, huddled close to the idling motor of his Ski-Doo, like a bear cub seeking warmth against its mother's body. It was mid-March but the temperature was still thirty degrees below zero. The ice leads, which would have made the tracking and capture of the seals possible, had not developed.

The flat, barren land was in a white-out condition. Swirling ice crystals made it impossible to separate the horizon from the shore. Except for the force of gravity, there was no way to distinguish up from down.

White-out had set in just after Takolik had seen The-Man-Who-Hides for the second time that afternoon— a man alone in the snow, cross-legged, with caribou horns growing from his head. It seemed to Takolik that the man was beckoning to him, and he stepped forward eagerly. There was a question still unformed in his mind, yet he knew there was something he had to ask the man. But then the figure disappeared behind the crest of an ice pressure ridge, and when Takolik topped the ridge he was gone and there was nothing but the vast flatness of the North Slope. Where the man had been there were vague depressions, as though of footprints, but they were quickly swept away by the wind, leaving only the smooth, perfectly white surface of the snow.

Takolik was hunting with the 1917 Springfield .30-06, which had been issued to some members of the Alaska Territorial Guard. It had been given to him by his father, who had begun to drink so much in recent years that he seldom went hunting anymore.

Takolik was particularly disturbed that the windstorm should come at that time because just before the white-out occurred, while he was looking for the tracks of The-Man-Who-Hides, he had found several large, clear polar bear paw prints. They were thin and high-arched —the bear was hungry after his long winter's rest. If the wind and snow had not come, Takolik could easily have caught up with the wandering bear and shot him. The skin, at fifteen dollars a foot, might bring a hundred to two hundred and fifty dollars at the store in the village. If he took it to the white men at the DEW line posts he could get three or four hundred dollars for it—cash he could well use in the months to come.

Officially the Inupiat—people of the North Slope —had been limited to a take of three hundred bears a year. Two hundred and twenty-five of these were to be taken by the white hunters—who came and chased the bears down with planes, then left the meat on the ice while people went hungry in the villages. Only seventy-five polar bears were allotted to the Eskimos. Nobody paid much attention to those rules, as there was only one law officer in the millions of acres of the North Slope.

Now, squatting against the gently throbbing iron monster that had brought him so far from the village, Takolik was waiting in hope that the storm would not last too long. He had packed two five-gallon Jerry-

8

cans of gasoline on the sled he trailed behind the Ski-Doo. The extra gas would have taken him much farther than he had any need to go, but when bad weather came it was necessary to keep the motor of the Ski-Doo running so that it would not freeze up. The wind would wipe out the bear's tracks, and the animal would probably dig into the snow to wait out the storm. Of course, if it was hungry—and bears at this time of the year usually were since they had been unable to catch seals during the long period when the sea was frozen—it might catch Takolik's scent and begin hunting *him*.

In the white man's world, Takolik was known as John Takolik. His father, Oquilluk, had been an "ice expert" with a Point Hope whaling crew. People said he could have been a captain. Oquilluk had an uncanny gift for predicting the weather. His word on storm and ice conditions and sea currents was believed over that of the broadcasts by the U.S. Meteorological service. It was said that he had the gift and balance to walk on thin ice where lighter men would crack it and fall through.

On the day John was born, his mother was traveling by skin boat from Jabbertown to Point Hope. The hunter's *umiat* was driven by a small, five-horse-power Evinrude motor, a pre-World War Two model. His mother, Pelowook, feeling the rhythmic pains of labor, had asked the men in the boat to stop and put her ashore to "go to the toilet." As soon as she was landed, a sudden gust of wind blew the *umiat* into the ice lead, and now, of all times, the motor sputtered and died.

Pelowook was not watching the boat. She had four children and knew what was involved. But each of them had died. Three had been born dead, and one of them had died at the age of two from influenza—one of the gifts brought to the Arctic by white "civilization," along with gonnorhea, alcoholism, and Christianity.

9

The midwife had felt Pelowook's belly only a month before, however, and had told her that this birth would go well. Now Pelowook squatted confidently in a pile of soft snow. She had taken off her outer parka and placed it under her to receive the newborn child. Its arrival was as neat and painless as a healthy evacuation. Holding the black-haired, squalling infant to her breast, Pelowook put on her parka and adjusted it so that it covered the child.

Then, using the cleaning knife she carried with her, she reached up and cut the umbilical cord. She tied it off with fishline, then scraped snow over the afterbirth until it stopped staining. Holding the baby under the parka, she ran up the beach to follow the drifting boat. The men finally solved the problem with the motor and the *umiat* put in to shore and picked up the two passengers without comment.

As the boat drifted off into the lead, gradually gaining control over the ocean current, Pelowook looked back to see a pack of white foxes sniffing and digging at the place where she had buried the afterbirth. The people in the village said this was why Takolik had grown up to be a strange and solitary creature who, even as a boy, would often disappear with his dog team into the tundra for days at a time, returning with no explanation. Older villagers looked at him in a bemused fashion, but always treated him with respect. They were convinced that Takolik was destined to become a shaman.

It had been more than a hundred years since the village had discarded the powers of the shamans and yielded to the greater magic of Christ, as represented by the Presbyterian Church. But there were still those who felt that this was a mistake. There were special qualities that indicated a man who would become a shaman—a quiet, somewhat sensitive man, a man who was creative,

10

who developed outside of the common horde. He would be a man of sudden flarings of moods—anger to sorrow to tenderness. He seemed always to be in some delicate emotional balance. Not infrequently he had some physical handicap—a bump, a clubfoot, a shriveled arm, a birthmark.

Some older men argued that Takolik, who was tall for an Eskimo, stocky, well-built and immensely strong, did not have the delicate physique of a shaman. But others pointed out that he must have suffered some psychic damage when the white foxes ate the placenta of his mother.

One thing prevented Takolik from being trained as a shaman. The last of the old magic men had disappeared from the village, driven out by Father McKenzie, the Presbyterian missionary. Father McKenzie was a strict moralist and could not abide the fact that the shaman's usual fee for curing an illness or exorcising an evil spirit was to spend a night with the wife of the man he had helped.

Oquilluk, and all the men of his generation, believed deeply in the powers of the shaman—that he could fly at will to all parts of the earth, even to the moon; that he could make himself so tiny that he could crawl through chinks in a hut or through a keyhole; that he could turn himself into a polar bear or a snow hare or a lemming; that he had a hole in his body that he could move about so that if you tried to pierce him with a harpoon or a bullet, the hole would magically appear and the weapon or projectile would pass harmlessly through his body.

Oquilluk and his friends swore that they had seen a shaman perform these miracles. While they admired his powers, they also feared him, for a displeased shaman could invoke disease, famine, death, or bad luck in hunting on a village. So they were content that he

11

lived away from the village. They sought him out only when they needed his help to heal the sick or to find somebody who had been lost on the ice and snow.

Sometimes they would ask him to tell them about the future, or even about events that had happened in the past, because the shaman could see past and future events by peering into the bottom of a bucket of water. Years later, Oquilluk laughingly referred to this as *Eskimo television*—but that was after the shaman had walked off into the snow and was seen no more. Father McKenzie was pleased. But the Inupiat knew that if a shaman dies he will arise again in three or four days. If a shaman walks off onto the snow, he is still alive somewhere, perhaps wandering around the drifts in another form—a snow owl, or an Arctic wolf.

When Takolik was twelve, he was sent off to the Bureau of Indian Affairs School at Wrangell. It was the first time he had been away from home, except for his solitary expeditions on the tundra of the North Slope. To get to the school he had to take a long airplane ride, changing planes at Fairbanks and Anchorage. Each time he changed planes, children from other parts of Alaska were added to the group. There were southern Eskimos—Aleuts and Athabascan indians—as well as Inupiat from other parts of the North Slope. And from the south came Yupik, Tlingit, and Haida Indians. There were only a handful of people from Takolik's village near Point Hope, but they stuck together and had to prove their independence by fighting the Indians and Aleuts from the south and even Inupiat from Barrow, Kotzebue, and other large villages.

The only person in the school for whom Takolik felt any affection was Irene Dodge, who taught art and science. It was 1957; the Russians had jarred America to its complacent scientific roots by putting Sputnik, the first earth satellite, into space. The Aleuts, in par-

12

ticular, took a perverse pride in emphasizing their Russian heritage, claiming some remote credit for the accomplishment. A small group of them from Little Diomede Island enjoyed pointing out that they lived only three miles from Mother Russia and that all of them had attended the Russian Orthodox Church. There was a lot of discussion about whether the Russians or the Americans would land men on the moon first, but all this talk seemed foolish to Takolik.

That night he worked hard on an art project for Miss Dodge's class the following day. It was a large painting entitled "The Eskimo Who Went to the Moon," but Miss Dodge found its contents puzzling. In the center sat a thin man, painted in pale colors but with the round face of an Eskimo. He was bearded and had heavy eyebrows; his close-set eyes seemed fixed in space, as though he were in a trance. Around one arm was a narrow thong. His neck was enclosed in a dog-collar-like arrangement from which dangled bear claws, animal teeth, and other amulets. In the background, to the left, was a drying rack with some headless fish hanging from it. A grinning human skull topped one of the wooden poles of which the rack was made. On the ground, at the man's feet, was a wooden cross. The sky above was quiet, but there are long straggling clouds of the sort the Eskimos know signal the arrival of high winds.

Miss Dodge spread the rolled-out piece of artwork before her and stared at it with a perplexed frown.

"I don't understand how this man could go to the moon. Who is he? An Eskimo? Someone you know?"

Takolik smiled a vague, distant smile. "No, he isn't anybody I know. He's just somebody I heard about; somebody they talk about in the village."

"But the skull, those amulets—do they have some special meaning?"

Takolik hesitated. In recent years he had developed

13

a disturbing stammer. Now the words didn't want to come. "He . . . he . . . he . . . is like . . . a man—not a man . . ." Then his lips seemed to press compulsively together and the words wouldn't come. In sudden haste he took back the painting, rolled it into a tight wand and went off down the school corridor, leaving Miss Dodge to unravel the meaning of this strange artwork.

It wasn't that he didn't want to explain things to Miss Dodge. It was simply that he saw things so differently he was sure she would not understand. This was a white man's school which told everything from the point of view of the outsiders.

History books told about what a marvellous purchase "Seward's Folly" was, how profitable it had turned out to be. Profitable to whom, Takolik wondered? Millions of dollars had been earned in gold, whale blubber, and furs, and still the Eskimo was poor. Poorer in many ways than before the whites came.

When he read the history of the West he began to see that the Indians (whom he had been raised to regard as outsiders, as dangerous and alien as the whites) had problems that were similar to those of his people. They too had their land, their way of life, even their magic, taken away by white invaders. Takolik always got low grades in history because he refused to answer questions the way the white teachers wanted, and continued to see things as they looked to people in the village. What was colonization, except another word for theft, Takolik wondered?

At the University of Alaska, where he was sent after the BIA school despite his erratic grades, because Miss Dodge saw some special intelligence and quality in his thinking—even with its unconventional presentation—Takolik still had trouble accepting what was presented to him. It too was a white man's place dealing with white men's problems. The only way a college educa-

14

tion could be of any use to Takolik was if he accepted the white man's way of life, moved to the city, and became one of *them*.

Nonetheless college wasn't entirely useless to Takolik. He became friendlier with Isaac "Ike" Samuelson a young Eskimo he had met at Wrangell. Together they explored anthropological books and discussed the impact of alien cultures on what the whites tended to call "primitive" societies. They began to meet with Athabascans, Aleuts, Tlingits and other native people and realize that they had many problems in common.

Takolik enrolled in a local branch of the American Indian Movement (AIM), and spent long hours in coffee sessions trying to understand how the new white radical groups such as the S.D.S. could relate to the problems of the Eskimos.

After a year and a half at the University of Alaska, Takolik quit to take a course offered to Eskimos by RCA. It was the white Company's way of training cheap labor that would be willing to work in the Distant Early Warning bases in the Arctic and on NASA projects in the North for which RCA had recently been awarded major contracts. The program was less than a success and failed in its second year.

But Takolik learned a great deal during his months in the course that had nothing to do with electronics. The company shipped his group to Jersey City, New Jersey for part of their courses. To avoid friction in white neighborhoods, RCA housed the Eskimos in black slum tenements. It was here Takolik learned about cockroaches, marijuana roaches, rats, cheap wine and blue ointment. He also learned about dignity—about what it was like to lose belief in yourself and your people—almost. It took a while before Takolik realized that the other students—the whites—didn't live in the Jersey City slums, only the Eskimos. It just confirmed Takolik's growing feeling that he could never live by the white man's rules. Half-way through the course he quit and went back to his village.

Now, ten years later, Takolik sat wondering whether the bear would find him, and whether he would see it in time to kill it with the .30-06 before it killed him. It was almost three in the afternoon and at that hour, in March, darkness came quickly. After an hour the wind died down and, as the swirling ice crystals settled, Takolik could again distinguish the horizon. On it he could see at a distance which might have been as much as ten miles, the bright blue and green lights of the Alamo Oil Company drilling tower. It took no mystic powers to know that the oil men were coming again. Already a series of oil companies had dragged their gear across the tundra, drilling holes and leaving tracks in the permafrost as they searched for the ancient energy-giving fluid.

British Petroleum, Atlantic Richfield, and many others had come, spent months digging expensive wells in the ground. According to the newspapers, each of the wells had cost nearly five million dollars. Even though Takolik's people had found oil seeping from the ground in abundance for thousands of years, and had used it to warm their huts and heat their food; even though one of the white explorers years before had found an entire lake of petroleum oozing from the ground; the drillers from the south—mostly Texans, Californians, and Oklahomans—seemed unable to find exactly what they were looking for: oil in sufficient quantities to make the commercial exploitation of the North Slope worthwhile.

They had also neglected to consult the people who lived on the North Slope as to their feelings about the scarred-up tundra, or the debris of torn-up paper, pieces of iron, and the ever-present forty-two gallon oil drums, which had come to be called "Alaska's State Flower."

In the village councils, Takolik had spoken about this invasion, about what it would mean for their way of life, of how their village ways would be destroyed—were in fact already being destroyed. How the game would be driven off, the seas poisoned, the land scarred and ravaged until the people would be totally dependent on the white man's jobs for their living.

His efforts had only reinforced the ideas of the people in his village that Takolik was in some way strange, different, outspoken and volatile. It was not the way of the Inupiat, who basically believed that aggressiveness and outright displays of anger were in extremely bad taste. Placidity, self-deprecation, and outer peace were more in line with the Inupiat character.

So they listened and speculated when Takolik spoke in his strange stammering rushes of words, but they did nothing. Instead, they thought, "They have punched all these dozens of holes in the tundra and they have found nothing. Soon they will realize that there is nothing for them here, and they will go away. And if they find oil—then we will demand jobs and payment for our land, and it will be good for all of us."

Now that the swirling snow crystals had settled, Takolik remounted his snowmobile and headed out over the ice, following the vaguely visible paw prints of the bear. The sea-ice was not level, but was broken up by innumerable pressure ridges where the ice had crashed together and risen forming miniature mountain ranges. Some of them rose twenty-five feet or more above the surface of the sea. Unfortunately, the bear could walk over these ridges; the snowmobile had to find its way through the flat parts, and Takolik was often forced to maneuver hundreds of yards out of the way in order to find a safe place to pass through. Then he would have to backtrack to pick up the dim trail of the rapidly traveling polar bear, who was probably miles away by that time, unless he was hiding somewhere among the jumbled slabs of ice in the pressure ridges—waiting.

Of course, on the snowmobile, he felt fairly safe. The bears, to this date anyhow, were still frightened of the snarling bright colored machines. Takolik had not heard of any cases where a man had been attacked while riding one.

Takolik gunned the motor to get up speed as he raced the snowmobile over a sloping slab of raised ice so that it could leap the three foot crevice separating a tilted flat area on the far side. The machine landed with a soft but jarring thud, then slid quickly and comfortably down the other side of the ridge.

Now, dimly across the long flat expanse that stretched before him, in front of the next ridge, Takolik saw a sight that made him feel that the precautions he had taken, of sewing the old-fashioned hunting amulets into his parka as the old men had showed him to do so many years ago, had been a wise one.

There was an open lead in the ice—the first he had seen that spring. Near it were several breathing holes. Normally Takolik would have been happy to wait at the breathing hole, motionless for hours if necessary, until a seal, it's oxygen exhausted, would poke its dark nose through the icy opening for a breath of Arctic air. Then, (even though it was still early spring and the seal had plenty of blubber and might float anyway) Takolik would follow the old custom of firing only a wounding shot from his .30-06 so that the seal would not die and sink out of reach before he could get his grappling hook on it to haul it out of the sea.

After what had been a fruitless and luckless day, it seemed that the animal spirits were smiling at him. Or perhaps The-Man-Who-Hides, recognizing a kinsman,

18

had sent him the luck. In any event, whoever or whatever was responsible, Takolik's eyes squinting against the brightness of the snow were rewarded by the sight of a large tapered sausage-like form lying on the ice. It was a seal cow lingering in the last light of the day—perhaps in hopes of finding a lover, for it was the beginning of mating season for the seals.

The snowmobile had been approaching for so long, and the sound it made had increased so gradually, that the seal had not been frightened by the whine of the motor. Takolik stopped behind a slight rise in the pack ice and dismounted, but left the motor running. This was not only to make sure that it would start again when he needed it, but also because a sudden silence might alarm the lolling cow.

The seal had taken a position between two bolt holes in the ice, either one of which would offer her a quick escape if there were signs of danger. She was tired, no doubt, from the long winter's siege, during which it was necessary to keep a crust open in the ice in order to breathe. Now that she had found some spring openings in the ice, she rested, nodding off into short naps no longer than a heart beat or so. Her head would nod like an old woman dozing over her sewing, then would snap up alert, twisting and craning in each direction, searching the landscape for signs of any bear that might be approaching.

Bears and men were her only enemies. A man, if he moved in the right fashion, could easily be mistaken for another seal—seals had notoriously weak eyes, although their sense of smell was good. But Takolik had smeared seal fat and seal skin on his body to smell like a seal long enough to get within rifle range.

He dropped to the snow-covered ice and began to crawl on his elbows toward the basking cow. He reached under his hood and pulled down some of his straight

19

black hair so it hung over his face, disguising the patch of pale brown skin that might have given him away to the seal.

Holding the rifle in the crook of both arms, with his feet crossed in imitation of the seal's tail, he inched forward. The game now was to see how close he could get and how sure he could make his shot before frightening the seal back into the sea.

When he had wriggled to less than a hundred yards from the cow, Takolik stopped, carefully pulled the barrel of the Springfield around in front of him, braced his arm in the sling, and took careful aim over the V sights.

The seal raised its head for a moment in seeming alarm and Takolik's finger tensed. He was sure he had been spotted. But then she scratched herself with a flipper, slid forward a few feet, and wriggled comfortably on her belly.

As Takolik shifted his body and spread his legs into a position for firing over the long distance, the seal became alarmed. Her head came up again, alert, as she scanned the horizon; she slithered a few feet as if to get a better view.

Takolik had to shift again to take careful aim over the old Springfield's wobbly sights. The seal's head was pointed at him—raised, quizzical, puzzled. Takolik knew that he had been spotted, that it would be only seconds before the seal lunged for the bolt hole.

Squinting one eye, he dropped the forward sight until he had a clean line on the seal's flipper where it joined the body, and carefully squeezed the trigger. The shot sounded flat and muffled by the surface of the snow. The seal, which had been craning up on its flippers for a better view of the approaching stranger, shuddered once at the impact and fell sideways on the ice, spewing blood from her half-opened mouth.

It was now almost as far back to the idling snow-mobile as it was to the seal. Takolik judged that it would be best to run to the seal to make sure that she could not escape to the bolt hole with a last surge of desper-ate energy. He ran toward the dying animal, which was now vomiting blood in a glistening red pool on the ice before her, struggling to rise on her weakened flippers.

Takolik dropped to one knee, and killed the seal with a single shot behind the ear. The impact of the bullet at that close range caused the dying seal to jerk and roll over on her back, like a restless sleeper chang-ing positions in the night. Takolik rose to his feet, slung the Springfield over his shoulder, pulled his knife from its sheath, and began striding with happy eager steps toward the cow—his first hunting kill of the spring.

He had been so intent on getting the seal that he had not noticed the white mound rising from the ice. It had appeared to be a small rounded snowdrift. It was the bear Takolik had been tracking. An old male as wily in the ways of hunting a seal as Takolik himself, he had covered his black nose with snow and apparently lain in wait, possibly mistaking Takolik for still another seal. Takolik's jogging pace toward the seal's body was sud-denly arrested as the big old bear, lean from the hard times of the winter, got casually to his feet and ambled toward the seal.

Takolik's heart tightened with excitement. Never could he have dreamed of such a lucky day. It seemed that the magic of his hunting amulets had delivered the seal only as bait for the much bigger and richer quarry of the bear. The range was good—about thirty yards—too far for the bear to reach him, even in a rushing at-tack, before he could get off one or two good shots.

He dropped to his knee and drew the sights down on the bear. As he squeezed the trigger he suddenly felt

21

a warning movement of air behind him—an eddy in the icy atmosphere—perhaps he also sensed the snorting sound of expelled angry breath. He turned quickly, tripping over the clumsy mukluks and rolling on his back, just in time to see the yearling she-bear raising on her feet behind him, her giant pink-tipped claws extended, her mouth drawn back in an angry snarl. She was close enough that Takolik could smell her fishy breath.

Tugging the rifle quickly from under him, without bothering to aim, Takolik pulled the trigger once. A red, geranium-like blossom erupted in the yellow-white fur of the she-bear's chest. She shuddered and lunged two more steps toward Takolik. Frantically, the frightened Eskimo pulled the bolt of the .30-06, ejecting the spent shell, and pumped another cartridge into the chamber. He pulled the trigger again, this time hitting the angry she-bear in the groin.

The animal stopped, looking stunned by the unexpected and puzzling pain. She staggered two more steps, her huge paws outstretched, and finally fell face forward, so close that one of the extended furry arms knocked Takolik's rifle from his trembling hands. Quickly he snatched it up and whirled to face the huge male behind him. Hunger had held sway over chivalry. The other bear, losing interest in his wounded companion, had disembowelled the dead seal, slashing it open with one swipe of his long claws. The gaping wound in the cow's belly revealed a pink-skinned unborn pup, writhing in the steaming entrails. As Takolik watched the bear took the pale delicacy from the butchered body of the seal cow, looked briefly back toward the man and the now-dead female, and then, with a seeming shrug of indifference, ambled off behind the ridge of pack ice to devour his sweetmeat at leisure.

Takolik clambered in pursuit over the jagged ridge of tossed ice slabs. But the bear was already out of sight, hiding in some fortuitous ice cave or perhaps dropping its quarry to circle back and stalk the hunting man.

Holding his rifle still at the ready, in case of a sudden attack, Takolik began to climb down the slippery ice ridge, anxious to get back to the snowmobile and bring it to the side of the dead female, where he could skin and pack it for the long trip back to the village. When that was done, he would retrieve what was left of the seal cow, and perhaps get another shot at the male bear if he came back to raid the corpse.

Takolik scanned the horizon briefly to get his bearings in relation to the snowmobile. From the vantage point of the high ridge, his eyes caught a sudden brilliant flair of orange and red flames to the east, lighting up the sky in the direction of the Alamo Oil Company drilling rig. Suddenly he knew that his worst fears about the oilmen had come true.

The flame he recognized, for he had done much research on the subject. The oil company had finally made an important strike and was now igniting it to determine the amount of the flow.

Takolik was no engineer, but even from where he stood he could see by the intensity of the flare lighting up the horizon that this was a major find. He knew that there would be even more Cat tractors, more airplanes, more helicopters, more drilling rigs—and with it, a massive invasion of the land in which his people had lived and hunted for more than thirty thousand years.

And the people—his own people—would welcome it because it seemed all of them now wanted money to buy radios and deep-freezes and Ski-Doos and white man's clothing and liquor. Soon the Inupiat, already reduced to a tenth of their former population by the diseases and vices of the white man, would leave their villages and go to the new oil camps, then to Fairbanks, or Anchorage, to spend the money or have it taken away from them by swarms of human wolverines that would descend on the north when news of the oil strike spread to the outside world.

Takolik realized that the Inupiat would no longer take pleasure from their old way of life; ranging the cold, dangerous land and polar seas; subsisting on the catch of whales and fish, seal, caribou, and the huge white bear.

When the oilmen came the old way of life would change. The Real People, instead of hunting for the creatures of the sea and ice would be following the spoor of the black sticky liquid and the blizzard of green paper money they knew would follow behind it.

"There are beyond question some honest people who made millions in oil, who never so much as paid or accepted a bribe. But if I as an oil operator were a normal but impressionable man, who found himself in a business climate where I was constantly seeing commercial piracy, mixed in with a little shrewdness and luck, being turned into huge fortunes around me, I might very well be tempted into playing the same game.

"If I were originally a honky-tonk bouncer or an ordinary clever chisler, the probability is I'd be hungry for power, and a display of power, and if I could keep out of jail I would get it. For I very likely would have told a thousand lies, worked skin games, been bribed and have paid bribes, have got quick millions in the first place. For into its fold, the oil business in Texas has invited and accepted some of the most talented, simonpure thieves that ever perjured themselves in any of the spectacular expansion periods of any of the new American industries."

—George Sessions Perry
Texas, A World in Itself (1942)

Chapter Two

W-Bar-S Ranch, Mitchell Mesa, Texas: March, 1968

Wilbur Steele was seated at the sixteenth century Spanish refectory table in the huge Moorish castle that was the main building on the W-Bar-S spread. He rose to drink the traditional toast to his deceased wife, Emma Bisset Steele.

As usual, the group around him was not a large one. It consisted only of the immediate family and closest friends. On his right sat his son, Larry Steele, looking uncomfortable in the Western-style dinner jacket, ruffled shirt and string tie, that Wilbur had declared *de rigueur* for the occasion. On his left, looking equally uncomfortable, in a black Victorian evening gown with an ostrich feather ruff, was his daughter Penelope "Penny" Steele, who had been persuaded to come back from the Berkeley campus for the occasion by the promise of a new red Thunderbird convertible.

In a wheelchair, at the far end of the table from Wilbur, was Whitney Bisset, the only one unable to stand for Wilbur's toast. He was Emma's father. Sitting up straight in the wicker and mahogany wheelchair, the old oil prospecter was almost as tall as the others. When Bisset had been a wildcatter in East Texas he had stood six-foot-five. He had been nicknamed "Tiny," and even now, seated and aged, he was a commanding figure.

Sitting next to Larry Steele, her face windburned and glowing from her afternoon's canter on one of the W-Bar-S's quarter horses, the flush now heightened by the three martinis she had consumed before dinner, was Deirdre Doheny. She was trying to keep a straight face through the toast while Larry Steele, looking seriously at his father, ran a fingernail up the side of her leg. Under his breath he whispered, "Just checking to see if you were still wearing your britches under that outfit." She was dressed in a simple, but stunning, light green floor length dress that complemented her tall, lean good looks, and set off her coloring gloriously.

Across the table was Mahlon Doheny, a long-time close friend of Wilbur Steele and his family, and Deirdre's father.

Doheny, as staunch, gray, and weather-beaten as a granite hitching post, listened mechanically, his mind switching off as soon as he heard the familiar words of the toast. He was preoccupied with another subject. How soon could Wilbur Steele come up with the necessary capital to finance his forth-coming Mexican oil explorations? The seismic and geological indications had been very promising but unless more money was forthcoming soon, Doheny's firm—Honda oil—would go bankrupt before a producing well could be brought in.

The only outsider at the table was Al Brandon, who was Wilbur Steele's right-hand man, chief executive officer, and well-paid companion. Brandon was tall, about six-foot-three, with close-cropped grey hair, and the shoulders-back bearing of a military man. The posture had been learned at VMI. It was one of the sorrows of Brandon's life that, prior to World War Two, he had been so skilled in drilling troops that he had been given a permanent assignment at Fort Devens, Massachusetts, training recruits into soldiers. He had not made it overseas until after the war. He first met Wilbur Steele while serving with the OSS, reprocessing Italian partisans in Rome and Naples.

Later, when Wilbur, fresh out of Wharton Business School, had started trying to expand Whitney Bisset's Alamo Oil Company, he found Brandon's OSS experience particularly useful in negotiating for concessions in foreign countries, both in Latin America and in the Middle East. Brandon knew who to contact and what sorts of pressure could be applied. He knew how to find out which men had influence, what their weaknesses or strengths were, and how to exploit them—and, if necessary, how to remove any obstacles that might interfere with Alamo's plans. Brandon stood at attention as Wilbur started his speech, as though he were listening to the opening bars of the Star Spangled Banner.

"To Emma Bisset Steele—a great and compassionate mother, an affectionate and beautiful daughter, a kind and caring friend to all of us—"

Wilbur's voice broke off, he blinked once or twice, then sipped from his glass of champagne to help him swallow the lump in his throat. Brandon leaned forward and said, "she was a wonderful woman, Wilbur."

Penny Steele glared at him, sweeping her auburn hair back from her brow in a gesture of weary disgust. "Why don't you knock it off, Brandon? My mother would puke at the sight of you."

She turned toward her father. "You know damn well she hated him, Wilbur." (Penny loved to call her father by his first name, because she knew that it irritated him, although he never would admit it.)

Larry Steele said nothing, but the corners of his mouth quivered with suppressed laughter.

Before Wilbur could answer, Mahlon Doheny interrupted in a tone of quiet rebuke. "Now you just cool down honey. That was down-right rude. Besides, you know Brandon was the one who took care of things around here during those last days when your Daddy was away."

"Yeah," Penny muttered. "I'd just like to know how much he *did* take care of."

Deirdre Doheny broke into a broad grin that she probably would not have permitted herself except for the three martinis she had had. "Daddy, there ain't any sense in you butting in. Everybody knows you're just trying to stay on Brandon's good side so he'll back you up on the Mexican deal."

Doheny's face flushed with anger underneath its leathery tan. "Deirdre! I told you hundreds of times that anything I say to you is strictly in the family."

"Oh, come on Mahlon," Larry said to smooth things over, "This is all family here, isn't it except for Brandon."

"And everybody knows," Whitney Bisset chimed in, "that Brandon's got more shit than the south forty."

Brandon's jaw muscles knotted with anger under the massed attack, but he maintained his military posture. Wilbur Steele watched them all closely, listening to

28

the exchange. His cold eyes gave no indication of what he was feeling. Without so much as a flicker of sympathy for Brandon, he raised his glass and resumed the toast.

"She was a heaven-sent bride and companion to me for nineteen marvelous years, during five of which, she showed more fortitude, courage, and down-right guts..."

Miguel Carreras, the butler, had entered at the beginning of the toast. He now stood next to Brandon, patiently waiting for a chance to claim Wilbur Steele's attention. Finally, unable to contain his excitement, he moved forward and whispered in Brandon's ear. Brandon turned apologetically to Wilbur, signalling that he wished to excuse himself.

Brandon walked through the carved Spanish oak doorway to the hallway outside. There, on the hall table, was a brass and mahogany chest, about eight inches high. Brandon opened the chest and removed a brown princess telephone from it. He pushed the lighted button for the extension on which the call was coming in.

It was from Vernon Lloyd, Wilbur Steele's chief geologist on the Prudhoe Bay well.

After six dry holes, costing an average of four to five million apiece, Lloyd had managed to persuade Wilbur Steele that it would be worthwhile to skid in a rig, borrowed from Golconda Oil on the adjoining lease, to a point fifty miles across the frozen tundra for one more try at the pool of oil convincing geological data, and every instinct in his well-trained geologist's brain told him must lay somewhere beneath.

Not all had been dry holes, several had in fact contained oil, but in insufficient quantities to make worthwhile the enormous shipping and construction costs of the north. There had also been several good shows of natural gas on neighboring leases, but still no large finds of oil. The tests had all looked promising, although there was no way to determine the exact location of oil from the seismic "jugs."

It had been more than a hunch that made it possible for Lloyd to convince Wilbur Steele to risk another five million on a possible dry hole. It was the accumulation of twenty years of experience, probing a mile, two miles, even more into the earth for the elusive ancient "black gold" that had made Lloyd's insistence seem plausible. It was also because Alamo was notably "crude poor," and would probably have to sell out or yield to a merger with a larger company unless it found new and important sources of oil. To Wilbur Steele the gamble made sense.

Brandon, picking up the receiver, could feel the excitement in Lloyd's voice.

"Wilbur?"

"Brandon here."

"Will you put this on scrambler please?"

Brandon fished into a pocket of his vest and slipped out a small pierced disk which he dropped into a matching slot on the phone.

Lloyd's voice came through from Alaska, disguised against eavesdroppers by a pair of whirling coded discs on either end. It was one of the security touches Brandon himself had suggested when he had joined Alamo fresh out of the OSS. He knew, better than anyone, how vulnerable phone lines were.

"I'd like to speak to Wilbur please," Lloyd said when the coder device had been connected.

"I'm sorry Vernon, but he's very busy right now. Tell me what it is and I'll give him the message."

Lloyd sounded irritated. "Look, Brandon, I don't want to talk to any second in command. This is big, and it's important, and I want to talk to Wilbur himself."

Brandon could hear the excited quiver in the geologists' voice, and, at this point, barely had to hear any

30

more. "Just a minute. I'll see if I can get him. It may be a while."

"Please hurry," Lloyd said. "We're on a radio patch through Fairbanks, and the communications are really bad up here. We're liable to get blocked out by electrical disturbance at any time. So make it fast. This is very, very important."

"I will," Brandon said.

He punched the hold button, and then pushed one of the five other buttons for an outside line. He dialed a 212 code, and when a voice in New York answered, he said, "This is Brandon, I want you to get hold of all the cash you can, sell out any other accounts I have. Buy all of the Alamo and Golconda stock you can get your hands on." He hung up and then went in to get Wilbur. He arrived just in time to hear the last part of the toast.

". . . Emma, darling, wherever you are, I know you are with us in spirit tonight."

He waited until the group had raised their glasses, drunk deeply of the Dom Perignon, and seated themselves before he approached Wilbur's chair and whispered in his ear. The misty, sentimental look on Steele's face disappeared as though a giant windshield wiper had cleared its teary ambience. The expression that replaced it was the stone-cold, impenetrable look that Wilbur habitually assumed in decisive moments of business. It was his poker player's face—impassive, uncommunicating, but with a sense of incredible activity seething beneath its surface.

"Excuse me, you all," he said, as he got up and strode through the oak doors into the hall. There was a phone jack just behind his chair in the dining room, but Wilbur was not given to sharing the contents of his business conversations with anybody—even the close members of his family. He picked up the waiting phone.

"Yes, Vernon. What is it?"

"Will? It is *big*. BIG! We're sitting on, at least, two billion barrels."

"Two million barrels?"

"No. Two *billion,* with a big 'B.' "

"You're joking. There hasn't been a find like that in twenty years."

"I'm not joking. The gauges tell it. It tests over two thousand barrels a day—and God knows how much gas. I don't know how big the pool is. We'll get a confirmation well started as soon as we can skid the rig in to the new site. But I want to tell you, this is it! I can *feel* it. I can *taste* it. The biggest thing that's been hit in North America since Dad Joiner brought in Daisy Bradford Number Three in East Texas!"

"Who knows about this?"

"Nobody but me and a couple of guys here on the platform know for sure. But we blew out a lot of mud, and I think some of it hit a plane that was going over from Golconda. There had to be a scout on that plane —this one's going to be hard to sit on. He probably saw the test fire too. Communication is lousy here, but rumors travel faster than radio waves."

"Okay. Shut it off as fast as you can and see if you can keep it as tight a hole as possible."

"I'll try, but don't forget we're talking on a radio patch."

"Okay do the best you can. I'll get busy on this end."

He hung up the receiver thoughtfully, his mind already on the hundreds of details that would have to be attended to to maximize the profits from this giant strike. It was the moment he had been waiting for his entire career. He knew that it would take every bit of capital that he could raise, beg, or borrow, plus a consortium of at least five or six other oil companies,

32

to bring in the whole field. There were leases in a patch-work gridded all around the slope—there was no way of telling how big the oil pool was, but there was no possibility of shutting out at least six others. The problem now was to make the most profit for Alamo.

Wilbur Steele returned to the table, his face still bemused and clouded with thought. Mahlon Doheny looked at him curiously. "Bad news?"

"No, It's not bad news, Mahlon. I think I could say it was good news for Alamo anyway."

Then, turning to the butler, "Miguel, have them bring out the cochinillo. I'm starving. And bring up one of the Jeroboams of Perignon. I have a feeling this is a big night for all of us."

"Each spring the whalers would pick up many young women from these villages to be used for their pleasure during the whaling season. Sometimes they were not returned until the following year, and then not all came home. This caused great anxiety and grief to parents and husbands. It was not until many years later that law and order was obtained through the Coast Guard. At this time many of the women were finally returned to their homes."

—Frank Topsekok, Alaskan Native

Chapter Three

Point Barrow—November, 1968

While Takolik was away at the BIA School as a teenager, a revolution started among the Inupiat.

In 1961 the people of Point Hope discovered that these pale images of men from the south were planning to blast an enormous hole in their harbor with an atomic bomb. It was a plan by the Atomic Energy Commission to create an instant deep water harbor.

As usual, the white people had consulted only each other; nobody had asked the eight hundred Eskimos who lived in the Cape Thompson area, where the blast was to take place. But the people of Noatak, Kivalina, and Point Hope—in the vicinity of the blast—began to question whether the fallout from this atomic explosion might threaten their hunting grounds or even their very existence. They organized, for the first time, a meeting of all the people from the twenty villages in the area. The meeting was called Inupiat Paitot—"the people's heritage." This was the first time the various villages of the Inupiat had attempted to act together, to confront the authority of the whites. They were well aware that Alaska had become a state in 1958 and, as a result, they were citizens equal to the others in the south. The white people, however, did not seem to grasp this.

The actions of the Inupiat Paitot at least forced a delay in the atomic explosion. Meanwhile, it was reported that Russian scientists had discovered that fallout from previous atomic tests *had* landed on the tundra, where it had been absorbed by the caribou that grazed there. Some Eskimos fed mainly on the meat of the caribou, and these Eskimos were found to have a much higher radiation count than any of the people on the outside.

When Takolik came back on vacation, Oquilluk told him what had happened. Takolik was interested and excited. At school he had read in history books how the whites had first come to control the land of the Inupiat, and it had angered him that his people had been so gentle and passive by nature as to allow this to happen. In the High School library, in *Bancroft's History,* he had read: "The chiefs were in favor of driving out the 'Boston Men' . . . the discontentment arose not from any antagonism for the Americans, but from the fact that the territory had been sold without their consent, and that they had received none of the proceeds of the sale. The Russians, they argued, had been allowed to occupy the territory partly for mutual benefit, but their forefathers had dwelt in Alaska long before any white man had set foot in America. Why had not the seven million two hundred thousand dollars not been paid to them instead of the Russians?"

This statement had tantalized Takolik. He wondered why the white men were able to take all of the gold and oil and minerals and timber from the land where the "real people" were expected to live only by subsistence—hunting and fishing. Was it because the Inupiat had never thought to demand the rights even the white men had admitted were theirs?

Takolik went back to the library in search of more answers to his questions, but what he found disturbed him even more. The average white Alaskan had an educational level of almost twelve-and-a-half years, where as only nine percent of the Eskimos had graduated from high school, and twenty percent of them had not gone to school at all. More shockingly, less than one percent of the Eskimos had ever graduated from college, and none had yet become a doctor.

The figures on native health were even more alarming. The rate of tuberculosis among Alaskan natives was twenty times the rate for the "lower forty-eight." Even compared to the American Indian, the figures were shocking. More than three times as many Alaskan native children died at birth as American Indian children. Ten times as many Alaskan natives died of respiratory diseases, such as influenza and pneumonia, as did Alaskan whites.

Diseases that could be easily treated, such as chronic *otitis media,* an infection of the middle ear which results in deafness and which afflicted between ten and fifteen percent of his people, were let to run their courses for lack of doctors, or even medically trained technicians, although such care is readily available to white Alaskans.

Stories in the villages, told by fathers to their sons, and to *their* sons, told of the time that the Inupiat first met the "Boston Men," the whalers from New England. This was back about a hundred years, but people remembered and told their children about how the land of the Inupiat was swept with endless waves of disease —smallpox, measles, diptheria, pneumonia, the common cold, syphilis, gonorrhea.

Point Franklin, which had eight hundred people when the "Boston Men" arrived, was wiped out entirely. Point Hope, which had two thousand people in 1823 when the "Boston Men" first came, had only three hundred and fifty, by 1890. Point Barrow, in that some period, went from a thousand people to a hundred. The people of the Shichmaref Inlet were reduced from a population of about fifteen hundred to only three houses.

It seemed more and more clear to Takolik that if the Inupiat did not rouse themselves from their natural passivity and acceptance of fate, there would soon be none of the "real people" left in the world and only the images would remain. There had been *some* aggressive Inupiat in the past. These were the shamans, who did not fear the whites and often spoke out against them—sometimes even won. But when the Christians came, they did away with the shamans—the Inupiat's only weapon.

And now that the land of his people was threatened by the descendants of the "Boston Men," this time after, not whale oil, but oil from beneath the ground, could the people of the Inupiat villages unite again as they had against the AEC? Could they stand fast and try to get back the land that was theirs?

Already the fifty-six million acres occupied by the Inupiat of the north had its population reduced from thirty thousand to less than five thousand. To the outside people the arctic was a vast white space, a wilderness practically unoccupied. Takolik's people knew it and used it all. They knew where the seeps of oil were and the coal cliffs, and even the mountain of jade. They knew more than eighty different kinds of snow—snow to build shelters with, snow to ride sleds on, snow in which one sank to one's waist—and they had words for all of these. They had hunting areas and sled trails and trading camps and trap lines, all of which went back thousands of years. And now the white men, with their huge, bladed Cats, their trucks and their planes, were tearing up the tundra as though it belonged to them and the damage they were doing would take another four or five thousand years to be repaired—*if* the land were ever left to rest again.

Takolik was determined to organize the people of the North Slope. He wrote to the leaders of all the villages and to their councils. He wrote to Wainwright, to Point Lay, to Point Hope, to Anaktuvuk Pass, to Colville, to Kotzebue, and to Kaktovik. And for once the "real people" agreed—with the exception of the people of Kotzebue, who wanted to go their own way.

Still, Takolik was able to call a meeting and to present the idea he had discussed with the others on his travels through the North Slope. The idea that before his land was all given away to be drilled in, chopped up, and rigged over by the whites, the Inupiat should put in a legal claim under the white man's law for the land that had been always theirs.

Isaac Samuelson, who had become a dynamic young Eskimo leader from Barrow—known by his Eskimo name, Angakok—joined Takolik in his struggle. After meeting with the group, Isaac wrote the following letter to Frank Peters, a native claims lawyer who had done a fantastic job for the Tlingit indians in the south:

Dear Mr. Peters:

We Inupiat of the North have organized a group of Eskimos whose goal is to secure our aboriginal rights to the land which runs north of the Brooks Range from the sea South of Point Hope and making a line that follows the divide of the Brooks Range to the Canadian border. We claim our ancestral rights to all land North of that line.

This area is now being developed for oil and other minerals by various groups, both private and government. My people and I wish you to advise us if we can obtain a Federal injunction to prevent further exploitation of our land. Our aim is to force this issue of native land rights to be heard in court.

We can prove that our ancestors have lived and hunted in this territory for at least 5,000 years. Our ancestors also used the oil deposits and coal of the lands in which they hunted and fished, and they knew of the other mineral deposits such as gold which they used centuries ago to make fishhooks and small toys for their children.

The injunction we seek is based on the fact that nobody but our people has a clear title to this land, and the Inupiat have never been adequately compensated for its use by outsiders, government or private. Therefore this

land cannot and should not be ex-
ploited until a proper settlement is
made with our people by a court
decision.

Will you please advise and counsel
us on this matter and also act as our
attorney as you have experience in
this area? Please tell us how much
it will cost, as we have not much
money, to act as attorney for our
group to be known as the North Slope
Native Association.

> Yours in brotherhood
> Isaac Samuelson
> (Angakok)

Takolik met with Angakok and other Eskimo leaders
including Guy Okakok, Herman Rexford of Barter
Island, David Takyak of Wainwright, Charlie Edwardsen, of Point Hope, and even Jack Ahgook, of
Anaktuvik, where the last of the inland Inupiat still
survived, and they all thought it was a good letter and
that it was important that the claim be made. But later,
Takolik took Angakok aside. His friend's face was con-
torted with pain because he had ulcers, and the emotional strain of the meeting was tearing him up inside.
Though both had been to the BIA school and spoke
English well as a second language, they spoke together
in the Inupiat dialect of the North Slope.

"Angakok, what you have done is good and it is important, but you studied history as well as I did and
you know that the white people will never give us what
we want. The oil people will come and they will take
what they want and they will tear up our land and they

will drive away the game and they will destroy our way of life. You know they will have the backing of President Nixon and everybody on his staff. What can we five thousand Eskimos do against the billions of the oil people?"

"We have the law on our side. The white man's law. They must obey it, mustn't they?"

"Why should they obey it now? They haven't in the past. If they were to obey their law they would return all of Alaska to the people who own it. Do you think they'll do that?"

Angakok, shrugged. "It's too late for us to get back all that really belongs to us—but at least we should get something out of the rape of this land."

"Yes, we should", Takolik interjected, "but the only way we'll do it is to show as much force and violence as the whites have shown to us. You remember the shelling of Angoon, and the rape and kidnap of our women by the whalers . . ."

"Yes, but we have no weapons, we are not fighters, and we do have the law on our side."

"We'll make the law ours only if we act, and there are people even now—Indians in the lower forty-eight and blacks—who've learned that people will listen if you take direct action."

"You will not get the support of our people in this, though I think sometimes you might be right about the need for force."

"Even a small group taking positive action can have an enormous effect. The Chinese taught us that and the students in America even now are showing that. You remember the people that came to talk to us at the University in Fairbanks?"

"The SDS?"

Takolik nodded. "Yes, those and the others. It is

41

from them we will learn the way to fight the enormous power of these oil people."

Angakok looked doubtful. "Do you have a plan?"

"It's not definite yet, but I'll let you know about it, if possible . . .".

The last temptation is the greatest treason:
To do the right deed for the wrong reason.

—T. S. Eliot
Murder In The Cathedral

Chapter Four

The yellowish-gray coyote paused in its steady trot across the stubbled cornfield and stared curiously back over its shoulder, looking for the source of the keening noise emitted by Larry Steele's varmint call. Hidden by a rock on the wooded hillside that bordered the narrow strip of arable land, Larry sighted along the barrel of the Weatherby .240 rifle and squeezed off a single shot.

The coyote leaped briefly in the air at the impact of the bullet, which caught it in the chest section right behind the front leg, and fell lifeless to the ground.

He slung the Weatherby, climbed down the rock-strewn hillside, and walked across the dry crackling cornstalks. Later they would turn the Longhorns loose in the field to finish off what remained of the stubble. It was a crisp, bright autumn day, not yet really chilly even at that mile-high altitude.

Raul Martinez, who had the job of looking after the quarter horses and the herd of Longhorns that had been Wilbur Steele's hobby for the last ten years, had told Larry the day before that two of the Longhorn calves had been found with their throats ripped out in the west meadow. "One of 'em was a bull-calf that the

43

old man had in mind keeping for breeding stock. He's going to be some pissed off when he finds out about this." So Larry had put the Weatherby in the rack on the back of the pickup before driving out for his morning swim in the little pond that overlooked the cornfield.

Now, as he stopped to turn over the body of the small, dog-like animal, there was the unmistakable rackety whine of a bullet, and a spurt of dust about a yard to his right. Larry hit the ground fast, unslinging the rifle, and squirming around to see who was shooting at him. There was the sound of a shot and another spurt of dust six feet behind him: still another report and a crackling that clipped the top off a cornstalk to his right and sent feathery bits of fiber scattering through the air.

Peering back at the hill, Larry Steele could see the blue sheen of a rifle muzzle. His pulse was racing, his adrenalin charging through his system, and he again felt the almost embarrassing spurt of anal excitement combined with gut-gripping fear which he had experienced so many times in the 'Nam, back in 1967.

There wasn't a shred of cover in the open field. Larry began to inch his way toward a small hummock that would at least give him protection from the line of fire on the hill. As he did so, he was startled to hear a high-pitched giggle of laughter, and then a shout.

"Whooooeeee, you motherfucker!"

Son of a bitch. It was that damn fool Penny!

Cautiously, Larry got to his feet. "Whoooeeee, bitch!"

Now he could see her standing on the rock, trailing the old Marlin .22, her head thrown back in wild laughter. She was wearing jeans and the fringed, beaded Indian jacket she'd acquired at one of the boutiques in Berkeley earlier in the year.

44

Larry sprinted angrily across the field and up the slope to where his sister stood, now holding her sides from laughter.

"Boy," she said, still gasping, "you were sure one scared mother. That must have been what those Vietnamese felt like when you were picking away at them with your M16."

Larry grabbed her angrily by the shoulders of her buckskin jacket and shook her viciously so that her head snapped back and forth. But the crazy grin remained on her face.

"What did you *do* that for? For Christssake, Penny, you could have killed me!"

"*Sheeit.* If I'd wanted to kill you, I would've hit you, right? What'd you shoot that poor damned coyote for?"

"Look. In the first place, it's none of your business. In the second place, it happens that he knocked off two of Dad's calves yesterday."

"Oh," she said mockingly, "I suppose you got his fingerprints."

Larry sighed. "Listen, let's not get into one of those Goddamned ecology things. Those coyotes have been hitting the herd all fall—in fact, since last spring. And I can't see dying because of your feelings about conservation."

Penny grinned again. "What's so great about living?" Then she dropped the subject. "You going swimming or not?"

"That's what I was fixing to do when the Goddamned coyote came over the field."

"It ain't too cold for you, is it little fellow?"

"Shit, Penny, I dove into that hole when there was a crust of ice on it."

"Ok," she said, "let's go. I think you're chicken."

Larry looked at her appraisingly. "What about you?"

"You'll see."

The pickup was parked in the clearing beside the pond. Larry opened the door, shucked out of his cords and shirt. Underneath he was wearing his old khaki shorts that served as a swimsuit.

He ran across the clearing onto the tall granite rock that served as a springboard, and without giving himself time to lose his nerve, jumped into the chilly pond with an enormous splash. He stayed under for a long time swimming out in a straight line toward the center of the pond, hoping that by doing so he would get used to the cold water sooner. He surfaced blowing and sputtering about twenty-five yards away from the rock, just in time to see a spinning slim, tanned figure launch itself from the top of the rock, all flailing arms and streaming red-brown hair.

"Keerist!" he said to himself, "she naked as a jay-bird!"

Penny came up sputtering and laughing about ten yards from where Larry was treading water. "Man, that *is* cold. My titties feel like a pair of Pecos strawberries."

"What are you doin' in here with nothin' on," Larry said. "Suppose somebody came along? They'd think we were a couple of creeps."

"Come on, Larry," Penny said laughing. "You've seen me bare-assed before."

"Yeah," Larry said, "but not since you're a grown-up."

She swam over and wrapped her legs around him so he could feel the sea-weed-growth of her pubic hair against his hip.

"You didn't mind fooling around when we were kids," she said. Her slender fingers crawled octopus-like over the muscled ridges of his belly, and curled themselves gently around his groin. Larry found himself responding with embarrassing eagerness.

"Listen, Penny", he said anxiously, "Let go, that was a long time ago. Let go now! You're really acting weird."

He shook her off and plunged to the bottom in a surface dive, then surfaced, swimming in long hard strokes toward the shore. When the water was waist-deep he stood up and ran splashing across the gravel pond bottom through the clearing to the truck, where he grabbed a large beach towel and began to dry himself off vigorously.

Penny followed languidly after him, stopping first in the ankle-deep water to squeeze the remaining drops of water from her long, straight hair. Then, still naked, she ambled up and stood beside him at the cab of the Cheyenne pickup.

"You'll have to lend me a corner of your towel," she said. "I didn't come out prepared for a swim—as you can see." She spread her arms and pirouetted on one foot.

Larry had detected the clue to her hyper-charged performance. He took her by the shoulders, looked into her eyes, and saw that the pupils were the size of a pair of beebee shots.

"Christ," he said, "you're stoned out of your mind again. What're you on now? Reds? C? Acid?"

"A little of each, I think," Penny said giggling. "Ain't it grand?"

Larry slid into his cords and shirt, grumbling in disgust. He searched around in the grass until he found Penny's jeans and jacket. "Here throw these on, for Christssake, before we get pinched for incest."

Penny grinned that vacant grin again. "Who knows," she said, "it might not be half-bad. You ain't getting any from that D.D., that's for sure." She slipped into the beaded jacket, which hung seductively just below

47

her crotchline, and jumped into the passenger's side of the pickup.

"Put on your pants, Goddamn it," Larry said angrily. "And what the fuck do you know about me and D.D.?"

"Listen," she said, "I can tell when people are getting it on, and you are nowhere with that woman."

"That's for damned sure," Larry said, throwing the Cheyenne violently into gear and starting down the rocky trail toward the main house.

"Daddy'll probably get into her pants before you do. If he hasn't already." Penny said mockingly as they jolted over the rocks toward the ranch house.

"Don't talk stupid."

"Well, you know Daddy talked her into going up to Alaska. Says he's gonna put her in charge of coordinating the ecological reports—that's a lot of bullshit and you know it. He's just not lettin' her get out of his sight. She's going to be working up there with him. And you're going to be down here, so how are you ever going to get into her pants?

"That's all you think about these days is dope and sex, right?" Larry said with disgust.

"No. I think about a lot of things it wouldn't hurt you to put your mind to. Like stopping the war. Like revolution."

"That's all bullshit. You think you and that gang of hop-head maniacs you were running with in Chicago are going to change things?"

"You think sitting on your dead ass watching *I Love Lucy* reruns amounts to a row of shit? At least we *did* something down in Lincoln Park. The newspapers paid attention. It was something they couldn't ignore."

"Did you do that to help the cause, or just to get stoned, screwed, and drive old Wilbur practically out of his mind?"

48

Larry couldn't help laughing despite his irritation with his sister. "Boy! He like to bust a gut when your picture showed up on TV throwing rocks at the cops, and him a Republican national delegate!"

As they walked to the entrance of the sprawling house, Penny threw an arm over Larry's shoulder and squeezed him affectionately.

"That's just *it*, Stringbean Big Brother. If I hated Ol' Wilbur as much as you say, Hell, I'd have bombed the *Republican* convention!"

Larry laughed and shoved her in the direction of her room.

"O.K. Hold off the revolution for a minute. Go up and shower and rest for a while. See if you can straighten out before dinner, or the old man may take the strap to you, like he did when you were a kid."

"The old fuck really enjoyed that, you know?" Penny said. Her tone was bitter, "I'd like to see the son of a bitch try it now! I'd *kill* him, I really would!"

It was no doubt the pills talking, but for a moment Larry could really believe she meant it.

D.D. was on the terrace with Grandpa Bisset when Penny and Larry returned. The terrace was built right to the edge of the tall cliff that bounded the mountain on which the huge, Spanish-style hacienda had been built. It faced west toward the Del Norte Mountains, and on a clear day, way in the background behind Cathedral Mountain, you could see the sharp tip of Bisset Mountain, named for Whitney Bisset's great grandfather. In the afternoon the old man used to like to sit in his elaborate wheel chair, staring out over the valley at the ancestral mountain—like a guru looking for a message from space.

D.D. had mixed them a Virginia Gentleman on the rocks in a huge fourteen ounce tumbler he favored.

Gratefully, the old man, his once-weathered face now going yellow from long days spent in the shade and shelter of the house, clutched the big tumbler between his thumb and fourth finger. The other two fingers were only stubs.

"You got a good grip on that glass, Gramps?" D.D. asked with concern.

"Shucks, I could straighten a horseshoe with those two fingers. I ever tell you how I lost them?"

"Well, you did, but I don't quite remember," D.D. lied.

"Well, I was running a casing crew in East Texas— you know, we were taking contracts to run the pipe down in the wells. I had maybe twenty, thirty men working for me that time. We had five to a crew and a lot of times we had five or six crews. Well, sometimes the crews would be short-handed, you know? So I worked as a stabber—that's the man that sits on the end of the walking beam and holds the pipe straight. You have to realize that these were cable tools at this time. Meanwhile, the rest of the crew, they screw the pipe together, put the elevators in a pipe, and drop it down into the hole. And I was doing this, I was stabbing this pipe, and I guess I was a little drowsy—I'd been tearing up the pea-patch a little bit the night before—and as those runner blocks come by I like to've fell off the beam—that would have been about a twenty-five foot drop to the derrick floor.

"So I stretch out and grab for anything in sight and —I grab onto the running line and the next thing you know, it pulled my hand right up into the shives of the running block. I just reared back, pulled my hand out and give a yell like a bull bein' gelded—it got these three middle fingers here just by the roots.

"I musta passed out.

"They tell me I pulled leaders out of my arm must

50

have been eighteen inches long. But I'm a fast healer. You know I was back on the job in about two months, but it took me a little while to learn how to work things with just the fingers I had left. Got it down pretty good, now, don't I?"

"You can do everything except play concert piano," said D.D. with a smile.

"It was just about that time," the old man reminisced, "when some oil man come by and he wanted to get a lease to drill for oil on that old dry farm I had out there in East Texas. Fellow says he was paying a dollar an acre, so I says, hows about ten dollars an acre and I want a stipulation that you drill the well on my ground? Well, it took them a couple of months to get started, but when they did it, they get down about four thousand feet and bingo they hit a three thousand barrel oil well. My share run around $750.00 a month and that deal lasted over thirty years. Wasn't too long ago she finally run dry. I got about $50,000.00 out of that well —I remember the last royalty check was about eighty-five cents. But the business has changed a lot now, I guess. Shit, you couldn't even start to spud a well for $50,000.00 today."

He took a sip of the mellow brown bourbon and whirled his wheelchair nimbly in a hundred eighty degree arc.

"Are you sure you want to go up there, D.? It's mighty cold in Alaska, from what I hear. No place for a woman anyhow."

D.D. laughed. "From what I hear, it's the *best* place for a woman. They tell me there's about five men to every gal up there. Besides, I'm not going to be out in the cold—I'm going to be working in an office. It'll be the same as working down in Houston, only I'll get a lot more money."

51

"Well, that Wilbur, I guess he can't find his ass with both hands without you to show him where it is."

"Don't sweat it out, Gramps," D.D. said. "I'll probably only be up there for a year anyway, and I'll come back every few months. They give you R & R you know—just like in the Army."

"Goddamn it, in a year or two, I'll probably be—gone. Six feet down in that old apple orchard over there with the rest of the Bissets."

D.D. put her hand sympathetically on his shoulder. "You've got a few miles left on you old boy."

"Shit," he said wistfully, "if they'd put sled runners on this old chair, I'd go up there myself."

Larry appeared at the end of the terrace, his hair still damp from the swim. He went to the chromium rolling bar and poured himself a straight bourbon. He brought it over and joined D.D. and Bisset.

"You're really going, D.?" he said. "You're going to miss all this." He gestured with his glass toward the sprawling mountain panorama, now turning purple in the valleys with an orange fringe around the crown of the hills.

D.D. nodded. "I'll miss this, all right, but I won't miss Houston. That's getting to be like a concrete playpen. Besides, Wilbur didn't *ask* me. He *told* me. It's either that, or I don't have a job."

Larry looked at her doubtfully. "Look, you don't need the dough. Your old man could take care of you any time."

"I'm not so sure of that," D.D. said. "He's tied up practically every nickel he could find or borrow in that Mexican lease, and he's waiting for some money that Wilbur promised him to go ahead. And you know Wilbur's stretching himself pretty thin now also. Daddy's real worried."

She quickly changed the subject.

"What are you going to do, Larry? You know he'd like to have you up there with him."

Larry strolled to the parapet, put a foot up on the stone balustrade, and looked out toward the fading sunset. "I don't know," he said. "There won't be much for me here once you're gone." He looked irritated.

"He don't want me working in the field up there. Says it wouldn't look good for the family. But I'll be damned if I'll take some tight-ass office job."

"You got the word, son," Grandpa Bisset interjected. "Them starchy sonsabitches he hangs around with call themselves oilmen. Shit, that son-in-law of mine never been on an oil rig in his life. 'Fraid he'd get his lily white hands dirty. And them popcorn artists he pals around with, they ain't much better. Learned everything they know about the oil business up at Harvard or some damn-fool place. 'Cept maybe for Rawhide Robertson. His Daddy started him as a tool dresser—same way I started. They used to pay me five dollars a day for a twelve hour shift, noon to midnight. But it was a whale of a salary at that time for a fifteen year old kid. That was back in 1915."

Larry laughed sheepishly. "Well, I guess you can't say that I started at the top either."

The old man reached up from the wheelchair and placed his hand near Larry's shoulder. "You done right kid. A fellow's got to go out and prove his manhood before he starts sharpening pencils and making paper airplanes, in some candy-ass office. You got out there and flew those little-bitty Piper Cubs there in Veet-nam, drove them big truck rigs out of East Texas, got your Teamsters card, and your Roughneck's card—so you've got all that experience now. You might as well get in there with your Pa and make the big buck, up there north of the Yukon."

Larry gently shrugged the hand off his shoulder. "If

I'd wanted to push pencils, I coulda done it long ago. I just didn't like being cooped up in an office all day. I guess you and I are more alike. I like all this," he gestured toward the mountains. "I like worrying about myself and not bossing a lot of other guys around; getting my paycheck and going to town—doing what I want with it. Besides I'm not sure I like what they're going to be doing up there. The way I hear it they're going to be chasing off all the game, tearing up the wilderness. Pretty soon the whole damn thing will look like Houston all over again. With all that stuff you've been spouting about conservation and ecology, D.D., I don't see how you can go along with it."

"That's just the idea, Larry. I told Wilbur I was worried about what they were going to do up there. And he explained that they've hired a whole ecological team to make sure the thing is done right. And I'm going to be in a position where I can check it all out—coordinating all the reports, from the government agencies and our own people. There's got to be *somebody* looking out for the seal puppies and the polar bears."

"Listen, D.D. I don't understand why you're so hung up on working for the old man anyway. Why don't we just cut out to Colorado or some place. Get ourselves a spread in one of them little towns up there . . ."

"I told you Larry . . ." D.D. looked uncomfortable under his assault.

"Well, I'm not letting you go that easy," Larry said. "Because I know you and me are going to work it out one of these days."

"Well we sure can't work it out with me up there and you down here," D.D. said.

"No, I've been thinking about that. I got a plan of my own, but I don't want to talk about it now."

"You can tell us, can't you?" D.D. said.

Larry shook his head, still staring over the valley.

It's something I'd just rather keep to myself, but I'll tell you one thing." He turned now, smiling. "You may be seeing me a lot sooner than you think. Just keep your eyes and ears open when you get up there."

"It (the oil industry's arrival) was like a military invasion
—another Normandy landing, only better equipped and
without so many scruples."

—Harmon Helmericks
Alaskan Bush Pilot

Chapter Five

Anchorage, September 10, 1969

Excitement in Alaska's biggest city had not been
higher since goldrush days. For weeks bidders on the
four hundred and fifty-one thousand acres of North
Slope oil land offered by the State of Alaska had been
swarming into "Anchor-town." Swaggering Texans in
big hats and pointy, high-heeled boots mingled with
sharp pin striped New Yorkers and shrewd, dapper in-
vestors from London.

The Anchorage Westward, the Traveler's Inn, and
the Captain Cook Hotel had all been solidly booked for
a month. Every two-bit motel and workers' rooming
house was fully occupied. A few oil executives, like
Wilbur Steele, had had the foresight to send huge land
yachts (super deluxe mobile office-homes) ahead of
them, up the Alcan Highway, to provide comfortable,
and above all, completely secure, accommodations.

Bidding on the tracts was expected to go to a billion
dollars. Alamo and Golconda, of course, were already
well situated, holding leases on the areas where the dis-

covery wells had been drilled—some bought for fifty cents an acre back in the fifties. But there were tens of thousands of acres surrounding the area of the discovery that would be drawing from the same oil formation. This is what the bidding was all about.

All over the city, company men, executives, accountants, geologists, drilling experts huddled together in private corners to plan their strategy. Those like Golconda, Royal American, and Alamo, who were already situated on the North Slope, were anxious to guard the geological information on which they would base their bids for the remaining acreage, while those who were not so fortunate had to assemble every tantalizing clue and bit of scouting information they could, in order to put together a credible bid on the various tracts without leaving too much "on the table."

In the lease areas scattered on either side of the two big Royal American and Alamo holdings, rumors and exaggerated tales spread like splashes of spilled oil as scouts and spies made repeated dashes to the North Slope, attempting to winnow out some further clues by observing stacks of pipes, and trying to estimate the depths of holes that were being drilled, watching the comings and goings of supplies and personnel and analyzing reports of test burn-offs. At one point, the tool pusher on Alamo's Crazy Horse Number One threatened to take an M16 and shoot down the next low flying plane to pass over his rig.

The state had put up North Slope land for lease four times previously, since it had selected a million acres in the form of Federal Land between Pet 4 and the wildlife range to the east in 1964. No company could be sure of what the others might bid for the leases offered. The sale was to be based purely on sealed bids with no open competitive bidding, although there were many who thought that the state would earn more in an open auction.

All of the participants were aware of the value of inside information. One careless word could cost a company billions in valuable leases. On one hand, a carefully planted red herring might confuse a competitor to the point where he might waste his resources by over bidding for possibly worthless leases. On the other hand, little-known leases might be picked up for a pittance—"pittances" were going for ten million dollars and up.

Each company had to plan carefully, as they had been allotted by their management a certain amount to spend on the checkerboard of leases sprawling across the North Slope.

All of the leases previously sold in Alaska had netted less than a hundred million. But predictions now were that the bidding would go to ten times that. The largest previous total bid had been six hundred and three million dollars, paid the previous year for three hundred and sixty-three acres in the Santa Barbara Channel off California.

Gamblers, pimps, whores, conmen, and scam artists of every persuasion were drawn to the scene like sharks sensing the thrashing movements of a potential victim in the water. Black, white, brown, and yellow whores cruised up and down Fourth Street in junk heaps, calling out "Want a ride, honey?" in silver-sweet, dollar-hungry tones.

The biggest lease sale in history was scheduled to open at seven A.M. in the Sydney Lawrence Auditorium. In addition to the seats held by subordinates for oil company executives, functionaries, and geologists, there were two hundred general admissions. The line of people waiting for these seats stretched halfway around the block by six a.m. NBC, CBS, and ABC TV crews were in the auditorium, as well as TV crews from

Japan, Europe, and the BBC in Britain. There were also reporters from most of the big East Coast cities and Europe.

The crowds jostled each other on the street, waiting to storm into the auditorium like opening day on the Cherokee Strip. John Takolik and other native leaders had been busy since the early hours of the morning. They had organized a group of high school students from the bush at the Anchorage Native Welcome Center and had them busy drawing up signs and nailing them to sticks. Ike Samuelson gave the kids their final instructions. "Take the crap," he said. "It's going to look nicer if people bully you. If they spit at you, don't react. We'll just take their names down. We're going to do this in an orderly fashion. If they ask about your rights, you know what to tell them."

Takolik listened to all this peace-making instruction and chewed his lip in frustration. It was Ike's show—for the moment. Later, he took him outside and remonstrated. "What is all this 'turn the other cheek' bullshit, Ike? You know you never get any attention that way! They just crap all over you. If you want action, you got to follow what the S.D.S. is doing down in the lower forty-eight, or the I.R.A., or the Palestinians. Throw some bombs. Act, don't talk!"

"Look, Ike said, "When the time is right for action I'm with you. But this isn't it. It's tough enough getting those Uncle Toms in the villages to go along with anything as it is. But now at least we've got most of them on our side. Hell you and I know that nobody but the young kids were willing to come down here and picket —and a couple of radical whites."

"But the Eskimos are protesting the wrong things. They're just asking for a big payoff when it all happens. That won't help. It'll still wreck the whole Eskimo way of life." Takolik argued.

Ike wasn't impressed. "Be realistic. The oilmen are moving in. We won't stop them, but let's at least make sure they don't screw the Eskimos the way they have in the past. You try and stop oil development entirely, and half the Eskimos will be down on your neck. They *want* a settlement, but a fair one—with Eskimos sharing in the royalties."

"Those villagers are all selling out to the white men. Remember before the missionaries came the shamans were the only ones to stand up and fight? Maybe the time has come again . . ."

"Look, Takolik," Ike said, "This is just the wrong time for that crap. The oil companies are the villains. The poor Eskimos are the heroes, and we have nationwide network television here to cover. How often do you think we'll get a chance like this to tell the people our side of it? If we get violent now—on television—we'll just make *ourselves* the villains instead of the oil people."

"Goddamn it Ike!" Takolik shouted, "It's going to be the same story all over again isn't it? The Eskimo takes shit and shit and shit from the white man, and comes up smiling and peaceful like he likes it. If you don't do something, I'm gonna take action myself."

Ike sniffed Takolik's breath suspiciously.

"In the first place you've been boozing again. You're never gonna accomplish anything if you keep that up. Besides you have nothing, no plan, no organization, no theory, just some wild-ass idea of violence. All you'll do is show up on coast-to-coast TV as another dumb drunken Eskimo. Just what we don't need right now."

Takolik seemed about to explode with rage, but he clamped his lips together, turned on his heel, and strode out of the Welcome Center.

By five thirty in the morning, Ike and the kids were marching up and down outside the Auditorium. Ike's sign said, "ESKIMOS OWN NORTH SLOPE." Other kids in blue jeans and khakis carried signs reading, "BAD DEAL AT TOM KELLY'S TRADING POST," "TWO BILLION DOLLAR LAND ROBBERY." By the end of the day there were two hundred and fifty people taking turns picketing. Some of them were even white government employees, who took time off to join the pickets. And yet a good many of the natives eyed Ike's activities with disfavor.

He was too pushy for an Eskimo—too loud, too vulgar. And many of them were afraid that in some way he would hold up the exploitation of the oil and therefore delay their own share in the expected forthcoming riches.

Every reporter, TV crew member and reporter entering the stadium had to cross Ike's picket line and there was no way to miss his message.

Inside the Auditorium, the sale was inaugurated with an appropriately folksy ceremony, beginning with the Pledge of Allegiance to the Flag, with all of the oil executives, investment counselors, geologists, and newsmen standing solemnly, their hands over their hearts in the civilian salute, mumbling the time-worn phrases . . . "and to the Republic for which she stands, one Nation, indivisible, with liberty and justice for all."

This was followed by a request for everybody to stand and sing the Alaska State Song. Unfortunately, none of the visitors and few of the Alaskans knew the words and the rendition came out straggling and puny.

Tom Kelly, the Alaska Commissioner of Natural Resources, who was serving as master of ceremonies, gave an opening pep talk that described the greatness of Alaska's resources, his interest in the conservation of the wilderness along with the development of these resources.

"Those of us who live in Alaska have a feeling for our lands," Kelly droned.

His act was followed by Larry Beck, "The Bard of the North," who was dressed in a parka and mukluks. Beck gave a modern version of "The Saga of Dangerous Dan McGrew," which turned out to be a tribute to the oil industry that he felt all would come to know and love.

Governor Miller spoke next. His last words were, "Alaska will never be the same."

Meanwhile, at a desk to one side, sealed bids were being accepted until eight a.m., after which a solemn community of clerks began assembling and opening the envelopes. At ten thirty a.m. the ceremony ended and the sale began.

The first bid opened and announced produced a gasp of astonishment in the crowd, followed by a roar of excitement. Royal American Oil Company had offered fifteen and a half million dollars for one of the tracts on the Colville River Delta. This was a hundred miles north and west of Prudhoe Bay.

In the next ten minutes, Royal American had bought more than fifteen thousand acres along the Colville River Delta, and had paid almost a hundred million dollars for those rights.

Sir Ian Plummer, the sleek representative of Royal American Oil at the conference, had found a seat in the press section next to London's Fleet Street team of crack journalists, sent to cover the event. Plummer was tall—six-foot-three or better—and slim in his Savile Row tailored suit. His face, with its predatory beak and keen restless eyes, suggested the visage of a peregrine falcon. When the bidding closed on the Colville River tract, he nudged Richard Kilian, the shaggy-haired correspondent from the London Express sitting next to him and said, "Hold onto your hat, old boy.

You haven't seen anything yet." And as the bidding opened up on the tracts where oil had actually been found on the North Slope, the bids began to leap in giant steps.

When bidding was announced for the leases in the Prudhoe Bay area, prices were offered that made Royal American's earlier bids seem like penny ante. Most of the excitement was saved for when bids were offered on Tract 57, which bounded the oil discoveries made by Wilbur Steele's Alamo Oil Company.

The first bid on the tract was by Atlantic Richfield and it was for twenty-six million dollars. Royal American brought this up to forty-eight million, and as bids were opened this seemed to be holding as the highest. The next bid, from Mobil-Phillips and Standard of California, for seventy-two-point-one million dollars caused the whole auditorium to break into a pandemonium of cheering and shouting. That seemed to close off the auction, but there was one more bid.

Nervously, the clerk opened the folded piece of paper and read from it. "Golconda Oil bids seventy-two-point-three million dollars for Tract 57."

The crowd seemed paralyzed into silence for a moment, and then broke into a deafening roar.

Ralph "Rawhide" Robertson, a sprawling, gawky looking Texan in a Stetson, grinned smugly as the bid was announced. Two men from the Mobil-Phillips-Standard group turned around in their seats and fixed him with a steely gaze. Robertson ignored their angry looks. It was clear to most of the insiders that in some way Robertson had gained access to the "secret" bid to be offered by Mobil-Phillips-Standard. Otherwise how could he have come so close? Certainly, when amounts of this magnitude are involved, an expenditure of ten or fifty or a hundred thousand dollars for information would be a well placed investment. And what clerk or junior executive could not be tempted by such sums?

That bid by Golconda represented the highest for the day. As the sale continued, however, Golconda continued to be the big spender, finally investing almost two hundred and eighty million dollars for eighteen tracts, some of them bid on in conjunction with other groups. Eagle Oil had made a heavy play, putting up one hundred and seventy-five million dollars for some twenty-six tracts.

Wilbur Steele sat in his land yacht parked in the West Fourth Street lot, which had been made from the levelled over rubble of the 1964 earthquake.

The vehicle was a sleek customized Cortez—a self-contained motor home that included a living room with a complete communications setup: radio, television, telexes and wire-service teletypes. In addition, there were two bedrooms with complete baths, and a bar.

Wilbur watched the proceedings on TV with a small smile on his face. Alamo Oil had taken only a minor part in the bidding, actually only placing winning bets on about nineteen tracts. After all, with Golconda, he owned over a million acres on the North Slope, and, to date, it was the *best* million acres. Wilbur was not interested now in laying out more capital when he already had—he suspected—more oil than he knew what to do with. His financial resources must be conserved for more important projects, such as exploitation of the find.

At the end of the day the successful bids put in for North Slope Oil Concessions amounted to $900,220,590.00—just short of a billion. The whole state of Alaska had been originally bought for two cents an acre, and on this day a tiny segment had paid $2,180.00 an acre, just for the oil and gas rights.

Reviewing the sale in his mind, Wilbur Steele wondered who Robertson had paid off, and how much, in order to get the information on which Golconda's staggering bid was so obviously based.

"That twisty so-and-so is going to get his hand caught in a bear trap one of these days," Wilbur said to himself as he switched off the TV.

Every phone line out of Anchorage that could connect to a brokerage house in New York was tied up for hours. Several of the speculators had held lines open for the entire ten hour duration of the auction. As soon as the lease sale closed, the certified checks that had accompanied each bid were rushed to a plane chartered by the Bank of America, which was handling the financial end of the deal. The plane was heading east, toward the rising sun, in order to deposit the checks as soon as each bank opened, and have that billion dollars earning interest by dawn of the same day.

Brandon came back to the land yacht at the close of the sale to change his clothes and help Wilbur Steele get ready for the big party that night at the Petroleum Club atop the Anchorage Westward Hotel.

"That son of a bitch Rawhide Robertson," Brandon said. "He shaved that bid pretty close."

"Well, our information wasn't so bad, and we only had to pay Robertson for a little of it."

Brandon looked surprised. "You made a deal with Robertson?"

"I only wanted those few tracts. There was no point in fighting him over it. We're going to have to work together in this project in the end."

"Can you count on him?"

Wilbur, lathering his face for a quick shave, stared at his reflection in the mirror. "Golconda'll help, because they're in on the deal. But keep in mind that we have a use for every barrel of crude we can get out of there, and the sooner we get it the better. We're talking about a probable profit of ten billion dollars according to my figures. And a quick ten billion to us is a lot better than a slow one."

"And what about Golconda—Robertson?"

"They got all the crude they can use right now. As far as they're concerned, they'd just like to keep this in the bank until the price goes up to make it juicy."

"You think all this oil dumped on the market will bring the price down?"

Steele buried his chiseled features in a hot towel. "We'll have to see to it that it doesn't, won't we?"

Brandon scratched his bristly crew cut speculatively. "That's a pretty tall order. How do you figure . . ."

The question was interrupted by the discreet buzzing from the Swedish-style modern phone on Wilbur's desk in a niche just outside the bathroom. Brandon picked it up impatiently.

"Brandon, base one." He was silent while a voice sputtered on the other end in apparent agitation. Brandon shot a worried glance at his boss, still mopping patches of lather from his freshly shaved face.

". . . I thought you were watching her . . . Didn't you have enough men . . . Oh. I see . . . Well, when she was arrested, why didn't you pick her up at the jail? . . . They did? Who? Who picked up the bail? . . . The S.D.S.? Isn't that the group that . . . Well, use as many men as you can. And get moving fast before she can get very far . . . You did? Okay. Keep on it. I want a report twice a day whether anything happens or not. I'll get back to you if Mr. Steele has any further instructions." Brandon hung up the phone thoughtfully.

Wilbur Steele, who had heard the last part of the conversation, looked up at him with concern. "Something with Penny?"

Brandon nodded grimly. "She was busted on the highway just outside of Berkeley—for transporting marijuana."

66

"But I thought we had her watched."

Brandon nodded wearily. "Our men were there, but the cops seemed to've had a hard-on for your daughter. Anyway, they wouldn't play ball. They offered the cops money—nothing doing. There's a lot of trouble down there these days, you know, with these hippies and the student groups. I guess the cops were really out to get her ass."

"Well, it shouldn't be so much of a problem," Wilbur said. "We can beat it in court, I'm sure."

"We could," Brandon said gloomily, "Except that before we could get our man down there, she was bailed out by somebody else, and somehow she got out of the courthouse without any of our men spotting her."

"Who bailed her out?"

"A radical student group—the S.D.S. She's been running with them for some time now."

"Well, what about this kid you've got planted there? Can't he help us out—help locate her?"

Brandon shrugged. "Not so far. The word is that the group took her out, bundled her into a car, and took off. Nobody knows where they are."

"That little bitch!"

"We'll try to get her, Wilbur. But I have to admit it's tough. These kids have their own underground, and once they go to ground, we can't seem to penetrate. There's others out there hiding too, and the only way they'll get picked up is if somebody rats on them. Even putting up a reward won't work."

Wilbur stared at his chiselled features in the bathroom mirror, as though searching out the genetic weakness that had caused him to produce Penny.

"The hell with her. Let her disappear into that freak circus. I got better things to keep you busy with than combing every junkie commune."

"Well, we'll keep our eyes open anyway." Brandon

67

looked at his wrist watch. "We'd better get over to the Petroleum Club before they run out of booze."

"I don't think we have to worry about that. I had them lay in a case of Dom Perignon for us before the sale. By the way, did you hear from Deirdre?"

"Yes. She's agreed."

"People of the same trade seldom meet together even for merriment and diversion but the conversation ends in a conspiracy against the public or in some contrivance to raise prices."

—Adam Smith
The Wealth Of Nations (1776)

Chapter Six

There were only fourteen men, aside from the crew, aboard the orange 707, which was on long-term-lease to the Trans-Alaskan Pipeline Service (TAPS), a consortium of three of the companies most deeply involved in the North Slope oil: Alamo, Golconda, and Royal American. Representatives of the four other major participants in the Prudhoe Bay oil fields had been invited to join the consortium and share the costs of construction of the pipeline, which would presumably be necessary to transport the oil from the inaccessible Arctic Ocean to a deep water port.

The men invited were top executives of the oil companies holding virtually all of the North Slope leases. Each had been asked to bring with him only one assistant, generally an executive right hand man. By mutual consent, there were to be no secretaries nor were any notes to be taken by anyone else during the trip. It had taken some persuasion to get these tycoons on the plane together—one of them had once refused to see Nixon when invited to the San Clemente White House saying, "He's got a plane. Let him come to see me." (Considering the money that each of the companies had spent on the Nixon campaign, it was not surprising that they regarded him as something of a hired servant.)

Each of the men, of course, had his own jet in which he had arrived at Anchorage. But, as Wilbur explained, by traveling in the TAPS 707 together they could view the entire pipeline route and at the same time have a valuable exchange of ideas. If they left at nine in the morning, they would be over Prudhoe Bay by Arctic daybreak. The 707 could then descend to a relatively low level and follow the route of the pipeline to its terminal. The whole trip would take less than three hours and at Anchorage International Airport, where the 707 would finally touch down, the men could transfer back to their company jets in time for lunch aboard —if they so chose.

The oil men themselves were primarily native Texans or, at least, adopted sons of that state. Five represented large independents, and two were allied with the so-called "Seven Sisters," the mammoth multi-national oil powers, without whom no project of this scope could be brought to fruition.

One was an Easterner, Albert Stern, of Grandee-Stern. He was Philadelphia, but not of the Mainline. There was speculation that he was of German-Jewish descent, but Stern himself was closed-mouthed on the subject. He had been at Wharton a few years ahead of Wilbur Steele, but the two had not known each other, since Stern was a "townie" and had not mixed with the free-swinging fraternity set of which Steele had been a part.

Stern had built a fortune for himself, starting with a chain of service stations that he modernized and stripped down, painting them all in a uniform ochre color and offering cheap prices and no services other than gas sales. Later he had expanded into the refining end and bought into some smaller producing companies, but even now his firm was top-heavy on distribution and transportation. (Grandee-Stern was one of the largest supertanker contractors in the business.) Like Alamo, what Grandee-Stern needed was crude oil. A lot of it.

The men were oddly assorted physically, but if they had anything in common—with the exception of Rawhide Robertson—it was a certain bland protective coloration. All seemed to follow Lord Chesterfield's philosophy of being neither the first in style nor the last to drop it. Their hair was long enough to be modish, but not so long as to be noticeable. Their suits were finely tailored in Rome, London, or New York, but with few flamboyant frills. Stern, who wore a small upturned cuff on the jacket of his brown whipcord suit, was thought of as something of an adventurer.

The only foreigner in the group was Sir Ian Plummer of Royal American. He was a former agent of British MI6 and had been knighted during the war for having been instrumental in uncovering the fact that Standard Oil of New Jersey, one of the Seven Sisters, was exchanging vital information with the Nazis, even after the German invasion of Europe.

(Standard Oil of New Jersey had swapped its patents on tetraethyl lead, vital to German's production of hundred octane aviation fuel, for I.G. Farben research on synthetic rubber. Anticipating this information, they had held back research in America so that, when the Japanese finally seized the Malayan rubber plantations, the Allies were left with inadequate research on synthetic rubber while the Germans were far ahead. To Standard Oil of New Jersey, international cooperation was simply a matter of business and had nothing to do with such mundane matters as war.)

As a result of the information developed by Plummer,

the U.S. Justice Department ultimately moved against Standard and brought an anti-trust action against it for attempting to control oil transportation through pipelines, and for its restrictive agreements with Farben.

While the Seven Sisters effectively controlled the world oil market, there were powerful independent oil companies in Texas that had felt distressed and orphaned at being left out of the "Sister's" many cartel deals and market-sharing projects. There were even those that said that Whitney "Tiny" Bisset, who was attempting to weld a number of Texas independents into a single powerful unit, with world marketing potentials, intended to force his way into the closed family of the Seven Sisters.

If this was true, he had not been successful. But Bisset was able to organize several small East Texas producers into a group that was later expanded by Wilbur Steele with the addition of a chain of refineries and gas stations into what was now Alamo.

Wilbur's ambition, however, was still bigger. He constantly reinvested the considerable income and capital of Alamo into trying to find more sources of oil, so that he would not be dependent either on foreign crude (controlled by the Seven Sisters) or competitive producers in East Texas.

A master poker player, Steele in the end had bet all his chips on finding oil on the North Slope. And it was, above all, because of this that he had to invite the cooperation of Royal American and Golconda, the other "Sisters" in the Denali consortium.

Though Wilbur was a gambler, he was not a fool. During the war, when the Navy was exploring an area of the North Slope, looking for a Naval oil reserve to guard the country in case of emergencies, Wilbur Steele, then the commander of a Navy geological survey team, had been one of the men—all of them in peace time allied with the oil industry—who had done the exploration of the area later to be known as PET 4 —the United States Naval Petroleum Reserve on the North Slope.

Wilbur Steele learned there was oil up there, a lot more than the U.S. Government had realized, even to this day. And he and the others knew that if they under reported or minimized their findings in PET 4, ultimately there would be a chance that they themselves would have a crack at what promised to be the biggest oil pool in North America.

Because the oil reserves were supposed to be so enormous in Alaska, there was an unspoken agreement among the large oil companies not to try to exploit them for fear that the new supply of oil would drive oil prices down. But Wilbur, unconventional, daring, and desperately in need of oil, had broken the gentleman's agreement—much to the irritation of some of the crude-rich Sisters, like Golconda.

Golconda was represented at the meeting by Ralph Robertson. Rawhide, as he was known as much for his manner as for his weather-beaten appearance, was one of those Texans who never, but never, removed his high heeled boots or his Stetson hat. On the rare occasions he was seen without the hat, a white line the color of a frog's belly, could be seen above the brim line. It was said that Robertson would die rather than reveal the fact that he had first come to Texas from Binghamton, New York. For Robertson was not only proud of his adopted state, but insisted that every leading member of his staff appreciate the "Texas way of life."

He entertained on a lavish scale at a big ranch at McAllen and had fought unions and government inter-ference all his life. Among the Seven Sisters he had always been regarded as a maverick and a loner. This was perhaps the reason he had been so easily induced to join Steele's Alaskan consortium.

Among the other four attending the unusual excursion was Sid Lathrup of Eagle Oil. He was a pudgy, seemingly easy-going man, scion of a family that made it big at Spindletop. It was only his eyes, as hard and cold as a pair of steel ball bearings, that revealed the strength that enabled him to keep a top seat against the machinations of three sisters and two scheming brothers.

Bart Cunningham, of Magnolia, had the bearing and aggressiveness of a fighting cock. His conservative gray flannel suit was styled by a Savile Row tailor who came over twice a year to check the seldom-changing measurements of Cunningham's compact fifty-eight year old frame.

Jason "J.J." Walters, of Star Oil, was a cool giant of a man, with buck teeth, and a laugh that always seemed too loud for the occasion.

Jack Farnum, of Western Oil, was a conservative in every way—in his politics, dress, in his life-style—it is said he didn't own even one Cadillac. Steele had met them all many times, either in Houston at the Petroleum Club or Luby's Diner, or on various oil junkets looking after business in Indonesia, Iraq, Iran, and the desert states of Arabia. Plummer he had seen less frequently, but they had cemented a solid friendship when the British oil man had helped Steele acquire several good buys in paintings by Francis Bacon in London.

Wilbur greeted them as they gathered in the plane lounge for drinks before takeoff. He wore an English herringbone tweed suit, a pale yellow shirt, and a Wharton school tie. The cuffs of the shirt were fastened by links in the shape of his W-Bar-S Ranch brand. The greetings were cordial but restrained. Wilbur leaned comfortably on the end of a wooden bar carved with Haida masks. His movements were easy, almost languid,

74

and with his hard, beaked nose and gleaming, carefully-waved, prematurely white hair, he quickly established a feeling of his territorial prerogatives.

He waved toward the bar. "State your pleasure, gentlemen. We've got it all. And for those of you who are drinking highballs, we're cooling them off with million year old Alaskan glacier ice."

There was a scarcely perceptible lurch as the airport tractor pulled the 707 out of its gate and into position to taxi for a takeoff on the sixteen hundred mile round trip to Prudhoe Bay.

"Take off your jackets if you like, gentlemen. Get out of your shoes. I figure we're going to have plenty of time to talk, figure out details, cut up a few old touches, and work out the bugs in this project. Three hours may seem a long time to be out of touch with the outside world, but I think you'll find it's worth it—first to get a look at the location and scenery of this strike, and, secondly, to hear some plans in which I think you'd all like to take part, for maximizing the profits up here in the month." He took a sip of his Virginia Gentleman, which had been shipped in case-load lots from Washington by his brother, Senator Fred Steele.

As the plane flew over Cook Inlet, Wilbur turned casually toward the assembled group. "You know, I was doing some figuring about that pipeline we talked about yesterday at the Petroleum Club, and I think it's going to be about as big a venture as any of us have ever undertaken. One of my engineers has figured out that it is probably the biggest privately funded man-made project ever considered."

Bart Cunningham of Magnolia Oil threw a hard, cynical glance at Steele. "You can cut out the window dressing, Wilbur. I sure hope what you have to say on the rest of this trip is more important than *that*."

It was clear from the looks exchanged, Cunningham

spoke for all of them. Sightseeing was something they could do anytime. What they were interested in was maximizing profits.

"I ain't even sure that Golconda wants to be in on this pipeline deal," drawled Robertson. "It's going to take a long time to iron out *all* the kinks."

"You wouldn't be trying to stall it, now would you, Robertson?" Steele said, fixing him with an icy glare.

Robertson, with apparent indifference to the hard look, replied, "I ain't going to be pushed into anything before I'm ready—that's for *damn* sure."

"One thing to remember about the energy crisis is that oil men come naturally to the mechanics of the squeeze play. The oil business has always been an international poker game in which the cartel giants hold all the aces. For half a century the companies have practiced muscle flexing on a global scale."

—Ovid Demaris
Dirty Business

Chapter Seven

As the plane swept past the shores of Knik Arm, the men, peering through the windows of the customized jet, could see the snow clad outlines of the Chugach Mountains in the forefront of the great Alaska Range.

Among them, only Robertson and Wilbur Steele had ever been to Alaska before. Steele had appointed himself host and guide. "On a good, clear day you can see Mt. McKinley over there, beyond this range. We'll be getting a closer look at it."

The men had loosened their collars, many of them had taken off their jackets. Even Cunningham had removed his suitcoat, revealing an English Tattersall vest. Jack Farnum, however, had declined to either unbutton or relax. He pulled a black briefcase from his valise, opened it, and started checking geological field reports. In addition to the seven top executives, the plane carried the seven "executive assistants" who had been invited for the trip. Most of these men were large, hard-bitten, and from a military background. A good many had started as pilots, drivers, or bodyguards but like Brandon, who was there to represent Wilbur Steele, they had worked their way up, largely through their confidential knowledge and indispensable ability to get certain things done discreetly and with a minimum of discussion.

Of this group, Brandon was certainly the senior man. He was widely respected for his active part in the CIA restoration of Shah Pahlevi of Iran at the time that Premier Mossadeq had tried to nationalize Iranian oil in 1951. The operation, under the direction of Kermit Roosevelt, was neat, efficient, and cheap, having cost the CIA — according to one source — only about $700,000.00, half of which was paid by the British.

In addition to operating in security and on a body-guard level, most of these assistants were in charge of the teams of scouts that roamed the oil country, endlessly spying on the operations of the competition. And occasionally indulging in something which, although not called that, had a close resemblance to industrial espionage.

Within ten minutes after takeoff, the 707 was flying over the beautiful sweeping Matanuska Valley, cradled between the Alaska Range and the Talkeetna Mountains.

"In about a month," Wilbur said, "this will all be as green as a stack of dollar bills. It's the best stretch of farmland in Alaska, and probably, in some ways, one of the best stretches of farmland in the country."

Farnum looked up from his reports. "Any oil out there?"

Wilbur smiled. "Nothing but salad oil for those cabbages. No, all the oil they've found in Alaska so far has been around the edges or out on the Continental Shelf."

Ian Plummer, sipping on a bourbon, looked up with quiet interest. "Correct me if I'm wrong, Wilbur, but isn't it true that there've been some excellent formations out to the south here, in the Gulf of Alaska?"

"There's people that say so. I must admit, it looks good down there."

"Then, may I ask why we have spent so much money drilling in such difficult terrain as the North Slope, where it's so much more expensive to find it, and so much more expensive to get it out?"

Rawhide Robertson interjected himself into the conversation. "I'll tell you why. Because all the Gulf stuff's on Federal land—cost us a fortune to get at it now. Fuckin' Commies turned everything over to the Government. Even up there on the North Slope, two-thirds of everything belongs to the Government, one way or another. And the fuckin' Eskimo slants are tryin' to get the rest of it. They already put in a claim saying they own the whole Goddamn state of Alaska!".

Cunningham looked concerned. "You mean there are going to be lawsuits on this?"

Wilbur was patient. "Look, we *always* have lawsuits. How long do you think some group of Indians and Eskimos are going to be able to hold out against our lawyers? Not to mention the pull we have with the Government. Nixon's not exactly our enemy—or he better not be, after all we threw into his pot.

"If we had to listen to all them gooks, we'd all be walking around down there in Texas in sombreros and eating tacos. You all just come up with the money and we'll take care of the Slants," Robertson said. He refilled his glass from a bottle of Old Worthy Scotch on the counter.

Steele ignored the remark and turned to Brandon, who was pouring over a loose-leaf folder of reports in a leather binder. "Brandon, would you sketch these men in on the preliminary results of our feasibility reports?"

The group settled into comfortable postures preliminary to hearing the report which they assumed was the root cause of the meeting—except for Robertson and Plummer, who were involved in a quiet discussion in the corner of the cabin. Of course, both of them, as major lease holders on the original North Slope holdings, were already familiar to a large extent, with the contents of Brandon's report.

"Gentlemen," Brandon began, clearing his throat. His voice was fluent, effortless, and deep and carried only a hint of his dirt farm, Virginia origins.

"Back in 1968, when those of us drilling up here realized there was going to be plenty of oil to export from Alaska—maybe even before that—Alamo, with the help of our colleagues at Golconda and Royal American," he nodded courteously toward the two oil executives still involved in their discussion in the corner, "conducted an extensive and careful investigation of every aspect relative to transportation of oil on the North Slope to suitable markets in the United States or elsewhere. I know that several of you have also given thought to this project. Some of the research goes back a long way, even to the time when the first oil finds were made on PET 4. We all know American petroleum needs have been increasing about four percent a year . . ."

Steele interrupted. "I think you can skip the preliminary details, Brandon. These gentlemen are basically interested in the transportation problems."

Brandon looked up, annoyed at the intrusion in his carefully prepared presentation.

"Very well. Of the principal route alternatives," he pulled down a large wall map of Alaska and from beneath the bar he produced a small flash-light pointer with which he illustrated his remarks, "the first possibility is a pipeline that would run a little less than eight hundred miles from Prudhoe Bay," he flashed the light on a spot on the North Slope of Alaska and swept it in almost a due south route to a point just east of Anchorage, "down to a port in this ice-free area of Alaska — probably Seward or Valdez, although our studies favor Valdez. Another alternative would be a route that ran east here from Prudhoe, along the edge of the Arctic Preserve, which lies just east of the Prudhoe strike, into Canada, then down the McKenzie Valley, and into the producing Province of Alberta. From the Edmonton area, this pipeline would extend to Puget Sound where oil destined for California refineries could be picked up by tankers, unless, of course, this pipeline were extended down the coast to California.

"The same pipeline could also be extended from Edmonton into the North Central region of the United States. Another possibility would take the pipeline west from Prudhoe Bay, along here through the Naval Petroleum Reserve, Number Four, and would terminate in the Chukchi Sea, near Kotzebue or maybe on the Bering Sea coast, near Nome.

"Other alternatives have been construction of an all-weather road following approximately the route of the pipeline as far as Fairbanks, then following the route of the Alaskan Railway. This would necessitate placing the southern terminal at Whittier, Seward, or Anchorage, where rail terminals already exist.

"Based on U.S. operations where it costs twenty-eight cents to ship a barrel of crude by pipeline from Oklahoma to Chicago—seven hundred miles away—and where comparable rail shipment on existing rails is two dollars a barrel, we have not seriously pursued the railroad alternative. This applies also to truck transportation. One of our cooperating oil companies," he nodded toward Robertson, "has already invested a considerable hunk of money in researching the feasibility of using ice-breaking tankers to bring North Alaskan oil to the eastern market. We are still waiting for a full report on this, but it seems at this point that while a ship might possibly get through in certain conditions it would be an expensive and vulnerable route."

Robertson looked irritated.

"Of course we have taken into account the possibility of loading oil directly in Prudhoe Bay, but Prudhoe lies on a very shallow shelf and is ice free for only a few weeks in the entire year, so this seems a highly unlikely possibility considering the volume of oil we would need to ship out of this field. Economics also favor using the pipeline for as long a route as possible.

"Some of the alternatives have a futuristic sound, and perhaps, in time to come, might prove practical. General Dynamics has been developing an idea for a nuclear powered super-tanker submarine in the one hundred-seventy thousand ton range. These vessels could cruise at depths between three and four hundred feet below the polar ice caps, but they require more time than we have for design and testing before there is a prototype ready to haul oil. General Dynamics has told us that they would need at least two or three years lead time for the nuclear power plant alone. An optimistic estimate for completion of the vessel itself—barring strikes and other problems—is about five years. Basically, I think we can forget about submarines for a long time.

"Other highway, tramway, monorail, and forms of surface transportation have also been proposed and discussed, but all would have limited tank capacities and would require enormous fleets of cars. Besides, such surface forms would be subject to rigorous weather conditions, with the possibilities of accidents.

"One proposal was to elevate the pipeline and use it to suspend an aerial tramway which would be used along the entire route as a transportation system for people and materials other than oil. Our study indicates that elevating pipelines, even on pilings, is a much more expensive system than constructing them underground or on the surface on a gravel berm. The higher the pipeline is elevated, the more costly it becomes. Additionally, such a line would have to withstand winds up to a hundred fifteen miles an hour, far out of line in expense.

"It has even been suggested that we might be able to move the oil from the North Slope by air-borne vehicles—lighter than air crafts such as dirigibles, rigid balloons, aircraft, or hovercraft. But none of these would be equal to the two million barrel a day movement which we envision as necessary for Prudhoe Bay.

"Two million barrels a day is about thirty times the total amount of tonnage of all freight and express carried by the U.S. airlines in the past year.

"We have come to the conclusion, therefore, that the most feasible method of all is a pipeline: and of the alternate pipeline routes, Prudhoe Bay to Valdez across the Brooks Range is the only conceivable one. A McKenzie Valley project would offer enormous obstacles from ecology-minded groups—even more than we will have traveling south through Alaska—since it traverses the Arctic Wildlife Preserve immediately to the east of Prudhoe Bay, and on entering Canada would have to deal with various governmental and ecological problems that could be raised by the Canadian provinces and the Canadian Federal government.

"As you know, there has been a socialist trend in Canada. The Province of Saskatchewan has already voted socialist and I don't think it would be very smart, in view of the national security situation, to subject ourselves to the possibilities of nationalization, or terrorism, in addition to everything else.

The pipeline will be mostly buried—out of sight, silent, secure, and all but invisible. A minor irritant to the sparse population of Alaska. We propose that the entire pipeline, including all related facilities, will occupy less than twenty square miles out of the 560,000 square miles in the entire state. There are, of course, some risks associated with this, as with any development. But we have all been involved in building pipelines all over the world—over the Alps, and the Andes, and elsewhere in the far north.

"These pipelines have been built under conditions very similar to those encountered in Alaska. The technology is available to us. I have had access—through my contacts with certain government intelligence sources—to the work of Czukek and Demek on problems of permafrost encountered by the Russians in building their Siberian pipeline. Between us and our other colleagues, we have at least two hundred thousand miles of successful pipelines in the States alone—most of it runs through areas of high recreational and environmental value, without disturbing these activities. In addition, our study of economic factors in Alaska indicate that both the Native and non-Native population will enthusiastically welcome the development of jobs associated with the construction of this pipeline; in fact, that they would deeply resent the shipping of their oil, or at least the oil originating in their state, by any other means. Since the pipeline might raise skills, provide jobs, and a certain economic independence in many areas where these benefits are now in short supply—" Brandon paused to shuffle through the few remaining pages of his report.

Steele cut in, "Thank you, Mr. Brandon. I think you've presented the case very well. Are there any questions gentlemen?"

"Well, I must say," Farnum said, closing his folder of geological reports, "it seems we are letting ourselves in for an enormous expense per barrel to get this oil out."

J. J. Walters fixed Steele with a toothy, sincere smile. "I agree with Farnum. I can't say I like the profit margin on Arctic oil at present prices. Perhaps we should wait a while until there's a more favorable price on oil."

Robertson's head nodded in almost imperceptible accord. Wilbur had noticed Robertson huddling several times with Walters at the Petroleum Club, and assumed the big Texan had offered to keep Walters well supplied with crude, apart from anything that came out of the north.

The plane was flying now over the Susitna Valley toward the Alaska Range and the looming majesty of McKinley.

"There *is* no workable alternative to this pipeline," Steele said calmly.

"Do you know what it's going to cost?" Farnum asked.

"Sure I do—a billion or so—maybe more."

Steele signalled with his eyes to Brandon, who handed him a folder. "Gentlemen, I suppose most of you already know this through your special sources of information—"

Robertson ventured a smug smile.

"—but our confirmation well, on the Colville River, which is a seven mile step-out from Crazy Horse Number One, indicates that there is a minimum of *ten* billion barrels in the Sadlerochit level. Actually, our objective in the drilling was the Lisburne formation underneath it. Certainly we knew that the Triassic didn't have much of a history of producing oil elsewhere in the world, much less in the United States. If anyone had told us we would find that kind of oil in the Triassic, we probably would have told them they were crazy. But the fact remains: we did drill, we did find it, and to the west, in the Kuparuk River sands, there seems to be another formation of maybe a billion barrels."

There was a long pause while the information sunk in. Of course, all of the men, through their own resources, already knew that the North Slope was a major find. And some of them were reasonably certain that it was in excess of two billion. But *ten billion!* That would make it bigger than the East Texas field—the biggest one ever struck in the States.

"You ain't just speeding on us, are you?" Latham asked.

"As a matter of fact," Steele said, accepting another highball from Brandon, "I'm underestimating."

"Can you really bring it in at a billion dollars?" Farnum asked.

No guarantees. We don't know what we're going to run into out there. I told you this was the big one. I can only say this, any one of you wants to sell out your leases, I'm ready to buy."

"Who're you kidding?" Robertson said. "You couldn't buy diddly-shit. You're stretched to the limit from drilling that well."

Wilbur looked at him coldly. "You want to try me? You're not the only Sister in the family.

"I wish you'd explain one thing," Plummer said. He was a rosy-cheeked man in rough tweeds and looked as though he'd just stepped in from a bird shoot in Scotland. "Would it not be more advisable—as you mentioned—to run the pipeline along the McKenzie River, across Canada, and into your Middle West? The land is much more level and the pipeline might be used to run Canadian gas or oil down also."

"Fuck that," Robertson said angrily. "And leave the whole thing up to the Canucks? Come around and Communize the whole thing, charge us to run our own damn oil? No sir, we ain't leavin' no pipeline in the control of no foreigners."

Plummer looked pained.

"He didn't mean you, Ian," Latham said. "You're one of the good ones, even though you are a Limey."

"Robertson's right," Wilbur said. "We're going to

have to battle conservationists, Native claims, state claims, and every damn thing, putting this pipeline through. It's bad enough to do it with the State of Alaska and the Federal Government looking over our shoulders, without taking on the Canadian government, and the Canadian Natives, plus all those Canuck radicals over there."

"Of course," Robertson said, "if any of you fellows don't like the plan, I stand ready to buy out your leases and maybe give you a good profit. Unlike Wilbur here, I know I can make the offer flat out with no help from anyone."

Walters glared at the big, tanned delegate from Golconda. "Don't try to puff yourself up, Robertson. You may work for a big outfit, but we know what you're pulling down. You're only taking out two hundred thousand a year. Just a salaried boy. There isn't a man here, except maybe Plummer, who couldn't buy you and sell you ten times over. So don't come on big, fella."

The other independents smiled in approval. While they regarded themselves as victims of the big, multinational companies, the fact was that each of their companies was largely family owned, and each of them had personal property in excess of a half a billion. Rawhide Robertson had to be content with his salary and whatever he could steal on inside information and stock speculations. It probably was the only business in the world where a man pulling down two hundred thousand dollars a year was thought of as a piker.

The look Robertson gave Walters was murderous.

"You say we're going to be bringing down around two million barrels of oil a day into some port down in the south—how are we going to market that without driving the bottom out of the prices?" Farnum asked.

Wilbur smiled sardonically and said, "I think we have

a plan that will enable America to handle the big petroleum crisis that's coming."

"What petroleum crisis?" J. J. asked. "There's no crisis. We got more fucking oil now than we can sell."

"Yes, but we haven't implemented my plan yet. It's a big one, and we're all going to have to cooperate on it. But believe me, it's going to be worth the trouble. If this project goes through, gentlemen, we'll be splitting up a pie of two to three billion dollars a year."

He turned to his hard-bitten executive assistant. "Brandon, will you sketch in some of the details for these gentlemen? You all remember Mr. Brandon's part with the CIA in helping us retain our holdings in Iran at the time nationalization was threatened."

"As several of you have pointed out," Brandon said, "a major problem with this North Slope oil is that it's going to be damned expensive to bring down. In fact, as long as Middle Eastern oil stays as cheap as it is, around thirty cents a barrel, there'll be hardly any point in developing this field. But Mr. Steele and I think it's time we were independent of these foreign pressures. Nationalization is almost certain in Venezuela, it's already started in Libya, and it's more than likely in Iraq, Iran and Saudi Arabia. You all know of course what happened to Shell down in Indonesia.

"Our country must be made to realize how important it is to develop our own oil resources. Congress has been resistant for a long time to the idea of raising the prices on domestic oil. But they don't realize the danger to our country. For instance, suppose the foreign oil suppliers should join together and form their own oil organization? Suppose they increase the price of oil to American companies? Such a move could really shake up those people who have not yet realized the importance of developing our own resources."

"And do you think there's a chance such a thing could happen?" Plummer said.

"With the agreement of you gentlemen, I plan a trip to the Middle East in the near future to investigate just such a possibility," Brandon said.

Stern rose and walked over to study the chart behind the bar carefully. "I don't see any way we can profitably get the oil out unless something happens to the prices," he said. "We all paid plenty for those leases."

By now it was after ten a.m. and the early sun was tinting the foothills of the snow covered Brooks Range a gaudy pink. From twenty thousand feet, the broad ranging, rugged mountains, sloping gradually toward Prudhoe Bay looked like a crumpled carpet of rosy-colored paper. Beyond it stretched the flat white expanse of the tundra, which blended almost imperceptibly into the waters of the Arctic Ocean.

The speeding plane began its descent toward the cluster of lights still blinking in the late Arctic dawn on drilling towers, temporary construction buildings, and tall cranes.

Brandon lowered a second map. "This is a numbered map of the leases if you want to compare. They're down there somewhere."

None of the men got up to look. They were interested in the money side, not the drilling.

"That little airstrip down there is Deadhorse, the one we've been using for the development of the Prudhoe area," Wilbur Steele said. "It got its name from a trucking company that nearly went bankrupt supplying us. The outfit called their company 'Deadhorse Haulers' to show us that they were willing to haul anything in order to stay in business. I must say, they're doing okay now, with the help of the pipeline service."

The plane had dropped in a descending bank, until it was flying only a few thousand feet over the dark thin line in the tundra that represented the haul road that had been bulldozed through for supplies going to Prudhoe.

"As you can see," Wilbur said, "the road itself is just like a thread running through the wilderness—it hardly makes any impression at all on the land. It's enough to make some of us Texans feel puny. If you superimposed a map of Alaska over the lower forty-eight, from the Aleutian chain to the pan handle, it would reach from California to the Carolinas. One of the glaciers they got down there could blanket up the whole country of Holland."

The plane swung wide over the Beaufort Sea, dropped down to a comfortable two thousand feet and began flying south toward the towering Brooks Range, along the Sagavanirktok River. Every twenty-five miles or so they flew over spaced construction camps—tiny dots on the landscape.

"We've got forty million dollars in construction equipment down there already," Wilbur told the group as they stared curiously out the windows. "It's just waiting for a go-ahead."

They flew over Galbraith Lake Camp, rimmed by velvet mountains in blue and white hues and snow covered lakes. Past the camp the plane gradually ascended into the heart of the Brooks Range, flying at seven thousand feet over the forty-eight hundred foot Dietrich Pass, which marked the highest point on the pipeline route. It was a fantasy land of sharp edged peaks, cathedral-like valleys, and billowing clouds.

Zooming out of the pass, the plane winged over the old mining camp of Wiseman, and then the Koyukuk River. Now they were out of the real Arctic and began to see timber, flecked with snow, along the way. Just north of the Yukon River the pilot dropped the plane in a low bank.

"If you'll look down there to the right," Wilbur said, "You'll see a caribou herd grazing. They come down here from the Brooks Range for the winter."

Several of the men went over to the side of the plane to look at the huge herd of thousands of horned animals moving slowly over the path of the proposed pipeline.

"Well, the haul road doesn't seem to bother them so far anyway," Walters said.

At the Yukon the road continued in a straight black line over the frozen ice of the river.

"That down there," is the ice bridge, made from logs tied together with cables, then frozen over with water from the river for added strength. It'll hold a full truck-load with no trouble."

South of the river the plane overflew rolling hills of frosted trees which sometimes so surrounded the slender strip of road that it vanished from visibility.

The plane continued south through Isabel Pass in the Alaska Range and followed the road where it dipped through the Copper Basin, the Chugach Mountains, and Thompson Pass and then squeezed through Keystone Canyon for its final descent to Valdez, a beautiful deep-water harbor ringed with steep, ragged, snow covered mountains.

Wilbur stood up as the plane headed westward over the Chugach Range. "I thank you, gentlemen, for your time. I think you can see our point about the pipeline."

"Yeah," Stern said, "we can see your point. But it all won't mean anything unless the price of oil goes up."

"For that, gentlemen, we will have to wait on Mr. Brandon's report on conditions in the Middle East," Wilbur said.

"While we the Native people are forced to wait and sit in spite of our screams of injustices on the proposed settlement for our land claim, the oil companies, the able few, and all awe-struck, would-be millionaires are fighting over the very lands that we have claimed, and to which we are legally entitled . . . Taking someone else's property knowingly and without consent is plain robbery, thievery, grand larceny. Call it anything—just plain stealing."

—Eben Hopson—Vice President
Alaska Federation of Natives

Chapter Eight

March, 1971; Fairbanks

John Takolik started systematically to drink at the corner of First Street and Noble Avenue, along the row of nondescript gin mills flanking the Chena River. He could tell almost from the start that it was going to be one of those tough nights. The street lights and the neon signs of the honky-tonk bars glowed with a peculiar luminosity in the thick night air loaded with ice crystals from the fog that rose over the Chena mixed with tar and carbon monoxide from the car and truck motors kept running constantly in the winter months, for fear that they would freeze up and be unable to start until spring.

The temperature in the windless streets had risen to zero. The week before it had been minus sixty. People were walking down the street in the snow, from bar to bar, with their parkas hanging open, in total comfort with the "warm spell."

It had been a long time since there were any signs in Fairbanks saying "Natives Not Permitted." There was no overt segregation, but there were bars that were simply not frequented by Eskimos and Indians. Takolik, in a combative mood, was determined that he would drink in each of them.

Actually the night was a gay one for most of the other Eskimos and Indians. Word had come down that Congress was going to pass a more generous Native land settlement than they had hoped for. In January, Bill Egan had taken over again as Governor from the crusty little Keith Miller. Most of the Native leaders were convinced that the Nixon administration was going to send to Congress a Native land settlement bill offering forty million acres of land for the Natives and a billion dollars in cash compensation in return for extinguishment of all Native Claims for the land.

The Tlingit, Haida, and other Indians in the south were delighted with such a scheme, which would give them a cut of a big piece of money without their having to relinquish any land. But where the oil was was Inupiat land, and Takolik, Charlie Edwardsen, Eben Hopson, and other North Slope leaders were not as happy with the idea. The Inupiat were getting screwed, Takolik felt, not only by the politicians and the oil companies, but by their own fellow Natives. What the Eskimos of the North Slope wanted was not the money but the land itself. Charlie Edwardsen had told the Congressional Committee the month before in Washington:

"I do not know what it is really going to take for those corporate pigs in the Senate and Congress to understand how we value our lands. They try to give us little economic development schemes — field welfare programs. But in Alaska we own the oil and we are in the way of getting that oil to market. 'It's the Goddamn Eskimos,' they say, and we Eskimos are just in the way."

In fact, the North Slope Eskimos had been so much "in the way," that the oil people finally appointed someone to work with the Eskimos to see if they could arrange a land settlement and get the pipeline started, since the Native Claims had now held up the building of the pipeline for two years.

Bernard Zander, an old friend of Ike Samelson's, had been appointed by the oilmen to try to help the Eskimos pull their act together and get a satisfactory settlement from Congress, so the pipeline could go forward. All the billions in revenue and development that Alaska was waiting for were now being held up by the persistence of the North Slope Eskimos in demanding that their claims to their own land be respected before the oil companies went ahead with tearing up and puncturing the tundra. But the oil companies, acting as a kind of super government, were not waiting for any Congressional or judicial decisions. They started to move men and supplies into the Arctic at such a rate that by 1969, the Fairbanks airport was handling more freight than any other airport in the world. And after the big lease sale, traffic of big Hercules transport planes bringing heavy equipment to the North increased.

The Eskimo claims, of course, weren't the only obstacles the oil companies faced in getting an okay for the pipeline. A special task force, appointed by then Secretary of Interior Wally Hickel, had run into problems to which no solution had been found, as yet: how to handle the permafrost; where would the gravel come from to insulate the pipeline from the ground; what would be done about possible earthquakes along the route (keeping in mind that the route followed—almost religiously—the path of epicenters of the most violent earthquake zones in an already quake prone area); what would be done about the disposal of human waste, (which does not deteriorate chemically in the cold of the Arctic, but remains in its original form for decades); how would the problems of water pollution from oil spills or tanker discharges be handled; and what would the effects be on wildlife of so much human activity in what had been wilderness?

Two members of the Interior subcommittee had taken a tour of Alaska and had come back furious at what they had seen: hilltops denuded of vegetation, a swathe cut through the wilderness for tens of miles, hundreds of drilling rigs operating on hundreds of square miles of ripped-up tundra. But what really angered the Congressmen was that all of this had been done without any permission being granted at all.

"After seeing all the work that's been done up there," Representative Saylor said, "this hearing is rather like coming to us after the horse has been stolen. The only thing left to do is lay the pipe—the rest's been done."

It turned out that the denuded hilltop Representative Saylor and his friends had seen had been gravel pits used for construction of a road to the Yukon.

Interior Secretary Hickel — a former Governor of Alaska—couldn't see what all the fuss was about. He pointed out that the pipeline would supply badly needed oil to the West Coast and bring much needed jobs to Alaskans. Asked how the Natives felt about the pipeline, Hickel replied cagily, "No Native village or association has reacted unfavorably to the pipeline project."

Conservationists screamed, Eskimos complained, but the oil companies, operating on some superpower level simply proceeded with their plans, knowing that, in the end, they had the clout to make what they wanted to make happen, happen.

A friend of Takolik's, an Eskimo woman named Lucy Ahvakana, had gone up to her fishing camp on the North Slope during the past summer. She found that Golconda Oil had taken over the shack that she had used for years, and was using her home for storage of its supplies. They had also built an airstrip nearby to keep the shack supplied and the traffic frightened away all the game in the area. Despite complaints, the oil companies just proceeded as if nothing had happened.

Emil Notti, a usually mild tempered Native leader and President of the Alaska Federation of Natives, finally was aroused to protest to the Governor: "We are extremely distressed at the interference of oil companies on the state lands of the Native people in the North Slope area. Two incidents have been brought to my attention by Mr. Eben Hopson of Barrow. The first instance, an oil company planted eleven barges of material near Beechey Point and took over lands that had been used and occupied by a Native family since 1920. There were buildings and a cemetery of eight graves on the lands appropriated by the oil company. They allegedly obtained a permit from the State Division of Lands, even though all maps show cabins located there, and the land was obviously currently in use and occupied by Natives.

"The second incident involved interference and threats to a Native man who was involved in subsistence fishing on Colville River. He was told to vacate his traditional fishing site and to move to another place."

John Takolik was only too aware of how useless these protests were. They would be published in the *Tundra Times*, the Native newspaper, and that was all the attention they would get. Meanwhile, Congress and the oil people kept talking about making financial compensation for any damage done.

"Goddamnit," Takolik muttered to himself as he trudged through the ice-hard packed snow of First Street. "Let them keep their fucking money! We want our land!"

The Northward Bar was one of those frequented

primarily by Texas and California construction men, and high-priced whores. John Takolik, feeling his nose turning cold, decided to turn into the long narrow, cavern-like room. He ordered an Oly—Olympia beer shipped up from Washington State—with a C.B. back. The Christian Brothers brandy had a reputation for getting the circulation going faster and more effectively than any other spirit. The bartender, a shaggy, curly haired big blond kid, looked at him coldly as he took the order and wordlessly served up the two drinks.

The bar was crowded and Takolik had taken the only available barstool, next to two sleek looking whores up from Vegas looking for some fresh blood. The girls had —apparently—been exchanging information with the bartender. "How are the cops up here anyway?"

The curly headed bartender shrugged. "We don't have much trouble with them. Besides, there's not many of them anyway—all they want to do is keep the peace, if you know what I mean."

"I think we do," the girl said.

"No, seriously. I've seen worse."

The talkative girl, who was dressed in a tight fitting red wool pantsuit with a head of hair to match its improbable color, snorted, "Down there in Vegas they're been busting me for everything from burglary tools to armed robbery. Anything to drag me away from work. And you know what those cops say? They say I'm too nice a girl to be in the life. They say they're only doing it to keep me from going wrong."

The girl, professionally alert, turned her eyes from the bartender for a moment to assess the sullen looking Native drinking the Oly and C.B. next to her.

The bartender shook his head in an almost imperceptible negative gesture. He leaned on the bar, cupping his hands carefully around his mouth, in a transparent effort to conceal his conversation from Takolik. "Forget about these guys. None of them have pipeline jobs, and they haven't got the kind of dough you're talking about."

"You don't have to go hiding your mouth from me," Takolik said, "I can hear real good."

"Well, why don't you just mind your business, then?" the bartender said with quiet menace.

"I *am* minding my business," Takolik said. "I live here. My parents live here. My grandparents lived here. My great-grandparents lived here. This *country* is my business. Not you people coming up from Texas and Nevada and . . . and those places."

The bartender, without flamboyance, reached under the bar and took out the shot-loaded pool cue he kept there, its end wrapped in tape to ensure a firm grip. "Listen, blubber-snapper, "I'm going to give you exactly ten to take your brown face out of here. And if you don't move, I'm going to split that thick skull of yours right down to your frigid, midget, digit."

Takolik's eyes clouded over with fury.

A burly Virginian, in a hardhat bearing the symbol of the Trans-Alaska Pipeline Service, was on Takolik's far side. He turned to catch the conversation and silently nodded complicity with the bartender. Takolik's strong white teeth were bared in a grimace so wide it almost could be mistaken for a savage smile. The tiny bristles in the sparse moustache that adorned his upper lip seemed to stand straight out in the stretched skin. Suddenly, in a lightning move, astonishingly quick for someone encumbered by a National Guard surplus parka, Takolik's two stubby hands shot out, and, before the bartender could lift the billy club, they fastened in a tight grip around his throat.

The bartender's eyes began to bulge like Ping-Pong balls from their sockets. His face, which had gone dead white, was beginning to turn purple.

Takolik's wide black eyes were squinted in fury, but

before the action could move into anything more drastic, there was a thudding sound and the tinkle of falling glass. The TAPS worker had broken the remains of a bottle of Oly on the back of John Takolik's skull. The Eskimo shook his head once in puzzlement, still hanging on to the bartender's throat, then he slumped gently to the floor.

The bartender, recovering quickly, leaped over the mahogany counter. Between him and the construction worker, they dragged the half-conscious Eskimo out the door and threw him over the high snowbank lining the sidewalk into the road.

The redhead looked on in horror. "Won't he freeze or get run over out there?"

"Christ, no," the bartender said, pouring himself a bourbon from the back-bar to settle his nerves. "Those guys are used to that. You'll see dozens of them laying around in the road and the snow. Doesn't seem to bother them at all—must be something in their blood. I even seen one of them get run over, just get up and brush the snow off his pants and walk away. This guy was a little unusual, you know," he said, wiping his moustache after downing the bourbon. "Mostly they're very peaceful. Just drink their booze, slide off the stool onto the floor, and lay there. Sometimes, if we got room, we just leave 'em lay—as long as they ain't in the way. Mainly they're peaceful little fellows—only fight among themselves. That guy's a little unusual. Guess he had some kind of wild hair up his ass. I don't know what gets into some of them. I guess its these long winter nights makes 'em go weird like that."

In the street, the cold was beginning to revive John Takolik. He sat shaking his head. Two short figures in blue down parkas approached him and stood staring down at him. One, who had her parka hood thrown back, was a white woman with a frizz of light blond

99

hair done in an afro style. The other, he could see now, was a little taller, had short dark hair, and intense black eyes.

"My god," the blond one said. "What did they do to you? You've got blood all over you."

Takolik reached up and realized that the sticky fluid running down his forehead and the front of his face was blood from the broken bottle. "Guess they cut me a bit," he said, woozily.

The girl took him by the arm and started to lift him. "Can you walk?"

"I guess so. Still a little dizzy, though."

"Marge, get his other arm," the blond commanded, and the darker girl complied. Between them they hauled the battered Eskimo to his feet.

Marge looked at her frizzy haired friend. "Where you want to take him?"

"Well, we better get him over to the Savoy where we can get a drink into him. I think he could use one. And we can get his face cleaned up," she said. "Come on along, fella. We'll figure what to do about that pig in there later."

Joined at the arms, the little troika moved off down the snow covered road, and through the parking lot that separated First street from Second street toward the Savoy.

"Each spring the whalers would pick up many young women from these villages to be used for their pleasure during the whaling season. Sometimes they were not returned until the following year, and then not all came home. This caused great anxiety and grief to the parents and husbands. It was not until many years later that law and order was obtained through the Coast Guard. At this time many of the women were finally returned to their home."

—Frank Topsekok, Alaskan Native

Chapter Nine

The trio stumbled past the straggling line of Eskimo, black, and peroxided whores drawn outdoors by the "warm spell." A few even dared to bare their goose-pimpled thighs to the cold breezes in hot pants and micro-minis. They stared with dead eyes as the profit-less trio struggled and slipped across the packed ice of the parking lot toward the bright lights of Two Street.

Two Street was the hub of Fairbanks night life and the walkway in front of the Flame Lounge, the only place downtown featuring topless go-go girls, was the parade ground for a colorful assortment of whores, pimps, and drunks, Native, black, and white. The Savoy, which advertised itself every week in the *Tundra Times* as "delightfully unique," was on the corner of Second and Lacey Streets, midway in Two Street's two block bright light section. It was the larger of two bars catering to the Native trade. The other was the Chena, immediately next door. The Savoy was a large room and supported a completely equipped bar along the right and left walls. In the middle there were pillars and booths. In front was a big pool table on which a number of drunken whores and prospective clients kept ripping up the felt with their misaimed pool cues.

The light was dim, and yellow—the air was thick. At

101

first glance, the scene looked like an old faded painting by Hogarth out of Remington. Seated at one table was a tiny fellow who was either one of the world's champion pimps, or was trying to impress the world as one. He wore an enormous white fedora, a flowered shirt open at the collar, a tight fitting pin striped suit—except for the shoulders which were improbably broad—and platform shoes. In the heels and the hat he probably still would have had trouble making five feet. A sign over the bar said "Happy hour six to seven. All drinks and Oly half price." Next to it was a sign for Olympia Beer with its motto: "It's the water that counts."

The crowd, aside from the whores, was largely Native and local, with only a sprinkling of the new influx of oil men and construction workers. In the gloom, several figures could be seen slumped on the tables or passed out on the floor. But no one seemed unduly concerned; those who were carrying their drinks from the bar to the booths simply side-stepped, or politely strode over, the obstacles.

The two women steered Takolik, still groggy and bloody from the blow on the head, to a booth near one of the pillars. The blond girl put her arms consolingly around the Eskimo's shoulders. What are you drinking?" she asked. "Marge, get him something from the bar."

"Oly. C.B. back."

The blond pulled a red bandana from the pocket of her wool lined denim dungarees, moistened it in a glass of water left there on the table by a previous customer, and began gently to rub the drying blood from Takolik's brow.

Takolik leaned back, closed his eyes, and yielded philosophically to her ministrations. The cut the bottle had made was above the hairline so that, when the girl

102

was through cleaning him, there was not much sign left except some tangled, matted patches of hair. The damage had not been that great. As the girl soothed Takolik's brow he mumbled a few words, which were swallowed up in the general din of the bar.

The girl leaned closer. "What was that you said?"

"I said," Takolik muttered, baring his teeth now in grim determination, "that I'll get that fucking, Texas-carpetbagging pig if it's the last thing I do."

"Right on, brother!"

Margie arrived with the drinks. Each of them took a bottle of Oly from the tray and lifted it in a toast.

"Up the people: fuck the pipeline," the blonde said.

"I'll drink to that," Takolik said solemnly.

They put the necks of their respective bottles to their lips. There were several serious swallows.

A huge, heavy-set man, in a red and black Pendleton wool shirt, with a bushy unkempt Santa Claus beard, walked unsteadily toward their table, reached across in front of Margie and clasped John Takolik's shoulder in a hand like a first baseman's mitt. "John-boy," he said. "How you goin'? Looks like you're doin' great—" He nodded his head in the direction of the women. "Will you have a drink?"

Takolik shook his head from side to side in a sulky, negative gesture. "Not with you, Baronian," he said. "I'm not drinking on oil company money."

Baronian roared with laughter, revealing a row of worn, tobacco-stained teeth, speckled here and there with gold caps. "Don't be stupid, man," he said. "Get it while you can. Besides, I'm boring from within—getting lots of information, pulling down fifteen hundred bucks a week. You'll be glad of my help one of these days."

"Who's paying for *your* drinks," Takolik said, "the Frito Banditos?"

"Look," Baronian said reasonably, "you know Ike Samuelson ain't paying for nothing. So Zander's picking up the tab with oil company money—what's the harm in that? You know he's on your side."

"He ain't on *my* side," Takolik said. "He's just trying to push the Native Claims Act through so they can get their fucking pipeline in there, without a lot of expensive delays."

Baronian shrugged. "Okay. Have it your way. But playing hard-nose ain't going to get you nowhere either. We work together, we might be able to come up with something."

"I'll let you know," Takolik said, dismissing him. He took the pony of C.B. brandy and poured it down his throat, wiping his lips with the back of his hand, as Baronian waddled off to join his group at the bar.

"Who was that?" the blond asked curiously.

Bobby Baronian," Takolik said. "He used to be a terrific wildlife photographer — even has a Ph.D. in something, I think it's marine biology. Claims to be a big environmentalist, but he sold out to the oil company. Now he says he's really against them, but he's working from within."

The blinde looked serious and interested. "I'd like to meet him again sometime."

Takolik suddenly had the feeling he had been taken over—acquired by these two women, like a stray dog in the street, and now they had a heavy length of rope around his neck and were leading him by it.

"Shit, Miss. I don't even know who you are," he said politely.

The girl hesitated. "You can call me Sonia."

"Funny," Takolik said, taking another swig from the Oly, "You don't look like a Sonia. All the Sonias I know are Eskimos."

A small, intense looking man, in a goose down parka,

104

had been watching the exchange with Baronian impatiently. As soon as the big man headed for the bar he slipped into the booth opposite Takolik and the girls. The parka was open and under it the newcomer was wearing an expensive looking beige camel's-hair sports jacket, and a casually elegant Vyella shirt. "John," he said, "I've been looking all over for you." He had a high dome-like forehead and a narrow, wedge shaped chin with hollowed out cheeks that gave his face something of the shape of an electric lightbulb. The words he spoke came through tiny rose-bud lips that looked oddly out of place in an otherwise ascetic countenance. "What happened at the meeting?"

Takolik looked at him dubiously. "The same as always. All the Indians were as pleased as shit to get a piece of money. They're all for the settlement, and most of the Eskimos too. All they can see is the dough and the jobs. They don't see what's going to happen later."

"What about Samuelson?" the man said.

"Ike's okay, even though he is taking the white man's dollar—indirectly. He wants to fight but he won't go far enough."

"Why? What did you have in mind?"

"You'd like to know that, wouldn't you? But you've joined up with them. Not fuckin' likely I'll tell you what I have in mind."

"You told me about that other idea, about taking over the DEW line outpost and holding it ransom until the Federal Government gave you back your land."

"That was Ike's idea. Or maybe a little bit both of ours. But anyway it was just talk."

The two girls were now listening to the conversation with intense interest, but Takolik made no effort to introduce them. The man himself paid them hardly any attention at all. A sallow faced man in an expensive looking gray Pendleton shirt slouched into the booth beside the man in the parka. Takolik interrupted his attack to look up a minute.

"Hello, Al," he said dully, and then turned back to the man in the parka.

"Besides, when I told you that, you were a newsman —and it seemed like you were a good one. Now, I don't know. All you do is put out these bullshit PR poop sheets for the pipeliners."

The man looked hurt. He had prided himself on his journalistic reputation. He had been the first one to get the news of the size of the North Slope strike and send it south where Alaska made front page headlines for the first time since statehood. He had expected a Pulitzer for the job, but somehow the credit had been dissipated in the newspaper for which he worked, and everything had been swallowed up in the more highly competitive stories of the Vietnamese war.

Takolik leaned back against the seat, studying the man facing him through hooded black eyes. He turned to the girls on either side of him. "This," he said, "is Brent Heywood. He used to be a hell of a newsman. Now he's a fucking whore. The other guy's Al Everhardt—he works for the *News-Miner* and so far, he's been a friend. But then Heywood *used* to be a friend."

Heywood's skin colored slightly with anger. He sucked pensively at his little cupid's bow lips, got up, and bowed almost formally to the women. "I'm sorry. I'll go now. I see I'm intruding. I don't like talking to him when he's in these moods—when he's been drinking. But you should know, he's really a sweet person." Heywood turned to the man in the Pendleton shirt. "Let's go, Al," he said. "Takolik's in a speech making mood."

Everhardt looked toward Takolik questioningly, almost as though asking if he were finished. Getting no

106

response he shrugged and followed the other man out of the Savoy bar.

The girls said nothing. Takolik looked up dully and said "Bye, bye, Heywood. Bye, Everhardt."

"You really know a lot of people, don't you?" Sonia said.

Takolik shrugged. "Before the pipeline came, everybody knew everybody else up here. There aren't that many of us. Christ, there's only five or six of us from the North Slope that's got the balls to speak up anyway. Everybody else is being a nice, quiet, passive, polite, Eskimo—like their grandpappies taught them." He reached down into the pockets of his parka, came up with a crumpled handful of bills, and put them on the table. "Let's get some more drinks. This party's getting too serious."

"That's okay," Sonia said. "We'll spring for the booze."

"Not on your life. I don't go for all that women's lib bullshit. I'm buying." He started to get to his feet, but Sonia pressed him down again.

"Okay," she said. "Margie'll get the drinks. We can just talk."

"Make it a double, Margie. No. Make it a triple. Saves walking back and forth."

Marge did some rapid mental calculations. "That'll be about fifteen bucks, right?"

"Whatever you say," Takolik said. "It's only money."

Margie carefully counted out the amount from the crumpled stack of bills in front of her—mostly singles with a few fives scattered in. When she had extracted the fifteen dollars there were only a couple of lonesome-looking singles left on the table.

"Might as well give them to the bartender," Takolik said, pushing the two remaining bills at the girl.

"But it's all you've got," she protested.

107

Takolik waved vaguely. "Don't worry. There's plenty more, plenty more."

Doubtfully Marge scooped up the untidy stack of bills and headed for the bar. While they were talking, Sonia had pulled an expensive-looking silver cigarette case from the hip pocket of her jeans. The case was engraved in a flowery script with the initials "SP" and inside the case, neatly lined up in a row, were a half a dozen hand-rolled cigarettes. Sonia held the case out toward Takolik. "Smoke," she said. "It's the real stuff. Matanuska Thunderfuck."

"Oh, man. You don't see much of that up here."

"Do you think it's okay to light up in here?" Sonia said.

Takolik waved carelessly. "They haven't got enough cops in this fuckin' town now to take care of the murders and the muggings, let alone somebody pulling on a few joints in public."

It took a long time for Marge to return with the drinks. And by that time Sonia and Takolik had smoked down about a third of the joints.

"Beautiful, beautiful," Takolik said, his eyes dreamy with delight.

Marge looked at them a bit acidly as she lay the heavy tray of drinks on the table. "You could have waited for me," she said to Sonia.

Sonia waved her hand carelessly. "Don't worry. There's plenty of this shit. You can catch up."

Matanuska Thunderfuck was powerful weed, grown in the hyperactive five-month summer of the Matanuska Valley. The smoke, on top of the C.B. brandy and beer, began to really blow holes in Takolik's mind. Probably he should have given up the drinking, once the joints were lit. But Takolik was essentially a drinker rather than a smoker, and he had downed three C.B. boilermakers by the time they lit the next joint.

108

Gradually he sank into a state not unlike a white-out. There were no horizons and no boundaries, except that, instead of freezing, he felt pleasantly warm, with a dullish tingle at his extremities. And it seemed to him that there was a warm hand groping at his crotch under the table. Or was it two? Or was it three?

As peaceful as he felt, he somehow almost got into a fistfight with Sammy Stevens, a Tlingit from Hoonah. It was Sammy's gloating over the five-hundred million dollar settlement that set Takolik off. The swing he started was so aimless and ill-timed, that Sammy easily slipped under it and gripped Takolik in a bear hug— more friendly than hostile.

"Don't be like that, Takolik. Remember, we're all brothers now."

"Yeah," Takolik said, "but some of you guys are more brothers than others." And he broke into a wild, high-pitched laugh. "That's poetry," he said. "More brothers than others." Then he remembered the girls, who were pulling him on either side into the cold night air. Soon they were in a taxi.

"You know, we have poetry," Takolik said, leaning back dreamily in the taxi seat, feeling the pressure of thighs and breasts, even through the layers of down. "We have our own stories and our own poems." He launched into a long story that he kept up as the taxi drove along the banks of the Chena to the first bridge and stopped before one of the old log huts, which now had a bright day-glow sign featuring "Swap-Shop, Second-Hand Goods, Books, and Antiques. Cheap." The sign was painted on the cut-out bottom of an old oil drum.

But Takolik hardly noticed, he was deep into his story of the Eskimo myths. "You know, we have a story up in the North Slope about the old days when everybody lived by hunting, and we all had this great

109

respect for nature. We figured everything had a soul—not just men and animals, but hills and streams and rocks—everything. Weather—that was a man walking around the top of the world. And the wind, it came from holes in the sky, but a shaman could sometimes close up the holes and make calm. The stars, they were human beings too, or maybe they were animals that had escaped from the earth. And if you didn't show respect to an animal, even after you had killed it, we believe that all the other animals would leave, and the Real People—the Inupiat—would starve. So even if we killed a seal, we would pour a dipper full of fresh water in its mouth. And if we killed a polar bear we would hang it out in the open for a couple of days, with different things, so that the soul of the bear could leave its body in peace.

"But there was one hunter. He was a really big deal. And he felt like it wasn't necessary for him to do these things. He didn't respect the souls of animals—even though they offered themselves to his spear or to his bow. And so because of this, all the animals went away from the land and the Real People began to starve. That hunter, he traveled across the ice for days and days, looking for food. And he went through a lot of bad times. And finally he was so weak from the lack of food that he couldn't travel any more. He laid himself down on the ice. So then the raven—that was the creator of the earth—came down and the hunter begged him for his life. But the raven pointed out that there was no food available, and he turned the hunter into a stalk of grass.

"The hunter was happy that way for a while. He laid there pretty warm. He was protected by the snow until the summer. But then a family of mice came along, and they were eating and pulling up the grass. The man became frightened, and he wished that he

110

were a mouse. As soon as he wished it, he changed into a mouse, and he felt that he was safe. But all of a sudden this big owl came and swooped around him. He was afraid again and wished he could fly.

"Flash! The minute he wished it, he changed into an owl. He flew out across the sea, but he got tired for a while and he had no place to land, except for a piece of driftwood floating there in the water. He rested on it and he floated until he came near to shore. There he saw two men and they had food with them. He immediately wished that he was a man again and he became one.

"He landed on the shore, but he was a stranger and the men were from another tribe. So they attacked him and killed him on the spot. And the minute he died all the animals returned to the land of the Real People and they weren't hungry anymore.

"That's a funny story, isn't it?" He turned to the girls, pleased with the story he had told them, but saw that they were asleep, one on either side of him, and that they were naked. The girl with the short chestnut hair was lying on one arm. The other girl was resting her head on his belly, breathing gently toward his crotch. They were on a big mattress on a floor somewhere in a log house. Takolik wondered if he had been away from his body—if he had flown away on a trip to the moon or someplace after he had smoked all of that weed. He looked down and the girl whose head was resting on his belly looked different. She had long auburn hair—not frizzy blond—yet she looked something like the girl he'd been with. Then he looked at the small, rough hewn table against the wall and saw on it a familiar mass of curly, frizzy hair.

"Fairbanks, Alaska—It's like a war, except there are no
guns and no particular enemy. The construction of the
Alaska Pipeline . . . will finally mean a steady flow of
oil each day from the edge of the Arctic Ocean south
to the ice-free port of Valdez. The project will also kill
hundreds of men, turn many women into whores, and
shatter the quiet lifestyle of the communities along its
798 mile route."

—Winthrop Griffith
New York Times Magazine

Chapter Ten

The living room of the log house on the Chena River
was warm, almost suffocating, due to the presence of an
unusual number of bodies in it. Every half hour or so,
somebody would open the door to let oxygen in to feed
the propane stove. Other than that, every crack was
filled with rags, fiberglass, cotton-like insulation, caulked,
nailed, or otherwise stopped to make the room almost
airtight. The furniture in the cabin was early Salvation
Army: a few battered kitchen chairs, an overstuffed sofa
with a greasy slip-cover out of which wads of upholstery
batting poked obscenely, like bits of fat flesh from a too
tight housedress.

The air was thick with the combined smell of cigarettes, Thunderbird, and Matanuska Thunderfuck. John

112

Takolik, who had not completely recovered from his drunk of three nights previous, was slung in the torn canvas hammock of a butterfly chair, staring blankly at the Che Guevara poster opposite him, hearing only a few of the words that were being spoken.

Sonia and Abby Maroon sat at a porcelain kitchen table at one end of the room. The table was covered with leaflets and ashtrays overflowing with cigarette butts. Maroon was a tall, round shouldered man, with a soft-looking olive-toned face, and a mass of straight black hair cut in bangs across his forehead and hanging almost to his shoulders. He wore mouse-gray aviation goggles, partly to conceal his dark sentimental eyes, which always looked slightly wet with tears, a feature he found embarrassing.

Sonia, who was co-chairing the meeting, pounded the porcelain table top with the glass snow-fall "Souvenir of Fairbanks" paperweight she was using as a gavel, causing the little white specks inside the weight to swirl in a mock meteorological crisis around the upright figure of the plastic polar bear inside.

She looked wearily at the small group assembled in the backroom of the second-hand shop. Useless as balls on a dairy cow—most of them—she thought as her eyes checked out her tiny revolutionary platoon. Even that erratic bunch of Weathermen in Seattle had been mire together than this. But she had not been able to get any of them to agree with her premise that the revolution was to be fought here and now, against the big industrial fat cats; that Vietnam was only a side issue.

They had called her a bourgeoise revisionist and other equally filthy names. Not more than one or two of them had known her actual identity. And those few —Marge included—could only think of getting at Wilbur Steele's personal fortune.

Rudy Rathman, who had found out who she was from Marge, was convinced that the group could make a fortune holding up Wilbur for ransom.

"You're his daughter, ain't you?" Rudy had argued. "That ought to be worth a couple of mil to him."

"Yeah," she had answered, "but there's one thing wrong with that—I would never take a nickel from that murdering son of a bitch."

"Even for a good cause?"

"Not for anything. Two; he already knew where I was at when I left. There's no way he's going to believe anybody's holding him up for ransom. Three; I think the cold-blooded fucker would just as soon see me dead anyway, even if I was held by real kidnappers. Believe me, a death or two in the family means nothing to him."

"It's really a shame," Rudy said. "We really could have used the dough."

She could see that he was not ready to let the idea drop. In fact, Sonia/Penny soon began to feel that Rudy had blabbed so much to so many people in the Seattle underground that her cover was blown anyway.

The whole group had been very excited, getting up for the Days of Rage riots in Chicago, which were to take place in October. All through the months before members of the collective were criticizing Sonia for smoking too much dope and risking a bust dealing pills.

"Fuck that," Sonia said. "Dope is political, don't you see? If we turn on the kids, they become criminals—part of the underworld. Anyway, you think any of these kids would join the revolution if you had a ban on dope?"

And then the fact that she and Marge had developed a crush on each other bugged the group. It was not the lesbian aspect to the relationship, but the fact that when they were making it with each other neither of them

114

wanted to have anything to do sexually with anybody else.

"Monogamy is out, right?" Rudy had argued. (Not mentioning that he'd been unsuccessfully trying to get into Sonia's pants since she had joined the group.)

All of the items in *The Fire Next Time,* the Weathermen's underground paper, were about the Days of Rage, and Sonia felt that she was getting further and further out on a limb.

For a while it looked as though Sonia might be able to take over leadership of the Seattle group. She set up a major riot at the Ave on the University campus. One group led by Marge trashed Captain Hook's, a deluxe men's clothing shop, while Sonia led a mixed gang of inner city blacks and university radicals against a TV appliance shop. It was exhilarating to feel the power of leading a group into such a major demonstration.

Later, Sonia organized an attack against the Pacific National Bank because of some involvement it had with the Vietnam war. That action really got important attention for the little revolutionary group.

But no matter how successful her capers were, there were two factors that continued to bug Sonia.

One was the chauvinism of most of the male leaders. It was clear that they just saw the girls as nice to have around for handing out leaflets, typing, and fucking, but resented it when any of the women began to exercise leadership.

The second was Sonia's gradual realization that half the group were just dilettantes, hanging out for the parties and dope and not giving a damn for the cause. Most of them were even anti-black and quarreled with Sonia's ideas about recruiting members in the ghetto.

"Shit!" Rudy said, "This is *our* territory. Let the spades trash their own neighborhoods."

The penultimate straw for Sonia was at a demonstra-

115

tion at the Sky River Rock Festival. Sonia's branch of the S.D.S. had set up a candy booth with a big sign "FREE HUEY NEWTON." (Some of the rock freaks actually thought that a "Huey Newton" was some kind of a candy bar.) Next door, a radical group that called itself "The Werewolves" had set up a revolutionary "Kissing Booth." The sheer chauvinistic gall of it infuriated Sonia and the rest of the women and they got into a real bad-mouthing session with the Werewolves (who were all freaked out on mescaline).

One of the Werewolf leaders came over to the candy booth and called Sonia a stupid reactionary cunt, and Marge belted him with a microphone stand. For a while it looked as though there was going to be a real slugfest —boys against girls, but Sonia and the Indian who ran the kissing booth finally cooled the scene. It all left a rotten taste in Sonia's mouth.

Finally, after a scathing self-criticism session in the collective's skid row tenement in Seattle, Sonia decided she had had enough. She wasn't going to the Days of Rage and get Maced, busted, and finger-printed for a cause in which she had very little feeling anyway.

That night she gave Marge an ultimatum, Alaska or bust up. Early the next morning they were on Route 99 with knapsacks, parkas, and sleeping bags heading for the Alcan highway.

In September the weather was brisk, but not freezing cold yet. The girls had no problem getting rides from the friendly truck drivers, many of them moving gear up the Alcan for use on the pipeline. The trip took three days, and only once did a driver try to make them put out for a ride. Ordinarily Penny wouldn't have minded. He was a big good looking guy in his early forties, with short graying hair, and a body that would have been slim and muscular except for a paunchy thickening at the middle. It was the fact that half way to Dawson City he had been talking about the deserters he had been running into while driving through Canada.

"If I had my way, I'd string those chickenshit bastards up by their balls and ship them back in a cattle car," the driver had said, spitting a wad of tobacco juice out of the truck window to emphasize his point.

When they left him Penny said to Marge "I don't mind fucking—but not for a Fascist pig like that!"

"Besides," Marge said, holding her arm as she got down from the trucks tall steps, "We've got each other now, right?"

"Right," Penny said in distraction. She had not yet decided that women were her bag, but it was interesting for the moment. At least with Marge she could run things the way she wanted. With men, she usually found that if they couldn't be the boss they couldn't even get it up.

Once they reached Fairbanks Penny had sworn Marge not to tell anybody this time what her true identity was.

"I don't want to run into the same kind of shit we ran into down in Seattle, with that turkey Rudy," Penny said. "This, what we're doing now, is something big. I'm going to call it Operation Cut off. Zap."

"Meaning what?" Marge asked.

"Meaning cut off the pipeline, the big iron pecker the oil biz is waving in our faces."

Marge smiled, glad to be part of the action.

Despite the so-called boom in Fairbanks, the fact was that there were few jobs to be had at the time, at least not on the pipeline. In the first place, if you were unskilled, or had no seniority in one of the big Teamster locals, your only chance was for one of the unskilled pipeline jobs and for that you had to have a *bona fide* certificate as an Alaskan resident. (Ordinary off-pipeline jobs just required the usual I. D.).

To qualify for the resident card you had to fill out a form giving date and place of birth, social security number, past address, voter registration card number (in Alaska), and other information that would establish that you were a resident according to Title 38 of the Alaska Land Act. Title 38 defined a resident as a person "who has been physically present in the state for a period of one year immediately prior to the time he entered into the contract of employment, maintains a place of residence within the state, and has established a residency for voting purposes." At the bottom of the application there was a statement in capital letters, "I CERTIFY UNDER PENALTY OF PERJURY THAT THE FOREGOING IS TRUE AND CORRECT," followed by a line for a signature.

There was no way Penny was going to expose herself to that kind of thing, but they had only two hundred and fifty dollars between them when they left Seattle, and they had spent fifty dollars on the road.

"We could always be hookers," Marge said, wistfully. "I hear there's pretty good money in that."

"Let's leave that for a last resort," Penny said sourly.

The first few nights they slept for ten dollars a night in a frame house out on Eighth and Noble Streets. The owner had put four cots into each of the three bedrooms, earning herself a neat hundred and twenty dollars a night on the deal. Linens were thrown in for free.

"Got to make something on this pipeline rush," she explained, collecting the cash in advance for the beds. "Those boomers from the lower forty-eight are going to be through here like shit through a tin horn. And we'll be all back eating Spaghetti-O's and beans."

Two days later, Marge was able to get a job as a

teller at the National Bank of Alaska, on Two Street. Penny, who called herself Sonia all the time now, had left Seattle without having found the time to line up forged papers and was unable to connect with anything legit. She finally had to settle for a job go-go dancing at the Flame Lounge on Two Street where for all the obvious reasons no embarrassing questions were asked. The pay was only two hundred dollars a week, but she was supposed to be able to earn a lot in "tips." She soon found that she could pick up between an extra couple of hundred dollars in tips by letting the girl-hungry construction workers grope her thighs and breasts in the darkness between dance sets.

One of the older girls showed her how to give a man a hand-job under the table and keep him in a state of excitation without ever quite letting him come. Between dancing and groping she was able to take home about four hundred dollars a week, all of it in cash.

The two of them were able to rent the two room log house on Clay Street near the Chena River, which was part of the second hand shop and bookstore owned by Abby Maroon on the front of the property. The house itself, Maroon explained, had been skidded to its present location on a sled from the town of Chena, up the river, to the Fairbanks town site in the winter of 1907. It was, in a sense, one of Fairbanks' pioneer homes, but it sure didn't look it.

Maroon seemed affable and friendly — even too friendly—and his long hair and weird eyes gave Sonia confidence that she was dealing with a genuine freak. Besides, the book shop, such as it was, showed where his sympathies lay, being loaded with copies of *ZAP* Comix, *The Rolling Stone, The Village Voice, Cahiers du Cinema,* and loads of eco-freak, nature food, and anti-war posters. If there were any soulmates in Fairbanks, Sonia and Marge were pretty sure that this was where they'd find them.

Once they had stopped all the chinks, augmented the spotty insulation, and bought a three hundred dollar second hand heater from Maroon to bolster his own shaky oil hot water heating system, the place was at least comfortable in terms of keeping out the frigid drafts, although aesthetically it left a lot to be desired. Maroon, out of the bigness of his heart, had given them several pieces of sagging and flaking furniture to tide them over until they had money to furnish on their own.

Sonia was immensely satisfied with the set up. As far as the Flame Lounge job was concerned, it was degrading and exhausting, but she just loaded up on Seconal and coasted through semi-conscious. Basically, Maroon's bookstore-junk yard made a perfect field headquarters for Operation Cut Off.

Denali had estimated that it would be at least two years from the time of pipeline approval until oil was flowing, so Sonia was certain she'd have plenty of time to line up reliable recruits. She'd learned a lot about organizing revolutionary movements from the Weathermen, and she'd given a lot of thought to her plan. In her mind she had her campaign divided into two segments. A., Dialectic; B., Revolutionary. In segment A she would assemble the good troops, selecting an inner core who would be valuable either for their dedication, their obedience, or for certain special skills that would be required later. During the first period the group would keep a relatively low profile, perhaps passing out leaflets, and doing research. It would be of the utmost importance to place members of the group in the pipeline work itself, or to enlist people who were already working there. In that sense, working in the Flame Lounge might some day prove handy. But so far, the type of Texas-Oklahoma hard-hat mentality she'd run into had not offered a promising field of recruitment.

By February Sonia and Marge had learned a lot about the folkways of Fairbanks. They'd learned about ice fog pollution, wind chill factors, headbolt heaters for cars, the cultural differences between Tlingits, Haida, Aleuts, Athabascans, and Eskimos. They had also gathered a small, but unreliable, group for Operation Cut Off.

John Takolik had been a great find, being both a radical and an Eskimo, which gave the group a certain interracial flavor.

"I wish we could find a black," Marge said. "But the only ones I've seen up here so far are hookers, and they don't want to be radicalized."

Van Taylor had a tendency to drink too much, talk too much, and goof off a lot, but he lived in Valdez, owned a fishing boat, and was very bitter about the coming of the pipeline terminal to Prince William Sound.

"In a couple of years, we'll be shipping back salmon already packed in oil," Taylor said bitterly. "It's a Goddamned shame."

Taylor was particularly disturbed because he had made his earlier living ponying cocaine and marijuana from Mexico and Colombia to the States. After several narrow escapes and one misdemeanor conviction, he had finally decided that the life was too hard, and with the proceeds of his last cocaine run from Colombia he had bought *High Hopes,* a sixty foot fishing trawler, usually crewed by a rag-tag collection of waterfront freaks and Indians recruited in the Club Valdez. Despite his loose and lackadaisical quality ashore, Taylor was a demon on the bridge, and a lucky and knowledgable fisherman. His crews usually went home at the end of the season with anywhere from fifteen to twenty-five thousand dollars as their share. And Van himself could usually bank thirty-five thousand a year. So he had a serious concern that the almost certain oil spills that would result from the loading of tankers in Valdez harbor would wipe out a prosperous, exciting, and, most of all, legitimate way of life for him.

From the beginning, it was obvious that Abby Maroon would be a part of the group. And Maroon recruited Ernie Mason, an angry radical young poet, whose work nobody could understand. Ernie worked as a bellboy and spy at the Chena View Hotel, which was now patronized entirely by Denali workers.

A couple of months after Marge and Sonia took the house on Clay Street, Marge ran into an old friend of hers from Seattle, Eli Hurwood. Hurwood's specialty was modern folk songs of social consciousness, talking blues, and a tremendously driving and aggressive style on the acoustic guitar, although sometimes slightly off-key.

"The Golden Fingers with the Tin Ear," Ernie called him.

Hurwood, who hailed from the West Bronx but sounded more Texan than Sonia, had known Marge during her early Weathermen days. One good thing about the group was, there was no need to make up any elaborate cover stories. Sonia acknowledged that she was underground, and simply wouldn't talk about her background. All this gave her an immediate aura of authority and importance. Some of them suspected that she was Kathy Boudin or one of the other refugees from the Eleventh Street bombing in New York.

It all served to encourage her primacy as the Dragon Lady of the Chena River radical movement.

Sonia rapped again with authority on the tinny surface of the kitchen table.

"All right, you guys, cool it," she said, waving her hand in front of her face to chase away the pervasive grass fumes. "And snuff those joints until the meeting is over. I'd like to get through this without everybody falling down in giggles."

Briefly and forcefully she outlined the preliminary stages of her plans for the first part of Operation Cut Off.

Sonia opened a manila folder and arranged some notes before her.

"Just by way of introduction—although I know you are familiar with these facts, or at least some of them— I'd like to go over some of the reasons why I feel we should fight the pipeline.

"In the first place, despite any propaganda the oil companies may have released, the creation of the pipeline and the trans-shipping of oil from Valdez, as now planned, would probably be the greatest ecological disaster on the face of this earth. We already know from the spills at Santa Barbara, the Torrey Canyon, and elsewhere that the oil business can *not* be counted on to police itself, no matter what kind of wild promises they make.

"The Coast Guard says that despite the supposedly increased precautions, there has been a five hundred percent increase of oil spills reported in the last five years, and you know damn well that they only report those spills that the public gets to know about. If they don't report them they have to pay a ten thousand dollar fine. Big deal! They make over a million on each shipment, so what's ten thousand bucks? It costs less to pay the fine than it does to take the precautions—or to clean it up.

"The tankers that will be working out of Valdez will be at least *five* times as big as the Torrey Canyon. You can imagine the effect it will have on the fish, the birds, the seals, and the whole food chain in the Arctic if one of those tankers spills. And believe me, it's not unlikely. It goes without saying that in the cold of the Arctic the dispersal of the oil will take much longer than it would further south. The hydrocarbons contained in crude oil—once they get into the food chain, even if they don't kill the fish—contain definite cancer-causing agents. It will probably be years before they know about damage caused in this way.

"Secondly, the hot oil system planned—as you may know the oil comes out of the ground at about one hundred and sixty degrees and the temperature would be kept up for the length of the pipeline by the actual friction of its movement through the pipe—would cause serious damage to the permafrost, irrevocably damaging the last virgin wilderness this country has.

"Thirdly, the route of the pipeline is through lands that are owned by Alaskan Natives; that have never been legitimately bought from them in the first place."

"Right on," Takolik interjected.

"Fourthly, the so-called national energy crisis by which the oil companies seek to justify this massive depredation is completely phony and a product of capitalist opportunism. I happen to know that only a couple of years ago all the oil companies were screaming like stuck pigs because they were afraid there'd be a great glut of oil that would force the prices down. It was only by limiting production that they were able to keep Americans from having cheap oil.

"Ultimately we know the only answer to this sort of manipulation is nationalization of all resources and returning them to The People!"

"Yeah! Right on! Hear, hear!" the group chorused in approval.

"To give you an idea of the kind of money the big oil pigs will be making from this rape . . ."

Sonia shuffled her notes and located the quote. " 'The anticipated rate of return to oil companies working the Slope would be forty-three percent—even if estimates of the pipeline cost double, the returns would still be nearly thirty-six percent.' This explains why these oil barons have been willing to invest millions without having a final okay from the government. They know that they *own* Washington. They own the *country!* And if it costs billions more it means only that it will take perhaps one more year to get a return on their capital.

"And now comes one of the most frightening things. I can't document this—we'll have to do some research on it. But I've heard that the polar cap now reflects about ninety percent of the solar energy that shines on it. If the polar ice cap—or any portion of it—becomes coated by oil, the dark color would cause it to absorb three or four times as much energy. This in turn would cause the ice cap to melt and shrink, and the less ice cap there is to reflect back the energy, the hotter the earth's surface will become. Ultimately, this will lead to greater and greater melting of the ice cap, which would substantially raise the sea levels throughout the world, causing flooding in all our ocean port cities and unimaginable damage to the agricultural food chain. In my opinion, there is no question that an Arctic oil spill of the magnitude that is possible from the Alaska pipeline could be the greatest man-made disaster known to history. Greater even than all the damage caused by all the atom bombs combined.

"For all these, and for many more reasons—"

Including some personal ones, Marge thought to herself.

"I urge you all to devote every ounce of energy, strength, and imagination you have to the final goal of Operation Cut Off. Stop that pipeline!"

125

The tiny congregation broke into a loud chorus of yips, yells, handclaps, and cheers of exhortation.

"What about Phase Two?" Ernie Mason asked.

"Let's just get finished with Phase One," Sonia said, "I can only promise you that it will be heavy—real heavy."

"I object to your autocratic approach," Mason said. "I think this should be done by democratic decision."

"How'd you like a fat lip to match your ass?" Taylor said, coming to Sonia's defense.

"Who from?" Mason said defiantly. "You and your cockamamy herring navy?"

Sonia banged on the table again with the paperweight.

"Okay, cool it everybody. Cool it. When the time comes, everything will be done by vote. I can tell you this, that the aim of our Operation Cut Off is to completely emasculate the capitalist pig pipeline!"

"Yeah, yeah, hear, hear!" Marge said and Abby joined in.

"I'd like to set up some *ad hoc* committees to get this show on the road" Sonia said. "Takolik, obviously you'll be Native affairs chairman. Abby, you will be publicity and ecological liaison. Van, you'll be Valdez delegate. Marge, you and I will be recruiting and personnel. And Ernie, well, you can be espionage."

"Ve haf ways to make you talk," Ernie said, acknowledging the appointment.

"Abby. I think you had some suggestions to make," Sonia said, turning to the dark-eyed landlord.

"Yes," he said, "I think there are a couple of guys who could be really useful to us. One is Al Everhardt—you know he works for the Fairbanks *News-Miner,* and he's been doing a lot of good work, exposing weaknesses in the pipeline set up."

Sonia seemed doubtful. "Well we can feed him information anyway. I know he'll be useful. We'll keep an eye on him, but we don't have to let him come into meetings of the steering committee quite yet. Who else?"

"Well, Baronian. The guy I told you about before. You know he's working on the pipeline and he knows a lot about ecology."

"He sounds like a real good man," Sonia agreed. "We'll have him to some informal gatherings and keep an eye on him. You know there's been a lot of FBI plants in these organizations. We had plenty of that down in the Weathermen, so we can't move too carefully."

"I don't know if I'd trust Baronian. He used to be a good man on ecology, but now he's working for the enemy—Denali," Takolik said.

"That's just the point, isn't it?" Marge said, "Now we can have someone boring from within."

"He's boring, anyway you look at him," Takolik said.

"This guy is my cousin," Maroon said. "I've known him all my life."

"Believe me," Sonia said fervently, "Relatives can be finks also." She surveyed the little group with satisfaction.

"Okay. I think this'll do for a first meeting. I want all of you to think about your respective assignments; we'll have some mini-meetings later in the week. In the meanwhile, pour the Thunderbird and," she raised her clenched fist, "up the Revolution; down with the pipeline."

Later Sonia, Marge, and Takolik opened a couple of cans of beer.

"Think it went okay?" Sonia asked.

Takolik paused.

"Basically okay. I guess. I mean, we don't exactly have the same goals. I want the land returned to my people. You want the pipeline destroyed and some kind of socialist revolution. My people already *had* socialism before the white man came. We took care of each other and we shared the whale, or whatever, with every one in the village."

"But you'll work with us?"

"Shit! At least you're working on some action. My own people, I can't get them off their frozen Eskimo asses. They think fighting the white man is undignified."

"They say you've got to live in Alaska three years to become a sour dough, but some of the guys come here —it's such a shock for them—it only takes them two months to go sour on the country and run out of dough. So I guess you could call them sour doughs, too."

—Texas Tool-pusher

Chapter Eleven

Nick Gordon was already sitting on the broad bench seat of the big Mack Thermo-Dyne 67 when Larry Steele swung himself up behind the steering wheel. The motor, which had been running ever since the truck had been started hours before in the heated garage at the Fairbanks terminal of Wheeler Transportation, was throbbing and vibrating, its fans sending big welcome drafts of hot air up along the windshield and down on the floor of the truck's cab.

Gordon was a big man, his face seamed and gulleyed by years of exposure to the outdoors. His age could have been anywhere between fifty and seventy. The fringe of stubbly hair that showed beneath the thrown-back wolverine brim of his parka was yellowy-white. He had a pleasant, bulbous potato nose and a wide gold-toothed grin.

"Heighdy! You've got a passenger! Name's Nick Gordon. Dispatcher said you'd give me a ride up to Old Man. I gotta pick up a Cat and drive it back to the Yukon to help them keep up that ice bridge."

"Steele," Larry said, extending a hand.

Gordon sized him up. "First trip?"

Larry smiled sheepishly. "First up here anyway."

"Well, maybe you're lucky you got me as a passenger.

I've driven this thing since '68. But now I'm in a different outfit. Got myself a card—Local 798—more dough driving the dirt-pushers than the trucks. Been doing that for about a year. You'd better start jamming gears," Gordon said, "if you want to get there in ten, twelve hours. You've got a hundred and fifty bad miles ahead of you. I'm figuring on sleeping over in Old Man and then going on to Prospect—that's where my Cat is —in the morning."

"I guess I'll be deadheading back about then," Larry said, shifting the big truck into low register and beginning to take it through its range of sixteen gears. The truck slowly groaned into action, towing its low-boy cargo of a forty foot Atco pre-fab unit, packed with communications gear. The load was a relatively light one, considering the capacity of the big truck, but Larry had been warned that it might be tricky because the Atco's high metal sides would make it extremely vulnerable to the high winds that could be expected after he came out of the Fairbanks basin.

The big Mack rolled easily over the Chena River bridge and onto the Steese Highway, heading toward Fox where the pavement ended.

"You can make good time along here," Gordon commented. "It's actually pretty fair until you get above Livengood."

"You've driven this road a lot?" Larry asked, his eyes roaming over the huge array of gauges in front of him. He had had only the previous night to familiarize himself with the interior of the truck, although he had driven other similar rigs earlier in Oklahoma.

"I guess I did it maybe ten, twenty times as far as Livengood, and I made that first season on the Hickel Highway before she all went to hell."

"What was the story on that, anyway?" Larry said.

"Well, Governor Wally was in a big-ass hurry to get

130

some trucks out there up to the North Slope. Your boss, the Wheeler Brothers, and some other big trucking companies was really hustling to get them some trucking business before the big Hercs flew everything up there and took all the trade. Anyway they put a lot of state road builders on the job from Southern Alaska —didn't know diddly-shit about permafrost, just bulldozed a flat road out from Livengood to the Yukon and then clean on up to the Brooks Range, through Anaktuvik Pass, and on down to Prudhoe. It was tough building too. Up there around Prospect, where I'm going, that's about the coldest place in Alaska. Sometimes gets down to seventy-five or eighty below. When they were pushing that road through back in January '68, they hit one of those cold waves. Man it was murder! Those hydraulic hoses was busting like uncooked spaghetti—dozer blades were snapping off, tires exploding —just shattering you know, they was so brittle in the cold. Finally they had to just hold up everything until the temperature warmed up to about fifty below.

"Trouble is, if they'd asked any experts they got up here, like Frontier Rock and Sand, they woulda done it right. What they did, they just scooped up all the dirt— vegetation and tundra and all that shit—packed it up on the road. When summer come, all those dark patches of dirt just pulled in the heat and melted all the snow. They kept throwing in more dirt and garbage, but it just kept melting. By the middle of summer, all they had was a big long lake. I understand it cost 'em about a half a million to fix it up again so's we can use it today—and I don't think it'll be any damn good at all after this winter. Then the only time you can use it will be when you got solid ice in there. Course, they have to put a quarter of a million dollars in each year to fix up that ice bridge over the Yukon too. She ought to be good and solid by now—probably a good sixteen feet of ice. Take this rig, no trouble. It's been taking some of them eighty foot lengths of pipe. Those go about a hundred thousand to the load. Not supposed to take more than sixty thousand across that bridge, but them oil company's got a lot of pull. Nobody's saying nothing to them. But I wouldn't want to go acrost behind one of them big fuckers. Don't like the sound of the ice when they're goin' acrost."

Larry Steele was glad for the company of the older man, who was cheerful and full of information. It would be a long, lonesome ride without him. Besides, if there were trouble on this first trip, it would be good to have an experienced hand along.

"How come they didn't fly you up to Prospect?"

Gordon grinned sheepishly. "I *never* fly when I can roll. I'm afraid of them damned planes. Awful lot of those guys get up, go down in a hole in the ice, and that's the last you ever hear of them. You got any idea how many of those little planes we lose every year? Been up here long?"

Larry shrugged. "All week." He smiled. "It took a little while to learn the ropes and get dispatched out on this job."

"You went down to the Local and stood on the line, right? Waited for a call?"

"Yeah," Larry said. "Is there any other way?

"Yeah, there are other ways." Gordon grinned. "If you want to lay out a century note to the right business agents. Course, if you're a woman you can get the same effect with a blow-job. Maybe even a man could, for all I know." He roared at his own joke. "It'll be okay onct you get your hours in—you get moved up to a 'B' card or an 'A' card, then you can get a job anytime. But it scares me the kids they put out on this road, without explaining anything about Arctic driving to them, the problems you get into in the cold. They're supposed to

132

put you through a special course, but nobody's got time for that now. Just a question of learn or freeze."

A couple of yellow Denali trucks passed them heading south from Livengood along with several yellow buses full of workers. On the front of the Denali pickup was a bumper sticker—"Let the bastards freeze in the dark." It was one of several Larry had noticed during his brief stay in Fairbanks; they expressed what seemed to be the Alaskan spirit of the day. Another popular bumper sticker read, "Sierra go home!" It too expressed the fear of many Alaskans that protest by ecology groups would hold up the construction of the pipeline, and the prosperity that they felt would follow.

Some stickers already expressed discontent with the invasion of workers from the lower forty-eight. One, Larry had noticed on a Dodge camper the night before, read, "Happiness is 10,000 Okies going south with a Texan under each arm."

"I learned how to Arctic drive coming up from Edmonton, even before they had the Alcan Highway," Nick said.

"Without a road?"

"Sure. In the winter we just made our own roads—right across the lakes and the ice. We just run Cats over the trail, pack it down, got it good and solid, push more snow onto it, until we had a good road. Then we'd go. "Course we tried to move in convoys and keep in touch with the C.B. radios in case we got in trouble. Usually there was somebody within calling distance if you got in a jam. But once I busted an axle and I had to walk out twenty miles into Bywash Landing."

Larry was content to let the older man ramble on with his yarns and reminiscences. He had decided to keep a low profile since his arrival in Alaska the week before. He left word with Grandpa Bisset that he was heading north. "Good move, Larry," the old man had

133

said, pounding him on the shoulder with approval. "God, I'd like to go up there where the action is! If I hadn't got these old knees smashed up, I'd be with you, boy. You telling your Daddy?"

Larry had sighed moodily, stirring his bourbon with his finger as he gazed into the roaring fire inside the huge ranch house.

"I don't think so. I reckon I'll get going tomorrow before he gets back from New York and Washington. I understand he's up there talking to Uncle Fred, trying to get some Congressional action moving on that pipeline okay. It's not coming through as fast as he'd like."

"Better come through," the old man said. "I understand they got damn near eight hundred miles of forty-eight inch pipe already shipped in there from Japan. They're going to look like some awful big dumb-asses if they get stuck with that stuff, and no oil to push through it."

"Well, I guess Daddy and those other oil companies must be pretty sure they're going to get the go ahead. They already laid out over a billion dollars. That's more than the whole job was supposed to cost in the first place."

"The kind of money they throw at those politicians, I guess they kinda figure they got a right to expect Congress to play ball."

"What I think they're really counting on more than anything else is Nixon," Larry said. "Daddy says he's just as much in their pocket as Johnson was."

"How come you're not telling your Daddy, son?"

"I just don't want him taking over; laying things out for me on a silver platter. I like to pick my own kind of work; I like to be in control of what happens to me. If he had his way I'd be stuck in an office like him. I'd never get out into the field to see what was happening."

134

"Well, there's a lot to what you say, Larry boy, but you're sure taking the hard way."

Larry sipped at his bourbon. "The thing is that Dad's idea of an oil man is a financier in a starched collar with a pencil in one hand and a computer in the other. I see it more like the way you did things Gramps. I mean, getting out there and getting your hands dirty. Anyway, there's time enough for all that paper-shuffling when I'm older. Right now, I like to be outdoors, learning a few things on my own."

In the few years since his discharge from the Army, Larry had managed to stay out of the corporate clutches of his wealthy father. He had driven trucks in Tulsa and in the Williston Oil Basin; had worked as a Rough-neck in the Louisiana area and in East Texas on the oil rigs; and briefly, with a couple of other friends from 'Nam had run a private air service, which was ultimately bought out by Braniff to be used as a feeder line. The money had been divided between wildcat oil leases—none of which had yet come in profitably —and municipal bonds bought at Brandon's advice which at least gave him the security to continue to vagabond from job to job until he found, as his father said, "what kind of work he was out of."

Despite the fact that he held a card in the Roughneck's Union and probably could easily have gotten a job in the Slope oil fields, Larry decided to try a trucking job first, using his Teamster's Card. It was highly unlikely that once he got among the actual oil workers he could keep his presence in the North or his whereabouts a secret. On the other hand, if he stayed with the private contractors who were trucking for Denali, it was improbable he would be recognized. Ultimately, he knew Wilbur Steele's intelligence system would track him down, so he wanted at least a headstart, to get his feet on the ground on his own.

The only one besides Grandpa Bisset who knew where he was was D.D. Doheny. He had stopped to see her at Denali Headquarters in Anchorage on his way up. That night they had dinner at the Top of the World, on the roof of the Anchorage Westward, the city's tallest building. The night, which in effect was eighteen hours long, was beautiful yet had a strange undertone of strain. They had danced to the music of Chick Soloway and his Bark Peelers, a rock group. They drank bourbon over glacier ice.

"Too bad we can't get any of that Virginia Gentleman up here," D.D. said, calling up memories of the ranch on Mitchell Mesa.

"If I know my Dad, he's had a carload shipped up from Washington and stashed here somewhere. He's down there with his brother Fred now, or so I understand."

"Yes, I know."

And now Larry realized that the undercurrent of tension in her voice was there only when they talked about Wilbur.

"Are you having trouble with Dad? You're not losing your job or something?"

Deirdre avoided his eyes and looked out over the sparse twinkling lights ending at the edge of the Cook Inlet. "No, the job's going well."

"Well, why do you sound nervous every time we talk about it?"

"It's just . . . It's a big job and there's a lot of responsibility. We're preparing a feasibility study now for congress and it's really complicated and there are a lot of questions to be answered that I'm not sure of."

"What about your Daddy, Ol' Mahlon—how's he?"

Deirdre seemed relieved to change the subject.

"Oh, Daddy's doin' great I guess. He was sure disappointed when that Mexican deal fell through, but it helped some when Wilbur gave him the job running Denali up here."

"No hard feelings—about Wilbur backing out of his promise to help capitalize Honda?"

Deirdre shrugged.

"That's oil business, I guess. They're both a couple of tough ol' rattlesnakes when you come down to it."

"Yeah," Larry said, smiling ruefully, "Only ol' Wilbur got a lot more poison."

Deirdre looked at him oddly, then laughed.

After dinner they sat at a bar beside the huge panoramic windows overlooking Cook Inlet for a nightcap.

"I have to get home soon," Deirdre said. "We're starting early and working overtime these days—every day. It makes for a good paycheck, but a lousy social life." She smiled apologetically, and put her warm hand over his.

"Can we go to your place now?" Larry asked.

D.D. smiled sadly and shook her head. "I've got a roommate at the moment, besides I don't think that this is the time to start that sort of talk."

"Well, what about coming down to my room?"

D.D. traced the pattern of small triangles on the formica top of the bar. "Larry," a lot's been changing between us. I guess we're not buddy-buddy anymore. I know you feel more than that, and I do too." She looked up at him. Larry was surprised to see that her eyes were bright, almost teary with intensity.

"I promise, Larry, I promise that we'll be together. But the moment just isn't right."

"For Christ sake!" Larry said, suddenly angry. "I've been chasing your little tail for twenty-four years—when is the moment *going* to be right?" He got up angrily, reached into his wallet, took out a fifty dollar bill and threw it on the bar. "This ought to cover it, and a taxi for you too."

"Larry, don't be a jerk," D.D. started to protest, but Larry was already disappearing through the swinging doors to the vestibule beyond, where an elevator swallowed him up before she could follow.

Downstairs he turned right on C Street and went over to Fourth. He had earlier noticed a tacky little row of bars, which were the only things in Anchorage that looked anything Klondike-like or had the boom town atmosphere he had expected. In the doorway of a pawnshop next to the Frontier Bar, which Larry noted ironically occupied the ground level of the Rough-neck's Union building, a round faced black-eyed girl stood huddling in her parka.

"Hey, Tex," she said, spotting the boots and Stetson "you want to learn dirty Eskimo?"

"Some other time, sweetie," Larry said, walking into the bar.

He ordered a double bourbon and shoved three dollars across the counter. As he did so he was aware that a figure had slid onto the bar stool next to him and a pair of slim fingers pushed another three dollars across the bar. "I'll have the same as my friend, Tex." It was the voice of a woman with an unmistakable down-home accent. Deirdre had followed him.

Larry started to protest, "Godamighty, D," but she interrupted him by placing a hand over his and holding it tightly. "When we finish these we can have just one more nightcap in your room at the Westward, okay?"

"The oil is going to be extracted and some of the country, hitherto unmolested, is going to be torn up in the process. Let's not fool ourselves. This activity is already far past the point of no return."

> —James H. Galloway,
> Vice President, Humble Oil
> and Refining Co.

Chapter Twelve

As they rolled out through Fox, across the Chatanika River, and out on the Elliott Highway, old Nick kept up low-keyed running comment that kept weaving in and out of Larry's thoughts of that night with D.D.

"You know kid, they lost so many trucks along this here road—especially where it gets winding up there and the wind picks up—they call it the Kamikaze Trail. They put a green kid on here with one of them long loads and it starts swaying and wobbling in the wind, next thing you know the thing's out of control and in the ditch. Maybe it falls on the poor bastard, pins 'im there—"

It had been good being together in that strange place so far from home—but it was also weird. They had known each other so long she was like a part of him and they'd had almost every sort of physical contact except love-making—wrestling and tackling each other in the green hills outside of the W-Bar-S. Once he remembered a steamy necking session out in the middle of a field of oats with the high grain-land rising around them on all sides, forming a little

private chamber in the middle of the field. But that
had been kid-stuff, above the waist, with no probing
behind the ruled-off surface of her plaid workshirt.
He remembered particularly the delicious slippery-
shiny surface of their skins as the sun baked into the
middle of the hot ripe fields.

But now, away from home, with the conclusion
almost preordained, there was a strange seriousness
and formality to their coupling. Larry remembered
being surprised when, after finishing her drink, with
unexpected swiftness D.D. asked him, "Do you have
an old pajama top, or a shirt?" She began pulling
out the pins that held her hair in a tight bun at the
back of her neck, letting it fall in long twisting yel-
low strands like unbraided manila rope . . .

Nick pointed to a road ahead as they passed Beaver
Creek. "You're going to have a real rough winding,
climbing trail now for about forty-six miles. Don't let
your brakes get over-heated here—you start sliding
backwards and you'll be in deep shit. Problem is, you
get on too steep a grade and you can get in a lot of
trouble."

Larry remembered D.D. coming out of the hotel
bathroom dressed in the top of his red flannel pa-
jamas—the ones with the W-Bar-S brand on the
pocket, which Wilbur had given him two Christ-
masses ago. She'd showered too, and with the light
bouncing off of the red flannel, she was as pink as
the dawn all over.

The older man, seeing that Larry was lost in a day-
dream, lapsed into a silence and switched on the AM
radio.

"We're switching on to Channel 10 on the C.B. later
when we turn off to Livengood, but I guess we can
just listen to KYAK here for a while, while we can

140

still pull in Fairbanks. It fades out pretty soon after a couple of miles."

They rode along for a few miles listening to the wandering crackling tropes of KYAK's predominantly country music fare. After a rousing version of "Okie from Muskogee" an announcer broke in.

"Now tonight's bush pipeline messages . . ."

"This here's a program they got for people out in the toolies," Nick explained. "They don't hardly get no mail this time of year, and without a high-powered radio they have trouble getting through to each other. So they just broadcast these here messages and anybody that hears them, well, they just relay 'em on when they run into those people. 'Course, the people that use it usually listen in."

The radio cracked and buzzed on.

"This message is for Mark—'I am leaving the Chena River Lodge today for L.A. Sending your food on tonight's flight, along with some nice surprises for Mary and a note for Harry and Erwin . . .'

"This is to Edna, from Jim at Tolchitna Lodge —'Will be over tonight in a red Piper, and will appreciate pick up. Will try landing on the bar next to the Lodge.' That one's signed, 'Al.'

"Here's a message to the Montana Creek Dog Musher Club members—'There will be a regular meeting Thursday at eight p.m. The race schedule for the coming season will be presented for consideration.' And it's signed, 'Leroy Davey, President of the Montana Creek Dog Musher Association.'

"To Allen Moore up in the Petersville Road—'I have your stovepipe.' That's signed, 'Carpenter's Hardware.'

"To Tony and Ellen at Curry—'Sorry I missed you on Fourth. Couldn't get in there with the Beaver.

I'm in Anchorage now taking care of Shirley, if you know what I mean. Just on R and R. Will be going back to Valdez for a while. Bucks here are just going too fast, as you can empathize. I'll see you when I get back to the camp. Tom.'

"This one's to Holly at Manley Hot Springs—'Got the job. Have to join the union. Will be going to Valdez to work as road-runner. First leave in the middle of September. Love, and miss you. Signed, Willy.' "

The radio began to sputter and skip, picking up the messages only in patches until Nick finally turned it off in disgust.

"That intersection we passed a while back, that's the road to Manley Hot Springs. The 'Road to Nome' they call it, but it ends at Manley Hot Springs right now. Got a hell of a way to go before they ever get to Nome. Son of a bitchin' fine hot springs they got there though. Been running a hotel out there since way back around the Klondike days, I guess it is."

Larry nodded, his eyes fixed on the winding white road ahead of him. He was taking the curves carefully with the big rig; the Atco was swaying and wobbling in the rear. Darkness had set in around three o'clock in the afternoon.

Nick looked sharply at the young Texan. "You sleepy, boy? Let me know and I can give you some bennies." He started reaching into his pocket.

Larry shook his head negatively. "No, I'm okay. It's just that I don't know the road and I find it hard to talk and drive. Might want an upper later, though."

He held out his hand and Nick shook out a couple of the triangular yellow pills into it. Larry slipped them into a small zippered pocket in his parka.

"Guess you're one of those quiet Gary Cooper kind

of Texans like they have in the movies," Nick said smiling.

"What have people got against Texans up here anyway? I see all these signs, and people are always making remarks."

"I don't know," Nick said. "I guess they're all right. Talk kind of funny. Always saying things like 'ass hockey' when they mean ice hockey and 'sad doah' for side door, but I don't mind 'em much I guess. A lot of 'em ain't like you, ya know. A lot of 'em have awful big mouths. I remember a fellow says to a Texan the other day, 'You don't shut your big mouth, we'll cut Alaska in two and make you the *third* biggest state.' "

Nick's gold teeth flashed in laughter at his own joke, which Larry favored with a polite smile, since he had already heard it at least four times in the week he'd been in Alaska.

Just past Mile 69 out of Fairbanks, the big Mack rolled through a little cluster of houses known as Livengood. Three or four miles past was a sign marked "TAPS Road, No Services."

"Well son, this here's the beginning of the North Slope Highway. They got a construction camp up ahead a couple of miles where we might be able to get a cup of coffee, but I think I'd rather pull into the West Fork Service. Maybe we can pick up a little package of interior anti-freeze there for the rest of the road. Come in handy, in case we get stuck in the frozen north, right?"

The West Fork, which was a medium-sized building built of huge stripped logs and featured gas, oil, groceries, liquor, and coffee. Larry indulged in several cups of hot black coffee and a Drake's Raisin Cake. Nick settled for a cup of canned chicken soup and a Yankee Doodle.

"Can't drink coffee," Nick said, sipping the hot soup, "gives me heartburn. Too many years on the road ruins

143

a man's stomach. You try to quit as soon as you can, you hear son? And you'd better take one of those bennies now. It takes about an hour before it takes effect, and you'll be getting groggy before we get up to Old Man."

Larry took one of the little triangles from his parka pocket and swallowed it with the black coffee. It tasted bitter when it passed over his tongue. He started to reach into the pocket of his Arctic down pants for his wallet, but Nick had already paid the tab.

By quick calculation, Larry figured it would be five p.m. by the time they had "lunch" but with a night twenty-one hours long, time acquired a topsy-turvy aspect. "Lunch" was simply the meal you had several hours after breakfast.

"They got a base at Five Mile for the guys who are building the construction camps. Chow ain't much, but it's all you can get between here and Old Man. This isn't exactly your Route 66 out here."

They had been traveling forty minutes out of West Fork Service when Larry noticed on a straight-away, just past Mile 110, where the road was beginning to slope downward toward the Yukon River crossing, a slight glow to his left toward the western horizon. At first it looked to be the reflected illumination from some town or camp, but there was a reddish tone to the light that was suspicious.

"Nick, what's that light up there? Is there a construction camp over that way?" Larry asked.

The older man studied it. "I don't know," he said. "Looks like a forest fire, but this ain't the right time of year for that." He reached over and switched on the C.B. radio, plucking the mike from its holder.

"Hello, hello," he said. Breaker One Zero. Somebody Southbound? This is Texas Wildcat at mile marker 110 on the TAPS Road. Looks like some hot pants over

144

there a mile, couple of miles, ahead of us. Anybody got anything on it? Come on, Good Buddy.

There was only an answering blare of static over the receiver.

"Not many trucks within range out this way," Nick explained. "But I thought I'd give it a try. I'm not sure I like the looks of that one. Could you put on a little speed? Don't take any chances, but there may be some trouble up there."

They were now on a dangerously winding and slippery downgrade.

"Whatever it is," Larry said, "I think it's going to have to wait. I don't think I can go any faster on this stretch."

Nick looked critically over the road. "Yeah, I guess you're right. No sense having any more trouble than we have to. How far do you figure that light is?"

Larry squinted at the horizon. "It's getting brighter all the time. I don't think it's any more than a mile away."

Two minutes later they could see by the flickering quality of the light that it was a fire, and a big one, that they were approaching. Within another minute they could see tall orange flames licking at the night sky.

Nick whistled appreciatively. "Whatever it is, it's a beaut. There's more than a truck engine going up there! Must be some hot cargo."

As they turned a bend around a long granite outcropping topped by evergreens, they saw what at first appeared to be a tiny piece of the sun that had fallen off and had settled into the snow covered gulley. It was shooting flames sixty to seventy feet into the air. Squinting through the light, Larry could make out the long tubular shape of a tanker truck.

"I think it's one of ours," Nick said. "It's a Wheeler fuel truck. I know I've seen it out here somewhere.

145

Don't look like anybody could of got out of that alive."

By now they rounded another bend and saw the tractor of what appeared to be a huge cab-over White freightliner, lying on its side its wheels turning lazily in the glaring light. The tractor was hung between a huge boulder and a long, exposed granite ledge. Apparently the fifth wheel assembly had become disengaged from the eight-thousand gallon tanker, which had rolled down the hillside and ignited.

"I don't see any driver," Nick said. "He's either still in there or . . . well, he's still in there, one way or the other."

As carefully as he could, to avoid jack-knifing, Larry braked the 18-wheeler to a stop. The tractor was lying on its side less than a hundred yards from the road and the sloping shelf of granite on which it was jammed had been blown clear of snow by the wind.

"I think we can get out there following that long ridge," Nick said, pulling on his long mittens and tightening up the parka. "Good thing we've got that. We'd never make it through the heavy snow otherwise."

Slipping and stumbling, the two men made their way down the outcropping of rock toward the tractor. As they neared it, both men yelled as loud as they could. "Anybody in there? Can we help?! Anybody theeeere?"

But the wind blowing through the sparse evergreens and across the sheet metal of the truck would have drowned out any reply. As they approached the capsized monster, its six wheels sticking up stiffly in the air like the paws of a felled dinosaur, Larry could see the truck's nickname painted on the right front fender, now towering twelve feet in the air—"Mighty Moe," lettered in brilliant yellow paint.

With an assist from Nick, Larry managed to climb up the rapidly cooling radiator grill. Inside he could see a man with a patch of hair as red as the fire burning

146

on the horizon. He was dressed in a Bombardier ski suit with the hood thrown back, and a knitted watchcap barely covering the flame-colored curls. A dangerous-looking, darker-colored streak was running down the side of the driver's jaw and into the neck of the suit. The man still had one hand gripped, almost in reflex, around the steering wheel.

With difficulty, standing on the sheet metal side of the truck, Larry managed to edge open the heavy door. Wedging it with one foot, he rolled down the window which was stiff with cold and yelled anxiously into the cab.

"Hey buddy, you all right? Hey, wake up! You okay man?"

The figure behind the wheel moved slightly and groaned. There was a distressingly final-sounding note to the man's expression of pain, like the last revolution of a stalling motor.

Larry clambered over to the fender and reached down to help Nick up to the top of the big cab, realizing that he would never be able to handle the man himself. Then he dropped down through the open window to see what he could do for the stricken driver, who was now beginning to show some sign of life. It was a slight fluttering of the closed lids. A tongue licked the half-open lips. Finally there was a muttered sound from the half-conscious driver.

"Shit, man! What happened?"

"Looks like you rolled her," Larry said, but the man didn't seem to hear him.

Nick peered down through the horizontal open window of the cab-over.

"Can you get him up where I can get hold of him?" Nick asked, his face ruddy in the flickering flames of the tanker.

147

"I guess I can, if he'll give me a hand. Can you move, buddy?"

The man put a hand to his head and Larry repeated the question. Finally there was an answer.

"I think so."

"Well, hold it. Anything broken?"

The man, dazed, seemed not to understand the question. At last he nodded. "Yes, I mean, no—no. I guess I'm okay."

"Then give me your hand."

Gradually, between them, Nick and Larry managed to get the man out through the open window of the tractor and into the open air.

Before he left the cab Larry took a fast look around and found some mittens and some other Arctic gear, which he tucked into his parka. Some fur garment was crumpled in a corner of the cab, but Larry already had all he could handle.

"We'd better get out of here," Nick said. "This thing's liable to catch fire too, any minute. He's carrying a hell of a load of gas in the fuel tank here."

The two men lowered the driver down the side of the tractor onto the snowy granite ledge. Nick pulled out the pint of Three Feathers he'd bought in the truck stop and gave the man a sip of whiskey. The harsh blend served to snap the red-headed driver to attention. He shuddered with appreciation and looked back at the truck.

There was a popping sound and a sudden roar of flames as the gas dripping from the tractor's ruptured tank finally caught fire in a huge whoosh.

The driver looked toward his ruined truck in horrified fascination, then suddenly his eyes took on a wild look. Before Larry or Nick had any idea what he was doing, he had pushed himself to his feet, and was running in a stumbling gait toward the roaring flames engulfing the tractor.

"My God," he yelled, "Sally is in there! Sally must still be in there!"

". . . But sparse attention has been given to one price of the pipeline, which can be labelled only with the phrase 'verging on the macabre': the human toll, a toll measured both in human despair and in injury and death. The casualty figures for pipeline related workers may well turn out to be higher than for any other major construction project in the nation in modern times."

—Winthrop Griffith
New York Times Magazine

Chapter Thirteen

"She's going to blow any minute!" Nick said. "Larry, stop that crazy son of a bitch!"

The driver was still stumbling along the rock ledge toward the flaming truck. Larry trotted towards him as fast as he could on the snow covered surface of the ledge, but the driver was within twenty-five feet of the tractor before Larry could tackle him. Nick, who had followed behind as fast as he could, joined him in subduing the flailing and protesting driver, who rolled with Larry into the deeper snow off the edge of the ledge. Nick reached down to give Larry a hand in holding on to the squirming man. The two of them pulled the trucker back onto the ledge and began to drag him away from the dangerously flaming tractor.

They had gotten only fifty feet from the spot where Larry had tackled the driver when the fuel tank exploded with a thunderous roar, the blast's impact knocking all three men to the ground. The driver turned back toward the truck. He was now near hysteria, screaming, "Sally! Sally!"

Between them, Nick and Larry dragged the gibbering driver to the shelter of the Mack, where he slumped in the upholstered seat, sobbing and mumbling incoherently. With difficulty, Nick forced a shot of Three Feathers between the man's lips. Finally he sat up, his reddened eyes staring blankly at the two flaming pyres that were all that was left of his rig.

Nick put a sympathetic arm around the man's sagging shoulders.

"I'm really sorry fella, but there was really no way to get anyone outa there."

There was a long pause and Nick said gently, "Was she your wife? Your girlfriend?"

The man looked at him for a moment, his eyes still wild and uncomprehending. Then he said dully, "No, she was my dog."

The men drove in silence the remaining ten miles, the last six or seven of which the road wound gradually down hill to the basin of the broad frozen-over Yukon.

Nick twiddled the dials of the C.B. radio again and finally was able to raise a dispatcher at the Five Mile Camp on the other side of the river.

"This is Big Ray at Five Mile; Big Ray at Five Mile. Come on Texas Wildcat."

"Big Ray. We got a ten-thirty-three here. Man rolled a Wheeler boom wagon belly-up over at Mile Marker 110. Can you get a chopper in? I think he could use some medical help."

"I'll try," Big Ray said, "but it's doubtful. I had the Cisco Kid on about an hour ago and he was heading for Old Man. Guy got blown off a crane up there—they think he's got a broken leg. I'll try to reach him for you anyway, see if he's through. What's your handle, Good Buddy?"

"This is Nick Gordon here. You okay Ray?"

"Yeah, we're fine. On the whole I'd be happier in Miami. Your man hurt bad?"

151

Nick looked at the driver who had now lapsed into a catatonic silence. "I don't know," he said doubtfully. "Might be a concussion here. We ought to able to make your place about a half hour. If you can get ahold of the Cisco Kid, tell him to hang in there and wait for us. Ten-ten."

Larry who was busily down-shifting to keep the load from getting away from him on the long downhill towards the ice bridge across the Yukon, looked questioningly at Nick.

"Who's the Cisco Kid?"

"It's Carlos Morales. He was really born in Spain but everyone around here thinks he's Mexican. He's a nurse."

"A nurse?"

"Well, he's really like a medic. He's the only doctoring help we can get around here. He works for Denali and mostly the guys call him Doc. I suppose most of them think he really is a doctor, but he's a registered nurse. Of course, he knows a lot more than most nurses—especially about Arctic survival and stuff like that. Denali has him flying around in one of these four-place DeHavilland Beavers. I guess he covers about fifteen hundred miles a week or so, just flying from one camp to another. There's always something to keep him busy. If it ain't a busted ass, then it's a belly-ache or a dose of clap. He's about the only guy available to some of these bush Indian villages up this way too."

"Aren't these Eskimos up here?" Larry asked.

"No. You don't get them until you get North of the Brooks Range. These here is Athabascan Indians. I met Carlos years ago when he was working in Harbor View Hospital Trauma Center in Seattle in the emergency room. He got plenty of experience there. That was back when I was trucking up the Alcan."

The big Mack rig eased down the final slope to the

banks of the Yukon where a long causeway was raised three or four feet above the frozen surface of the river. Larry scanned it speculatively.

"Looks safe enough. Is that ice solid?"

"Oh yeah," Nick said, "by now she's a good fifteen, sixteen foot thick. It was Frontier Rock and Sand figured out how to do this—at least they were the first ones to put it in over here. Just keep her in the middle register. Don't go too slow or too fast. Actually, at this time of year, there's no worry anyway, just like a regular road."

Taking Nick at his word, Larry eased the truck onto the long straight-away. The river was more than a mile wide at this point. A half hour later they had engineered the winding road leading away from the Yukon and pulled into the welcome lights of the construction camp at Five Mile, which glittered like a frozen fairy city. Closer up, though, it was just a cluster of pre-fab Atco units pulled up in a U-shape. It reminded Larry of frontier camps of covered wagons.

To the left of the Administration shack was another Atco where someone had lettered a cardboard sign saying "Five Mile Club—Open all night." A chunky figure in a blue down parka came out of the door, a white coffee cup in hand.

"Bring him in here," the man said. "I can look at him just as good here as any place else, and you guys can get some coffee."

"Ok, Doc," Nick said.

Between them the two men steered the still dazed and stumbling driver into the mess hall.

"Do you know this man?" Nick asked the medic.

"I seen him. Wheeler took him on about a month ago, but it really takes a while to get used to these roads —especially with a tricky load. I don't think he's hurt too bad. Feeling any pain, mister?"

153

"Nah, I guess I feel all right."

There was a stainless steel counter with racks on it containing sandwiches, pies, fruit salads, desserts, and several big urns containing coffee, hot water, and milk. Next to the sandwiches was a steam table with several containers of soggy-looking breaded veal cutlets, ravioli, beans, and coleslaw. Larry took a couple of the cutlets, some ravioli and some beans and a big cup of coffee. Nick just took the ravioli and a glass of milk.

"I used to have an appetite like yours before I started driving," Nick said smiling wryly. "Now they tell me that if I don't start taking it easy, they're going to have to slice a piece out of my pie-lorus."

The Formica table at which they sat to eat their lunch had a row of condiments on it that must have been almost two feet long. A-1 Sauce, Worcestershire Sauce, Steak Sauce, Catchup, Chili Sauce, Mayonnaise, Hot Mustard, Regular Mustard, Soy Sauce, Garlic Pepper, Regular Pepper and Salt, grated cheese.

"Goddamn," Larry said, "you could make a meal just out of these condiments."

"Well, it gets monotonous up here, and guys like to jazz up their food a little, put a little originality into it. To tell you the truth, when I say the chow's not bad what I mean is that there's plenty of it and it's nourishing. But as for taste . . ."

Larry bit into one of the soggy cutlets. "Well, it's an *interesting* taste," he said. "Kind of like a cross between a boiled football and a plastic sponge. *Good* though," he smiled.

They left the driver being bandaged up by Doc Morales. "He'll be okay," the pudgy nurse said. "But I think we'd better fly him down to Fairbanks, get his head x-rayed. Might be a little concussion there. Otherwise, he seems to be a little hysterical."

"Well, he lost his dog, Sally, in the crash," Larry said.

"Oh, I'm sorry, that's real tough," the nurse said with deep sympathy.

Feeling warm and nourished, and beginning to be comfortable with the rig and the ice conditions, Larry made the remaining forty-five miles to Old Man Camp in a little over two hours. They were assigned a room together in one of the transient quarters.

Each ten by ten foot room contained two cots, a couple of lockers, a pair of bedside tables, and some shelves.

Larry was bone-weary. The hundred fifty mile trip had taken twelve hours. Larry realized that he should feel grateful. From what he had heard in the union halls everybody up there was looking for just that—seven days of twelve hour shifts. That was the way to pile up the money. He wasn't entirely sure of the rate, but the way he figured it, he'd made somewhere between a hundred and thirty and a hundred and fifty dollars that day.

"Quite a day, quite a day," he said, lacing his arms behind his head and closing his eyes wearily.

Nick looked at him with amusement. " 'Bout average I'd say."

"By agreeing not to strike, the powerful Teamsters and other unions won fat contracts that allow workers to put in as many as 84 hours a week with everything over 40 hours counted as time and a half or double time."

—*Time Magazine*
June 2, 1975

Chapter Fourteen

In the morning, his stomach warm and full from a construction worker's breakfast of juice, flap-jacks, sausages, oatmeal, milk and coffee, Larry supervised the unloading of the big Atco unit from his low-boy trailer. Bob Willy, who was the resident camp manager, stood by as a pair of giant Caterpillar loaders pushed the unit into place.

"Boy, we really needed that," the RCM said. "Main generator went out the other day, and we damned near froze our asses off here until we got it fixed. With this reserve I guess we'll be covered."

"How many of these camps you got up here, Bob?" Larry asked.

"Let's see now," the manager said, "we got Prospect, Old Man, Coldfoot, Wiseman, and Prudhoe—I guess we got five camps. A fellow says they put twenty million dollars into these so far."

Larry whistled. "Boy, that's a lot of dough—considering that they haven't got an *okay* to put in the pipeline yet."

Bob Willy looked at him with quiet amusement. "You know the kind of billions we're talking about here? You think these guys are worried about a lousy ten or twenty million? That's a drop in the bucket compared to the profits they're going to make when this thing starts going. Believe me, they wouldn't do it if they didn't know that they were going to get it built. You ought to meet some of these big-wigs sometime. Cold as ice, all of them. And sure as God."

Larry smiled grimly and made no comment as he gathered up the cables that had held the Atco and stowed them in the trailer.

"Oh, listen," the RCM said, almost as an afterthought, "you'd better come back to the office. I got a note for you."

Larry followed the burly man back to the administrative shack identified by a sign over the door—Birdwell Construction Company. Birdwell was the subcontractor working on the building of the camps for Denali.

Hanging on the wall behind Willy were several photos, one showing him in a hardhat standing on a giant Caterpillar earth mover with date palms in the background. He noticed Larry staring at them. "That there was taken in Saudi Arabia. Pretty funny going from the hottest damn place on earth to practically the coldest. I guess that's what I like about this kind of work—sure always has a challenge."

The second photo showed three young people in western gear mounted on Quarter horses.

"That other picture's of down home. You're from Texas too, aren't you?"

Larry nodded.

"Got a couple of sections down near Waco. I let the kids raise the horses—keeps 'em busy and makes a little extra money, so I can take the whole place off on taxes."

Between the pictures was a hand letfered sign that said:

157

"WE THE WILLING, LED BY THE UN-
KNOWING, ARE DOING THE IMPOSSIBLE
FOR THE UNGRATEFUL. WE HAVE DONE
SO MUCH, FOR SO LONG, WITH SO LITTLE,
WE ARE NOW QUALIFIED TO DO ANY-
THING WITH NOTHING."

The RCM shuffled around among the papers on his
untidy desk and came up with a small folded slip of
paper. It had the Wheeler Trucking letterhead. It said,
"Steele, take the Mack 36 to Prospect with Nick Gordon to pick up the D-6 Cat after he has fixed it. Deposit Gordon and Cat at Base Camp in Prudhoe."

Larry whistled. "Well, looks as if I may get 7-12's
this week after all! They want me to take that Cat all
the way up to Prudhoe."

"You start traveling on some of those roads," Willy
said, "and you'll be glad you've got the Cat with you.
You'll need it to plow on ahead of you or pull you out
of some jams."

Outside, although it was nine o'clock in the morning,
it was still pitch-dark. Nick, who had slept late while
Larry unloaded the truck, was lingering over a cup of
coffee in the mess hall when Larry came in.

"Looks like we're going to be roommates for a while,
Nick," he said as he threw the note on the table.

Nick scanned it quickly. "I figured they might do
something like that. They're going to need a lot more
heavy equipment up on the Slope when this thing gets
going. Stuff up here breaks down at a fantastic rate.
'Course, they've been flying a lot of construction equipment in on Fat Albert."

"What's that?"

"Thats those big Lockheed C-130 Hercules planes."

"They're big enough for one of them DC-8 Cats?"

"Hell, they'll handle it easy. They carry a twenty-five
ton payload and they got a cargo compartment that's
about ten feet wide and nine feet high, and runs about

forty feet. You could put a bunk house, a Caterpillar, or a whole pile of thirty-one foot lengths of drill pipe in it. One time they even cut up a whole drilling rig and flew it in in sections—up to Sagwon. That was back in '66—an Alamo crew cut the rig into Hercsized pieces, built a runway out of snow—that's what they had me doing there, pushing that snow around with the Cat. We had to build it strong enough to handle a hundred and thirty thousand pounds, that's what the plane weighs with the payload. That there Fat Albert made seventy-two round trips up to the drill site. Brought in damn near two thousand tons of rig, pipe, fuel, trucks, drilling mud—all the Goddamn shit they need for spudding a well. Those Hercs flew in there in snow storms, dropped in when the temperature was down to seventy below, in the dark, and it all went off as slick as greased owl shit. Didn't have an accident until the last load came in and a cable snapped in the cold on one of the loads. It busted both legs on a Cat-skinner, Tommy Lee. By that time I think he was glad to get out of there. He's working as a dispatcher now for Birdwell. Still walks with a cane though."

"Well, we better get this load of post holes up to Prospect," Larry said, "so we can get that Cat fixed. You can tell me some more stories when we're rolling."

The truck, which had been idling all through the night, was warm when Larry and Nick got into it and pulled it over to the insulated gas pump.

"How much gas you use up idling like that?" Larry asked.

"Hell, it could run for a week idling. But if you're working, one tank would be enough to get you up to Prudhoe probably. Tank holds two hundred and fifty gallons—it's made special."

Five miles out of Old Man Camp they passed the

sign that said, "You are now entering the frozen North, courtesy Denali Pipeline Construction Company."

"That's the Arctic Circle son. We're really up there now," Nick said chuckling.

The terrain, which had consisted of rolling hills, began to get rugged. Huge jagged peaks appeared on the horizon.

"We're into the Brooks Range now," Nick said "and you're going to learn a hell of a lot about mountain driving before we get down out of them. It's three hundred miles from here to Prudhoe."

They made Prospect in less than an hour—it was twenty miles to there from Old Man. For the last five miles, Larry drove aided by the light of a brilliant sunrise above the mountains on his right.

"Sure is beautiful up here," Larry said, his eyes roving appreciatively over the apparently endless mountain range. "It reminds me a little of home, only bigger."

"That reminds me of what an Eskimo girl said when a Texan tried to explain to her what a penis was. She didn't get the idea so fast, so he whipped the old wanger out of his union suit and laid it on the table in front of her. The Eskimo girl takes a look at it, and she says, 'Just like a cock, isn't it—only smaller.' "

Larry had heard the same joke about a Cockney girl and a Yankee, but he smiled appreciatively. The older man's rambling talk helped to keep Larry from getting drowsy. This far north it was rare to pick up any transmissions on the C.B. and the broadcast band was completely out, so it was a choice of listening to Nick or complete silence.

At Prospect, Nick discovered that the big Cat tractor had a long, barely visible crack in its blade.

"Son of a bitch Olsen was driving this last. He probably hit a rock with it. I told him a hundred times, to watch for them damn things. In this cold, these blades'll snap like a Saltine. This here's the coldest place in Alaska you know. Set a record a little while back— seventy-nine degrees below, and a hell of a lot of wind too. We're lucky it's warm today—only about forty below. Guess we got here just in time for the hot spell."

The disabled Cat had been kept in a closed shed so it didn't take too long to get the motor going, with the help of a Herman Nelson heater. There were no suitable welding rods available to repair the crack and in fact there was no welder on duty at the camp.

"Them guys will be coming up later. They're from that hot-shot 798 local down in Tulsa. But I don't guess the shop steward will pull everybody out if I do a little welding myself here. I'm in that local too."

Nick searched around the machine shop and found a piece of discarded spring steel, which he used with a portable electric welder to run a long bead sealing off the crack and protecting the blade from further damage.

Larry stood by and drank a cup of coffee with a shot of Nick's Three Feathers in it. He admired the neat and casual way in which Nick Gordon laid the bead down on the shiny metal. They laid a couple of skids onto the Low-Boy and Nick drove the big Cat onto the trailer.

Larry walked around the truck checking the lights and lashings, tires and snow chains. When he had satisfied himself that everything was secure, the two men crawled into the cab and Larry eased the truck out of Prospect Camp, headed north on the winter haul road.

"It should be a little bit easier driving with the Cat on the back there. She doesn't take the wind so much as the big Atco did. You'll be glad to have the old Cat along before the trip's through. At times these roads get drifted over or you get into a white-out and you can't find the damn road at all."

"If it's this bad down here, I can imagine how bad it will be up ahead."

"Not necessarily," Nick said. "Actually the worst spot is right around here—up here in the mountains where the wind goes through. Like they say down in Arizona, it's dry, dry cold here. They don't get anymore rain here than they do down in the Mohavey Desert, or snow, I should say—three or four inches a year. But it just blows and blows and piles up, and also the stuff doesn't melt much, it just accumulates. You have to realize that sixty below is common here, and even like it is out now, fifty below with a thirty-five mile an hour wind, that makes the chill factor about a hundred and thirty-five degrees below zero. If you get outside here, look out about taking off your gloves or touching any metal. Your flesh'll freeze in thirty seconds in this weather. It's so cold up here," Nick said, "that for a long time thermometers wouldn't even tell you—they'd just run right out the bottom. Then this old sour-dough named Leroy McQuestin—he had a place back in the Klondike days on the Yukon River— found out that a bottle of quicksilver would freeze at forty below, kerosene at fifty below, and Jamaica ginger extract at sixty below. Perry Davis Pain killer turns white at sixty below, crystalizes at seventy below and freezes solid at seventy-five below. I'm not kidding. This stuff's been confirmed scientifically.

"Other guys have other ways of telling the temperature. A lot of 'em say if you poke a stick in a can of kerosene and it leaves a hole, then you know it's seventy below. I guess you heard people talking about a one dog night, or a two dog night or a three dog night— that means, a man's got to have that many dogs in his bedroll if he expects to survive until morning.

"Of course, you can't do that if you're driving a Snow-Go. I guess you could keep the motor going and cuddle up to that — that's probably equivalent to a three dog night. But, hell, it gets as cold in Fairbanks sometimes as it does here. I remember one year it was so cold the ground was cracking open, just like there was an earthquake. Big wide cracks in the ground, busted open a bunch of natural gas lines and they had gas leaking out. It exploded three houses. I guess this is what you could call the fairy tales of the frozen north, except it's all true. You'll find that out."

"What about earthquakes—I mean, real ones?"

"Oh, we don't think about them much," Nick laughed. "I guess we get an average of forty, fifty a week up here. It's in the papers every week. I think the least we ever had was about thirty-three one week."

"You're kidding!"

"Nah. You don't really notice them much out here in the bush. And most of them are small. Of course we've had a couple of beauts. That one in Anchorage in '64. And Valdez, when the whole city fell down. And there were some back in the '30's I guess."

Larry, coming to a steep downgrade after having crested one of the Brooks Range peaks, tapped his brakes gently to avoid going into a skid but was surprised to find that there seemed to be no response. He hit the brake pedal a little harder as the truck began to pick up speed. And then he shifted into low register to slow down their velocity.

"Oh, yeah," Nick said. "I forgot to tell you. We must be about fifty below here now. Brakes just aren't any good at that temperature. I've got so used to it, I just plain stopped using them myself anyway."

"Well, what *do* you do? Outside of downshifting."

The truck was gradually slowing to a safe rate of descent.

"Well, if you really get desperate, you can always drive off the road into a deep drift, and haul yourself out with a cat. Basically, though, after you've got a little experience, you won't have any trouble driving this road. The main thing is, on these roads you ain't likely to run into any fast traffic—anything that's coming, you can see a long way off. So, you don't really need brakes that bad. As long as you watch your speed and don't let the load get to swinging and swaying so's you get out of control, you'll be okay. Even if you roll her or rhubarb off the road, we've got the old D-6 Cat on the back to pull us out."

"What do the other drivers do, if they don't have a Cat with them?"

"Well, they just radio for help, if there's anybody nearby. Or else, they just sit here until somebody comes along. This time of year there's at least ten, twenty trucks a day, so it ain't that much of a worry. Here comes one now. See way down there?"

He pointed down the bare mountainside, where the road zig-zagged into a valley.

"Right now he's crossing a stream down there."

Way off in the distance, perhaps two miles away, Larry could make out an occasional flash of chromium in the light of the sun, which had now managed to lever itself a few inches above the horizon. Ten minutes later they passed a big Diamond T, pulling what appeared to be a load of scrap iron in its stake-bed trailer. The driver flashed his lights once in recognition. Larry signalled back.

As they passed each other, Nick picked up the C.B.

"This here's Texas Wildcat. How's the road up ahead? Come on, good buddy."

"A-Okay, Wildcat, good buddy," the radio crackled back. "But you'd better watch the ice on a couple of them rivers. They're froze deep, but they got currents and deep spots."

164

"Ten four. What's your handle, good buddy?" Nick asked.

"This is Diamond Head, here. That you, Nick?"

"Yeah, just dead-heading up, with my good yellow Cat on the back. Will I see you on the bounce around?"

"Mercy, no, good buddy. I'm headed for R 'n R. Fairbanks, Wahoooo! Here I come."

"What's happening?"

"Nothing much. Some little Native boy got his head squashed night before last in Galbraith."

"Hurt him much?"

"Yeah. Killed him."

"I always figured 'em Eskimos had heads like bowling balls," Nick said. "How'd it happen?"

"He was fixing the wheels on one of the Cats—laying down there—and I guess somebody got in and backed up without looking."

"You buy that?" Nick asked cynically.

"All kind of accidents happen up here, Nick," Diamond Head answered, the voice growing fainter as the trucks pulled apart.

Nick turned up the volume and continued the chatter for the next twenty minutes, until the Diamond T drew out of range. Finally, after a period of intermittently fading signals, he clicked off the C.B. in disgust.

The road, which had dipped slightly to an iced-over river crossing, now began to climb in steep, hair-pin zig-zags. Far ahead, Larry could see a small hand painted sign and an access road leading off to the right.

"That's Coldfoot up there," Nick said. "You want to stop for some coffee?"

"When's the next stop? I like to keep going as long as there's daylight."

"Well, there's a little construction camp at Dietrich. That's just about thirty-five miles up ahead, right after you cross the Bettles River. I guess maybe, two, maybe

165

three hours — depending on your luck. Be dark by then."

"Let's go for it. Do you mind?"

"Hell no. Not as long as I got a little of this Three Feathers left. But she ain't going to last until the Continental Divide."

"Can't you pick up some in one of the camps?"

"Shit, no! No booze, no women, no gambling. That's what they say, anyhow. Oh, you can usually find a bottle around somewhere, in somebody's footlocker. And as far as gambling, there's no way they can easily stop that—they just play with markers, if there's a company hot-shot around."

"What about women?"

"Well, there's getting to be a few around—bullcooks, and such. The way I hear it, there's going to be a lot more before it's finished."

Three hours later, an hour after the sun had finally set below the ragged skyline, they pulled into Dietrich. It was identifiable for miles before they actually saw it by the cluster of lights glowing below in the valley where the Bettles and Dietrich Rivers joined.

As they passed along the stainless steel chow line, built exactly like the ones Larry had seen further down, Larry noticed a typed sign hung from one of the metal shelves over the steam table. It said:

"FROM: DENALI PIPELINE MANAGEMENT

TO: ALL EMPLOYEES

RE: GENERAL HEALTH

REGULAR BATHING IS A MATTER OF COM-
MON POLITENESS. NO MATTER HOW AT-
TRACTIVELY A MEAL IS PRESENTED, A
PERSON'S APPETITE MAY VERY WELL BE
RUINED IF AN UNWASHED PERSON SITS

166

After a couple of doughnuts and a fast cup of coffee,
Larry and Nick hit the road again. They had been less
than two days on the road, but to Larry it seemed like
weeks. Hardly an hour passed without some kind of
minor crisis: a broken tire chain, that had to be welded
or replaced with a repair link; a patch of spongy sagging ice at a frozen river crossing that caused little
beads of fear-sweat to pop out on Larry's brow. At
Kanooti Flats the truck ran into drifts that completely
covered the haul road. Larry had to wait while Nick
unloaded the Cat, pushed a vague path through the
snow, and finally hauled the Mack along behind it for
five miles until they were through the drifts and over
the next mountain peak. Once, sickeningly, the truck's
rear tractor tires sank as Larry drove across a frozen
creek near the Atigun Canyon. For a minute Larry
thought the whole truck was going to disappear beneath the water, but fortunately the stream was shallow at that point and the truck only settled two or three
feet before hitting bottom. Nick, always cheerful, taking
each mishap as a matter of course, rolled the big D-6
off the Low-Boy, and onto the ice. By pulling around
the spot he was able to cross to the shore. The Cat,
of course, with its wide tracks and lesser weight, had no
trouble negotiating the ice. Larry attached the heavy
tow chain to the tow hook on the front of the Mack
and gradually Nick pulled the big truck onto the shore
and to the far slope of the river, but then the rear drive
wheels were frozen, and they had to unlimber the Herman Nelson heater from Nick's Cat and thaw the
wheels.

One of the tire chains had broken in the pull. While
Nick thawed the frozen wheel, Larry worked on the

chain—something he discovered it was impossible to do in a pair of heavy mittens. Finally, in disgust, holding the repair link briefly between his teeth, he pulled the mittens off, figuring that he could manage to attach the link in several short spurts, each of them less than the thirty seconds he had been warned was the danger point for frostbite. Unfortunately, he'd forgotten Nick's warning about not touching metal. When he went to take the link from between his teeth, he found that it had stuck, painfully, to his lower lip. He did not find this out until he had pulled a sizeable patch of lip and flesh from his half-frozen mouth. Ignoring the pain, he managed to insert the pin and attach the chain link in only six thirty-second spurts of bare-skinned exposure to the cold, between which he warmed his fingers on the idling truck motor to bring back circulation to the frost-whitened fingertips.

Once they were under way again, in the warm truck, Larry began to feel considerable pain from the torn skin on his lip. Nick covered it and soothed it somewhat with antiseptic ointment from the truck's first aid kit, but Larry was aware of the nagging raw-edged pain for the rest of the trip.

At Galbraith Lake Camp, just beyond the Atigun Canyon, they pulled in for supper. The Camp was in a wide barren valley, which, according to Nick had been favored as a campsite thousands of years before by nomadic hunters from Mongolia who had wandered across the Bering Strait when it was still solid footing.

Galbraith was a good stopping place, since they had just gone through the highest mountain pass of the trip —forty-eight hundred feet. Larry took advantage of the break to visit the camp medic. The medical facility consisted of one room and a partitioned-off area with an operating table for minor surgery. The Medic, Artie Palmer, was a tall, thin, nervous man—probably no

168

more than thirty years old, Larry thought, but his face already showed signs of worry lines and strain from the unexpected responsibilities of the job. Palmer took a fast look at Larry's lip, which was now swelling and motioned him to a chair.

"You'll have to wait a minute now, so I can take care of these two welders here. They got thrown—both of 'em—off the platform of one of those front loading trucks."

Larry looked into the operating room and saw two men stretched out. One of them was apparently unconscious, and the other was moaning in agony.

"That one's got a fractured skull and his arm was practically torn out of his shoulder socket."

The unconscious man's face was completely swathed in bandages.

Palmer gestured toward the other man.

"He's got five broken ribs and a punctured lung. I had to put a tube in to drain his lung, and God knows I'm not trained to handle that kind of thing."

Palmer looked pale and near exhaustion.

"I'm just a para-medic you know. But I have to handle everything—traumatic fractures, gonorrhea, angina, insomnia, dehydration. You know, you got to drink a lot of water up here. Keep that in mind. Somehow, in the cold weather, your body just dehydrates. I've had a few dead ones too, here. I guess I've put three men into body bags in the last three months. Going to run out of plastic bags before I'm done, that's for sure. And I hope I'm done pretty soon. Or at least that they give me a camp further south. Maybe I could take the work if I didn't have the cold riding my ass all the time. *All* the time. *All* the time."

After comforting the two men as best he could, the harried medic was able to turn his attention to Larry.

"You still on your way?"

Larry nodded.

"Well, I can't give you any pain killers—you'd only fall asleep on the road. I'll put a fresh ointment on it and that'll kill the pain for a couple of hours. And you can get some Darvon or something when you get up to Prudhoe. It should heal over okay. Not too many germs around when you get up this way."

As the Medic dabbed the soothing analgesic ointment and salve on his lips, Larry stared over his shoulder at a poster showing a cute white fox. The legend on the poster read, *"The fox looks friendly, but he may be rabid."*

Palmer noticed him reading the sign.

"Pay good attention to that one. We've got a real epidemic of rabies up here. It's endemic, in fact, to these animals. I'd say ninety percent of the foxes and wolves up here have rabies. In case you don't know it, rabies is one disease that is just about incurable when it takes hold. And by incurable, I mean fatal."

"I get the picture. I swear never to feed a fox."

Palmer held his eyes for a moment in a bitter stare.

"It's nothing to joke about."

An hour later, after a huge meal of braised steak, soup, fruit salad, bean salad, and apple pie, Larry and Nick again boarded the truck for the hundred and thirty-five mile stretch remaining to Prudhoe.

"How long you think it'll take?" Larry asked.

Nick pursed his lips, calculating mentally. "Anywhere from six hours to forever, depending on how much trouble we have. We're on the down-hill side now, and the last eighty miles is pretty flat. So we ought to be in there tomorrow early morning some time. Think you can hack it?"

Larry felt warm and drowsy from the meal. He held out a hand to Nick.

"Think I'd better take another one of those cockle burrs."

Nick doled out a pair of the yellow amphetemines.

"You be sure you get plenty of sleep once you get up to Prudhoe. You can't go forever on these things, you know. They'll make you sick and crazy."

"I know, I know," Larry said, swallowing the pills with a slug from Nick's rapidly vanishing pint of Three Feathers.

Three and a half hours after they left Galbraith, they passed the Happy Valley Camp, but Larry, now coasting on speed, felt no need for either coffee or food. He just wanted to put on miles. The slopes had fewer hairpin turns to them and were less steep as the Brooks Range flattened in its northern face approach to the Arctic Ocean. Twenty miles after they passed Happy Valley the mountains flattened out until there was nothing but tall bluffs interrupting the white flatness of the tundra.

"Now this here is what most people talking about when they say 'the Arctic,'" Nick said. "Nothing but this flat white. In the springtime there are little lakes here, but they're not really lakes, just puddles. Other than that, it's just this flat tundra. Millions of acres of it."

"I thought I'd at least see some igloos."

Nick laughed. "The only place you see them is in geography books. These here Eskimos live in shacks— tin shacks, wood shacks, Caribou hide shacks, anything they can throw together. Them igloos is for when they're hunting far out, away from home. Maybe hundreds of miles away, if they need shelter and there's the right kind of snow around, they dig it up and build one of them igloos. I been up here a long time, and I ain't seen one yet."

At four o'clock in the morning, almost nineteen hours

since they started, Larry spotted the lights of the Prudhoe Bay Camp, stretching out like a miniature metropolis across the tundra. From a distance it looked like a major city, with lights sprawling for miles in either direction, as though thousands of stars had fallen from the clear polar sky onto the flat white blanket that merged invisibly into the Arctic Sea. In the darkness, the white and blue lights, which ran for eight or ten miles in every direction, reminded Larry of Odessa Texas, deep in the oil fields.

Larry and Nick, bone-weary and balloon-light from the chain of amphetemines and Three Feathers that had kept them going, checked in with the Wheeler dispatcher and were assigned bunks by the personnel office. It was two or three hours before Larry, hypercharged from the pills and over-tired, was able to get to sleep. He played two games of Foos-ball with Nick in the recreation hall and finally, with the help of a few Darvons from the Medic on duty, was able to drowse off. Just before he fell asleep he mumbled to Nick, "Quite a day, quite a day. What's next, I wonder?"

"Nothing much," Nick said. "You get yourself eight, ten hours of sleep, load up the big Mack, get some gas, turn her around and start south. Probably empty. Only difference is, this trip you won't have me and that big yellow Cat to help you out of trouble."

"Terrific, I can hardly wait."

"Don't forget you earned yourself damned near two hundred and fifty bucks today, and that ain't pinfeathers," Nick said.

But Larry was already snoring.

"For the first time in history, the alternatives are absolute. There is an untouched wilderness on one hand and an enormous natural resource on the other. Industry has never had such a clear opportunity to develop the resource and still preserve the wilderness. There are two causes to be served. Perhaps with unusual thought and care both can be served."

—Robert Cantwell
"The Ultimate Confrontation"
Sports Illustrated

Chapter Fifteen

Deirdre Doheny turned her swivel chair, abandoning the heap of folders and bound reports on the desk before her, and stared out through the double insulated window of the eight-story Denali headquarters at the western outskirts of Anchorage. Her window faced east and from it she could see the sparse, newly developed skyline of downtown Anchorage, and the patchy brown and white sprawl of new construction partially covered by the melting snows of April.

Spring was approaching and in celebration of the day Deirdre had changed from her usual warm wool pants suit to a bright Tartan plaid skirt in soft textured mohair. She felt a compulsion somehow, while waiting for the greening of the short Alaskan spring, to herald its arrival with a burst of color, like a patch of early blooming forsythia. And spring seemed a good time for reappraisal, too. She had just completed her R and R trip back to Texas for the Easter holiday, where she had filled in an eager Whitney Bisset on the progress she had made in the past three years working as public relations liaison and consultant in the Ecology Sector of the pipeline operation, a division not initially conceived as a major part of the pipeline plan, but one that had become almost dominant since the passage of the National Environmental Policy Act in January of 1970.

The oil companies would never forgive Wally Hickel for the fact that during his brief reign as Nixon's Secretary of the Interior, he had thrown up just enough dust about the construction of the pipeline to delay it until the NEPA went into effect. If approval of the pipeline route had been obtained before that it would have saved Denali and its owner companies billions of dollars. Since the passage of the act, it almost seemed as if Denali was as much in the ecology business as it was in the oil business.

Deirdre's job, originally conceived of by Wilbur Steele as a pleasant sinecure and a lure to bring her north, now became the hub around which a good many of Denali's activities revolved. All of the various departments were obliged to check in with the ecology experts. The people who specialized in law, engineering, geology, oil production or government—none of them could afford to be ignorant of the ecological impact of any of their actions.

When Mahlon Doheny had been installed as an Executive Field Director of Denali some two years earlier, Deirdre had had to fight the attitude that she was simply a decorative, nepotistic flower in the business-like truck garden of the pipeline administration. But during the last year, her devotion to the job, willingness to work long hours, and mainly her ability to act as a lubricant and soothing influence between the abrasive personalities that seemed to occupy so many of the steel-walled cubicles in the Denali building had made her a valuable—almost indispensable—member of the team.

174

If Michael Harrison, the civil engineer assigned to Denali by Royal American, had his feelings hurt in an argument over the routing of the pipeline through the Atigun Canyon, it was Deirdre who would bring him a cup of properly brewed tea and take him to a quiet corner, where she would explain that the fact that Jack Keefer had called him "a dumb limey son of a bitch" was not meant to be offensive. Harrison would sip his tea reflectively, adding to it a few drops from the bottle of Glenlivet Malt Whiskey in his drawer and stare dolefully at Deirdre with his pale cat-like amber eyes.

"You know," he'd say, "I never have understood you Americans. And up here, where you all seem so quintessential, so typical, it's as though I'm living in some sort of animated cartoon version of America, with everything heightened and exaggerated."

Deirdre patted his hand.

"Cheer up Michael. By the end of these long winters we all get a bit of cabin fever. You'll feel better, and maybe you'll even convince them about the Atigun Canyon routing."

"Look," Michael explained patiently, as though he had not been over and over it again in the meetings. "I know that the routing in the Atigun Canyon looked very atractive to the engineers in Houston, but my dear girl, they simply have never been there. Have you flown over the Atigun Canyon? It's nothing but enormous, impassable boulders, sheer rock faces, and spring floods that are beyond belief. It is an absolute engineering impossibility to send the pipeline through there. The fact that it's twenty-two miles shorter than my suggested route might make your father and his cronies ecstatic, but my dear girl—it simply will not work. It is an engineering impossibility."

"Okay," Deirdre said. "You can bring it up again at the next staff meeting. I'll talk to Keefer and ask him to

175

try to control his temper and remember that this is a meeting between professionals."

"I'd appreciate that," Harrison said quietly as he added another inch of the liquor to his tea.

As Deirdre dropped her styrofoam cup into the wastebasket and left Harrison to return to her office, she reflected that at least part of the reason that the frustrated British engineer always seemed to be so sweet and thoughtful was that he was usually half smashed by eleven-thirty in the morning.

"If you want to have a good meeting with the limey," McDade had told her, "you'd better call it before lunch. After that he's as useless as tits on a boar hog."

She swiveled her chair again and returned her attention to the heap of documents on her desk. It was spring cleaning time and moving day for her. In appreciation for her growing importance in the organization, McDade had assigned her a new and larger office in Fairbanks, where she would be closer to the field activities with which she was becoming increasingly associated.

In taking over the new job she had to assimilate all the various memos, files, and reports on staff meetings in Anchorage and Fairbanks—top level meetings which she never previously had been invited to attend, although sometimes she had been allowed to see abridged reports of the meetings. They made an impressive heap on her desk. It took at least twenty minutes to organize the material by date rather than by subject. She quickly skipped through the early formative memos in late 1969 and early 1970 during which time she had been in the field, getting familiar with the area, setting up the offices, and accompanying Wilbur on what he called his "orientation tours."

(In those days she often had been the only woman in the camp, although that was gradually changing now. Wilbur had always insisted that they have adjoining

176

rooms for "her protection." She supposed it hadn't done much for her reputation, but having his brand figuratively stamped on her flank had at least saved her a lot of trouble from men in the field when later, on various ecological assignments, she had to travel the camps alone.

The first item that caught her attention was the minutes of the first management meeting:

DENALI PIPELINE SERVICE CO.

Minutes of Management Meeting

Number One

December 15, 1970

Present: M. W. Doheny, J. R. Keefer, R. M. Baronian, B. W. Heywood, F. X. McDade, M. Q. Harrison, A. Vaughn, E. C. D'Ablaisio, J. Quinn.

Guests: W. F. Fawcett, Royce and Rogers Advertising Agency; A. Brandon, representing Wilbur Steele.

McDade 1. This is the first of weekly meetings of office and department managers at the Denali/Anchorage offices for the purpose of exchanging information and improving communication.

2. Al Brandon is going to Washington, D.C. tomorrow to clarify the strictness of adherence to which Denali will be kept in respect to NEPA stipulations on our project.

3. We are retaining a lobbyist in Washington, D.C.

That sure opened a can of warms, Deirdre thought.

177

Doheny 4. Mr. Brandon, from Houston,
is in Anchorage on special assignment
to review our office procedures.

5. The unabridged monthly status report will be circulated to the Anchorage staff by division vice presidents,
who will distribute an abridged
monthly status report in Alaska.

Here followed reports from personnel, legal, labor,
and ecology. Deirdre read Vaughn's summary with
interest.

Vaughn 11. D. D. Doheny is reviewing
the new Alaska State Conservation
bill, which we hope to distribute
next month.

12. The Ecology Department is checking models and other visual equipment
to be used in the Congressional
hearings.

13. A study on the entire environmental situation is underway.

14. A consulting arrangement with
about ten environmental consultants
is under development.

15. We are investigating a request
from the Polar Research Institute to
publish data which has been generated through Denali's efforts.

*That one came as a surprise to Deirdre. She had al-
ways thought research institutes did their own research.*

16. An environmental study involving
operations in the Valdez harbor
has begun.

Quinn 17. Highest priority work is continuing in the effort to secure a pipeline.

18. Plans are underway to employ a lawyer and a government liason man in Juneau.

19. Work is underway to develop special legislation which will be introduced in congress to handle the Native Claims problem.

That explained good old "Uncle" Fred Steele's trips to Alaska that summer with Wilbur and Brandon. And the sudden spurt of conferences that made Wilbur's appearance in Washington so urgent.

D'Ablaisio 20. An update on the labor situation in Valdez: The labor union has placed pickets at two of three entrances to the pipeyard. The entrance used by Wheeler Trucking has not been picketed. Picket signs read "Wardell Construction Company pays sub-standard wages."

21. Wheeler drivers have stopped driving. Teamster local officials have indicated that they should decide what to do individually, according to their conscience.

22. The ships continue to unload pipe, which is being stored temporarily behind the warehouse adjacent to the dock until we can get access to the pipeyard.

23. Meeting adjourned.

The day after that first meeting the information leaks

had started. A story about the labor trouble by Al Everhardt appeared in the Fairbanks *News-Miner* the next day. They couldn't have gotten that one alone; the details were suspiciously accurate. Reporters were at the office asking about the identity of the environmental experts and the house lawyers hired in Juneau. And a reporter from the *Anchorage Times* called to ask when the conservation film would be available. It appeared that somebody had distributed entire copies of the minutes liberally to the press. From then on, all minutes were headed "Confidential" and an effort was made to limit distribution to stop the leak. Also, Mahlon Doheny's secretary, Susie Wing, who typed up the summuary of the proceedings, would submit a draft to Doheny first, who would check it to make sure that confidential details of the meetings were not included.

Brent Heywood was warned to be guarded in all dealings with the local press, especially, since Alaskan newsmen tended to be much more inquisitive and well-informed than the out-of-staters, and to check all meeting summaries with Doheny's office before distribution.

But still matters appeared in the report that, if fully understood, might have interested the press. A cryptic mention from Heywood, for instance, that said: "The Fish and Wildlife Section of the Department of the Interior's environmental draft statement has been rewritten and several other sections have been modified and submitted to the Department for approval."

A sharp-eyed reporter would have quickly caught the fact that some of Denali's crack writers in Washington were actually writing and modifying the Department of the Interior's Environmental Statement. It would have made a column head in the *New York Times*.

Another item in the same report indicated that the Polar Research Institute had agreed to publish Denali's environmental findings "for a price." (No explanations were needed.)

Deirdre, through office gossip, and her good connections, was aware of much that went on in the company. But still, operations outside of Alaska often surprised her by their range and thoroughness. Often the only evidence available in Anchorage or Fairbanks were tiny notations and remarks from visiting executives, such as the entry attributed to Brandon in the second staff report: "Our Washington lobbyist, Mr. Forester, is preparing a recommendation on Denali's game plan for encouraging and influencing Congressional legislation on Native Claims."

On February 4th, Heywood reported: "Presently, most of the public relations effort is aimed at getting ready for the hearings in the Environmental draft statement. Due to the attitude of the Department of the Interior, which is to deliberately understate Denali's presence at the hearings, we plan to establish our press office across the street and to display our models of the planned instrumentations there."

Deirdre studied Heywood's report thoughtfully. She had not known that such an intimate relationship existed between the Department of the Interior and the oil companies. The minutes of the March 15th meeting in 1971 —meeting number ten—made the relationship even clearer. McDade, Executive Director under Dohney, had reported:

1. The Department of Interior has indicated that they would like our active participation in the writing of the final environmental statement. Tom Hastings will be the prime Denali contact at Interior. Since we understand that they are shooting for July 1st finish date for this statement, it will be August 1st before it gets to Russell Train (the Under-Secretary of the Department of the Interior, Alaskan Pipeline Task Force).

On that same day, Gus Vaughn announced that he had planned a caribou migration study using a snow fence to simulate the pipeline, at an approximate cost of $150,000.

That month Heywood started producing Denali Pipeline Service Company "News-line" communications for employees. The first one led with a photo and message from Mahlon Doheny, followed by a number of bright features about how Denali was helping the Natives with various business and cultural programs. There was a feature in it by Deirdre Doheny called "Digging up the Past" that described the work of the archeology teams who followed the construction camps to make sure that none of the priceless Eskimo heritage was disturbed. It also contained a feature about a survival course for Arctic travelers and an article describing the new campaign of full page advertisements in newspapers across the nation, written, the "News-Line" said, "to inform and assure the general public of the research and technology that have gone into the Denali Pipeline Project."

The first ad in the series showed an Eskimo dressed in a National Guard surplus parka holding up a giant graduate full of oil. There was a big headline, "Do We Need It?" and a thousand words of small print copy explaining why America *did* need the oil.

Bill Fawcett, the account executive from Rogers and Royce Advertising Agency, which handled the Denali account, had explained that long copy gave a more sincere look to the ad and conveyed the impression that Denali was trying to explain fully what it was doing to the public. Part of the copy read, "We have already spent millions of dollars finding out whether or not the pipeline could be built without damaging the environment. We've conducted experiments in the north with both hot and cold pipe. We've studied the wildlife— its breeding and migratory habits. We've carried out far-reaching botanical experiments to determine the best methods for re-seeding and restoring the tundra. We've even examined our entire proposed route to be sure that we will not disturb areas of archeological importance. In short, we have done our home-work.

"Now we feel it is time to move ahead. We need permission to use a right-of-way fifty-four feet wide and approximately eight hundred miles long. We must touch a wilderness, but we will touch it as carefully and gently as possible."

Deirdre smiled grimly and remembered a remark once made by Al Everhardt, "A virgin wilderness which has had an eight hundred mile, four foot thick pipeline rammed up its middle is not exactly a virgin anymore."

Deirdre also had a clipping in her files in which Doheny had announced in Washington that if legal and administrative hurdles could be cleared by summer, oil could start moving through the pipeline by late 1974. Otherwise the movement of oil might be postponed at least until late 1975. The news item was dated February 5, 1971. *That was before the Sierra Club and all those others got on our back,* Deirdre thought. *At this point things seemed very different.*

Two weeks later, Governor Egan of Alaska went to Washington to announce that the prosperity of the 49th State, and of all of its people, hinged on approval of the pipeline. But an Eskimo delegation cramped Egan's style by appearing at the same meeting chaired by the new Secretary, Rogers Morton. They announced that there would be no pipeline until there was a settlement of Native claims.

After the hearing, Morton, who at first had been expected to leap in with his approval of the pipeline, and then had worried Denali and the rest of the pipeline backers by stalling in order to appear not completely in the hands of the oil interests partially soothed Denali's

183

collective wrinkled brow by this statement: "I cannot endorse the philosophy that we must impose a moratorium on resource development forever in the Arctic."

Next in Deirdre's file was the first of those memos from Heywood, which Mahlon Doheny always scornfully called the "Gadfly memos." It was attached to a pamphlet put out by the Wilderness Society that was called "Russian Roulette in the Arctic." The pamphlet began: "A group of oil companies hopes to start work this spring on what could prove to be one of history's most fool-hardy and costly undertakings. A game of Russian roulette with man's natural environment.

"Seven major oil companies—six American and one British—have applied to the U.S. Department of the Interior for permission to thrust heavy construction equipment into the Federally managed public lands of Alaska in order to build the world's most ambitious pipeline."

A few paragraphs down there was a subhead that said, "BREAK WOULD BE A NIGHTMARE," followed by:

"A break in such a huge hot pipeline would be a nightmare of destruction and ugliness unparalleled in history. Should a break occur, the hot oil would quickly spew out over Alaska's beautiful and fragile tundra and forest land, into its streams and rivers, melting the permafrost and triggering a whole series of disastrous effects—perhaps for hundreds of miles. Such a calamity might easily happen in a terrain forbidding to human technology because of its severe cold, treacherous instability and frequent earthquakes . . . The oil companies say they have devoted intensive study to the environmental hazards and know how to surmount it. The truth is, however, that only in recent months, after court injunctions obtained by conservation groups and Native Alaskan villagers prevented the start of con-

struction, have the pipeline sponsors begun to acknowl-
edge the adverse environmental aspects of the project.
The best they can now promise is to 'minimize the
damage.' "

D.D. looked at Heywood's covering "Gadfly" memo:

To: Mahlon Doheny

From: Brent Heywood

Re: Our telephone conversation
    yesterday

   If you haven't read the attached, you
should. It may give you added insight
into the nature of your adversaries.
The Wilderness Society, I believe,
has a membership of about 9,000.
Each of them undoubtedly got a copy
of this and a high percentage will
respond with letters supporting the
stand the organization is taking.
   As I mentioned, I am willing to
write in opposition to that stand,
providing I can get facts that will
help to form a rebuttal. What I would
like to have is a description of
studies that have been made, the
names and credentials of the people
who made them, and something in the
way of data that will support the
conclusion that the pipeline is a
good idea.

   Poor Brent, Deirdre thought, always tilting at oil
derricks.

Following this Deirdre discovered a clipping from the Wilmington *Delaware Evening Journal*. It was an article by Stuart Udall, distributed widely by the Los Angeles Times Syndicate. It was headed, "Wheeling and Dealing with Alaskan Oil," and included what Udall described as a "highly disturbing scenario of the future of oil" that had been developed by two economists from an organization called "Resources For The Future, Inc.," a non-profit Washington, D.C. research group.

Udall stated: "The oil companies, having conned the United States into believing it had an overweening need for more crude from the North Slope, instead had found that the West Coast could not possibly absorb the 2,000,000 barrels a day . . . nor can they economically transport it to other markets in the United States. Therefore, the surplus oil, most of it, in fact, is sold to Japan. In return for this oil, the companies would get Interior Department licenses to import an equal amount of oil from the Persian Gulf and Venezuela, and, presumably, Saudi Arabia. Congress could not object that strategic considerations were involved since the Alaskan oil could always be diverted to U.S. markets should there be an emergency. Under the import quota program, which artificially raises the price for imported oil, the new exchanged oil would come to the U.S. from the Middle East for approximately twice the price that the Alaskan oil would have fetched domestically. Thus the . . . consortium would make a financial killing by dumping the Alaskan oil on Japan while selling an equal amount to the United States. It could, alternatively, sell its import licenses to other companies. Either way, the United States consumer would pay handsomely for the privilege of the big oil companies to make an undue profit and desecrate the Alaskan environment."

186

Mahlon Doheny had scrawled savagely across this in a broad-tipped black felt pen, "Who is feeding information to these Commies???" It was unlike him to be so unrestrained. But the notation was meant only for Deirdre's eyes.

In any event, as a result, Denali had hired Royce and Company, the public relations subsidiary of their advertising agency, Rogers and Royce, to prepare a full-fledged public relations program. Up to now the owner companies had been used to operating behind the scenes with the lobbyists and subsidized politicians, who gave as little information to the public as possible. But now every part of their program seemed to be springing leaks—the public was being flooded with unfavorable information. If the leaks couldn't be stopped, then the acid flood of adverse comment must somehow be neutralized.

Royce's report (incidentally making a pitch for a huge P.R. budget) put the case strongly:

Alfred Royce and Company
PUBLIC RELATIONS
Denali Pipeline Service Co.

INTRODUCTION

Despite reported assurances of administration support for the pipeline and ultimate granting of the permit, mounting opposition calls for Denali and its owner companies to launch a massive crash program to mobilize national public support. Every possible source of communication, convincing information, and persuasive argument must be utilized to rally this support.

We must win enough support among opinion leaders—and negate the growth of opposition—so that the issuance of the permit is politically feasible. For the Alaska pipeline is a political issue. The National Election Campaign is only months away. A permit may be possible for the

187

Administration to grant in 1971; but questionable in 1972.

The opposition is organized. It is a powerful political force. It is more aggressive than we are. Thus, practical issues of economics and U.S. energy needs are being subordinated to the emotional arguments of the ecologists and the environmentalists. As a national public issue, the pipeline case in Alaska parallels that of the S.S.T. in many respects. *The public* killed the S.S.T.

The report went on to recommend a comprehensive series of actions, including a public opinion poll, a survey of the attitudes of various members of Congress, a summary of selected members of Committees that will have an influence on Interior Department appropriations, environmental issues, and the Native Claims legislation; members of the Executive Branch, the Interior Department itself, the Environmental Protection Agency, and the White House.

A segment of the press the Royce Report felt it would be impossible to convert—leading papers, like the *New York Times* and *The Washington Post*. It recommended a survey of editorial positions to be run by a leading journalism school. "If results are heavily anti-pipeline in the news columns, they might be given to Vice President Agnew as one more instance of a biased press. Current press criticism of Agnew aside, he is making the press more self-conscious and defensive."

The report then went on to recommend an extensive program of public information justifying the position of Denali and trying to show how careful Denali planned to be with the environment. This would be supported by a massive advertising campaign.

"This is no time to be timid, or to fear the broadsides that advertising will elicit from the enemy. If a substantial portion of the press is against you, *buy* your way in with your side of the story. As public relations counsel we endorse an advertising campaign designed to discredit every opposition argument, kill every argument for delayed decision, and sell every critical need for Alaska's oil."

I don't suppose the fact that Royce is owned lock, stock, and barrel by our advertising agency had anything to do with that recommendation, Deirdre thought.

There followed a series of proposals for publicizing Denali's cause on radio, television, and with the production of a film such as the one already backed by Denali, but which would come out as produced by the State of Alaska, and would be featured on public television in unpaid-for time. What was more, Royce recommended that a book be commissioned for publication in paperback as soon as possible.

In its final summary, Royce stated: "It is generally agreed that the public relations program for Denali must enter a new 'campaign' phase of all-out warfare. Our organization has the Denali, Alaska, and national background and capability to carry out the kind of program outlined here. We have the enthusiasm and key manpower for the battle. We believe it should begin immediately." The report was signed by Alfred Royce.

The Royce report was well-received. Its implementation was accelerated as attacks on the pipeline began to increase.

Jack Anderson, quoting a report from the National Oceanic and Atmospheric Administration, charged that the Interior Department had neglected to investigate the effect of oil spills on marine life. "The inevitable spills at Valdez," Anderson warned, "would destroy the spawning waters of the salmon, gum up fishermen's nets, and poison shellfish and wild birds. In addition, the oil shipments into the Puget Sound area (if they ever got there) would present an ever greater danger of oil spills. The Interior Department also did not consider adequately what ocean currents could do to offshore oil spills . . . While salmon, crab, oysters and scallops are endangered inshore, such fish as cod, roc, flounder, perch, herring, and others may be fouled in the oceans."

Of course, not all the press was hostile. There were occasional bright spots in Deirdre's pile of clippings, most of the support coming from the *Anchorage Times*. Tom Kelly, the former State Commissioner of Natural Resources, who had conducted the nine hundred million dollar oil lease sale in 1969, spoke up in Vancouver for the pipeline. "I don't say that I believe it, but with the passage of time and witnessing the thrust of the opposition and the direction that economic progress has taken in Alaska, which is in reverse gear, I perceive more than altruism in wanting to protect Alaska's natural environment. The basis of all wealth stems from production, and if productivity can be squelched then the American system is very vulnerable to collapse," Kelly said. But Kelly's cries of red herrings in the woodpile were only picked up by the *Seattle Times* and ignored by the wire services and television networks.

Ultimately, Denali decided to spend, for starters, twenty million dollars on its new P.R. advertising counter attack, of which ten million dollars was to be disbursed for national advertising. But the ink was still wet on the ads when the press began to attack the campaign itself. The *Boston Globe* called it "eco-pornography, an ad creating an image of ecologic sensitivity for corporations that are continuing to pollute land, sea, and air."

One of the new high pressure programs in which Deirdre was asked to participate was "Speak Up

Alaska"—ostensibly a state-wide citizens committee trying to win public favor in the lower forty-eight for the pipeline, but actually financed by an initial grant of twenty-five thousand dollars from Denali. Unfortunately, Alaska's independent citizens, once they'd been launched were not that easy to control. Robert Reeve, for instance, owner of Reeve Aleutian Airways and Chairman of the Speak Up Alaska committee, spoke on a public affairs TV program in Anchorage.

He labelled Interior Secretary Rogers C. B. Morton, "Public Enemy Number One" for not immediately approving the Alaska Pipeline; criticized Alaskan Representative Nick Begich for voting against the supersonic transport; and took verbal swipes at Cordova fishermen, the National Rifle Association and others.

A memo from Heywood on Deirdre's desk asked, "What's Phase Two? Shut-Up, Alaska?"

Somehow this gag also leaked to the press, giving the anti-pipeline public a good laugh at Denali's expense. Doheny was furious. (Of course, Heywood may merely have repeated a current gag making the rounds in the bars.) But the problems caused by anti-pipeline people, most notedly the ecological group, were really beginning to be a serious obstacle.

The pipeline really should have been started long ago. Now the eight hundred miles of pipe was laying scattered in yards all over Alaska rusting: the camps were being reduced to maintenance forces; and drilling and construction were gradually coming to a halt as the member companies began to drag their heels about putting further money into the exploitation of the pipeline until a permit was granted. Each move made by Denali had to be approved by a majority of the owner-members, and it was in staff meetings, usually held elsewhere—in Houston, Washington, or New York—

that certain differences between the members became apparent.

Rawhide Robertson, the rough, tough Texan from Golconda certainly showed a surprisingly tender sensibility toward ecological problems. "I can't see us doing diddly-shit," he had told a member meeting "without we square away these wilderness boys. Shucks, I'm a member of the Sierra society myself and I've been a conservationist all my life, ever since I shot my first elk." Vaughn, the ecologist, had been Robertson's suggestion for the staff. Vaughn had previously worked for the Boone and Crockett Club on conservation matters. The Boone and Crockett club was a group of trophy hunters, deeply concerned lest wilderness areas be eroded and no animals left to hunt.

Of course, there were those who said that Golconda was willing to go along with the ecological protest movement because it already had ample supplies of crude oil domestically, whereas Steele's Alamo oil was in desperate need of the new crude supplies that would come from the North Slope.

In June of 1971 the caribou started moving into their summer range, and Denali's hundred and fifty thousand dollar snow fence was ready to test whether they would ignore the obstructions, go around or over it, and in what fashion their movement would be affected. At the staff meeting on June 15, Vaughn reported, "The test fence for caribou blew down last week as a result of a forty mile per hour wind. It should be repaired quickly since the environmental impact committee will be visiting the area with Rogers Morton next week."

What a screw-up, Deirdre thought. At first she had been deeply impressed with the professionalism of her fellow team members and the money that was spent. But she soon realized that fancy titles and big spending didn't always necessarily mean that the results were perfect—or even competent. Official sounding institutions, like the Polar Research Institute, turned out to be easily paid off. Well-credentialed scientists, who were also well paid by Denali, had a way of interpreting facts in such a manner that they were favorable to the pipeline. It was Heywood himself who had pointed out that even a respected professor, who had been previously earning $12,000.00 or $15,000.00 in some rinky-dink college, would think twice before making a report to Denali that would blow the forty or fifty thousand a year he was now making from the oil company.

Also, despite the reams of technical reports that had been made in preparation for the pipeline, it now turned out that the permafrost—through which much of the pipeline would run—would not support the hot oil line in most areas. In fact, it now looked as though the pipeline, instead of being ninety percent buried, would be very likely more than half on the surface or elevated.

By the end of June the expected caribou herd had not arrived, at least not in any great numbers, but Vaughn reported that three crossing had been reported so far—two under the fence and one over a ramp. In July the FCC had scored a big point for the Wilderness Society and other antipipeline groups. Deirdre noted Quinn's summary in the minutes of the July 6 meeting. "The FCC has ruled in the case that conservation groups should be provided equal time to answer commercials on NBC which endorse the trans-Alaskan pipeline. This is a new concept which could require equal time for an adverse party when an 'idea' or 'cause' is being presented affirmatively."

Deirdre remembered the look on her father's face when he had called her into his office to show her Quinn's memo. He was puffing furiously on his ever-present cigar. He had said nothing as she read the report, Deirdre remembered, but had angrily mashed out the stub and bit the end off a new cigar as if it were the head of Brock Brower, the leader of the Wilderness Society, and in a gesture of unaccustomed crudeness had spit the severed end out on the carpet.

Deirdre watched him anxiously for signs of the tell-tale flush that would indicate that his blood pressure was going up again, but Doheny caught her glance and smiled placatingly. For a minute she thought there was a trace of a twinkle in his steel-blue eyes. He was a complex man, and as well as she knew him, Deirdre was never entirely able to predict his moods.

She had always wondered, for instance, how her father had been able to accept, with relative calm, the complete shafting he had taken from Wilbur Steele on the Mexican oil deal. Now that she knew more about Denali it was obvious to her that Wilbur had withheld capital from Doheny's Honda oil deal not only because he was strapped for capital but also because he had wanted to maintain pressure on Congress for approval of the pipeline. The development of a new source of crude oil in Mexico would have relieved that pressure. The fact that withholding the promised capital had financially ruined his friend was not the sort of thing that impeded Wilbur's action—not that the job he had given Doheny as head of Denali was exactly that of an office boy. Mahlon Doheny's salary, Deirdre was sure, exceeded $100,000.00 in a budget made up by the owner-members. *But still,* she thought, *it must have been hard for Daddy to take working for other oil companies instead of being an independent boss of his own outfit as he always had been in the past.*

In July still another headache imposed itself. Charlie Edwardsen, who was President of the North Slope Natives Association, and was becoming increasingly prominent as an Eskimo leader, had consulted with other Eskimo leaders in the Barrow area and had come

194

up with the idea of organizing the Slope area, which included Prudhoe Bay, into an administrative Borough that would have the right to tax all the oil company property in the leased areas.

Denali's Juneau lobby and legal team were mobilised instantly in a frantic effort to combat this move. Hugh Gallagher, who had been working as liason with the Natives trying to get Native Claims settled so that the pipeline could proceed, reassured Denali that Edwardsen was not out to stop the pipeline, but simply to get from the oil companies what he felt was proper compensation for the lands that had been appropriated from the North Slope Eskimos.

But not matter how you sliced it, the North Slope Eskimos were the biggest barrier to an early settlement of the Native Claims. Most of the other Native groups —the Athabascans, and the Tlingits in the south and the Aleuts—were near to being ready for a settlement. In fact, Edwardsen was stressing his claim that not only the Prudhoe area, but PET 4, the Naval Reserve, and the Arctic Wilderness Preserve to the east of PET 4— which long-range plans had targeted for development too—were also part of the ancestral land of the Inupiat and it was obvious that he would demand compensation for them too when the time came. Still it was hoped that some kind of settlement would be reached by congress by the end of 1971.

In August, Vaughn gave a summary to the staff meeting of the caribou experience. Deirdre read it from the minutes of the August 3, 1971 meeting.

<u>Vaughn</u> Experience to date with the caribou fence. In a recent windstorm about twenty per cent of the fence was blown down. We are now considering the advisability of either repairing

the damage or taking the fence down
entirely. About 845 caribou have
approached the fence so far. The
behavior of these was as follows:
  —13% went over the fence
  —3% went under the fence
  —20% went around the fence
  —64% turned around and went back
      in the direction from whence
      they came.

Needless to say, Deirdre was not asked to put out a
press release describing these results. *How long can
they go on covering up every unfavorable fact,* Deirdre
wondered.

On August 24 there was a cryptic notation from
McDade:

> The project summary has been delayed due to
> a decision to make a significant change in the
> pipeline route. However, it will be available for re-
> lease shortly.

What change? Deirdre wondered. *Probably, it was to
abandon the Atisun Canyon route following Harrison's violent objections that this was impractical. But
in order to make the change, wouldn't it be necessary
to prepare an entire new Environmental Impact Statement? That could take six months or more. How much
more delay would the owner companies take? They
seemed to be digging in their heels and refusing to put
up more money. It was only because they had more
than a billion invested at this point that they could
not pull out. And also because the ultimate profit
would be so high that almost any expense could be
tolerated.*

Over a beer in the Westward lounge, following a
lunch in which the two had entertained a journalist

from the *Scientific American*, Heywood had explained the situation to Deirdre.

"Don't forget, deary," said Heywood, "that the State of Alaska is bearing a lot of these expenses. Their share of the oil is based on the well head prices, meaning the price of the oil when it is loaded on tankers in Valdez *minus* the cost of transporting the oil, and that includes the amortisation of the pipeline expense."

No wonder the State of Alaska has been even more anxious than Denali sometimes to get the project underway, Deirdre thought.

In August a bulky booklet, with huge fold-out maps and diagrams, called "Project Description of the Trans-Alaska Pipeline System" was put out by Denali. It was an impressive looking document including sections covering plans for all contingencies, such as spills along the pipeline route, safety precautions in the Valdez terminal, steps taken to protect the pipeline against the effects of earthquakes, tsunamis, permafrost melting, and other natural phenomena. It was a thorough and sincere document in appearance. The only thing that puzzled Deirdre was the fact that no mention of the new routing of the pipeline away from the Atigun Canyon was made, neither was this fact shown on the elaborate fold-out maps in the report. Yet the new route, Deirdre knew, was at least twenty or thirty miles away from the route originally described in the Denali project.

Deirdre knew that this omission was not accidental. *Could it be possible,* she wondered, *that they were going to relocate that thirty or forty miles of the pipeline without informing the Department of the Interior? Or getting government approval for it?*

In the file of clippings and press reports for September Deirdre found a mimeographed submission from

Radio-TV Reports, Inc., a New York outfit that monitors radio and television stations and sends summaries to its clients. It was a transcript of a news broadcast on station WNYC in New York:

Report on Pipeline

NEWSCASTER: While waiting for Emperor Hirohito to land at Elmendorf Air Base in Alaska, President Nixon rode into Anchorage for a reception at the home of Walter Hickel, the former Alaskan Governor he fired as Interior Secretary. The two men smiled and put their arms around each others shoulders as if no rift had developed.

An estimated 45,000 persons turned out along the route in downtown Anchorage to greet the President. Among the welcoming signs were a number of placards protesting the underground nuclear tests at Amchitka Island in the Aleutians. Don Fulsom reports from Anchorage that the President hinted that a trans-Alaska pipeline will be built.

DON FULSOM: In a statement which seemingly favors construction of a trans-Alaskan pipeline, the President says he does not think the apparent conflict between the oil interests and the environmentalists represents a permanent impasse. Mr. Nixon says Interior Secretary Morton is committed to the development of Arctic resources, is making progress toward balancing the equation of environment

versus technology, and that the final
decision will be made some time this
fall. Most conservationists claim
that the pipeline will seriously
damage the Alaskan ecology and that
it will cost less in the long run to
use an alternate route. Don Fulsom
with the President in Anchorage.

In December of 1971, just before Christmas and a
month after the expected okay, President Nixon finally
announced the passage of a Native Claims settlement.
It gave forty million acres of land to the Native's Association and just under a billion dollars (962.5 million)
to be invested in Native corporations.

Everyone at Denali had breathed a sigh of relief that
the native land claims settlement had gone through in
1971. 1972 was an election year and things were
bound to be fouled up. All the politicians would be
dancing this way and that, attempting to accomplish
their purposes without offending one block of voters
or the other.

Wilbur Steele, who was Republican National Com-
mitteeman from Texas, became so busy in the campaign
that he had little time, apparently, for the pipeline and
appeared rarely in Anchorage. This is not to say that
Wilbur's political involvement was entirely idealistic
and unrelated to the benefit of his company. Alamo Oil,
for instance, sponsored a CBS special on President
Nixon's visit to Peking. One Texas newspaper wondered
editorially if this could not be regarded as a little advance campaign contribution.

Alamo's sponsorship and its possible connection with
important Alaskan decisions went relatively uncom-
mented on in the States. But Al Everhardt noticed the
connection and commented acerbically:

By a strange set of circumstances, the man most concerned with Nixon's decision on the routing of the pipeline is the same man who sponsored the special on that Chinese trip. Within a few months, Nixon's advisors will drop a pile of recommendations on his desk concerning this decision. Steele will of course understand the President's dilemma at this point. Only a few days ago, Nixon's own Interior Department brought out a report on the environmental effects of the Alaskan pipeline. Much to the surprise of all the big shots in Nixon's own Interior Department—and God knows how it happened—but the report seems to indicate that it would be safer to build the line through Canada.

According to the report, in most environmental areas that are important—such as oil spills, earthquake zones, and so on—the Canadian line will pose less of a threat than the Alaskan line. Now we all know that Wilbur Steele of Alamo is just as interested in the environment as anybody else. In fact, last year he was appointed to the Secretary of State's advisory committee on the Stockholm Environmental Conference. Of course, some people who are not entirely kind noticed this appointment and wondered whether Steele's giant campaign contribution to Nixon had anything to do with it. It certainly is a problem for someone who is advising on the environment to actually want something that would damage the environment to an incredible degree.

But to get back to that Interior Department Report, it does present a problem. You see Nixon almost certainly never saw the report itself. What he saw was a neat little digest—maybe four or five pages long. That is all he needs. After all, it is not what the report actually says that counts—it's what people *think* it said. Unfortunately, the Washington Press corps, exactly the ones that Steele and Nixon were hoping would be impressed, took the trouble to read the entire report. And now, officials of the Interior Department, no matter how they try, have not been able to convince them that the report does not favor the Canadian route. These newsmen keep pointing to a page that says, "No general route is superior to any other in all respects," and what is worse, the reporters keep pointing to a little chart way back in volume five that says the Canadian line is superior in most respects.

It's gotten so that Interior officials are not quite sure what the report says themselves. Why, only the other day Interior Secretary Rogers Morton himself went on television and he said, "The Canadian line would face just as much risk of earthquake as the Alaskan line ..." It's funny nobody else can find a line about this in the Interior Department's report.

The networks were less sarcastic, but no less critical. A radio-TV report of a Walter Cronkite—CBS newscast from that same period was in the file.

WALTER CRONKITE: "For two years a court injunction has held back construction of the proposed Alaskan oil pipeline, pending a Government report on possible environmental damage. Well, today that report was made public by the Interior Department and supporting the claims of Environmental groups it warned that the oil pipeline could kill vegetation, drive away animal wildlife and thaw Alaska's permafrost. The study also indicated that alternate routes through Canada would have less destructive potential. However, the Interior Department stressed that it is not proposing a Canadian alternative. It also points out, that without Alaska's North Shore oil, America's energy crisis will get

worse. Daniel Schorr reports that a
final decision by Interior Secretary
Morton is being delayed probably, he
says, until after the November
election."

A reporter from NBC interviewed William T. Pecora
of the Department of the Interior on the subject of the
environmental report.

Pecora: "The work involved represents an effort
equal to the twelve labors of Hercules. Certainly this
is the most thorough, complete environmental impact
statement ever prepared."

Reporter: "Dr. Pecora, what is the Department's
disposition with regard to the request by eighty-two
members of Congress and conservation groups that a
public hearing now be held?"

Pecora: "Public hearings are optional completely."

Reporter: "I realize that."

Pecora: "Under the guidelines and under the act.
The Secretary at this time has felt that public hearings
are not necessary and as a matter of fact, would interfere with a more thoughtful and rational analysis of
this complex document."

Announcer: "Barring court delays it appears certain
that Secretary Morton, who is known to favor the
Alaskan route, will approve it."

Well, lots of things fall into place now, Deirdre
thought. *It certainly must have helped that Denali itself had prepared large parts of the Interior Department
Report. What I hadn't before realized was how large
Wilbur Steele's contributions had been, or how cal-
culated, or how important Fred Steele's influence had
been in Washington.*

Anyway, it seemed as though Denali was reasonably
sure that everything would go well, and the pipeline

would be started in 1972, provided Nixon won the election—or, maybe even if he didn't. A certain amount of money had been laid out on Senatorial and Congressional races by the various member companies. And this would certainly help in any ultimate Congressional decision. Not all Democrats by any means were opposed to the construction of the pipeline.

Even before the Interior Department statement, Deirdre had helped in the preparation of a huge and beautiful hundred page, four-color brochure, featuring lots of cute pictures of caribou, polar bears, Dall sheep, Peregrine Falcons, and other local fauna. The introduction to the booklet began, "The trans-Alaska pipeline will pass through some of the most hostile and most delicate country to man . . ." So it would begin to appear that the pipeline would finally get underway in 1972, the year originally planned for its completion.

There remained, however, one more obstacle—the Environmental Defense Fund, an ecology group that had filed a suit in a Federal court to halt the pipeline, so a court decision would have to be handed down before work could proceed. In the meanwhile, the EDF presented Morton with a counter-impact statement. Its conclusions were that the Canadian pipeline was preferable because of the ecological damage the Alaskan pipeline would cause and it called the Interior Department report "a passive document that blandly accepts at face value the fundamental premises of the oil companies."

Morton got the EDF report on May 4, and four days later they were distributed to Interior Department experts who were given two days to read, digest, and comment on the EDF objections. On May 11, Deirdre was sitting in Heywood's office. Heywood had his coat and shoes off and was drinking coffee, as they argued out the question as to whether public hearings would eventually come off, and if so, how Denali could get its point of view before the public. The phone rang. It was one of Heywood's sources in the office of Representative Nick Begich. He said that a statement was due any minute from Morton concerning the pipeline, but that he didn't know what it was. Heywood called all around to newsmen, to Washington, to lobbyists, but he wasn't able to get an advance statement.

Finally, in disgust, he hung up the phone.

"Excuse me, Deirdre," he said, turning to his typewriter. "I'd better get a statement ready for the press."

"On what?"

"Expressing our pleasure and gratification at the intelligent decision made by the Secretary of the Interior. What else?"

Deirdre left the room. Two hours later she turned the radio to KYAK news broadcast and heard the mellifluous voice of the tall and dignified U.S. Secretary of the Interior.

"I am convinced that it is in our best national interest to avoid all further delays and uncertainties in planning the development of the Alaskan North Slope Reserves by having a secure pipeline located under the total jurisdiction and for the exclusive use of the United States."

So far, so good for Denali, Deirdre thought. *Now if they can convince the environmental groups, the courts and the Natives.* Somehow she had the feeling this was the beginning, not the ending of the battle.

"The oil industry spends an estimated 50 million dollars every year for lobbying and promoting its role in the defense of the nation's security—more recently in publicizing the energy crisis. Millions of dollars are funneled into political campaigns, with millions more going into sophisticated payoffs such as law fees and stock options. In times of great corruption the artifice is discarded and the cash goes out in straight unadulterated cash—cash in a black bag or even in a paper sack."

—Ovid Demaris
Dirty Business

Chapter Sixteen

Wilbur Steele was a very different man in the company suite atop the Madison Hotel at 15th and M Streets Northwest in Washington than down at Mitchell Mesa. But Wilbur was a man who always had a sense of the appropriate — he had separate wardrobes for Houston, Dallas, and the ranch. In the suite in Washington, he lounged in crocodile slippers and a Countess Mara smoking jacket with foulard to match.

Brandon, steady, reliable, unimaginative (but more imaginative than Wilbur realized) had not changed his Brooks Brother button-down shirt image since he left the service (or the uniformed branch of it, at any rate).

It made financial sense for Alamo to maintain a full-time suite in Washington; it made security sense too. Brandon had supervised the decoration of the suite and at the same time insured its absolute protection against any electronic eavesdropping devices. As in the offices in Houston, the walls, behind the red colored brocade wallpaper, were quarter-inch steel. Neither room service nor maids were allowed keys to the suite. All the service was taken care of by Phillip Escoda, the Phillipino houseboy.

Still, there was no hint of business-like austerity about the rooms. With the exception of several large, comfortable suede-covered sofas, all the furniture was classic Eighteenth Century American, esteemed by Wilbur to be not only gracious but an extremely attractive investment. A Rhode Island block front highboy, for instance, which had been selected for the room by Deirdre Doheny only two years earlier, had almost doubled in value and would now have brought at least fifteen thousand at auction.

As Phillip gathered the dishes from the meal they had enjoyed, in front of the Eighteenth Century Georgian fireplace, Brandon lit a cigar and began to pace morosely around the room.

"Did you hear what that guy Morton said today at the Committee hearing?"

"I heard about it," Wilbur said. He picked up the brass tongs and stirred the fire thoughtfully. "We don't own Nixon outright, you know."

"Well, we own his goddamn . . ." Brandon glanced at Phillip who was sweeping up the last crumbs on the table and was about to wheel the trolley of used dishes from the room.

"The terrapin was fantastic, Phillip," Wilbur said, "it had a kind of a Chinesey flavor, but I didn't recognize it as any regional cooking. What was it?"

"Hee, hee," Phillip said. "It was my own recipe from the Phillipines. I learned to make it when I worked for Admiral. At Subic Bay. Damn good. You want me to pour more brandy before I go?" the houseman asked solicitously.

"No, no, Phillip, we'll take care of it," Wilbur said. "But get out a bottle of my brother's Virginia Gentleman before you go and put it on the bar over there."

206

"What time's he coming, anyway?" Brandon said, looking at his watch.

"As soon as the caucus is over. He should be here soon — before we finish drinks. It's only ten now, anyway."

When the doors had closed behind the Phillipino houseman, Brandon let out a long sigh of suppressed anger.

"I mean, after all, Goddamn it," he said, "after what you did for old Tricky Dick in the campaign—not to mention the contributions from the Bahama Corporation—I should think we'd be able to depend on him for something."

Wilbur smiled, mirthlessly. "There's only one politician I count on, and that's the man who's coming here tonight. And sometimes I'm not too sure about *him*. A man has to have time to examine the issues and I think that Morton will see the light shortly.

"Yeah," Brandon expostulated, "but last month he said he was for the Canadian route."

"What about Perry Dodge, Senator from Wisconsin?"

"He's got a right to his opinions I suppose, although I'm none too happy with them."

"Do you think anybody listens to all that stuff about the government exploiting all its own reserves and breaking up big oil, and all that crapola?"

Wilbur shrugged. "I'm afraid there are quite a few people who listen to it these days. Things are changing. That's one of the things I started talking to you about at lunch the other day. You know, *big* oil has never really meant *us*, at least until now. And it won't mean us until we get that oil flowing down from Prudhoe.

"The way these ecological freaks are carrying on, we may *never* get that stuff down. Those guys are costing us a fortune with their nature stories about the seals, and the caribou, and the precious tundra."

"I must admit," Wilbur said, "Even I didn't count on the impact of that. But of course, with the Santa Barbara channel spill, and the Torrey Canyon and all that stuff, everybody's at panic stations."

A discreet amber light glowed on the intercom box on the table to Wilbur's left. The oil man depressed the button and listened.

"Mr. Fred is on the way up," Phillips voice said.

"All right."

"You want to pour him a drink, Al? You're nearer to the bar." Wilbur had a gift for making his commands sound like requests, or even vague suggestions. Brandon had a gift for interpreting Wilbur's suggestions as commands.

Minutes later Wilbur Steele pressed the door release button to admit his older brother, Frederick Wakefield Steele, United States Senator from Texas—also a senior member of the Senate Finance and Budget committee and Chairman of the Ad Hoc Energy Emergency Commission. At first you would not have taken the two men for brothers. Wilbur, quick, hawk-like, urbane, giving an air of enormous tension, perfectly controlled. Fred, older, more comfortable looking, more of an owl, his jowly face settled into the easy smile lines of a practiced politician. His clothes were subtly western tailored to soothe his constituency, his laugh and humor, contagious and genuine. Only in their eyes did the two come to resemble each other—calculating, cold, and grey as river stones.

"Sorry I'm late, fellows," Fred Steele said, accepting a drink from Al Brandon. "Ehrlichman buttonholed me in the corridor and I couldn't shake loose for a while."

"What about?" Wilbur asked.

"Well, he was trying to explain why Nixon went for that cutdown in the depletion allowance. It seems like he's really sweating the elections coming up and he figures he can't afford to lose the Jew vote."

"Yeah," Wilbur said. "That was a tough one. The thing is, it hits us worse than it hits the big boys. They're getting all their money from foreign oil—that way he can come on like a big friend of the poor and still be kissing the ass of the Seven Sisters."

"Well," Fred said, "we can't afford to cut him loose at this point. He's the only President we've got and I figure he's a shoo-in for '72. We just have to lean on him a little. But Ehrlichman promised me that they'll explain the situation to Morton and tell him to get off his high horse. That stuff about Canada was only for public consumption anyway."

"Well, they'd better promise us something. His bag man was around the other day and they're expecting plenty of help in '72. Certainly, I'm going to cut down unless they show us a little more appreciation."

"What do you hear from the kids?" Fred asked solicitously.

"Well, Larry's knocking around somewhere up there in Alaska. I'm giving him a little rope, letting him shake himself down. I think the boy will straighten himself out. He's got good stuff in him."

"A hell of a good kid," Fred agreed. "What about Penny?"

"Al here had her traced to some radical bunch on the West Coast up in Seattle, but she managed to give his guys the slip again."

"I swear," Brandon said. "I think she's using disguises. I'm not kidding. Some of those other radicals you know have even gone so far as to have plastic surgery. Once they get into the real underground it's very hard to penetrate."

Wilbur looked very sour. "Well you must have the right contacts, for Christssake!"

"Yeah," Brandon said, "but mine are basically in the 'company,' and the FBI hasn't been giving us all the cooperation we could use these days. But I imagine I'll pick up something soon."

"And Deirdre?" Fred said, savoring the fumes of the bourbon which he drank straight in an old-fashioned glass, without ice. "You know, you ought to drink it this way sometime, Wilbur," he said. "It's better than cognac, and it's all-American. You owe it to your country, boy."

"You get the country to switch to American oil and I'll switch to American whiskey," Wilbur smiled. "About Deirdre, she's working for her father on Denali up in Anchorage."

"They-all all right?" Fred asked.

"Yeah, she's right as rain. I think she's really happy working with those ecologists up there. God knows its beginning to be an important part of our work. I had never figured it would become as important as it is right now when we first gave her the job."

"And Doheny?"

"He's pitched right in up there. 'Course, I think he was pretty hurt about the Mexican deal ending up a duster. But he's doing real good there and, if I know that boy, he's tough. He'll be on his feet in a year. In any case, he's pulling down better'n a hundred grand a year on this job, and Mexican food never agreed with him anyhow."

"You sure he ain't sore at you for pulling out of that Honda oil deal?"

Wilbur shrugged. "We're all in business. He knew I just didn't have the cash. He knew this Alaskan deal was pulling every nickel I had . . ."

". . . and he knew that you weren't anxious to have any new supplies of oil coming up from south of the border to queer the Alaskan deal."

"Okay, so he knew. It's a tough business and we all play by the same rules—"

"Which are none at all," Fred said, smiling.

Wilbur looked at his brother speculatively. "As a matter of fact, Fred, one of the things I wanted to talk to both of you about is that—I think I'm about to break some more of the 'club rules.' "

"Getting to be something of a maverick, aren't you?" Fred said, laughing. "That's the old Steele blood. You always were the bad boy in the family."

"Well, I know I didn't make the big boys any too happy when I broke their silent agreement to leave that oil sitting up there in Alaska. That's okay for them—they've got crude coming in from the Middle East, from Indonesia, from Africa, South America. We just got a bunch of these little bitty oil wells in Texas and Oklahoma. Now that I forced their hand it looks to me like Golconda's just trying to drag their feet. Far as I'm concerned, Rawhide Robertson will do anything to hold up the completion of that pipeline. He figures if he hangs in there long enough, he'll starve us out.

"What are you planning to do about it?" Fred asked.

"Well, there's something I was discussing with Al here a while back. Haven't got it completely worked out, but you remember his background."

"You mean, before Alamo? He worked with you on some of those spook deals in the Middle East, didn't he? CIA?"

"Well," Wilbur said, "I was out of it by then, but we were more or less in touch on the Mossadeq deal in Iran in '53."

"I always wanted to ask you Al," Fred said, "if you had any theories about that fellow Mattei that disappeared. You remember, the Italian fellow who was going around offering all these good deals to the Iranians and later on over in the Middle East?"

211

Al laughed. "Not my parish. Ask the guys at Exxon sometime. They had a lot of dealing with him."

"Crashed in a plane, didn't he—back in '62?" Fred asked. "Curious."

Al looked at the Senator trying to appraise his underlying meaning. "Not any more curious than any air crash."

"What's this all got to do with the price of cow cakes?" Fred asked.

Wilbur swirled the cognac in his glass and let the fumes ascend gently, sniffing in appreciation before he answered.

"You know, there are only two major companies up there in the frozen north who give fuck-all about getting that oil out in a hurry. That's Alamo and Royal American. And as for Golconda, it's pretty funny that an old red neck like Robertson is suddenly so interested in the life cycle of the ptarmigan and the caribou. It's all a stall, and now, with these ecology guys throwing up road blocks, and some of these senators, like your friend Perry Dodge—"

"Not my friend."

"Let's just say colleague. Anyway, if somebody doesn't take some positive action that damn pipeline is liable to be held up for five years or more. By that time Alamo could starve to death for want of crude."

"Keep talking," Fred said. Although the Senator's stocks were all in an escrow account, he knew very well that his financial fate was tied directly to the future of Alamo.

"You know, one thing Al learned—or *thought* he learned when he was over there in the fifties—was that there was no way those little bitty Arab oil producing countries and the rest of them out there were going to get together. And that's the power Golconda and the others have over them. Every time they try to get

212

together and ask for a little bigger piece of the pie, the big boys just freeze 'em out, one at a time—just refuse to buy their oil, cut them off, treat them like a bunch of hungry orphans lucky to get a handout. The big boys have counted on that for years. But things are different now."

"You mean nationalization?"

"Not so much that, except maybe in Lybia soon, but *participation*. That's the name of the game now. And as soon as those boys learn how to pull together they're going to really put the screws to big oil."

"Yeah, but they *won't* pull together—or at least, they never have."

"That was before. Since the war they've sent some very, very bright men to Harvard, to Washington University, to Oxford, and Cambridge. They spent a lot of time learning the rules of the game—Western style. And now those boys are ready to grow up. Look at that Sheikh Zakhki Yamani. The man's just past forty and he's getting to be one of the most powerful men in the world. A Harvard man too, but different from the kind they had around in my day. An Arab in my college days was some coffee-colored creep in a Cadillac who spent ninety percent of his time in New York, and usually got thrown out of school for failing marks in his second year. Tell him about your friend from Washington University, Al."

"Yeah, Dr. Jamshid Khatami. Studied hydraulics. Had a beautiful German wife. Sharp, clever, good sense of humor. Sophisticated. I met him at school and then, when I was taking a post-grad course. Later I got in touch with him in Persia."

"He's Minister of Finance, isn't he?" Fred said.

"*Used to be*," Al smiled. "He's got a new job now. He's in charge of oil policy. He and I had some good times together. Before he was married and even after."

"Now," Wilbur said, "the biggest weakness that OPEC has had up until now has been the fact that Iran wouldn't give full support. And after Saudia Arabia, Iran's got more oil than anybody. It's just that they need the money more and they were never able to hold out. Iran's got a lot more mouths to feed than those Arab sheikhs. But I think if somebody really independent—somebody with no stake in Middleastern oil, like for instance, Al Brandon—were to talk to somebody like Khatami, he might make him see that in the end there'd be a lot more money for Iran to stick in with the rest of OPEC in making big oil cough up a fair share for the oil they're taking out of there."

"Well, if they do pay more," Fred said, "they'll just pass it along to the public."

Wilbur's eyes lit in amusement. "Right, right! And what do you think people are going to say here when the price of gas goes up to a dollar a gallon? Do you think they're going to be *happy* sitting on maybe twenty-five billion barrels of oil up in Alaska, just because it might upset some caribou and some seals in the virgin wilderness?"

Senator Fred Steele sat down heavily in one of the suede armchairs and held out his empty glass to Al Brandon for a refill.

"It's big. It's very big," he said thoughtfully. "We're not dealing with simple desert sheikhs anymore, the way we were years ago. These are clever men. Most of them know the value of their influence. They're not easily manipulated. And then it's not easy to figure out what side they're on, or even what country they represent. You're going to have to pay through the nose to stir up the kind of action you have in mind." He looked at Brandon. "You'd know about that, wouldn't you Al?"

"Maybe," Brandon said, noncommittally. "Funny, you know. I was just thinking of taking a holiday trip to Beirut to get some sun, ski a little, maybe, play some tennis, visit the hot spots. It'll be convenient, because I hear my old friend Dr. Khatami will be there at the same time next month, visiting his money."

"No way it could hurt," Fred said, but his voice was doubtful.

Brandon, who was pouring the Senator a new drink, suddenly broke into a sharp, staccato barking laugh.

"What's so funny?" Wilbur asked coldly.

"No, no," Brandon protested. "I wasn't laughing at *Fred*. I was just picturing Rawhide Robertson's face if he ever got wind of my vacation plans for next month."

"Oil is for the Arabs! Why do you not exploit your lost wealth which is being plundered by the aliens? Remember that the oil which flows under your land is seized by your enemy! Remember oil, your lost wealth! Oil is for the Arabs!"

—Radio Cairo slogan

Chapter Seventeen

It was a good, late winter day in Beirut, a bit chilly for swimming but bright and crisp—not quite cold enough to discourage some of the braver, youthful types. Al Brandon lay back in his deck chair and let the sun collect in warm pools like melted butter on his eyelids.

He was half-asleep when he was jarred back to consciousness by a copious sprinkling of cold water. A bright-haired girl in a string bikini, with a seasoned caramel tan, ran by him and then stopped so suddenly that her breasts bounced an extra two beats after she had halted.

"Ah, pardon, Monsieur. J'espère que je ne vous ai pas derangé."

"Quand c'est quelqu'un comme vous, c'est mon plaisir," Brandon responded gallantly.

The company-sponsored course he'd taken at *Alliance Française* years ago had been one of their best investments, especially in the Middle East and Africa, where so many areas had fallen under French Colonial domination. It was more than a simple matter of communication. Most of the people he dealt with spoke English anyway. But they felt that anybody who could not speak proper French could not be terribly civilized. Al had been a good student and had augmented his

classroom lessons with sessions in *"L'Ecole D'Oreiller"*
—the pillow school.

The girl flattered him with a look of approval and
then skipped on to join her friends at the poolside bar.
A short, heavy set man in wrap-around dark glasses
dropped onto the chaise next to Brandon.

"You don't see much of that stuff in Alaska," he said,
nodding in the direction of the girl. He had long curly,
iron-gray hair, a cultivated tan the color of a camel
saddle. His body was as shiny and hairless as a cor-
dovan boot. Brandon did not seem surprised to see him.

"Not hardly, Abe," he said. "How's the culture
business?"

Aram Ajootian—"Abe" to his friends—was an old
friend, dating back to the hectic fifties in Tehran. Abe
and Brandon had bunked together at the "company
farm" in Camp Peary, near Williamsburg as junior CIA
trainees. Only Brandon had the impression that ultimately Ajootian, who had majored in archeology at
Brown prior to signing up with the CIA, had transferred out of clandestine services into OSI division (the
Office of Scientific Intelligence) after his marriage.

"Cleo takes all my time now," he had confided one
time to Brandon, "and the hours in CS were just too
irregular. Besides, my nerves were always so much on
edge, I couldn't get it up half the time."

"Occupational hazard," Brandon laughed.

That had been in the days when they were all riding
high after reinstalling the Shah and kicking out Mossadeq and his nationalized oil business.

Ajootian waved to the bar boy and ordered himself
a drink and a refill for Brandon.

"Arak?" he asked, noticing the milky liquid in Brandon's short glass. "I hate the stuff myself."

"I like to stay with the native sauce when I can.
Besides, it's cheaper," Brandon said.

217

Ajootian looked at him quizzically. "You're joking, of course. I don't imagine they ride too hard on your expense account at Alamo."

Brandon laughed. "No, I guess not. Habit, I guess."

As time had passed there had been fewer and fewer people that Brandon had found he could laugh with. Most of them had been Company men. Certainly nobody in the oil business. In the Company, despite all of its nervousness and intrigue, there was a certain mutual loyalty. In the oil business, no matter how much they all pulled together for their mutual interests, there was always the knowledge that everyone was looking out for Number One.

Even Brandon had been surprised when Wilbur Steele practically knifed Doheny in the back over the Mexican oil deal, in order to grease the way for the North Slope operation. But at least Wilbur had not left his pal stranded on the beach, and, with the Denali job as a springboard, it was certain that Mahlon Doheny would be on top again.

"Are we in business tonight?" Brandon said, turning his attention to the stocky, bronzed man beside him.

Ajootian leaned back, stretching sensuously in the sun.

"Is Michele a friend of yours?" he asked, ignoring Brandon's question.

"Who the hell is Michele?"

"The blonde over there, by the bar. The one that splashed you."

"I never saw her before in my life."

"Stay away from her."

"I didn't have any plans, although I wouldn't mind . . ."

"She'll only make trouble. You've got your business here. Stick to that. Sex and oil don't mix."

"I wouldn't say that," Brandon started to protest.

218

"Well, not in this case, anyway." He changed the subject. "Your friend'll be at Bacchus tonight. He'll have someone with him."

"Now wait a minute . . ." Al said.

"The friend talks business," Ajootian explained. "Khatami is too high up to get involved in any direct discussions."

"Now listen," Brandon protested, "we're talking about big numbers . . ."

Ajootian interrupted him. "Need to know, need to know." he said. "I'm strictly in the culture business these days. Phoenician ruins and that sort of thing. Have you heard about our dig out at Eshmun?"

The Hotel Bacchus itself was an obscure middle class hostelry on Wadi Abou Jamil frequented by middle class students, budget tourists, and opportunistic Palestinian refugees. The help spoke only Arabic and a smattering of French, so it attracted few Americans. The hotel belonged to Pepe Abed who also owned the Fishing Club in Byblos and the small inn and restaurant in Tyre, or Sur, as the Arabs called it.

Next to the unprepossessing entrance of the hotel was a huge oak, iron-studded door. A small bronze plaque on it read simply "Club Bacchus." Brandon pushed the small brass bell set into the doorframe and after a few minutes the door was answered by a very black man with the stripes of Senegalese ritual scars across his cheeks. His face broke into a broad smile when he saw Brandon's bulky figure.

"Hello, Joseph," Brandon said.

"Ah, Mr. Brandon," the Senegalese said. "Welcome back! Pepe will be pleased to see you."

He led the way down a massive, spiralling stone staircase into a large ancient vaulted cellar dug out of the Roman ruins that underlay the foundation of the hotel. The Club was a private one, a hobby of Pepe Abed's, run at his whim. Members were whoever he asked, or welcomed. Food was served casually, or sometimes not at all. Every niche, corner, or shelf of the room was occupied with antiquities—largely dredged from the sea by Abed, who was an avid collector of all things prior to the time of Christ. Some said he was a pirate.

In a prominent space against an old carved pillar was a ritual Roman phallus, about three feet high, shiny with the patina of many curious, caressing fingers. The room itself was nearly empty—apparently there had been no dinner party that night. In a remote dark corner a couple sat picking at a lavish tray of *mezzeh*, Another table was occupied by four boisterous Mexicans (Pepe was honorary Mexican Consul in Beirut).

Joseph held up the bottle of *arak* in a questioning gesture and Brandon nodded.

"You see?" he said, "I remember. Mr. Pepe will be very glad to see you. I called him."

Brandon was less than pleased. He would prefer complete privacy for his discussion that evening. But it was too late. The massive door behind the bar, which had been constructed from an old fishing boat, opened and Pepe rushed out to enfold him in an enthusiastic *abrazo*.

"Brandon! *Mon ami! Que pasa, amigo?* Where have you been?" Abed spoke French, Spanish, and English —usually in equally mixed proportions, no matter who he was speaking to. He was dressed, as usual, in a striped Basque fisherman's shirt and a yachting cap.

"Come," he pulled Brandon by the arm, "and I'll show you my new treasures."

He led him to a vaulted crypt, set back a little from the main dining room and guarded by massive iron gates. This was where he kept his more valuable archeological finds and the jewelry he fashioned from old lead sarcophagus flowers, ancient amber beads, bits of ivory and gold, and other ancient artifacts. (He always protested that these were not for sale, but usually could be persuaded to let a "friend" have them at "cost"— usually at least five hundred dollars.) He touched a switch beside a small niche carved in the thick stone walls and several pin spots lit up to illuminate a collection of about a half a dozen statues ranging from about six inches to two feet. They were all of the same subject, a standing woman in drapes reaching to the ground, one hand bent at the elbow, its palm held out in greeting, the other clutched across the chest, apparently holding the robe closed. Some of the heads and feet were missing, but they seemed to be in remarkably good condition.

"The Goddess Tanit," Pepe said enthusiastically. *"Tres* sexy. Phoenician Goddess of fertility. I found them diving by the old walls in Tyre only last week. But I don't think we can dive much there any more. Either the Palestinians are shooting or the Israelis are raiding. It's become impossible. *Conyo!"*

"Don't buy anything from him. He's a pirate." The voice was cultivated, with only a trace of a Middle-eastern accent.

Brandon turned.

"Jamshid, you old son of a bitch. How are you?"

The two men clasped each other in the European style embrace. Brandon had gotten used to that, but he still couldn't manage the kisses on two cheeks. He stood back to look at the dapper Iranian.

"Son of a gun, you must be swimming in it."

Khatami was dressed in a Pierre Cardin jacket, with what were obviously real gold buttons. He wore a cashmere turtleneck and carmel-colored Gucci loafers. On his right hand was the Washington University ring and in his lapel his Phi Gam pin. Brandon realized that the pin, at any rate, had been put on for his benefit.

"Son of a bitch," he said marvelling. "You look better all the time."

And it was true. In the twenty years he had known the dapper Iranian he seemed to have aged very little. If anything, the naked avarice and ambition that had shown so brightly from his face in younger years seemed coated and veiled by years of subtlety. "He's like a honey-covered hand grenade," Brandon thought.

"You're looking great, also," Jamshid said. "Big business must agree with you."

"Are you alone?" Brandon asked casually.

"No, no. I have my friend with me. He's at the table. Come and join us."

Pepe eyed the two men appraisingly and decided to be discreet.

"I'll see you later," he said. "I've got some Mexicans to talk to."

A round faced young man was at the table. He didn't look over thirty, and had a small tuft of beard on his chin and long lashed eyes like a camel. He rose as the pair approached the table.

"Nasser Ferouze. This is a very old friend, Al Brandon. We were at school together. You can trust him."

"Of course, of course. I am delighted to meet you," Ferouze said, extending a plump, damp hand.

"Nasser is with the Arab Bank Ltd., the Saudi Arabian branch. I am sure he will be very interested in what you will have to say. We are always glad to hear the opinion of American oil people."

"Of course," Brandon said. "You know, I'm with Alamo. We don't have any investments out here at all."

"Exactly, exactly," Jamshid said, enthusiastically. "That's why we value your opinion. Since those that do have investments have a habit of sticking together, it can be distressing—to say the least. And yet, when *we* chose to stick together with OPEC now they're all getting bugged with us."

"I think you are taking the right step, Jamshid. You know, it's no skin off of my nose, but I've always thought that you fellows have let yourselves be pushed around for too long—that if you ever got together you'd have terrific power. But in the past, you've let those big people put the squeeze on you, one at a time."

"Yes," Jamshid said smoothly. "But I think I've persuaded the Shah that it's time we took a stronger step. Don't you agree Nasser?"

The young man was pudgy and shiny as a Buddha, but underneath the long lashes his eyes were clear and calculating.

"So you've been telling me, Jamshid. And basically I agree," he said. "But you know, it is so hard to reach some of these sheikhs and Faisal, well, he's a very strong man. Of course, you could say that I have his ear right now in regard to the oil matter."

"Exactly why I felt you two should get together."

The plump young man looked at Brandon with an appraising air. "It could be very expensive to reach the right people . . ." he said. "In the oil business," he spread his palms expansively "what is not expensive?

His accent, Brandon noted, was British—probably one of those London School of Economics boys. But whatever the accent, Brandon had no trouble following the drift of the conversation.

"Of course," he said, "we understand. And naturally we realize that diplomatically speaking, it would be wise if we moved our deposits from the Morgan Guarantee to the Arab Bank, Ltd., if only to facilitate transfer of funds, should that be necessary."

"But of course," the Saudi Arabian said, smiling

223

noncommittally. "If you wish, that would be very nice. And, as you know, our bank is solidly backed with gold. With the world currency going to hell in a hand basket, it's not a bad place to have your money."

Khatami watched the two men, his head cocked on the side like a bright cockatoo, his eyes swinging from face to face.

"I am sure," he said, "that we all see things the same way. I know that in our case, the Shah is convinced that it is time to make a positive move in the Middle East. He said to me the other day, 'if the oil producing countries suffer even the smallest defeat, that would be the end of OPEC. Then nations will not dare to gather together and to rise against these giants.' And I know that—in the case of my country at any rate—we are prepared to go all the way against the oil cartel."

He turned toward Ferouze. "If your people stand behind us, we will have the overwhelming bulk of oil production in the Middle East to bargain with. Without you we are nothing. And even Mr. Brandon, who after all has no stake in the affair, can assure you that the time *is* right.

Ferouze nodded brightly. "I understand, I understand perfectly. But it may be difficult to explain it to Faisal. It may take time—and money." His eyes flicked for a microsecond in the direction of Brandon.

Khatami cast a diplomatic eye on his gold Phillipe Patek watch. "I have a few phone calls to make, from Pepe's office. But I am sure you two will find much to talk over."

On his way to the office behind the bar, the Iranian stopped at the table where the young couple was still lingering over their *mezzeh*. The girl stood up and kissed Khatami on both cheeks. Brandon was surprised to see that it was the blond who had splashed him at the St. George pool that afternoon. Ferouze's shrewd eyes followed his gaze.

"You know the girl?"

"No," Brandon said. "I wish I did."

"She's Belgian. With the PLO. They live in the ruins, near Saida. She can travel in places and be accepted where the Palestinians are not welcome. By tomorrow they will all know where you've been and to whom you've been speaking. Before noon Qadaffi will be informed. If you wish a woman I can arrange it, but I suggest you look elsewhere. Although, as you say, for the present we are all hanging together."

"Too bad," Brandon said, regretfully.

Ferouze folded his plump hands together in front of him on the table like a school boy awaiting a teacher's instructions.

"And now," he said, "I believe you have some suggestions regarding the financing . . ."

"The Chance of A Lifetime is here. At least 35 Grand a year. Room and board free. Laundry soap too. Someone even makes your bed for you. After taxes, say twenty grand clear. We're right up there with the fat American Corporate Lifers . . ."

—Ron Rau,
"Alaska: Changing face
of the Last Frontier"
TRUE magazine

Chapter Eighteen

Larry Steele was, in many respects, different from the others who had come north to work on the pipeline. He did not come to Alaska to get rich. He was not running away from anything (except maybe boredom). And he wasn't one of those gung-ho oil men who follow the camps from Saudi Arabia to the Andes to the Ultima Thule of the north.

Driving the big trucks had intrigued Larry, when the road was not quite yet finished and he had to travel cross-country, being pushed and towed by bulldozers, battling through drifts and across spongy ice, crossing the Yukon on rubber-flapped air-cushioned vehicles. But the novelty had worn off quickly and traveling up and down the line of camps began to give Larry Steele the feeling he was more an observer of this historic event than a participant.

Shifting out of the Teamsters into the Tulsa local, as a heavy machinery operator, had certainly brought him closer to actually *doing* it, but before he had made that shift completely, he'd had to take a few dispatches in the Laborer's Local 942, also. It had been a long stretch in the early '70's when the pipeline was being constructed in only a desultory fashion. Construction camps were being built, access roads were being pushed through, but the pipeline was still being held up, debated in Congress, litigated over in the courts, and argued over in barrooms.

By the time Larry went down to Local 942 he already had a preferred status as an Alaskan resident, having been in the 50th state for more than a year. This entitled him to a spot on the first list, the preferred list for actual Alaskan residents. After that came nonresidents with experience, and then the infamous third list, for which anybody could sign up, resident or not. This was where most newly arrived boomers wound up. It was said there were thousands—some said three, some said four—on that list, and at the time that Larry went to the hiring hall at 305 Noble Street, not one of the third list people had yet been hired as a laborer. Some had waited as long as three or four months and were becoming broke or desperate.

There was a stir in the oddly assorted group of waiting job aspirants, as the business agent in a wool Pendleton shirt and a snap-brimmed felt hat, came self-importantly from his glasswalled office in the rear.

"Ok, men, look alive," he said. "We've got nine jobs here on the North Slope."

"Anything for the third list?" a man yelled out hopelessly.

The agent looked at him with scorn. "We got over three hundred guys waiting for jobs on the *first* list. Why don't you guys go back to New Jersey or whatever?"

The jobs were a mixed bag—even the laborers' union included some skilled occupations. This time they wanted two powder monkeys, a couple of drillers, a stake hopper, and four jobs for straight camp labor.

The agent began to read the names on the four lines

in the first list. A lot of them were of people who were long since dead, or gone to Mexico, Bolivia, or California or jail. Larry had none of the skills required, but he was a first priority man for the camp labor job and got his pick of camps. Having traveled the line, he knew the distinctions. Valdez, as far as climate is concerned, is less demanding than the northernmost jobs. And there is the temptation of town also, but Larry had had enough of the towns. It was April, the days were getting longer, soon it would be spring—Larry picked Galbraith, probably the most physically beautiful camp in the whole string, and while it did not actually resemble the country around Mitchell Mesa, Texas, there was something about its setting on a flat plain ringed with mountains, with the pure blue reaches of Galbraith Lake stretching out behind the camp, that reminded him paradoxically of home. Perhaps it was the fact that, with only the white painted camp buildings to compete with the scenery, he would not be subjected to the depressing sight of street after street of tumbled down, jerry-built shacks and trailers which had come to dominate Valdez and Fairbanks.

Fairbanks was okay for getting drunk, laid, roistering around, and generally blowing off steam, but you wouldn't want to live there (at first Larry had actually thought that the omnipresent notices "No alcoholic beverages allowed" in the camps were real, but he soon discovered that people got as drunk in the camps as they did in Fairbanks, only more discreetly.) What the notices *really* meant was that if you showed up for your ten or twelve hour shift egregiously drunk or hopelessly hungover, and if the boss didn't care for you very much in the first place, you could be terminated without having any appeal to the union. Basically the feeling was that once you were put on dispatch for a job you were supposed to go out and get double or triple drunk-laid the night before and show up for the charter plane trip north with as ostentatious a hangover as possible—preferably from a two or three day toot. Each of the men would try to outdo each other in bragging about how overturned they were with nausea, fatigue, and a general fuckedout feeling (even those who had spent the night watching "Lucy" reruns in the King Eight Motel and drinking Pepsis, Larry suspected).

The charter plane only took five or six workers up to Galbraith: a cook, a teamster, a pipeline welder, and a timekeeper. Everybody was talking, when they weren't discussing their hangovers, about what kind of shifts they'd get.

"I hear they're only working seven tens," one man said, "but they'll be doing seven twelves when it warms up."

"Shit, I hear that they're in such a hurry to finish this job that we'll be working seven fourteens by this summer," a timekeeper said.

Even at laborer's pay, which was under nine dollars an hour, Larry knew that seven fourteens would amount to forty-five thousand dollars a year. He was not greedy for the money but he couldn't help but think about the account he had started in the bank in Houston. Working a little under a year on the truck route he'd been able to salt away fifteen thousand dollars. But working up in the actual camps, he'd probably be able to earn more, and save more. In five years, he might have made enough to start a little shuttle airline back in Texas, or maybe if things settled down, he'd go back to the Far East. He hadn't cared much for the war, but Bangkok was a place that had a lot of possibilities, a place which, at that moment, flying over the tumbled up, white-coated mountainous terrain beyond the Yukon, seemed even further than the end of the earth, if such a thing were possible.

By now the ten by twelve typical room in the Atco trailer with the unchosen and unknown roommate was a familiar sight to Larry, who had stayed in so many of them as a transient. Each was exactly like the other—two bunks, two closets with wood-looking plastic walls, one desk to be shared, two chairs and one window looking out on the next Atco unit. Larry's first roommate was a lank-haired, bearded New Yorker, known as Schlong. Schlong was an incinerator man, and it made him happy, since he was basically very concerned about the environmental impact of the pipeline.

The incinerator man, Schlong reasoned, was undoing some of the damage that might have otherwise been done, and had been done at many camps in the past, by dumping raw garbage on the outskirts of the camps, where it attracted wolves, foxes, and other wildlife and disturbed the natural balance. Everything, solid and disposable, went into the maw of Schlong's incinerator—kitchen slops, scrap lumber, pieces of Gypsum board, cardboard boxes with air freight tags, cans of Diet Pepsi, plastic bags full of wastepaper from the offices, endless Xeroxes of useless memos, cans of starting fluid—which would explode unexpectedly, sometimes shooting like missiles out of the open door of the incinerator—used oil filters, oil-wiping rags, plastic antifreeze containers, food scraps. The sign outside the incinerator shack read: Internal Residue Service. On the wall near his incinerator, Schlong tacked a Baby Ruth wrapper. Underneath was a printed sign, "One way ticket to Fairbanks," followed by a notice from the RCM on Denali stationery, "This wrapper was found on the access road outside Shop Building Two. Anyone caught disposing of such waste material in this fashion will be terminated without notice. Signed, J. Bagley, Resident Camp Manager." Sometimes they would even bring Schlong an oil barrel filled with dirt scooped up from some teacup oil spill on one of the work pads. Schlong was very impressed with this diligence, but he knew as well as Larry and the rest that these mini-spills were only scooped up if a camp supervisor noticed them. Otherwise a couple of quick shovel-fulls of dirt would cover over the damage, easily.

Once you were in a camp and assigned a job, the routine set in—eat, work, an hour or two of pool or reading or TV (on cassettes shipped up from the south, including the previous day's news). Everything became a matter of rote—get up, shit, shave, shower, smoke, eat, work, eat, work again, eat again, watch the TV news, (never noticing that the events are already a day old, but treating them as though they are actually happening), shoot pool, brush teeth, sleep, wake, shit, shave, shower, and so on.

Everything became so routine that Larry even found himself whistling the same song for weeks on end. Once, he remembered, for three weeks he couldn't stop humming the theme song from the old Little Orphan Annie radio show, which he had learned from Grandpa Bisset as a child. Another time he hummed the Coca-Cola theme song, "Things Go Better With Coca-Cola," for almost a solid month. Even the food, abundant though it was, grew dull—steak, steak, steak, with a lobster tail on Friday.

"Can't we ever have a Goddamn hamburger?" Schlong complained. "I'd give my left ball for a good, old, greasy, White Tower."

No matter how many flavors of ice cream were offered at the mess hall, somebody was always unhappy.

"They used to have great banana pistachio at the Tastee Freeze in Brattleboro," a sideload operator grumbled.

Even from the earliest day a mental rigor mortis would set in. Men would get the Arctic Stare, focusing

231

their eyes at nine feet in a six foot room. Everybody would get a little dingy. You would talk to someone and they would seem not to hear you but sit staring out at that nine foot focal point, dreaming. About what? About hot thighs wrapped around their ears, chili tacos in San Diego, surfing off Pismo Beach . . . who knows? After a while, most of the workers would develop strangely possessive attitudes, not only about their personal property, but even about their vehicles or tools, to the point where they would watch anxiously if a repair mechanic so much as loosened a bolt on a pneumatic hammer.

There must have been some wits around the camp, although you would never have known it to listen to the table talk. Somebody must have spent valuable hours (probably at Denali's expense) composing the regular stream of satiric memos that appeared on walls and bulletin boards to lighten the days' woes.

BULLETIN

TO ALL EMPLOYEES !
SUBJECT: DEATH OF AN EMPLOYEE
It has been brought to our attention that many employees are dying and refuse to fall over after they are dead.

THIS MUST STOP !

On and after June 4, 1972, any employee found standing up after he has died will be dropped from the payroll within ninety days. If, after several hours, it is noticed that an employee has not moved or changed position, the Supervisor will investi-

gate, because of the highly sensitive
nature of employees and the close
resemblance between death and their
natural working attitudes. The investigation will be made quickly so as
to disturb the employee if he is only
sleeping.

Supervisors note: If some doubt exists
as to the true condition of an employee, a pay envelope will be extended
at the alleged corpse. If the employee
does not reach for it, it may be
assumed that he is dead. In some cases
the instinct is so strong, however,
that a spasmodic clutch or reflex
motion may be encountered.

But the work went on, studded with gradually short-
ening lay-offs, as the point of actual construction of
the pipeline approached. The days lengthened with
the stretches between the brutal red and orange sunrises
and the endless salmon pink and rose sunsets gradually
backing into each other until they merged at midsum-
mer, leaving only a reddish glow and a darkened horizon
to mark the passing of a night.

On some of those nights, Larry Steele would sit on
the wooden steps outside the double Atco unit housing
the rec hall and make mental deals with himself. "When
the account in the old Houston Pioneer Bank gets to a
hundred thousand I'll lay it on D.D. No more fooling
around, no more sudden assignments, unexplained
absences, and mysterious ailments. Shit or get off the
pot. 'I beg your pardon M'am, but not wanting to rush
things after a mere twenty years of courtship, would
you be willing to bolt your piggyback camper to my

Ford pick-up semi-permanently so that we might, kind-of be all-in-the-same-place at the same time?'

'Why, Larry Steele, I've been fond of you since Noah was a rag doll. But if you had the sense that God gave a rubber duck you would know there has to be something wrong with a couple that's been engaged for fifteen years, without putting brands on each other.'

'But, M'am, I've been a diligent paplahner and I done stored up a hundred thousand dollars worth of solid gold nuggets for kind of a nest egg.'

'Well, what on God's green earth difference could that make? I've been a paplahner myself for as long as you have.'

'Okay, then, I'll tell you what. We'll wait until the Goddamn paplahn is finished. Then we'll do it, one way or the other.' "

So that was settled (in Larry's mind, anyway). All he had to do now was finish the Goddamn paplahn.

"The pipeline's gonna go straight under the road, a quarter mile from my cabin," said a young goodlooking freak from just outside Fairbanks. . . . "They've had the surveyor's stakes out for six months. We took 'em out once, and they came back in two weeks.

"It's going to be buried, they say. Well, I think there's two things we can do. One is, if it keeps the ground thawed, we can plant the longest truck garden in Alaska. Or we can blow it up . . . Somebody's going to try to blow it up man, that's for sure. I guarantee you."

—Michael Rogers *Rolling Stone,*
"The Dark Side Of The Earth"
(May 22, 1975)

Chapter Nineteen

The paperweight with the swirling snowfall in it had been accepted as a gavel at the meetings of Operation Cut Off. Sonia slammed it with authority on the kitchen table in the back room of Maroon's bookshop. Troops present, besides Sonia, were Abby Maroon; Ernie Mason; Eli Hurwood, the tin-ear guitar player; Bobby Baronian, the newest member; and Takolik, who was in Fairbanks on leave from his job as security guard at Alamo's Prudhoe Bay base camp. Missing were Marge, who had gotten a job as a warehouseman at Pump Station 5, and Van Taylor, who was still in Valdez.

There had been a considerable delay in pipeline construction while the Native claims settlement and various ecological suits were in the process of discussion. But by now, two years after the scheduled starting date, serious work on the pipeline had finally commenced.

"Ok, now, simmer down," Sonia said. "And stash the

grass and juice until after the meeting. I want clear minds right now."

Ernie Mason, who was smoking a King Kong bomber of Matanuska Thunderfuck, sighed loudly, pinched the end out, and carefuly stowed the remaining joint in a flat tin box beside an assortment of yellows, reds, seeds, and a couple of short roaches.

"Smoking lamp is out," he said, unnecessarily.

"Now, here's the situation," Sonia began when things had quieted down. "The corporate state under Nixon has decided to continue its immoral cooperation with the military-industrial complex. There are a couple of ecological suits in the courts, but with the entire Nixon administration more or less on the payroll of big oil, it is doubtful anything could stop the pipeline now—except us!

"Ernie, has your group come up with a good name?" she asked. "I don't want to keep calling it Operation Cut Off. It doesn't have a revolutionary sound."

Ernie pulled a dog-eared piece of cardboard from his pocket on which he'd written a few notes.

"We kicked around a lot of ideas, but with the revolutionary groups going around with a lot of initials, like S.D.S. and S.L.A. and all that bullshit, I still thought the strongest name would be an acronym."

"Acro-what?" Hurwood asked.

"You know, a word where every letter stands for something, but it all makes up one word."

"Like Weathermen? Abby asked.

"No, no. Weathermen doesn't have any initials, it's just a word. I wanted to have a word that has a meaning. Anyway, after some talks I had with Takolik, I think I've come up with the word: SHAMAN."

"Isn't that what Captain Marvel said?"

"No," Mason said scornfully, "that was Shazam."

"What's it mean?" Sonia asked.

"Well, some of you, if you've talked to Takolik, know that the shamans were the bearers of magic, the mystery men in the tribes. When the white men came, it was only the shamans who had the power to face up to them. Finally, in order to break the power of the shamans, it was necessary to Christianize the tribes and take away their magic, and if necessary, drive the shamans from the community."

"That's right," Takolik said. "But there's still plenty of them around, only the white man does not know."

"Well, that's not bad," Sonia said. "But what does it stand for?"

Mason turned the card over. "I kicked it around a lot, and I figure it stands for 'Save Heartland Alaska, Manumit the Alaskan Nation.'"

"What the fuck does 'manumit' mean?" Sonia asked.

"You know, like when Lincoln freed the slaves—manumition. It means to free the slaves."

"Oh, that's heavy," Hurwood said.

Sonia nodded in agreement.

Maroon raised his hand. "Listen, why do we need this name anyhow?"

"Because," Sonia explained carefully, "we're going to be sending notes and messages and we have to sign a name that people will recognize. Every revolutionary group has to have a name, right? Okay now, anybody opposed to Ernie Mason's suggestion that we call the group S.H.A.M.A.N.?"

Then, barely waiting for any murmurs of protest that might arise, Sonia rapped her paperweight on the table.

"Okay, Abby, you're secretary, right? Write it down. We are officially adopting the name S.H.A.M.A.N."

"Great. Now we can order up jackets and t-shirts," Maroon said, sarcastically.

Sonia gave him a withering look as her answer.

237

"Now is the time we've got to come up with the real plan for the operational phase. You all know what our goal is—to completely fuck up the pipeline so that it can never operate. We've been doing some research on this—both from public information and from a few people we have with the company, like Bobby Baronian there, and Marge, who's working up at a pump station, and Takolik who's been hired by NANA as a security guard at Prudhoe. If possible, as many of us as can do so should try to get a job on the pipeline itself so that we can establish a steady flow of inside information and operate more effectively. Besides that, it's a pretty good source of money. Right now we are getting contributions from all the members — especially Marge and Takolik—and now Bobby Baronian has agreed to turn over five hundred dollars a week to help the operation."

There was an enthusiastic spattering of applause.

"Welcome to the group, Bobby."

The big, bearded ecologist favored the assembled crowd with a gold-capped grin.

Sonia continued.

"Some of the ideas we talked about in the beginning just won't work, such as scattering comrades all along the line and peppering it with rifle shots. According to our weapons man, Eli, that wouldn't do any good. Right, Eli?"

"Well," Hurwood said in his mock Texas twang, "the exposed part of the pipeline is damn near a half inch thick of special steel. And all that is wrapped up with a couple of inches of outer tape and insulation. You'd have to hit it with an armor-piercing projectile to do any damage at all. You'd just have to pepper the whole length of it endlessly and even then it would only let out a little stream of oil. Mess up the countryside some, but you wouldn't stop the flow. Soon as they saw enough of a drop in pressure, they'd be down there and plug up the hole easy. Anyway, there'll be flying chopper patrols up and down the pipeline once it's built, and as far as the northern parts are concerned, there won't be easy hiding places or easy access. All and all, I figure the sniper approach is worth diddly-shit."

"Well, what about if we blow up some of those check valves that they have every few miles? Any ideas on that Baronian? You're familiar with the construction aspects."

"Well," Baronian said, "you could do that, but those are big heavy cast iron things. It would really take quite a blast to blow one apart. Even if you did, all they'd have to do is hook in a by-pass until they could get a new valve in there, and it wouldn't really stop the flow enough to make them any difference. Just cost them a couple of thousand dollars—maybe ten or twenty-five thousand."

"Well what about the wells? Aren't they vulnerable?" Sonia asked.

"Of course, the Christmas Trees, where the oil actually comes up, are pretty closely guarded. But I suppose an inside man would be able to get pretty close to them. There again, if you blew up the Christmas Tree, you could slow things down for a little while, but the problem is, they've got a lot of them. You couldn't just blow one or two up—you'd have to blow them all up. There're maybe ten or more oil outlets up there, and there're going to be more once the pipeline gets going. If you're going to explode them, the best way would be to drop a charge right down the tube. That would cost a couple of million maybe to replace. Trouble is, you see, they know where the oil is. All they'd have to do is sink another shaft. If we're going to use that approach, we'd have to pack that Prudhoe Bay camp with our own personnel, and that would be a big risk as far as the security factor is concerned. The more people you have, the more likely there'll be a leak somewhere. I figure, to simultaneously blow all the Christmas Trees, you'd need a crew of about a hundred people."

He looked around the small crowded room.

"As you can see our strength is nowhere near that."

"What about at the other end? What about Valdez?"

Baronian shook his head. "Somebody could get one of the tankers, I suppose. We'd have to have somebody on the crew, or get to somebody on board. But that wouldn't stop the pipeline, just spread a lot of oil around Prince William Sound. They got a whole bunch of holding tanks there but even if they're blown there's a big earthwork dike around them to contain the oil. Denali'd just get some hoses in and transfer the oil elsewhere."

Sonia began to look discouraged. "Well, anybody got any other ideas?"

"We could work through the unions," Hurwood said. "Pull a general strike and freeze the whole thing up."

Takolik looked scornful. "Are you kidding? You haven't been up in those camps. Half the unions are tied into the bosses with sweetheart contracts, like that Tulsa 798. And the Teamsters are locked in too. If you ask me, the Teamster bosses are paid off. Anyway, they might make some trouble, but there's no way they're going to give up those heavy paying jobs. The last thing you want to do is let any of those union people know what you're up to. They'd nail you to a vertical support member, and leave you out in the night to freeze."

"How about arson?" Maroon asked tentatively. "Isn't there any way we could burn the whole thing up? After all, oil is inflammable."

"You could do a lot of damage with some fires," Baronian acknowledged. "But it's the same thing as the Christmas Tree deal. You'd have to start an awful lot

240

of them to be really effective. In most cases, each of the camps or pumping stations has its own fire department and emergency crews and those guys get out fast. There've been a couple of bad fires, after the labor troubles last month. Some people think it was some wildcat members of 798 that set them after the company laid off about a hundred of them. One of the fires resulted in a power cut-off in Happy Valley Camp for a while, but they got the alternate units going pretty fast, and in the end it was just a small hold-up in the operation. Fires could hurt all right, but I don't think they could completely stop the pipeline once it was in operation."

Sonia's eyes darted restlessly around the group. "There must be a better idea than that. Something that would completely put the pipeline out of commission. Force them to build it all over again."

There was a pause, and then Baronian spoke. Working at a top management level, he was the most valuable recruit the group had enlisted. He had access to all sorts of technical data and top-level memoranda.

"There is one thing," the burly, bearded man said slowly. "If, in some way, you could stop the flow of oil during the cold weather for maybe eighteen or twenty hours, the oil inside the pipe would solidify and pretty soon you'd have nothing but an eight hundred mile long licorice stick."

"Wow," Sonia said. "You mean the oil would solidify—like tar—in the pipe?"

"That's right," Baronian said, "and they'd probably have to either build a new pipeline or at least take it apart in segments and clean out each segment of pipe separately. It would be one hell of a job."

"That would be fantastic," Mason said, "but how in the hell are we going to do that?"

Baronian was carrying a beat-up pigskin briefcase.

"I've got a copy of the complete engineering plans here. All together there are ten pumping stations that will move the oil across the mountains and down to Valdez. From talking around it seems to me that if we could tie up three or four of the pumping stations—maybe only three—and cause a problem at Prudhoe and Valdez, we might be able to create enough trouble to stop that oil for twenty-four hours."

Hearing the news, the group sat mute for a few minutes, trying to comprehend the magnitude of the project.

"It's big," Baronian said, "but I think it could be accomplished with no more than two or three men at each post. It would mean a group of fifteen to twenty people total. Not too many to handle. Of course, there'd have to be people with access to the pipeline installations."

Sonia's face was a mask as she listened to Baronian's plan. Obviously she appreciated his expertise and knowledgability. But there was an overtone of authority to his voice that gave her an uncomfortable feeling that he might take over the whole operation if she did not continue to exercise her dominance. She rapped with the paperweight on the table.

"Ok, Baronian, we'll take your suggestion under advisement. It's obvious that whatever we do, we first have to do two things. Get more of us working on the pipeline—most of us have residence stakes here by now—and recruit people that are already working there. How do chances for recruitment look to you, Takolik?"

The Eskimo shrugged. "Not so good. It's not exactly a revolutionary cell up there. There are no freaks or hippies. After all, to stay in there you usually have to work twelve hours a day, seven days a week. I'm not sure how many of you people can handle that," he said, casting his eye over the oddly assorted group. "Also, those workers aren't up there to make waves. Why the hell would they join in the destruction of the pipeline when they're making a minimum of a thousand a week—maybe as much as twenty-five hundred? I figure any guy caught sabotaging the pipeline would be very quietly taken care of by some of those tough union men. The only time they ever stop work is to get more money or more privileges. But they sure as hell don't want the pipeline put out of business."

"What about the natives? They're not getting such a good shake."

"Listen, I've been working on that angle since 1969. The fact is, the Natives want the oil royalties, and they want the work. If they get paid, they don't want to stop things any more than the white Alaskans. Even Charley Edwardsen and his group settled down pretty well once the Native claim thing went through. That's why I ditched the North Slope Native Association and joined you guys."

He looked around him with an expression that indicated that he wasn't entirely convinced the change had been for the better.

"Ok," Sonia said then, "for the moment we'll go ahead on Baronian's scheme. Can you find out how many pumping stations would have to be put out of commission, and which ones, and how we should go about it?"

"Couldn't we just blow up the power house in each case?"

"That would stop them all right," Baronian said, "but each pump station has two standby power units and you'd have to blow them all. Again, it gets to be a very big, complicated procedure."

"Well, how long will it take you to get us some kind of report?"

243

Baronian waggled his beard and thought. "Maybe two or three weeks."

"Okay," Sonia said, cutting off Baronian as he seemed about to launch himself into another suggestion. "Next meeting will be two weeks from today. In the meantime, see if you can recruit some good reliable members. But be careful—make sure you don't bring any finks in. We hope to have a report from Marge and one from Van Taylor in Valdez at that time. Meeting is adjourned. Let's take a grass and juice break."

Hurwood slid an eight-track cartridge of Carol King's *Tapestries* into the machine and turned the volume up loud. Ernie Mason came over with a couple of jugs of Boone Farms Apple wine and settled into the sagging sofa beside Sonia. They sat silently for a while, digging the music and taking turns puffing on the big joint that Mason had relit following the meeting.

"This stuff is really down," Sonia said dreamily. "Better than anything I ever had in the States."

"Yeah," Mason said. "Gets all my brain cells kind of flattened out, so I can sort of think in one special level and just ignore a lot of the other things. Like just sitting here smoking I had this fantastic insight."

"Yeah? What's that?" Sonia asked, beginning to feel lazy from the wine and smoke.

"Bobby Baronian is some kind of spy."

On the cassette, Carol King sang *"You sat down on a river rock and turned into a toad."*

". . . Pitting the consuming block against the producing block not only would harden issues, but would inevitably inject politics into the issue of energy, which should remain essentially a commercial issue.

"This is one of the major contributions made by international oil companies: they keep politics out of energy matters."

—Rawleigh Warner, Jr.
Chairman, Mobil Oil
in a speech to
Mobil Oil shareholders
May, 1973

Chapter Twenty

Wilbur Steele closed the leather-bound folder of reports in front of him and stood quietly looking out of the twenty-sixth floor window of his office at the Houston skyline. From where he stood he could see the big forty-six story Exxon building, the two Shell Plazas, the Gulf Building, and the sleek modern building of Golconda. Interspersed among these were the bank buildings that made the whole thing possible. Among these top U.S. corporations, Alamo had not yet made the magic top twenty, of which at least seven were competing oil companies. But if the vast and complicated problems of the Alaska oil fields could be settled, Wilbur was sure that he would soon be able to finance a building that would top even the Exxon tower.

Aside from the problems of the Native land settlement, which looked like they were soon to be solved, there was the even more serious problem of the various ecological pressures—both lawsuits and legislative action—which had to be solved before the long delayed pipeline could be built.

The voice of Miss Martinez, one of Wilbur's gestures toward Tex-Mex integration, came softly over the intercom.

"Mr. Brandon is here."

"Send him in," Wilbur said, crossing back to the desk and opening the folder again. He gestured Brandon to a seat opposite him at the big Chippendale antique partners desk.

"Good trip?"

"Yup."

"Drink?"

"Nope. Later maybe."

"There are a couple of things I'd like to go over and then we can go to the Club for lunch. Did you read this report on the election?"

"Yup."

"What do you think?"

"Well, I like that idea they had about investigating the extent of coordination between these different groups, like the Sierra Club, Friends of the Earth, National Audubon Society, Isaac Walton League, Zero Population Growth, Student Environmental Confederation, Wilderness Society, Environmental Coalition of North America, the Conservation Foundation—seems to me that maybe there's somebody who's pulling their work all together. I think that the report is right on that. In fact, I already have some men checking on it."

"What do you think about this suggestion about getting a liaison for Denali in Washington?"

"I think it's a must," Brandon said. It was clear he had done his homework. "I've been talking with Fred on it and he has a few ideas. He'll be sending you a memo in a day or so.

"Well I want you to pick somebody in the next couple of days. I think we have to get busy on a big P.R. program. Only a couple of years ago they killed a big dam project up in the Yukon in Alaska with some of this ecological propaganda. I don't want that happening now. We've got too much invested."

"It won't.

"Now, what about the elections?"

"Well, as usual," Brandon said, "in the state I think we're okay. Briscoe looks like a favorite to me, although Grover may give him trouble. Anyway, both of them are good oil men. There's a couple of Democratic liberals here in Houston who might give us trouble— like Barbara Jordan, a black woman—but overall I think we have good power on our side in Congress and Tower looks like a shoo-in on the Republican side for the Senate. I know we can always count on his vote. You've got most of the other states covered in that report there. I don't think there'll be too much trouble."

"What about Alaska? You've been up there again."

"Well, whoever is in, is going to be in favor of putting the pipeline through. The question now is who will make us pay the most taxes. Right now the Democrats are leaning on us most heavily. You know Egan has been opposing the well-head price. Claims it'll net Alaska a big fat zero, if the price of the pipeline goes too high."

"Well, that'll be their incentive to see that it doesn't, now, won't it?"

"Yup, but we've got to pour plenty of money in up there to make sure that the right people get in. We have good indications though that lots of people are in favor of our line. Terry Miller, the Republican, is supporting the existing oil legislation. This fellow Orbeck, who's in office now, is opposing us. My figures show that Miller is going to win, but we should give him all the help we can. In general I think we're better off with the Republicans up there. Of course, if McGovern gets nominated . . . we've been putting a lot of money behind his primary campaign, and between us I think that

247

the Committee to Reelect the President is doing a little work to encourage McGovern as the choice too. They don't want to run against Muskie."

"That's wise."

"I suspect that's what the Watergate break-in was all about—something to do with making sure that the right Democratic candidate gets put up."

"Well, I don't want to get mixed up in what CREEP is doing. I've heard about some funny things. Give them the money, but let them spend it the way they want. It's important to us that Nixon gets elected."

"I think that's a pretty safe bet," Brandon said. "Especially if he runs against McGovern. Ted Stevens has been doing a good job in Alaska fighting for the pipeline, and I think he stands a very good chance of getting reelected Senator. That's a powerful factor. Of course, Governor Eagan is still there, and he's something of a problem. Some people say that he was brought up in a fishing region, where the economy was controlled by outside fishing interests who brought in crews from the outside, and took them south again at the end of the summer for the payoff. This has made him a little bit sour on the pipeline operation.

"The thing is, he's been against us all along and I think he'll continue to be a problem. All he wants is to be a Governor for Alaska and the Alaskans—nothing else. He's just not interested in being rich—and furthermore, his wife isn't interested in social position.

"Overall, though, I'd say on the elections that if Nixon gets in he'll sweep men in on his coattails who will be in our favor. And it looks as though he stands an excellent chance. As you know, we already have a pretty sure okay from Nixon that Morton will be on our side—or whoever he appoints next in the job."

"Well, you know what to do. Spread the grease

around as discreetly as possible and try to cover yourself in the clinches."

"Haven't I always?"

"How about your Middle Eastern operation? How is
that working out?"

"All according to plan," Brandon said. "As you
know, I met with the Iranian in Paris. He's all set to
go."

"You told them to hold off until after the election?"

"Of course. Any kind of oil hold-up from the Middle
East before then could tip over the whole apple cart."

"Well, I'd like to see some action as soon as possible
after the election. Did you make the whole payment?"

Brandon shook his head. "No, it was agreed—fifty
percent on agreement, fifty percent on completion of
the deal."

"You're sure it got to the right place?"

"Several places," Brandon said. "Yes, I'm sure."

"How long do you think it will be after the election
before we can get something going? You know, the
longer we wait, the higher the cost of the pipeline.
We're going to have to get a major rise in oil prices now
to cover all that."

"Well, it's a very big proposition," Brandon said.
"You can't just suddenly pull it off. The Iranian said that
they'll have to wait until some crisis that will justify
suddenly cutting off U.S. oil. But he figures something's
bound to come up in the Israeli situation in the near
future—that's always a hot spot anyway. I know lots of
times in the past those A-rabs have considered the idea
of cutting off the oil on account of U.S. support of the
Israelis but they've never been able to get their dumb
brown heads together. Now they've got a lot of those
Harvard Business School types and Wharton graduates
over there and they're getting a lot shrewder."

"Well, the sooner the better, as far as I'm concerned." Wilbur said.

"Do the other Denali clients know?"

"Just in a general way—I'm expecting you to fill in the picture as much as necessary. The fewer details, though, the better."

"I wish we could get them to kick in on the pay-off. But I guess a million or so won't break us. And I'd rather not have any more people involved in this than necessary."

"I agree," Brandon said.

Wilbur snapped the report folders shut and put them on the corner of his desk. "Well, we can go over this in more detail tomorrow. Have there been any further reports about Perry Dodge?"

Wilbur stood with his hands resting on the desk and stared at his executive associate. Brandon's eyes were open in that bland and innocent way that signified pure dishonesty. Wilbur had become accustomed to having his wishes miraculously come true. He had only to suggest at times that he wished such and such an action take place and it seemed as though some on-looking God—or demon—would see to it that it was done.

Perry Dodge, who had been one of the biggest thorns in the side of Alamo in Congress, had gone to Alaska on an inspection tour and had disappeared on a flight over the Gulf of Alaska more than ten days ago.

Wilbur made it a policy in these cases never to ask too many questions. But he always wondered, remembering back to the final illness of his wife Emma, whether those same Gods or demon had been responsible for the disconnection of the plug to her respirator when she was in those final months of near-vegetable existence. Wilbur supposed that he had truly loved Emma, but of course by the time of her death she was a curled-up sixty-five pound fetus, living, and breathing only by the power of life-support systems. He could hardly regard her as a human being, let alone as a wife.

In the end it was the additional voting power of the stocks he inherited from Emma that had given him the surge he needed to push up from thirtieth place in American Corporations to a point just below the top twenty. And now, as successful completion of the pipeline loomed, he anticipated moving up into the magic circle of the Seven Sisters.

"Was there really a shortage? Consider these facts. According to the census bureau, oil and gasoline exported from the United States in September and October of 1973 were five times the normal export traffic. The bureau's records conveniently omit the identity of the sellers and buyers, nor do they list the selling price. The figures do not include the oil cargos that were literally sold while the tankers were on the high seas. Many tankers bound for the United States were diverted to Europe where the oil was sold at a higher price. As far as the Arab embargo was concerned, it appeared as phony as the rest of the energy crisis story."

—Ovid Demaris
Dirty Business

Chapter Twenty-one

For almost four years after the discovery of oil at Prudhoe Bay, there was a continuous swelling pressure built up by accumulation of reserves of material, labor and talent in Alaska: preparation of the rights of way for the pipeline, the building of camps, and the capping of oil wells were completed. But, with the passage of the National Environmental Protection Act in 1970, the initiation of Native Rights lawsuits, the actions of the Sierra Club and other ecology groups, big oil seemed stymied. Then with all the drama of a Western thriller, help came, thundering on a herd of camels out of the east.

OPEC, the sleeping giant, inspired and fostered originally by the Seven Sisters, finally decided to lower the boom on western nations by declaring an oil embargo in the wake of the 1973 Yom Kippur war with Israel.

The embargo acted like a miraculous cathartic to the stopped-up progress of the pipeline. With a great show of anguished hand wringing over the state of "National Security," the oil bigwigs, their lobbyists, and their paid representatives in Congress and the Executive branch finally conspired to stampede an okay for pipeline construction.

But even when construction started things didn't go smoothly. Ditches dug in the ice-rich permafrost caved in almost as soon as they were excavated, and new methods of digging them had to be designed. Test borings along the route had been inadequate and it was now discovered that the pipeline, which was to have been buried for all but fifty of its eight hundred miles, would now have to be elevated on vertical support members for more than half its length—another major re-engineering job.

Deirdre Doheny, having to put out releases and answer questions about an ever-changing set of rules, began to wonder for the first time whether her father and Wilbur Steele were the supermen she thought them to be. Their statements at the time of any given crisis were concise, authoritative, and positive. But then why did events so often proved them to be wrong? And if they were wrong about the engineering of the buried pipeline, and they were wrong about the impact of the environmental groups and their ability to hold up the pipeline, then isn't it possible that they were wrong when they assured the public that the pipe they were using in the pipeline was able to withstand any stress—that there would never be an earthquake capable of disrupting the line—that leaks would automatically be detected and stopped before so much as a cup of petroleum touched the virgin tundra? Each time she was questioned by members of the press, she would turn back to her own or to Denali's environmental and engineering experts, and always they would come up with positive and reassuring answers.

Too often, however, their answers proved to have flaws in them; for instance, when they started drilling holes for the vertical support members, which were to elevate the pipeline above the permafrost, the ice melted in the holes and the holes would cave in before the support members could be set in them, until finally a way had to be found to refrigerate the pipes around their base to keep the permafrost from thawing. Deirdre remembered the great snow fence fiasco, when the fence meant to test caribou migration blew down before the caribou had a chance to find out what it was all about.

When Wilbur was away, and her father wasn't around to lend moral support, Deirdre often found herself beginning to have severe doubts about the validity of the entire pipeline project. Her talks with Baronian and Heywood didn't help much either, as both of them were even more cynical than she was, confessing that they were only hanging in there because of the good dollar that was being paid.

Al Everhardt was also a gadfly. His probing questions and uncanny inside information—all of which Deirdre knew to be true—were becoming a serious annoyance to the big wigs at Denali. Strings were pulled and Everhardt was mysteriously relieved of his job at the *News-Miner*, only to pop up again on the staff of the *All-Alaska Weekly*, a peppery little paper edited by Tom Snapp, a rotund drawling son of Dixie, gentle and mild mannered at first appearance, but a hard-digging editor with an acid pen. Snapp made a weekly column available to Everhardt and without fail the caustic diatribes provoked rage and chagrin at the Fairbanks headquarters, and in Anchorage as well.

What was more disturbing is that the columns often were picked up by wire services and spread all over the country.

Mahlon Doheny was particularly resentful of Everhardt's attacks.

"I'd like to know who's financing that little pipsqueak," he said. "There's no way Tom Snapp can be paying him enough to make a living wage, just for that little bitsy column."

"Maybe he's got money of his own," Deirdre said.

Doheny looked at her scornfully. "Don't you think we've checked that out? He doesn't have a nickel."

What had particularly roused Doheny's ire was that morning's Everhardt column. The columnist had interviewed McDade, Denali's Vice President of Operations and the man who would probably be running the pipeline after construction was completed. He had asked McDade just how much money Denali would make out of the pipeline. McDade had been ready with an answer.

"The Interstate Commerce Commission limited the profit on the pipeline to a modest seven percent—it isn't very much, if you figure you can get more than that in municipal bonds, and almost as much in a savings bank."

But Everhardt had apparently not been satisfied with the answer.

"Modest?" he wrote. "Yes, it's a modest profit if you accept McDade's figures. But he didn't quite give the entire story. The seven percent profit figure is based on the total cost of the pipeline. But the owner companies actually put up only ten percent of that cost. The remaining ninety percent is borrowed under Government subsidy, and the interest on the loans is included in figuring the cost of the pipeline. So you see, the rate of return on the oil companies' actual investment is actually seventy percent of their cash outlay—not seven percent. Not a bad return on an investment.

"In other words, if you, dear citizen, invested a hundred thousand dollars in the pipeline (not that anybody asked you to) you would be returned a spiffy $70,000.00 a year for your investment. In two years you would have paid for your entire investment and had a forty thousand dollar profit to show for it. And after that you could sit back and rake in $70,000.00 a year for the rest of your life. Not such a pittance at that, is it? No wonder Denali doesn't mind if they have to fly a monkey wrench into Prudhoe Bay in a Hercules! And these figures aren't strictly Alaskan bonanza figures. The ICC reports that the average annual return on pipelines in the United States, between 1968 and 1972, was about forty percent of the equity. And one pipeline— Colonial—made seventy percent *after taxes* in 1970. No matter how you slice it, a pipeline is good business —if you own it.

"But some people say, aren't the oil companies entitled to make a big profit? After all the risks they take? I can only quote Senator Floyd Haskell of Colorado who said once, 'What risks? With a ten billion barrel field and an exclusive market—give me a franchise and I'll resign from the Senate and run the operation.'

"Let's point out also that the pipeline is only part of the profit that the owner companies will make in Alaskan oil. Whenever you, dear citizen, buy oil to heat your home or gas at the service station, you'll be paying for the cost of the oil, plus profit on the transportation, as well as the production, the refining and the distribution.

"How much money will the pipeline make? No matter how dumb the management and wasteful, the price will always be added onto the oil and deducted from the money paid to the State of Alaska, which, unfortunately, signed a stupid contract based on the wellhead price, which means the price delivered in Valdez. Every escalation of costs comes out of Alaska's pocket and the pocket of the public.

256

"As for Denali, it will more than double its investment, whatever it may turn out to be in three years. Not a bad deal, hey readers?"

"Now where does that son of a bitch get that stuff?" Doheny said. "I don't even think anybody *here* has that information."

"They say he's a hell of a reporter," Deirdre said.

"He's a Goddamn Commie, if you ask me," Doheny said, his face reddening. His thin lips pursed and then puffed as though inflated by air pressure from behind. He let out a sputtering sigh, and seemed to go from a state of apoplectic rage to one of relaxed good humor.

"Ah, the hell with it. I shouldn't let myself get stirred up by stuff like this, huh? Come on, let's get a Coke from the machine," he said, taking his daughter around the waist.

Then another embarrassing story broke on the front page. In it Everhardt told how Denali had bought twelve enormous specially designed Radmark back-filling machines at a cost of ten million dollars, only to find out once they got up to the Arctic that workers using conventional methods instead of this fancy equipment could back-fill at twice the speed. It turned out that the special units had never been tried in the field, even though six of them had been transported from Portland Oregon to various points along the pipeline.

The machine had been planned to straddle a ditch, via a conveyor system, but it now seemed that they would rot like giant metal mastodons in the far reaches of the Arctic.

The story did nothing for Mahlon Doheny's blood pressure, but he was not really as excited as Deirdre had expected him to be. It seemed that gradually he was learning to roll with the punches and conserve his emotional energy.

But the revelation of the foul-up did nothing to bolster Deirdre's confidence in the efficacy of the Denali organization. She developed a deep belief in Murphy's Law: if a thing can go wrong, it will.

Not everything went fatally wrong. The bridge Denali had contracted to construct over the Yukon river to replace the annual ice bridge was finally built with only the redesign and construction of one troublesome pier to be contended with. The new design added four and a half million dollars to the cost of the project, which had at first been estimated at twenty-four point eight million dollars. Gradually, the cost of the pipeline had escalated from the original estimate of nine hundred million dollars to six and a half billion, and it looked like it was still going up. All it would take was one major mishap—like a labor dispute—to shoot the price up somewhere near ten billion.

The frequency of engineering miscalculations was leading Deirdre to feel that Michael Harrison's concern about the impossibility of routing the pipeline through the Atigun Canyon had been well-grounded. In fact, there had been a series of meetings concerning this, about which she had seen no memos, nor any charts or maps—so she assumed that the pipeline was still being laid in the precipitous, rocky canyon. Strictly speaking, financing and engineering were not exactly in her department, although she had to answer questions about them to the press. Deirdre's responsibility was ecology and the conservationists would have preferred to by-pass Atigun Cayon anyway.

True they had ferreted out the fact that a film put out by the state of Alaska lauding the nature conservation practices of Denali had actually been financed by the oil companies—but that was before Deirdre's time. She was glad, at any rate, that nobody had yet leaked the fact that the Polar Research Institute's report had also been subsidized.

In any event, the only case the conservationists had been able to make so far was the threat of oil spills to the various forces of nature. They had not been able to show that the pipeline itself discouraged the migration of the caribou or disturbed the nesting habits of the peregrine falcons, although these were facts yet to be proven.

But this was not what concerned Deirdre. She found herself increasingly worried about the question of earthquakes. Superimposed on a chart of the epicenters of earthquake activity, the pipeline seemed to follow these points, almost like the connect-the-dots they used to carry in the comic strips. It is true that the pipeline was engineered to withstand an earthquake in excess of eight points on the Richter scale, larger than any Alaska had yet suffered. But two factors bothered Deirdre about that. First, who could say that an earthquake measuring more than eight points on the Richter scale would not come along? The figures upon which Denali had relied were only measurable earthquakes in recent history.

Secondly, in view of the many engineering snafus already uncovered on the pipeline, how could anybody be sure that the long line really could resist tremors as claimed?

Deirdre was sitting at the dressing table in her apartment in Fairbanks behind the Traveler's Lodge. She had just bathed and was drying her tawny hair with a portable dryer as she read a disturbing piece in the *All-Alaska Weekly*.

"Increasing amounts of steam being emitted from the summit crater of 14,163 foot Mt. Wrangell are being watched closely by scientists of the U.S. Geological Survey and the University of Alaska . . .

"Mt. Wrangell has been a special target for observation for the past ten years because the heat flow has been slowly increasing and the number of fumaroles in the mountain's summit calders (a large basin-shaped volcanic depression) has increased steadily during that time. This year, however, the flow of heat and the amount of steam being emitted increased at a much greater rate and a much larger number of fumeroles have developed indicating an increasingly 'restless' volcanic mountain."

The article went on to discuss the observations being made by the U.S. Geological Survey on the mountain. Toward the bottom it continued: "The scientists report that the recent activity at Mt. Wrangell is marked by an increased melting of snow that has destroyed ice dams that do not normally melt. The ice dams had held back water in one 150 foot diameter lake in the caldera. With the destruction of the ice dams, the water from the lake had been released into the surrounding ice fields. Another sign of the increased volcanic activity this year, the scientists said, was the increased height of the steam columns coming from the fumeroles. Steam observed from one fumerole reached a height of about 100 feet. If the heat continues to increase, several mud slides could develop, scientists said. They strongly emphasized, however, that if mud slides should develop the slides would not pose any immediate threat to people or property. The nearest town, Glennallen, is about 150 miles to the west with a population of about 2,000. A closer area, about 55 miles to the west, is now undergoing intense development because of work on the Alaska pipeline. About 6,000 people are in construction camps in that area."

Her reading was interrupted by a sharp rapping at the outer door. Unhurriedly Deirdre passed the dryer through her hair a few more times, reached into the closet behind her and took out a white ruffled pinafore dress with a flaring skirt. It was unlike any other in her wardrobe.

Slipping into it, she called out, "Just a minute. I'm coming!"

The pinafore, apparently, was to be her only garment. Pulling it into place and zipping it behind her, she tip-toed to the door in her bare feet and opened it. Outside stood Wilbur Steele in a beaver coat with a hat to match. It was October and the "termination dust"—the first flakes of winter snow—had already arrived but not yet the deep chill of winter.

Wilbur stood with his hands plunged into his pockets and his shoulders hunched against the early cold.

"Aren't you going to let me in, girl? It's cold out here."

"Of course," she said, "come in my lord." She dropped a neat curtsy.

Wilbur came in and she helped him out of the beaver coat and hat and hung them in her closet. From the freezer compartment she took the two bourbon high-balls which she had put there so that the glasses would frost.

"Everything ready, I see," Wilbur said, nodding in approval. He sipped the drink appreciately and slumped into the reclining Eames chair.

"Shoes."

"Yes, my lord," Deirdre said, slipping the Gucci loafers from his feet. It was almost as though it was a rehearsed routine.

"Jacket." It was a command.

He sat up straight and Deirdre managed to wrestle the Italian-style pin-striped jacket from Wilbur's shoulders and hung it in the closet. She returned, loosened his tie, removed it and folded it neatly; unbuttoned the Turnbull and Asser shirt to the beltline, and slipped her hands inside of it to the warm, hairy chest. He bent his head diffidently and she placed one hand behind his neck and favored him with a very long penetrating kiss.

"All right. Get busy."

"Yes, my lord."

There was a long Spanish chest—oak bound with iron—in a corner near the window. She went to the chest and lifted the lid. Inside it was an assortment of ropes, leather bindings, halters, riding crops, hand-cuffs, and whips.

"The black ropes."

"Yes, my lord."

Deirdre was moving in a trance-like fashion, different from her usual quick bird-like movements. Her lips were set in a strangely fixed smile, and her cheeks were flushed with excitement. She removed the ropes from the chest and brought them to Wilbur, who was sitting up in the Eames chair.

"Turn around—put your hands behind you."

Deirdre did as she was told and Wilbur began to wind the thick strands of silk rope around her thin, tanned wrists.

Deirdre's eyes were now bright with excitement.

"Is that all right?"

"Tighter, milord. Pull it tighter!"

"VALDEZ, Alaska — The pipeline boom has arrived. Liquor sales are up, so are taxes. Schools are overcrowded all day and bars are packed on weekends. Cocaine is here. Prostitutes work the bars. Rents soar, raw sewage pours into the bay..."

—Wallace Turner
New York Times

Chapter Twenty-two

August 15, 1975

Dear Sonia:

Here is the "Letter From Valdez" you asked for to be included in the first issue of the S.H.A.M.A.N. Newsletter. Hope you like it. Attached is another letter with a more personal view for the eyes of you and the gang only. Am sending these by reliable messenger to avoid any possible mail-checks by you-know-who.

Your Southern star,

Van Taylor

LETTER FROM VALDEZ

If you keep your eyes on the mountains when you pull into Valdez, and if it happens to be a clear day, you might think it's the most beautiful harbor in the world. Stark, snow covered hills—even in the summer

263

—many of them rocky and without vegetation, slope down steeply into the
water. There's a lot of conifers and
pinetrees that also come down to the
edge. But if you let your eyes drop
down from the mountain peaks what you
see is the biggest village of
Winnebago campers, shacks, jerry-built
houses and honky-tonk bars that you've
ever laid eyes on. This is new Valdez.
Old Valdez toppled into Prince
William Sound in 1964 during the big
earthquake and tidal wave. The new
village was built a few miles up the
Bay here on solid bedrock, they say.

Back in the beginning of the oil
boom there were only about eight
hundred people in Valdez, most of
them making their living from fishing
in the choppy and fog-bound waters of
Prince William Sound and the Gulf
of Alaska beyond it. As soon as the
Valdez citizens heard that the oil
people were looking for a deep water
southern port, they put on an enormous
campaign to win that privilege over
Seward, Cordova, and some of the other
southern towns that were scheming for
it. And they finally won out, but
now that they have it, many of the
locals aren't sure they want to be the
terminal of the Alaskan pipeline.

By the early fall of 1975, the
population had quintupled. And that
was only since January of 1974. Before
the oil boom you could get a building

lot for four or five hundred dollars;
by 1973 it cost $4000.00 and by 1975
it took $10,000.00, and for a large
lot, even $20,000.00.

Now that the boom is on, there's
not enough of anything. There aren't
enough places to sleep, there aren't
enough schools, there aren't enough
paved roads, there aren't enough
sanitary facilities, so that even
now the sewage is beginning to flow
into the formerly virgin waters of
Prince William Sound. There's only
one grocery store and people have to
stand in line for milk and juice.

The only thing there's enough of is
trouble. There are certainly enough
whores to service a population of
5000. There are six bars that stay
open from 8 a.m. to 2 a.m. There are
Winnebago trailers set up as gambling
parlors, tattoo parlors, and whore
houses. Even the taxis operate as
whore houses. One man arriving in the
airport got into a taxi and asked
where the nearest bordello was. The
woman cab driver turned around, gave
him a gap-toothed smile and said,
"You're in it, buster."

Fresh water is scarce. Gas stations
charge $7.50 for enough water to wash
a pickup truck and a dollar or two for
enough water to fill a thermos.

This is the end of it. The grand
cloaca of the pipeline. This is where
the big tankers will pull in and suck

up their share of the precious oil
flowing in from the north, hopefully,
without spilling too much of it on
the heads of the salmon, crab, ducks,
and other sea denizens that frequent
these waters.

Sitting in the Club Valdez you can
squint through a picture window and
see the lineup of fishing boats
fortunately still able to ply their
trade in the Bay and beyond. Climbing
up the hills on the other side of the
Sound you can see the outline of the
huge holding tanks and the big cranes
dropping in footings for the piers
that will accommodate the super
tankers that are already being built
in Japan and other ship-building
centers.

The oil companies have assured concerned conservationists that there
will be no spills, that Prince William
Sound is one of the most sheltered
deep-water harbors in the world and
that every precaution will be taken
against accidents. But Lieutenant
Commander William R. Hudson, who commands the Coast Guard cutter that
patrols the area, says that winds of
up to 110 knots are not uncommon in
the approaches to Valdez harbor. Waves
aren't very high in the sheltered
harbor, but the Sound is consistently
choppy. And in the winter, sunlight
lasts only six hours, sometimes less.
It is rare that you have two con-

secutive days without a heavy snowfall, a rain, or a fog.

The approach to Valdez, through the
Valdez Narrows, is flanked by steep
stone ledges. A hump called Middle
Rock rises above the water in mid-
stream. At the narrowest stretch of
the channel, Commander Hudson figures
the passageway at this point to be
only three hundred yards wide.

"Oil spills associated with storage, deballasting, loading, and
shipping disasters could have a
devastating effect on the ecosystem of
Prince William Sound and Valdez Arm.

In a discussion of tanker accidents
that have taken place around the
world, a Commerce Department report
said: "Most of these accidents occurred under more benign climactic
and geographical conditions than
those found in Prince William Sound
. . . Because of both the nature
of known navigational hazards within
Prince William Sound and the lack
of data concerning possible submarine pinnacles, uncharted currents,
and the absence of suitable holding
grounds, the risk of collision or
stranding is magnified."

Cordova, across the sound, has
fishermen whose names come right out
of a Robert Service poem: Black
Barney, Goat Mountain Smith, Mattress
Lil.

The Cordova fishermen formed an as-

sociation called S.O.S., for "Save
Our Seacoast." But the Valdez folks
say the Cordova people are only angry
because they didn't get the port
themselves.

The people at Prince William Sound
are far from Prudhoe Bay. They don't
worry much about what's happening
in the north.

"Tundra ain't good for much, anyway. But why ruin this? There's no
other place like Prince William
Sound. Why don't they use Cook
Inlet? They've ruined that already."

That's what Tom Parker, who runs
the air taxi service out of
Cordova has to say.

But not everybody is opposed to
bringing the oil people in. Mayor
Arthur P. Knight of Cordova has this
to say, "It may sound a little
crass, but on a deal like this, I'm
inclined to go along with the
dollar."

                    Valdez

                    August 15, 1975

Dear Sonia and Fellow SHAMANS:
    Well, it's really getting to be a
hell of a situation down here.
I've leased out my boat on shares
and according to plans have gotten
a job with Wackenhut as a security
guard at the main terminal base,

which is located straight across the bay from Valdez.

I got myself a Winnebago, which I keep camped outside the gates with a bunch of other Denali fellows. I use that to live in when I get some days off—which isn't often.

Met a nice girl by the name of Sue Anne Dalton, who works in the Club Valdez, which is the toughest bar in town. But it's mostly frequented by pipeliners, and she is a hell of a source of information. So I guess I'll have to go along with the fact that she had a tendency to peddle her patootie on the billiard table after 2 a.m., when the bar closes.

To give you an idea of the kind of place it is, Spider Hoffman, who owns it, put an ad in the paper for a big bouncer. "Preferably six foot eight tall, 280 to 300 pounds, ugly, tough, and mean."

Of course, Hoffman hasn't been here long, and maybe he scares easy —or maybe the whole thing's a publicity stunt. But I've seen some pretty rough fights going on in there. A couple of weeks ago there was a fight between some of the Fluor Construction crew people and a bunch of guys from Denali. They only got eight cops in the town now—that's up from the three that they used to have a couple of years ago. When

the first cop came in to break up
the fight, they took away his Mace,
gun, and shield, and threw him out
into the street. The same thing
happened to the second cop. Last cop
finally managed to bring the group
under control, but no arrests were
made. So maybe Hoffman isn't exag-
gerating that much.

Of course, it does get pretty
hairy, because about half the people
around here carry a rod. The
souvenir shop in the Sheffield Motel
has got more pistols than it has
postcards. And whoever isn't carrying
a rod is definitely carrying a big
four inch Buck sheath knife or some
other kind of sticker.

Anyway, it's pretty here this time
of year, if you don't notice the
dust in the streets, the dirt on the
people, and the ramshackle buildings.
Sometimes we get a day or two without fog, well, it's not really fog,
it's more like a storm cloud. It
reminds me of Orange County in
California. The clouds just get into
that basin, like a large cup over
the sound, and they can't get over
the mountains, so they hang there
until they unload. I try not to
bring the Winnebago into town too
often because the roads are so
ditched and rutted and muddy, I'd
stand a pretty good chance of breaking my axle.

I tried to call you all a few
times, but the situation is hopeless
as far as phones are concerned. To
get a call through from here to
Fairbanks, I'd have to start at about
one o'clock in the afternoon and,
if I was lucky, I might get through
by about six p.m.

Prices here are higher too—even
than they are in Fairbanks. A tiny
apartment will run you five or six
hundred dollars. And the cheapest
motel rooms around are about thirty
bucks and that's in a mobile home
annex. I'll say one thing, though,
you can get all the dope you want—
ups, downs, Columbian, coke, heroin.
Anything you can get in a big city,
you can get here. You pay a bit more,
but then everybody's _got_ more.

I would say that there's more guys
here getting rich on card games,
crap games, and dope than there are
getting rich on the pipeline, not
to mention the world's oldest
profession.

The hookers down here have some
funny ideas about booze. A lot
of them drink what they call a
"money pool," which is a plain
glass of ginger ale, with no booze
in it. The money for the booze goes
into a glass behind the bar for the
girl. I heard a girl last night down
at the Pipeline Club ask for a "long
slow screw." It turned out what

she wanted was a screw-driver, made
with sloe gin, and in a tall glass.
You get any orders for that kind
of thing at the Flame Lounge, Sonia?

The classiest joint in town is the
Totem Lodge. Used to be a motel, but
now all the units are rented out
to pipeliners and people here for
the oil boom. They got a piano there
and a piano bar. On the bar there's
a sign that says "Dance on the
piano bar at your own risk." And
another one says, "No shoes on the
piano bar." That, as I said, is
the class joint.

I forgot to mention that a lid of
lousy grass here goes for about sixty
bucks. What are they getting in
Fairbanks these days?

The excitement ain't through here
by a damn sight. They figure they're
going to have 3500 men in the terminal
camp across the bay by the time this
thing is really going full blast, in
addition to all the boomers and
hangers-on here in town.

The only way you can take the
crowding and the hustle around here
is to keep on drinking. A fellow I
met the other day said, "The reason
you have to drink so much here is
so to stay as wet on the inside as
you stay on the outside—that way you
won't warp." But I think I'm beginning to warp.

At least it's not cold this time of

year. The weather's around 60-70
most of the time. Gets up to 80 once
in a while. Of course it's only
dark a couple of hours, but the bars
all keep their shutters closed and
the shades down so's you get the
impression it's nighttime. Otherwise
people feel guilty about being in
there.

Valdez this time of year looks more
like Texas than Alaska. Or maybe
someplace up in the Rockies. A fellow said to me the other day, "Do
you know the difference between a
farmer's boots and a Texan's boots?"
"No," I says. "Well, a farmers boots
got the bullshit on the outside,"
he says. Ha, ha. No offense, Sonia.
And I hope that phony Texan Hurwood
doesn't take it personal.

In terms of our project, I have
not made that much progress. I have
made friends with an Aleut security
guard named Harold. He's very dreamy
and writes poems all the time when
he's on duty in the security shack.
I have not got around to talking to
him about our project, but he might
be good material.

There's probably more freaks down
here than there are in Fairbanks, but
they're all more interested in the
all-mighty dollar than they are in
doing anything to save the Sound.

We have a little fun around here
everytime they set off a blast when

they're building the revetments for
those big holding tanks. All the fire
alarms in the joint go off and the
emergency fire crew comes running out
and racing around like a bunch of
Keystone Cops trying to find out
what the trouble is.

I have gathered a good deal of information about the setup out here
at the terminal camp, which I am
forwarding by personal messenger
under separate cover (you can't trust
the mails that much.)

How about one of you trying to
get loose and come down here—keep
a poor old fisherman company. Ha,
ha. I am only kidding. Sue Anne
keeps me plenty busy when she is not
in action on the billiard table, or
in some taxi cab. But I keep thinking
some day my joint will turn black
and fall off, what with the viruses
she has been exposed to. Washing is
not exactly a favored activity around
here, even if they didn't charge for
water.

I'll close with a thought for the
day. There's a joke that's been
making the rounds down here about
what's going to happen the day they
open the pipeline. The way they
figure it, the President, the Secretary of the Interior, the Governor,
and all those officials will be assembled down at the dock. There'll
be brass bands playing and everything

will be ready for the first gallon
of oil to flow. Somebody will throw
the switch and in two minutes,
Valdez Harbor will be sucked dry
and the water spit out in Prudhoe
Bay. You don't suppose we could pull
that off, do you?

> Your friend in crime,
> Van Taylor

"Thousands of tons of gravel were removed from the North Slope streams, coastal beaches, to serve as a base for roads, airstrips, drilling rigs and buildings. Beaches were turned to mud, river channels blocked and silted, spawning areas of the migratory fish destroyed.

"Miles of Cat tracks and seismic trails crisscross the area, resulting in thawing and erosion of the tundra. In places the ruts were deep enough to hide a man. Garbage and debris were left to rot in the cold, dry climate, where it takes fifty years for a tin can to turn to dust. Frozen lakes were popular sites for winter camps. In spring the sites were not hard to find—the melting ice being well-marked with the garbage, fifty gallon drums, and often, raw, human sewage."

—Congressman Wilbur Mills
December 1969

Chapter Twenty-three

Driving the pipeline route in the winter was boring for Larry Steele—if a thing can be boring and threatening at the same time. No matter what the news magazines had to say about the luxurious camps on the North Slope, they were little better than deluxe trailer camps. Recreation consisted of a G-rated movie every night, some Footsball or pinball games, a little quiet gambling, and, rarely, a fast fuck in some temporarily vacant corner of the crowded Atco units that served as barracks.

After the first few years, more and more women began to work in the camps. At first they only came as bullcooks, essentially chamber maids, keeping the quarters swept and clean, and handling laundry. A few came as secretaries and clerical workers. And then later some came as warehouse helpers, computer operators, or work dispatchers. Still, the bulk of the outdoor work, the hard physical labor, was left to the men. A lot of the women didn't set foot outdoors for an entire shift, or if so, only to go from one group of Atco buildings to another.

Several of the girls worked double shifts, one for Denali and one on their back for cash. The way Larry figured it, an ambitious girl working that way could put away $100,000.00 a year and pay tax on only half of it. Most of the girls, of course, were straight, but since Larry rarely spent more than a transient night in any one of the camps, he was seldom able to make much headway with them. Usually they were spoken for by one or more of the permanent help, who guarded them jealously—from the mess hall to the recreation hall to the sleeping quarters, if possible.

Usually Larry worked six straight weeks of twelve hour days, and then was given a two week paid R & R. Once in a while he would fly back to Texas to see Grandpa Bisset and some of his old friends, but more usually he would try to spend his time in Fairbanks with Deirdre.

The mood of his visits with her were as unpredictable as the Alaskan weather and sometimes just as frosty. After a year or so he was able to break them down into three categories in his mind. One: just like old times, good old buddy days, when they would cruise around the different bars on Two Street, or maybe go out to the Sunset Strip, or the Rendezvous on the edge of town and bugaloo to the rock groups. They would come back to her apartment, or sometimes his hotel, tired and drunk, and the love-making would be casual, friendly—nice, but yet without much passion. Still, Larry liked it that way, and in those days, even in the mornings, Deirdre would be like a warm purring kitten, pressing herself to his side, her soft breath moist on his skin. Larry would lay awake for long hours —his arm falling asleep with her head closing off his circulation but not wanting to move for fear she would change positions and he would lose her.

Two: Larry would arrive and she would be tense, nervous, frequently "busy," with all sorts of company affairs. There would be endless meetings that would take up her time at night and she would send him off to cruise the honky-tonks along the Chena River or along Two Street. More often than not on those nights, he would wind up in a fight with other pipeliners or with some of the townies.

Three: there would be those times when, unable to stand her enigmatic quirks, Larry would blow up with anger, and once or twice, drunk and furious, he had slapped her. Later, when they made up following these scenes, it was always Deirdre that would take the lead in the sex, and suddenly she would seem like a different person—avid, eager, hungry, never seeming to be satisfied, and wildly passionate. Several times on those occasions she would ask him to bite her or spank her, and her movements were always wild and uncontrolled. Larry was often wary of her moods, because sometimes she would bite *him*. Angrily he would slap her in retaliation, only to find her more passionate than ever.

Things had grown easier between Larry and Wilbur during those years, and they would see each other for lunch or dinner once in a while during Wilbur's occasional visits to Alaska. Wilbur had learned not to push his son, but would only look at him with sad eyes and drop some remark, "Anytime you're ready to move on up, Son, we could sure use you. I'm not getting any younger, you know."

Larry looked at him and laughed. Wilbur was in his early fifties and looked ten years younger. His face was thin and tanned, his muscles taut and finely tuned, cossetted with regular exercise—riding, swimming, and massage.

Occasionally Wilbur would ask him what was going on in the camps and Larry would tell him what he could. There was a lot of unrest in the unions in the early years when, after the big pipeline push of 1969, things slacked off and many of the construction workers and drill hands had to be laid off. All of the companies held back on doing more exploratory drilling until the E.P.A. and Native claims settlements were through, even though equipment continued to pour into the country and the Japanese ships pulled in regularly to the port of Valdez with a monthly shipment of the huge forty-eight inch pipes to be sent out for distribution to the construction camps along the route.

But Larry didn't like to answer many questions about the work. It was too much like being a company spy. There were things he heard about resident camp managers taking kickbacks from suppliers of food and equipment, of fights between the different union locals —especially the Teamsters and the Tulsa welders— about thefts of equipment, up to and including huge D-8 Caterpillars, and complete trucks, and down to petty thieving from the commissary. One man in the Franklin Bluffs Camp, had been found with his entire foot locker filled with little paper-wrapped pieces of toilet soap. What he planned to do with them nobody knew.

As far as gambling, bootlegging, prostitution, and dope dealing, Larry figured it was pretty much the same as it was in any other medium-sized city—well, a bit more considering that most of the help was either single or living away from home. Larry didn't feel he had to go running to the old man with every rumor he heard and he was pretty sure Wilbur wouldn't want to hear about things on that level anyway. He supposed that if something really big (like what? he wondered) happened, family loyalty would come first.

What it all reminded him of more than anything else, in its waste and stupidity and bureaucratic duplication, was the Army—a bit less bloody than Vietnam had been, but almost as stupid.

The weather began to warm up around May, and by mid-June even the tundra had turned into a soft, springy mass of vegetation: tiny flowers and midget willow trees—three and four inches tall. In the northern camps they enjoyed the relief from the cold weather, but they still couldn't travel far from the base, except on the dusty roads linking Alamo's camp with Royal American's. The tundra itself was too soggy to walk on, and vehicles were prohibited for fear of tearing up the fragile insulating cover, leaving the permafrost below exposed to melting and erosion, as had happened in some of the previous exploratory oil camps. In some cases, Cat tracks had eroded away to a depth of eight feet in the tundra, and it was estimated that it would take thousands of years before the damage would be repaired.

In the northern camps, summer or winter, it was pretty much work, eat, and sleep. But down toward Fairbanks and below, the land seemed to bloom almost in obscene haste. Pink, yellow, and purple flowers popped up alongside the roadside, elbowing each other aside for a place in the day-long sunshine. The rivers and creeks and edges of the glaciers were all fringed with eager tourists and campers, boaters, fishermen, and hunters. Seeing the vacationers along the road, it was hard to realize that, beyond that thin strip in which the highway paralleled the pipeline all the way to Valdez, were millions of square miles of virgin wilderness on either side.

In those days, Larry would often sing country and

western songs to himself or play bluegrass on the portable eight track tape player he carried with him in the various trucks. There was something beautiful and lyrical about winding your way through those huge mountains, past dozens of enormous glaciers—some, they said, the size of the entire country of Hungary. Camps, like Dietrich, or Isabel Pass, were located high in mountain valleys that would make Aspen or Gstaad look downright shabby. But Larry was getting tired of spending every night in a different bed, and wanted at least the illusion of permanence that came from working in one camp for a few months at a time.

He would stop to see Nick Gordon whenever he could. Nick tended to shift jobs every few months himself, and had worked every camp from Prudhoe and Franklin Bluffs, down to Sheep Creek, Tonsina, and the Valdez terminal. In the few spare hours he had, Larry would frequently take instruction from Nick on handling the heavy equipment—the Cats and the fork-lifts, and even the big, fast, alligator-clawed lifts that could carry an eighty-foot, double-jointed section of forty-eight inch pipe at twenty miles an hour across the stockyards stacked high with pipeline steel.

Ultimately, Larry was able to work his way up to a "C" card in the Tulsa 798 union, and then to get himself dispatched to the Glenallen camp, a sprawling and comfortable location near the junction of the Glenallen Highway and the Richardson Highway. The Wrangell mountains rose magnificently to the east, there was plenty of grayling fishing on the Tolsona River, and red and King salmon up to seventy pounds to be caught in June and July on the Gulkana River. There was a little roadhouse out through the gates of the camp and a couple of miles up the road. A bit further, at the highway junction, was a big raffish bar called Smitty's, where he would go sometimes, if he wasn't too tired after work, to quaff a few beers.

The gang at Smitty's was rough and irritable with fatigue. But Smitty managed to keep reasonable control with a lead-lined billiard cue and a small bowling pin. Smitty had been in Alaska for thirty-three years and had done everything from running traplines to crab fishing and dog racing.

"I'll be glad when you rookies and roughnecks get your ass out of here and leave things simmer down to where they was," Smitty used to grumble. But guys in the camp said he was socking away three to four thousand dollars a week. A beer ran a dollar and a half at Smitty's joint — an Oly — and he would look at you funny if you asked for a glass with it.

Larry had acquaintances in most of the camps up and down the line from his truck driving days, so he was reasonably at home no matter where they dispatched him. Still, his only close friends were Nick Gordon and Deirdre. One of the pipeline welders had bought a Mustang II, which he kept in the private car parking lot on the edge of the Glenallen camp. When he got his R & R in mid-July, Larry borrowed the Mustang to drive to Fairbanks.

He had tried to call ahead to set up a date with Deirdre, but after five unsuccessful attempts to get a call through, decided he would start driving, and get in touch with her at some point along the way.

Since 1974, the tempo of work had picked up and already fifty miles of pipe had been laid. Larry had been operating a giant back-hoe, digging trenches for the pipes, which were to be underground for a considerable stretch, south of Glenallen. Six weeks of seven twelves had left him feeling bruised and wrung out. The first thing he planned to do when he got to Fairbanks was to go to that massage parlor on the edge of town and get himself rubbed and stroked all over, soak in a hot tub, and washed down with one of those loofas. He wondered as he turned north on the Richardson Highway for the two hundred fifty mile drive to Fairbanks whether any of those girls actually knew how to massage any part of a man that wasn't between his legs. At least in Vietnam you could have a choice of actually getting a massage or an around-the-world. Maybe he'd be able to get through to Deirdre and persuade *her* to rub his back.

About a mile before Paxson, Larry hit the brakes of the Mustang, swerved and nearly slid off into a ravine when a moose cow and calf suddenly broke out of the evergreens and jumped onto the road in front of him. *It's a good thing I missed them,* he thought. Besides wrecking Kelly's Mustang he probably would have faced a five hundred dollar rap for killing the cow. They said you could get in more trouble for killing a cow moose out of season than you could for killing your own girlfriend if you found her with another man. In fact, killing an unfaithful spouse was generally considered within the game rules and was referred to as a Spenard Divorce—after a section south of Anchorage, where such activities were popular.

At Paxson Lodge, Larry stopped for a cup of coffee and again tried to get through on the phone to Deirdre. After a forty-five minute wait, during which he consumed three two dollar hamburgers and two thirty cent coffees, he finally got a line through to Deirdre's Denali office in Fairbanks. Deirdre's phone was answered by a girl with the accent of an oil princess in the Petroleum Parade.

"You just missed her, Suh," the girl on the other end of the line said. "She's gone up to Prudhoe for an ecology meeting with Mr. Vaughn and Mr. Wilbur Steele."

Larry felt a burning surge of discontent in his mid-section—or was it the three greasy hamburgers?

"When do you expect her back?"

"Don't rightly know. Ought to be back by the end of the week. Who should I tell her called?"

"Just tell her 'Larry.' I'll be in Fairbanks at the King Eight or the Chena View."

Sadly, he hung up the receiver and listened to the waterfall of small coins dropping into the box.

Chapter Twenty-four

An hour out of Paxton, Larry began to pass over countless spring-swollen streams fed by glaciers in the surrounding mountains—Snow White, M'ladies' Mountain, White Princess, Black Cap, and Old Snowy. A few miles later, to his left, he passed the famous Black Rapids glacier, with its mile-wide front. Old time Alaskans had told him that in 1940 the glacier suddenly moved four miles from its base toward the road—for no reason that anyone could fathom. Then, as rapidly as the sudden motion had started, it stopped.

Now that it was spring, the roads on both sides were lined solidly with wild sweet pea, bluebell, lungwort, and purple lupine. At some points the fruity penetrating odor of the sweet peas filled the car.

Just outside of Delta, which was something less than a hundred miles from Fairbanks, Larry pulled off to the side of the road to see if he could catch sight of any of the buffalo that used the salt lick on the far side of the Delta River. The herd had been transplanted to that area in the 1920's and had multiplied to the point that it was a nuisance to the farmers. The salt lick was an attempt to keep the three hundred buffalo on the far side of the river.

Larry was tempted to have a hamburger at the Club Evergreen ("Entertainment and Dancing in the Lounge —featuring BIG NAME Groups and popular personalities"). Because of the pipeliners and occasional visitors from Eielson Air Base, there was usually quite a bit of action in the Evergreen. But it was early in the day, and Larry still had hopes that Deirdre might return to Fairbanks before the weekend. He drove on through, stopping only to pull off the road to look for the buffalo. There were a few vaguely moving dark brown spots on the range across the Delta, but it was too far to see clearly and there were no binoculars in the borrowed car.

From Delta the road degenerated into a dusty, accordion pleated, frost-heaved stretch—much of it unpaved or under construction. Local folks like to say, "If you could put two big bulldozers, one at each end of this highway, they might be able to hook onto this road and stretch it out between them, and you'd probably have enough pavement left over to pave the rest of the way to Fairbanks."

For a stretch the road paralleled the Tanana River and was lined with birch trees, making white zebra-like stripes against the background of green spruce.

Three hours later, Larry pulled into the North Pole Trading Post to stretch his legs and have a cup of coffee. There was a public phone there, but Larry again was not able to get through—either to Denali or to Deirdre's home number. North Pole had nothing to do with the actual North Pole—it was only fourteen miles out of Fairbanks and was a commuter base for many workers in town. It was named by some homesteaders in 1944 in the hope that some toy manufacturer would build a plant there and advertise products as being "Made in the North Pole." So far, that had not happened.

With Deirdre away, Larry wondered how he would spend his R & R. He had long since wearied of the typical round of boozing, brawling, and belly-bumping. Gambling was not much fun when you were going up against professionals most of the time—professionals never lost. And Larry had long ago exhausted the tourist possibilities—the stern-wheeler Riverboat tour down the Chena and Tanana Rivers, a visit to the Musk ox Ranch at Oomingmak, Alaskaland (the big phony version of old-timey Alaska), and the tourist gold mine tours. He thought he would see if Nick or one of the boys was in town and would like to run up to the Arctic Circle hot springs resort for some swimming and fishing. Or maybe they could charter a riverboat.

The waitress, a tall, clean faced blond with an outstanding bosom, returned with three dollars change from the five he had given her for a hamburger and coffee.

"Going to the races tonight?"

Larry thought for a minute. "I might just do that."

There was a stock car track—the North Pole Speedway—just outside town. Larry had been there once or twice before. It reminded him of some of the dirt tracks in Oklahoma. On summer nights the North Pole Speedway was almost as big an attraction as the Glacier Pilots baseball team. It boasted a grandstand that held about twenty-five hundred people and was usually full.

There was still an hour until race time but Larry drove the three or four miles anyway. The beer bar underneath the grandstand was usually open ahead of time and he planned to pick up a couple of brews and

287

wander around in the pit area looking over the cars. Usually you had to have a pit pass to do that but Larry found that if you went early enough, nobody made much fuss about it.

He parked the Mustang in the muddy parking lot where the spectators were already gathering. Some of them were enjoying a pre-race tailgate picnic, others were playing cards or yarning, many of them in net camping tents to keep out the mosquitoes.

Larry ordered an Oly and a bag of chips at the bar. Next to him was a girl in a beaded buckskin jacket and jeans. She had light hazel eyes with green glints in them. They were a peculiar almond shape, subtly slanted, and her hair was light brown—almost honey blond —and hung straight to her shoulders, where it curled in ringlets.

"I'll have a six pack of Oly," she said to the bartender. "And make sure they're cold."

"That's a lot of beer for one girl,' Larry said. "You must have a heck of a thirst."

She had a good smile. "They're for my cousin and the pit crew," she said. Her chin was a bit too long but the teeth and the smile made up for it, Larry decided.

"Hey, have you got a pit pass?"

"Sure—got the loan of one."

"Mind if I come along with you? I wanted to get into the pits and look over the cars before the race and I haven't got a pass myself."

"Come along."

They paid for the beers and started off across the muddy infield toward the pit area.

"You from around here?"

"No," the girl said. "Anchorage."

"Up here on a visit?"

She nodded.

"Visiting relatives?"

"My cousin Angie. Her husband works on the pipe-line. You a pipeliner?"

"Yup."

"I figured."

"Mind?" Larry asked.

"No. I guess there's no way to stop it. Besides, so far, I've gotten a couple of thousand dollars out of it."

"How's that? You working on the pipeline?"

"No. Native Claims settlement."

"Native Claims?"

"Yes," the girl smiled. "I'm one-quarter Tlingit Indian." (She pronounced it "Klin-kut.")

"You sure don't look it."

"My father was a Scandinavian fisherman down in Hoonah. You know, near Haines?"

Larry knew that Hoonah was in Southeastern Alaska, not far from Juneau.

"My mother was half-Tlingit, half-Russian," the girl explained further. "But among the Tlingit, descendence is based on the mother—we're matrilineal, you know."

"Is your cousin Indian too—the one who lives in Fairbanks?" Larry asked.

"Yes, she's a quarter. Same as me. The difference is, I was raised in the village, in Hoonah. We have all the old artifacts and relics stored away there and we have ceremonies and dances—even potlatches. I was raised to know about my Indian background. My cousin Angie, she was brought up in Juneau and they used to tell her that her mother was white. She didn't really know that she was Indian until a couple of years ago. Now she's really happy about it, and besides, she gets a piece of the Native action. She's been asking me to help her study up on Tlingit customs and so on. We're of the Raven clan. You know, that's the most aristocratic one."

"No," Larry said. "I didn't know that."

The girl was named Ruby Karsian. She was married to an Armenian lawyer in Anchorage, but she didn't sound as if she were madly in love with him. She was planning to stay for the long weekend ahead in Fairbanks and return three or four days later.

"You got a place to stay?" Larry asked.

"I'll be staying with my cousin. She's got an extra room."

Angie, as it turned out, was dark and petite—more Indian looking than Ruby—with striking violet eyes and a trim, provocative figure that was outlined in a tightly-fitted cream-colored racing coverall with a blue stripe down the side. Over her left breast, the name "Angie Belson" was stitched in blue; over the right breast was a "Purolator" patch.

She shook hands gravely when she was introduced to Larry and did not seem surprised or curious that her married cousin had a boyfriend.

Her car was a blue and cream colored, battered Cougar, with the top chopped down so low it barely cleared her dark, curly hair when she sat behind the wheel.

Angie turned the Cougar over to her pit crew and joined Ruby and Larry in the stands, which were already half-full. It was a sunny day, around sixty degrees, and the crowd, glad to be rid of cumbersome winter gear, was dressed in a brightly colored assortment of jackets, sweaters, T-shirts, and sweatshirts. Men and women wore peaked fishing caps or western style hats to keep off the sun. Some had bought straw sun hats with miniature replicas of beer cans along the rim. Ten and twelve year old kids clambered through the stands, hawking beer and peanuts.

They had a few beers while examining the program —there were ten races that day. Bill Belson, Angie's husband, was in the second and fourth. Ruby was in the seventh. Larry and the two women returned to the pit area to meet Bill, who was busy with his crew, seeing to the adjustment of the carburetor intake. He grunted impassively as Angie introduced Larry and Ruby.

"Larry is a pipeliner too," Angie explained.

Belson, a swarthy, thick-set youth with an unruly dark-haired cowlick flicked an eye appraisingly over the Texan.

"What union?"

"Tulsa."

"I'm Teamsters 959," he said. It was as though he had just drawn a line in the dirt and was daring Larry to step over it. Ever since the start-up of the actual pipeline operation in 1974, there had been a number of bad clashes between the Tulsa pipeline union and the Teamsters.

Basically, the pipeline men were from Oklahoma, and California. The Teamsters were of more scattered geographic origin. Most of the Tulsa group had worked on pipelines around the world, whereas the Teamsters were in an assortment of occupations covering a large spectrum of work at the camps. The other important unions were the International Brotherhood of Electrical workers, the Culinary, the Plumbers and Steamfitters, and Local 942 of the Construction and General Laborers.

The Tulsa local and the Teamsters were by far the most powerful. The highest paid men in the camp were the men from the Tulsa union—the pipeline welders and other specialists. They were regarded by the other unions as having a sweetheart contract and being entirely too cozy with Denali management. Fights erupted frequently between members of the two unions over a variety of subjects—union jurisdiction, personal animosity, and racial slurs. The Tulsa local, consisting largely of southerners, was lily-white, while the Teamsters, though

291

not exactly racially liberated, included a number of blacks and Natives.

Pressure had been put on the Tulsa union by local officials and reluctantly they had added a few Native trainees and token blacks, but while the laws of integration may have become enforceable in the southern states of the lower forty-eight, wherever the Tulsa pipe-liners ruled, races other than white still rode in the back of the bus. This provided grounds for several camp conflicts, as the buses loaded with workers from various unions were boarded for trips out to the worksites. Several times the disputes resulted in work stoppages, picketing, and, sometimes, brutal fistfights.

All the fighting and violence in the camps was not between unions. Several times workers had gone on a rampage over the quality of the food or working conditions. They had beaten or nearly killed suspected pilferers or gambling cheats. There were several outbreaks of violence over the Denali policy of searching out-going luggage for possible stolen material and incoming luggage for liquor or dope. By 1975 Denali had to yield to union pressure and accept the fact that the men were bringing in drugs and liquor. The company gave up its privilege of searching luggage.

"If men want to drink in their rooms," McDade had told the press, "Denali won't be too strict, as long as we don't know about it. However, we will not tolerate drunkenness on the job and it will be cause for termination."

Larry held the hostile race-driver's eye briefly. He debated whether to point out that he had also been a Teamster, then decided that it wasn't worth it. Angie seemed embarassed by her husband's surly response.

"He's always like that—tense, before the races," she explained as they walked back to the stand. "The fact is," she said more to Ruby than to Larry, "he's not one of your all time social butterflies. If I hadn't gotten into racing myself, we wouldn't have had a hell of a lot to talk about."

"You working?" Ruby asked.

"Oh, yeah," Angie said. "I'm a barmaid down at the Rendezvous Club, on the Steese Highway."

Larry looked at her with renewed interest. The Rendezvous Club was a sprawling concrete block structure outside the Fairbanks city limits—a huge, raucous dancehall catering largely to pipeliners.

"You like the work?" Ruby asked.

Angie shrugged. "It's pretty good, and the tips are terrific. Some guys just off the line throw down a fifty or a hundred dollar bill before they leave."

"What do you have to *do* to get *that?*" Ruby asked.

"Just serve drinks, although I get asked plenty of times about the other. Of course, we got plenty of rounders out there, and some of the waitresses peddle a little ass on the side also."

"You must really be socking it away," Ruby said enviously as they clambered back into the stands and to their seats.

Sitting there in the sun, surrounded by two pretty girls, and warmed by a third round of beer (which Ruby had insisted on paying for) Larry felt relaxed and happy for a moment, and he forgot his gnawing irritation with Deirdre.

"We would have saved about $50,000.00 last year," Angie explained, "but all of that went for the house and lot. We paid cash for that. And baby-sitters up here get about four bucks an hour, so a lot of money goes on that when Bill's out on the pipeline and I'm working."

"Is it hard to get sitters?" Ruby asked. "It's hard in Anchorage."

"It's worse here. Lots of people, if their kids are

eight or nine, leave them on their own. Some of them even leave nine and ten year old kids in charge of the household while both parents are away working on the pipeline—for weeks at a time."

They stood up as a scratchy record blared the Star Spangled Banner over the loudspeaker and the races started. Looking at the crowded, colorful stands, and the track, soggy with early spring mud, Larry could as easily have been in one of the millions of stockcar dirt tracks he had visited through the south and midwest in his roustabout days. The racers were all local, and the crowds wildly partisan—with much good-natured shouting and jeering. Bill took a second in his first race, which was good for a two hundred dollar purse. Several people in the crowd reached over and shook hands, congratulating Angie. The Belsons were minor local celebrities.

Watching the race, and getting high on the beers, Larry noticed that Ruby, after an early spurt of family gossip and girlish chatter, was paying more attention to him. Her leg was pressed against his, closer perhaps than the crowded stands required, and in a moment of excitement she had a tendency to drop her hand to his thigh and squeeze it enthusiastically. *Not the worst way to start an R & R,* Larry thought.

The track was barely a quarter of a mile around. The events lasted for ten laps of banging, smashing, close-contact racing. The cars looked like refugees from a wrecking yard, and on the small track the top lap time averaged slightly under seventy miles per hour. Belson managed to take first in his Dodge Charger in his next race and collected a three hundred dollar purse.

"Hey, you're really getting rich today!" Larry said.

"Yeah," Angie agreed, "we usually make out pretty good. But we got to split with the sponsor you know.

Bill's sponsored by Pete's Surplus, and I'm getting a ride from the Rendezvous Club."

"Hey, Angie," a puffy-faced blond yelled from two rows below, "you going to make it a family parlay?"

"Going to try, honey," Angie said, as she put her beer down and stood up to make her way down to the cars. "Gotta go now," she said. "Join us later in the pits for a couple of beers."

She turned to Larry, and said, "I'm sure you and Bill will get along once you, get to know each other. He's tough, but he's a good guy . . . I guess."

Ruby looked after her with a frown as the trim figure disappeared into the crowd and passed through the gates into the pits.

"Something wrong?" Larry asked, as he handed her another beer. But the brief cloud of concern had passed over, and she turned to him with a sunny smile.

"No," she said, "everything's all right—for now anyway. Right, Tex?"

Larry smiled and clinked beer cans and kissed her on the mouth. Ruby's breath tasted of beer and Fritos. Her mouth opened in tentative response and then she pushed him away.

"Take it easy, Tex. We've got a long night ahead of us."

Chapter Twenty-five

After the races, the drivers, pit crews, and friends gathered around a bar in the base of the grandstand and stood around in their racing suits, dangling crash helmets from their free arm, their zippers half-way open, their faces still crusted with the mud and dust of the track. Some of the drivers worked on the pipeline, others were garage mechanics, owned shops, or had various jobs around town. Bill Belson seemed a bit more relaxed than he had at the beginning of the race—but he was not what one would call cordial.

It was now eleven o'clock at night and the sun was still as bright as noonday in Houston. In the years Larry had spent in Alaska, he had never gotten used to the midnight sun. Going to sleep while the sun was bright outside just didn't seem to make any sense. As a result, people got very little sleep during the summer season. Larry, drinking Oly from the can, drifted around the little group, which was leaning against the bar and lounging against the pickups and trailers onto which the stockcars had been loaded.

Larry said very little, listening to conversations, sipping slowly at the beer, wondering what his next move with Ruby would be.

". . . You know how that sumbitch got his dough? There was this old gal, you know, she was seein' Don Sheldon—the pilot? Well, Sheldon flew the route back in '68—he laid out the whole route for the pipeline companies. And that little old gal, she heard from Sheldon where the route was going to be. Next thing you know, she was working for old Bob and he starts to ask her about what Sheldon told her. That sumbitch went out and bought a hundred thousand acres along the pipeline route and got in some good leases up north. Must be worth about four or five million by now . . ."

". . . The thing is, all you see is them goddamn yellow Denali trucks around the streets now. You know what they used to say when they had the dog teams, 'never drink yellow snow.' Well, I'm beginning to think them trucks is making the snow yellow around here. Goddamn it, I'll be glad when them fuckers is out of here and we can have a little peace . . ."

". . . Maybe some folks is getting rich out of this, but it sure ain't me. I can't get no help in my store, the prices of everything is going up, and I can't raise my prices fast enough to keep up with them . . ."

". . . I go down to that damn union hall everyday and there's still 700 people ahead of me on the list. I'm a fine bulldozer driver, but I'm gonna run out of money before I get a job, looks like. You don't suppose I could slip a few bucks to the B.A.? . . ."

". . . We save enough dough on this damn thing and I'm gonna buy me a hundred acres down in Kansas and get the hell out of this damn country. Shit, me and my kid used to hunt moose down where they got that Denali construction camp. Now you can't hunt or fish worth a damn anywhere within ten miles of the road—

'you've got to have a plane to fly in to one of those lakes in the interior . . ."

". . . I understand eight people went to the hospital after that fight in the Wainwright camp, including the trooper they sent to bust it up . . ."

". . . I parked my pickup in the lot near the Flame Lounge on Two Street and would you believe I got propositioned six times before I got out of the lot? . . ."

". . . I kept waiting for my elevator over at the Chena View Hotel and I finally walked up. You know what was holding up the elevator? There was a line all the way out and down the hall. Pipeliners and soldiers standing there with their money in their hands. Two girls were working the elevators between floors—about ten minutes a go. Nothing but blow jobs. They must have picked up five hundred dollars apiece in the elevator before somebody got it started again . . ."

Larry had had about three more beers and felt drawn back to Ruby. She was glad to see him. She took him by the hand; Her fingers were warm and the touch was tender. She surprised him with a sudden wet kiss on the ear and he could feel her warm tongue probing nearly to his ear drum. Larry felt a turgid rustling in the crotch of his tight jeans.

"You want to get out of here?" he whispered. "I've got a place at the Chena View."

Ruby opened her big shiny mouth in a delighted laugh. "Wouldn't *that* be fun, though? But we'd better cool it for now" She wagged her head toward her cousin Angie, who was sitting on the running board of the pickup surrounded by several drivers discussing a change in the regulation of the track.

"Anyway, we're all going over to the Sunset Strip and get some breakfast."

Larry looked at his watch and was surprised to see it was well past midnight. The sun was still hanging low on the horizon, but bright enough to give you a tan. Pickups and jalopies were racing their motors and several cars had already started out. Bill Belson took the pit crew in his pickup and Angie rode along with Ruby in Larry's Mustang as they headed for the old Richardson Highway and the strip of dance halls and honky-tonks that lined it about a half mile outside of the city limits.

Larry knew the place well—a big raucous dance hall with a rock group in a darkened room to make you forget it was still sunny outside, and another room where they served "Pipeliner's Breakfast" (a pint of juice, a steak, two eggs, an English muffin, and a pot of coffee) twenty-four hours a day. The breakfast was six dollars.

On the way over Angie and Ruby exchanged reminiscences of life down in the southeast.

The Sunset Strip was jumping when the group got there, full of the usual mixture of construction workers, drivers, laborers, bush pilots, hookers, good time girls, hustlers, gamblers, and pimps. Larry waited a few minutes until a table for eight was cleared and sat down with the girls, holding places for the rest of the group, which was still on its way.

Sizing up the crowd, Larry decided to put both girls on the inside of the booth, away from the milling half-drunk patrons. It was just as well. A rat-faced kid of about twenty, with long, uncombed blond hair, stumbled up to the table.

"I guess you don't need all this space. I reckon I'll sit down."

"Taken," Larry said.

"Says who?"

Larry stood up and picked up the ketchup bottle by the neck from the table. "Says me."

As quickly as Larry moved, the blond kid reached his hand toward the sheath on his belt. He pulled out a straight bladed Buck knife. But before he had a chance

299

to utter a threat, Larry broke the ketchup bottle on the kid's wrist, sending the knife clattering to the floor. There was a stir of interest in the corner as several other youths in green coveralls with "Fairbanks Air Freight" patches over the pockets came over. Larry had the blond kid by the shirt-front and was holding the ketchup bottle by his face.

"Okay, Mister," one of the two newcomers said. "Take it easy. Herbie, maybe we better get you home. You just been doing nothing but getting into trouble."

The men took Herbie by either arm. Suspiciously Larry let the blond kid go. By now two uniformed security guards had managed to get through the crowd to the scene of the action.

"What's the trouble?"

The men in the green coveralls signalled Larry frantically with their eyes.

"Oh, nothing officer," Larry said. "The kid stumbled against the table and broke this ketchup bottle. His friends are taking him home."

The guards, one of them a cheery round faced Eskimo, looked with humorous doubt from one to the other, shrugged, and went back to their post by the door. The stumbling, rat-faced blond was helped out of the room by his friends.

By the time Larry sat down again, Ruby had gotten some towels, and wiped the surface of the table. A small circle had formed during the heat of the action possibly hoping to see a good fight. In the crowd was Bill Belson and some of the other drivers. Larry wondered if they would have helped him if the kid had come at him with the knife.

Belson and the pit crew slid into seats in the long booth. Belson looked over at Larry, his thick lips struggling to form the words that were on his mind. Finally ne slapped the menu shut and said, grudgingly, "Thanks for saving us a seat, fella!"

Larry sat close to Ruby, holding her warm hand under the table, as others talked excitedly about the next week's races.

Around three a.m., and many Olys later, the group broke up.

"Don't forget," Angie said, as the others staggered from the table, "tomorrow, one o'clock at the Rendezvous, we're going to roast Herman."

"Who's Herman?" Larry asked Ruby.

"Herman's a pig," Ruby said. "You want to come and watch them roast him?"

Larry shrugged. He wondered if Deirdre had returned yet. Finally he said, "Sure, why not? What have I got to lose?"

"Happiness is a hundred Texans going home with an Okie under each arm."

—Fairbanks graffito

Chapter Twenty-six

Larry woke up at noon the following day feeling surprisingly fit, considering the night he had been through. His memories of the end of the night were vague, but he did remember some sexy fumbling with Ruby on the front seat of the Mustang. He reached for the phone and then realized too late that he had not taken the phone number of Bill and Angie Belson. He looked in his wallet and took out the card with Deirdre's number on it. He tried both the office and her home. It was Sunday, so, if she were in town, she would most certainly be home. But there was no answer at either place. He got a busy signal a couple of times on Deirdre's home number, but that always happened in the Fairbanks. The busy signal had become known as "the song of Fairbanks."

Lazily he showered and shaved, wondering how he would get in touch with Ruby. Then he remembered something about a pig roast—was it "Arnold" or "Herman" the pig? And where and when was it? One o'clock, he remembered it was someplace that had burned down. He went down to the bar of the Chena View where a tough-looking brunette in leotards was tending the bar. There were about a dozen pipeliners there, already well started on their Sunday observance. A couple of them were still wearing their hard-hats, as though they were afraid the ceilings would fall in.

"Hey, Shirley," said a red-faced man to the barmaid, "you know, if you was a blond, you'd be a *dumb* blond? Whoever heard of putting a cherry in a Martini, for christ sake!"

"Well, we were out of olives," Shirley said petulantly.

Larry had a Bloody Mary, with plenty of tabasco to clear away the morning fog.

"Shirley, do you know someplace, some big dance hall or bar that burned down recently?"

"Gee, I don't know. I've only been here a week."

"I think you're talking about the Rendezvous," a curly haired kid in a Bechtel T-shirt said. "Part of it burned down a couple of weeks ago. Its out on the Steese Highway. You can't miss it, it's where the Farmer's Loop joins the highway. A big purple building."

After some searching, Larry found the Mustang parked about two feet from the curb, on First avenue, near the river. There was a drunk Indian lying on the sidewalk, his head cushioned on a pint bottle of Thunderbird. As Larry stepped over him, the Indian waved his arm in a gracious gesture. "Pass, stranger," he said.

Larry drove down First Avenue, past the Cushman Street bridge and the big log structure that was the Chamber of Commerce headquarters. There was a little parking area next to the Chamber of Commerce and a sign that said, "Parking for Chamber of Commerce Only," over some garbage cans. Seated on the garbage cans were an Eskimo and a blond, curly-haired man with a seamed and filthy face. They were solemnly passing a bottle of C.B. back and forth between them.

A typical Sunday morning in Fairbanks, Larry

303

thought. There was still a little cotton floating around inside Larry's skull, and he missed the turn on Noble Street, which would have brought him to the Steese Highway Bridge. Instead, he followed First Avenue to Clay where it bordered the Chena and had to double back to the left past a cluster of log homes, one of which sheltered a second-hand store brightly proclaimed on a sign cut from the top of an oil drum.

The road led out of town past the Teamsters Hiring Hall on the far side of the river. At about Mile Marker 5 the highway broke out of the ramshackle suburb into an open, level stretch, with brilliant fireweed, pink plumes, and mountain marigold bordering the road. At Mile Marker 9 the sharp intersection formed by Farmer's Loop Road and the Steese Highway, there was a large cinderblock building painted a garish shade of lavender. The parking lot was full of campers, Winnebagos, pickups, Volkswagon vans, and yellow Denali trucks. It looked like it was *some* party! Five dollars paid at the door got Larry a ticket entitling him to a full dinner, including a helping of Herman the Pig. Drinks could be had at the bar at regular prices—two dollars a shot.

Inside, the place was as packed as on a Saturday night. A rock group called the Northern Lights was on the stand and the blinds were drawn on any available source of light so that, from the moment you passed through the door, you were in the land of perpetual midnight. To the right there was a u-shaped buffet table. Scotty White, the proprietor, was supervising a crew that was sawing a four hundred pound barbequed pig, its chubby, friendly face nestled in a bed of greens, into manageable fist-sized chunks of pork. On another table was a halibut that was four feet across and about a foot thick. Also available were baked salmon, reindeer sausages, caribou stew, and an assortment of cole slaw, salads, and condiments. Larry filled a tray and looked around for the group. The crowd consisted of town pipeline and construction workers, hookers with their men and, frequently, their children.

He finally found Ruby and the Belsons with their three children at a folding table in the far corner of the room. Ruby looked surprised but pleased to see him, yet she greeted him with a decorous peck on the cheek. With her eyes she signalled toward the Belsons and the children and Larry understood.

"Managed to find your way here, huh Tulsa?" Belson said, his voice still truculent.

Larry grunted and put his tray down. He took a slug of Oly. The pork was spicy and tender; the reindeer sausage was tasty. Larry confined his appetite to these delicacies, and said little.

Belson was sitting with a couple of his driver friends. None of them made any effort to talk to Larry. He made small-talk with the girls, who were more subdued than the day before. Later he had a chance to talk with Ruby when they danced after the heavy lunch.

"What's the matter with *them?*" Larry asked, indicating the group at the table.

"Well, Bill is pissed because Angie's pit crew didn't tighten up the nuts too well on her wheel and now they're going to have about five hundred dollars worth of body work."

"But that's not all, is it?"

"No. They're not too crazy about me having you along. Belson's a friend of my husband Arnold. It's none of his damn business, but he knows Arnold and I haven't had anything to do with each other since we had Florie. It makes him angry anyhow. Besides, I don't think he likes your union."

"Damn it," Larry said, "I don't like it much myself.

A bunch of rednecks, but it's where the money is. I've been apprenticing to be a welder the last few months. They pull twenty-five hundred a week. I'll put up with a lot of rednecks for that kind of dough."

Ruby nodded. She had been around oil-boom Alaska long enough not to be terribly impressed by the size of the salary.

They went up to the bar and had a couple of Bloody Marys. Most of the men were paying for their drinks with brand new hundred dollar bills from folded wads as thick as a hotel Bible. It was considered tacky to spend soiled or mussed up hundreds.

One man bought a round for the entire bar with three hundred dollars in small bills. "I won 'em last night," he told them, "playing Monopoly with real money. Great game;"

The barmaid, a sweet-faced forty year old blond with hair like brass lathe turnings, stuffed the money into the register. "Goddamn show-off Texan," she muttered, ringing up the round.

"Hey, Sweetie," the Monopoly player said, whistling through his teeth, "come here."

Resignedly, the barmaid returned to his place at the counter.

"Here, take these," the Monopoly player said as he grabbed up another hand of tens and twenties and stuffed them into the front of her Vee necked knit blouse. She had an ample chest but there must have been room for sixty or seventy dollars in bills.

Larry wondered if the low-cut blouse was designed to encourage tips in the cleavage. He laid a hundred on the bar and bought a round for the table, including three Shirley Temples for the kids. "Keep the change, blondie."

"Thanks, buster."

"You going to be in Fairbanks long?" Larry asked as they wove their way back to the table.

"Depends," Ruby said.

Larry felt a warm glow in his groin. To hell with Deirdre.

Back at the table, Belson and his cronies accepted the round without comment. Angie, who was beginning to feel herself again after a few Bloody Marys, smiled and toasted Larry. "Here's to you, Tulsa," she said.

"Goddamn it, my name ain't Tulsa. And I'm not *from* Tulsa," Larry said. "If you want to be insulting you can at least call me Tex." But his voice was easy, and Angie took no offense.

Larry was finishing his dessert when the bikers started sifting in. There were eight of them, a square-set, hairy, scabrous-looking crew. Their shiny black leather jackets hung open in the steamy room. All of them wore or carried black helmets with gold Mercury wings painted on the sides.

Three bikers proceeded directly to the TV set which was against the far wall, not far from where Larry and his group were sitting. The leader, who was bearded, with a heavy paunch overhanging his black garrison belt, switched the set to the baseball game between the Goldpanners and the Glacier Pilots, and turned the volume up loud. He pulled up an iron folding chair, turned its back away from him and straddled it, facing the screen.

Snowbird Eddie, leader of the Northern Lights, was just remounting the bandstand after a short beer break. He looked with irritation toward the group of bikers clustered around the noisy TV.

"Hey, fellah," he remonstrated. "Turn that down, will ya? We're doing another set."

"Up yours," the bearded one said, not bothering to turn around for his answer.

307

"Come on, man," Snowbird Eddie urged. "We can't play with all that fucking noise going on."

The biker turned around lazily. "How'd you like a Quasar TV up your roly-poly ass?"

One of the other bikers was approaching from the bar with a tray filled with beer.

"Explain things to the man," the bearded one said over his shoulder, returning his concentration to the color TV, which showed grainy purple figures playing on a red grass diamond. The beer-bearing biker put his tray of Olys down on a nearby table, sauntered up to the bandstand, grabbed Snowbird Eddie by his scarlet-sequined Eisenhower jacket, and shoved him backwards so that he went sprawling into the spread-out snares, tom-toms and timpani.

· Bill Belson turned around in irritation. "Cut that out, Goddamn it, you motherfuckers! We wanna dance."

"He wants to dance," the bearded one said incredulously. "Ain't he cute?" He reached over and turned the volume even higher.

Belson pushed his chair back, walked past the portly biker, and turned off the TV. The Belson pit crew got to its feet with a harsh sound of scraping chairs. A lanky biker, his face purple and shiny with acne scale, started to approach Belson from his blind side.

Harry Abel, a tall crew cut member of Belson's pit gang stopped him with a punch behind the ear. That pulled the string. The bearded one leaped to his feet and cleared a circle around himself by swinging the iron folding chair he had been sitting on around his head. Two of the bikers began to unstrap chains and garrison belts from their waists. There was the sound of tinkling glass as several onlookers broke off bottles in anticipation of the brawl. Hostility spread through the room like a flashfire, and, suddenly, everybody was in motion. Each table, it seemed, had had its eye on some other group as a target for potential hostility, and when the fight broke out the source of the argument was quickly forgotten.

Teamsters aimed their punches or beer bottles at pipeliners. Townies jumped Teamsters. Eskimos worked off grudges on Indians. The whole cavernous dance hall seemed to break up into a maelstrom of swinging fists, clubbed broken-off chair legs, smashed bottles, chains, belts, and knives. As yet there was no shooting, but Larry knew it would just be a matter of time. He'd been present on such occasions before.

He grabbed for Ruby's hand. "Come on, let's get out of here. We don't need all this shit."

The brassy-haired barmaid reached over and hit the nearest biker with a sawed-off billiard cue, which was kept under the bar. The biker merely shook his head dazedly and then, whirling his helmet around his head, threw it across the bar into the stock of whiskey and cordial bottles, shattering three or four of them and smashing the mirror.

Outside, in the distance, Larry could already hear the sound of approaching police sirens. There was a push-broom standing against the wall, a few feet from the table, and in lieu of a better weapon, Larry grabbed it. and used it to clear a way for himself and Ruby toward the exit door.

He could hear the sound of scattering gravel as police cars, their sirens still screaming, pulled into the parking lot beyond. Larry was too preoccupied with pushing his way through the boisterous, flailing crowd toward the exit to notice a girl in a pale Afro battling her way toward the same doorway. But the girl noticed Larry, and suddenly changed her line of direction, with some effort, against the surging bodies. Sonia—Penny Steele—managed to battle her way against the human stream and head for the far door near the bandstand.

As Larry reached the fire exit, he found his way blocked by a grinning, helmeted Alaskan trooper.

"Take it easy, folks," the trooper said, smiling. "Nobody's going nowheres."

"Every spill that ever comes out is an exception to the industry! This is a standard ploy of the oil industry. If there's any damage, they say, 'well this is atypical, this is a special case.' But we have 10,000 special cases each year."

—Scientist quoted in
Audubon Magazine
May, 1971

Chapter Twenty-seven

Deirdre was lunching with Bobby Baronian and Brent Heywood at the Bear and Seal in the Traveler's Motel. She was beginning to feel a peculiar sense of alliance with these two outcasts from the corporate structure. Sometimes Michael Harrison, the Royal American man, would join them but he was away at Dietrich camp that week.

The second round of cocktails, which they had ordered while they were looking over the menu, arrived. Heywood and Baronian were drinking Martinis on the rocks, but Deirdre confined herself to a less potent Bloody Mary.

"Here's to the first two hundred miles," Baronian said. Solemnly the three Denali employees clicked glasses.

"Just think," Heywood said, "only five years since they said we'd have the job finished, and already we have twenty-five percent of it done!"

"And don't forget," Baronian said, "it's only going to cost ten times as much as they figured. *If* we're lucky. It's a good thing this business is swimming in money. I see that you got that feature into the Denali Reports about 'the most challenging construction effort in history.'"

311

Heywood shrugged modestly. "It was nothing. After all, I'm the editor of the reports."

"Well, they picked it up in the *All-Alaska* today. Gave it a five column spread with a two column cut."

"Yeah," Heywood said, "and they don't even *like* us."

"Well, I don't know," Deirdre said. "I think Tom Snapp likes us all right. Or at least he doesn't mind the pipeline as long as we do it right."

"Yeah, well that sure makes a problem," Heywood said moodily. "You hear about the new oil spill up at Galbraith?"

"You mean the one out of the Dietrich camp?" Deirdre asked.

"That's right. I got a funny feeling," Heywood said, scratching his bulbous forehead, "that one's going to be another spot of trouble."

Baronian roared with laughter. "A spot of trouble! You know how many gallons actually *leaked* up there?"

"I don't know. I'm waiting for a report from Harrison," Heywood said. "Then I guess we'll have to put out some kind of release about how it didn't do any harm, and we've got it confined, and all the usual bullshit."

"Yeah, well, the way I get it there's well over sixty-five thousand gallons that went out of that hole."

Deirdre was appalled. "Sixty-five thousand gallons! How do you know?"

"I was up there the other day," Baronian said. "Nobody would have even have mentioned it, if one of the newsguys hadn't gotten hold of the story."

Deirdre wasn't certain, but she thought she caught the glimmer of a wink. It was hard to see Baronian's eyes behind the fat layered cheekbones.

"If they're leaking this much *now*," Heywood said in despair, "and we don't even have the Goddamn pipeline *working*, you can imagine what's going to happen when we have crude actually going through it."

"How did it happen anyway?" Deirdre asked.

"Well, there was a leak," Baronian said, "in one of the underground diesel fuel lines. I was photographing the bear-lift. I was up there with Vaughn and Mel Buckholtz—you know, the State Fish and Game man."

"Did you get any good shots?" Deirdre asked.

"Oh, sure," Baronian laughed. "You know old sure-shot, always gets his bear. I got some good stuff on film of Buckholtz hitting a big, old yellow grizzly with a tranquilizer and then loading him on the chopper and then releasing him about a hundred and fifty miles away —stuff like that—you know, tagging the ears and everything else. That bear's probably half-way back to camp by now. Those fuckers can really travel, and they've got a homing instinct like a pigeon."

"Well," Deirdre said, "if the men wouldn't keep putting out food for them and everything, they wouldn't hang around the camps."

"Listen," Baronian said reasonably, "the bears are bored and the pipeliners are bored. It gives them all something to do. Those guys are all getting cabin fever up there. The bears are at least some kind of entertainment. You hear that they found one of the little blackies in the shower room down in Valdez in the terminal camp?"

"Yeah," Heywood said, "I had some cute pictures of that. They ran them in the *News-Miner* and the *Anchorage Times.*"

"I wanted to talk to you about that," Deirdre said. "You have to be careful how you release that kind of stuff. Those eco-freaks are ready to jump on anything."

"Well," Heywood said defensively, "I think it got good play and it pointed out that we don't let anybody kill the bears and that we have a policy terminating anyone who gets caught feeding them. Besides," he argued, "you're the one who always says that we have to put out the news as it happens, that we can't sit on it. Otherwise it'll get out anyway, and we'll have to come up with answers."

"Yes," Deirdre sighed, "I've tried to explain that to Daddy, but he's one of those old-line oil men, who figures the less the public knows the better."

"Well, they sure underestimated the power of the public on this one," Heywood said sourly. "Between the conservationists and the Eskimos they've managed to hold up the big, bad oil companies for five years."

"Sometimes," Baronian said, stirring his Martini with a thick finger, "I think it's going to be like the great Pyramid of Cheops. It'll just go on and on and on and on. Endless fuck-ups, endless hold-ups, endless delays."

"Well," Deirdre said. "At least you're getting well paid—the longer the job goes on, the more money you put away. What'll you do if the project is really finished in 1977 like they say it will be?"

"Fat chance," Baronian said. "There'll be something—a labor dispute, a legal hang-up—something, you can count on it. They'll be lucky if they can finish at ten billion. Like now, all of a sudden, we're getting all this sabotage and crime around the camps, union troubles, disgruntled workers, the whole bit. You heard of that bunch of electricians that damn near tore up the whole place at Happy Valley camp the other day. Just over some dumb labor dispute."

"It was about the food, wasn't it?" Deirdre said.

"Well, whatever. What about that Teamster the other day throwing roofing nails all over the parking lot out at Wainwright?"

Deirdre shrugged. "When you've got fifteen thousand

men working away from home, these things are bound to happen."

"What about those stolen x-rays?" Brent Heywood asked. "That's a kind of funny one."

"What happened actually?"

"Well, over at the Delta pipeline camp, somebody broke into the radiology shack, into the x-ray reading room and stole three hundred and fifty-eight x-rays of pipeline welds, and also about fourteen x-rays of VSM's. Nobody can figure out why."

"Maybe they're going to hold them for ransom," Baronian said. "I heard it would take about a half million dollars to reshoot all those x-rays."

The x-rays were taken along each weld of the pipeline and of the welds on the vertical support members, which held much of the pipeline above the permafrost, to insure that no faulty welds would be permitted—welds that might later crack or split, spilling the hot oil content of the pipeline on the ground.

"If they were going to hold them for ransom," Heywood reasoned, "we would have heard from them by now. That doesn't seem likely."

"Then why were they taken?" Deirdre asked.

"I have a theory—or at least I've heard rumors," Heywood said. "Some of the x-ray teams and some of the camp managers who were anxious to make good figures, were concealing x-rays of faulty welds and replacing them with duplicate x-rays of good welds."

"You have any proof of that?" Deirdre asked.

Heywood shrugged. "Just a rumor, and it's not my department anyway."

"Well," Deirdre said, "I know Daddy wants to finish the pipeline on time, but I don't think that he would approve anything like that."

"It doesn't come from up above," Heywood said. "It's just ambitious or crooked sub-contractors on the lower levels who are anxious to get through with the least amount of trouble. The same as all those small leaks they are always trying to cover up, until somebody finds out."

"Certainly Denali is anxious to finish the project on time."

"Denali may be," Baronian said, "but there's plenty of people working on the pipeline who don't give a rat's ass *when* they get it done. They'd be happy to keep working until the year 2000 at these rates." Heywood waved at the waiter for another Martini.

"Don't you guys ever feel like opening up and telling everything you know? Blasting the whole deal?"

"I don't see *you* doing so much for the 'cause' lately," Heywood said defensively. It was an inner circle joke among the three maverick Denali employees, all of whom were becoming embittered by the endless lies, corruption, and inefficiency they were witness to but could not always report on.

"Hell," Baronian said, "I'm no revolutionary. I got thousands of dollars of terrific equipment from Denali —I'm shooting miles and miles of film—learning more about Arctic nature photography than anybody ever knew. I'm satisfied. And besides, I . . ."

"Besides what?" Deirdre asked.

"Besides nothing," Baronian said, burying his face in the drink.

"Besides," Baronian continued, when he had finished swallowing his words, "you are not exactly the great crusading journalist you once were yourself, Heywood. One could even say that you've sold out to big business."

Heywood looked hurt. "Somebody's got to do the job. And better somebody who tries to handle the material honestly . . ."

"Don't give me that line of bullshit," Baronian said. "You're a whore, all of us are whores. If you'll excuse the expression M'am." He had turned to Deirdre. "Only figuratively speaking."

The food arrived and the waitress, a sunny, freckle-faced girl from Sioux Falls, Iowa, whose husband was a bullcook at Sheep Creek camp down at the southern end of the line, made a big show of unscrewing the top of a bottle of California wine and pouring a few drops for Heywood to taste.

"Pour the wine, Goddamn it," Heywood said irritably.

"That's how they *taught* me to do it," the freckle-faced girl said contritely. "You're supposed to taste it and see if it's got cork."

"For heaven's sake, it's got a screw-cap with a wax-lined inside, so how can it be corked?" Heywood said in disgust.

"Your Dad is pretty upset about all these leaks, isn't he?" Heywood said to Deirdre as they began to eat.

"Hey," Baronian said, laughing. "Did you see that funny phoney memo old Wilbur put out? I didn't think he had it in him."

There had been so much interior turmoil about leaks of Denali information to the press that Wilbur, in a fit of whimsey, had issued a memorandum warning the staff against further leaks, especially of memo number M404. M404, as it turned out, was a non-existent memo. Wilbur's idea was that the spy would go bananas trying to find it, but instead the mock memo itself was leaked along with a complete explanation of its purpose. It had appeared in Xerox form on bulletin boards in most of the administrative offices of Denali by the day following its issuance. Fortunately, Wilbur Steele never got to hear about that, so he could enjoy his little joke in peace.

"Hey," Baronian said, stuffing his cheeks with the turbot, "I ran into that good old Texas boy, Larry

Steele, down at the Elbow Room last night. You still seeing him?"

Deirdre blushed and looked confused. She busied herself stirring around the morsels of Crab Louis left on her plate. Heywood looked at her with sympathy.

"I . . . I'm not seeing him so often anymore."

"You seeing him this week?" Baronian asked.

"Not this week."

"Seems like a nice guy," Baronian said, "considering he's the boss's son. How many people you figure know that?"

"Not many," Deirdre said. "He doesn't talk about it. And not that many people up here actually know Wilbur."

"Yeah," Baronian said, "but they know who he is, all right. How come Larry isn't working at some better job? He told me he was learning to be a welder now, but hell, even that doesn't pay anything like the kind of work he could be doing for his old man."

"He never liked office work," Deirdre said. "He's more of a doer than a thinker. I guess he's always avoided intellectual challenges or emotional problems. He likes to model himself on his Grandpa Bisset, who was a wildcatter in East Texas in the old days."

"Boy," Baronian said, laughing, "can you imagine old Wilbur all touted out in greasy coveralls, working the string on some well up in the slope?"

The image of the dapper Wilbur Steele with so much as a dab of petroleum on his patrician nose was incongruous enough to bring guffaws from all of them.

"But seriously," Baronian continued, "if I were in the business of putting out news, I know one thing that would be the biggest Goddamn scoop yet. But we're not about to put it out."

"What's that," Deirdre asked.

Baronian, who was out in the camps, up and down the line two out of three weeks, was an excellent source of information much of which didn't reach her from official sources until weeks after she had learned it from the big, hairy photographer.

"That pipeline route. The one through the Atigun Canyon that your boyfriend Michael has been complaining about all this time?"

"What about it?"

"It was rerouted more than a year ago. It's running about thirty miles away from the original route—down around the south end of Galbraith Lake and rejoining the original pipeline route below the Dietrich camp. But if you look at the maps of the pipeline route you'll never see it on them."

"Why is that? Wait, don't tell me, I think I know. EPA, right?"

"Right," Baronian said. "They changed the route, but they never told the EPA. It would have cost millions to do a new feasibility study and a new impact study on the route, so they're just going to go ahead and do it, and if the EPA ever finds out and squawks, they'll just fight it out in the courts. It'll be cheaper and besides, by that time, if there was any ecological damage involved, it would already be done."

"But they're taking a terrible chance aren't they? If the news ever gets out, it could really put a big crimp in the schedule."

"To a shower of gold, most things are penetrable," Heywood said, in an oracular fashion. "That's Thomas Carlyle."

"That's funny," Baronian said, "I could have sworn it was Wilbur Steele." He turned dramatically toward Deirdre. "You're not going to defend him again, are you? Or are you giving up on that gambit?"

Deirdre mopped up the red Crab Louis sauce with a piece of roll and said nothing.

"I notice you have less and less to say about what a great guy he is these days," Baronian said.

Deirdre blushed, which was strange. She was not normally a wilting southern belle.

"Leave her alone," Heywood said protectively. "You're embarrassing her. Don't forget, Steele's practically a relative."

Baronian finished his wine in three swallows and looked at his watch. "Well, I'd better be going. I have a meeting to attend to at three o'clock."

Heywood looked up in surprise. "A meeting? I don't know about any meeting. I was planning . . ."

"No, no," Baronian said. "Never mind, it's just a . . . a meeting. A private meeting."

"Can I give you a lift?" Deirdre asked. "I've got the car and I'm going back to Wainwright to pick up some things."

"No, no," Baronian said. "Somebody's picking me up."

The whole thing sounded peculiar; Deirdre wondered who "somebody" was. It was not like Baronian to be so secretive about his activities.

"I have to go too," Heywood said. "But I'll just walk downtown. I'm meeting a friend at the Polaris. And I think the walk will do me good. I'm getting a little tummy there," he said, patting his flat, almost-concave sternum.

"Then, I guess we're all going different ways," Deirdre said, "I'll see you all later."

She went through the long corridor and out the rear entrance to the parking lot where she climbed into the yellow company car for the short drive back to Denali headquarters.

Baronian went out through the main lobby of the

Traveler's Lodge and out the front entrance where a man with dark liquid eyes and long black hair was waiting for him in a Ford Bronco. The man reached over and threw open the door of the vehicle and Baronian climbed in.

"Well," Baronian said, cheerfully expansive under the influence of the three Martinis and the bottle of white wine, "how's it going, Abby? The troops all assembled down in the junk shop of yours?"

Abby Maroon grimaced at the reference to his establishment, which he preferred to think of as a recycling center.

"Everybody's there," he said. "You got the envelope?"

"Right here," Baronian said, patting his breast pocket. "I'll give it to you later."

Maroon threw the Bronco into gear and drove off down Noble Street toward the Chena.

Back in the Traveler's Lodge, Brent Heywood was at the pay phone in the lobby. He called the Polaris Hotel and asked for room 943. A sleepy voice answered.

"Is that you, Gill?" he said softly. "Are you awake? It's three o'clock."

"Yeah, yeah," the voice said. "I'm awake. I had to get up to answer the phone anyway. Where are you?"

"I'm at the Traveler's. I can be down there in a few minutes."

"Well, hurry," the voice said. "I've been waiting for you all day. All shaved and showered and pretty as a picture."

"Well, just stay where you are," Heywood said, his face pink and flushed with excitement. "I'll run all the way."

Deirdre, when she returned to the Denali office, stopped only long enough to pick up her messages, return a few calls, and freshen her makeup. Then she went downstairs, climbed back into the company car, and drove back in the direction of her apartment in the residential district behind the Traveler's Lodge.

Sitting in his usual spot in the red upholstered, wingback chair when she let herself into the apartment was Wilbur Steele, sipping a Virginia Gentleman on the rocks and reading the Fairbanks *News-Miner*. The color of the red silk dressing gown he was wearing with the W-bar-S monogram over the right pocket blended so subtly with the chair's upholstery that he looked for the moment as though he was part of the apartment's decor. He glanced with irritation at his Phillipe Patek watch as Deirdre let herself in.

"You're eight minutes late."

Deirdre stood there in the doorway unbuckling her raincoat. *"I wonder,"* she thought, *"if I'll ever be able to break free."* But aloud she said, "I'm sorry. There were some calls I had to take care of."

"In times of revolution, just wars, and wars of liberation, I love the angels of destruction and disorder—as opposed to the devils of conservation and law and order."

—Eldridge Cleaver
1969

Chapter Twenty-eight

Sonia's plan to stop the pipeline by sabotage was beginning to take form. Members of the SHAMAN group had worked at almost every camp from Prudhoe Bay down to the terminal in Valdez. Takolik had worked as a security guard in most of the camps in the north, where NANA controlled the security. Eli Hurwood had been in the Culinary Union for over a year and had worked largely as bullcook up and down the line. Marge had started as bullcook but was now a warehouse man, and also had worked in most of the camps, as had Ernie Mason as a general laborer in the Laborer's Union. They had managed to obtain membership in most of the open unions, but had had less success with the Tulsa pipeliners, the pipe-fitters, the electricians, the plumbers, and other craft unions.

Gradually, sometimes by purchase and sometimes by stealing from the camps, they were acquiring the necessary arsenal of tools and weapons.

Financing had not been a problem despite the heavy expenses of operating out of Fairbanks. Members of the group were all making good money and whenever serious expenses were involved, Abby Maroon could be counted on to dip into some limitless pool of financial assistance. Baronian was a big help in supplying money, company documents, diagrams, and photos of the various installations.

At times it was hard to keep the group in control. Eli Hurwood wanted to make it into a people's crusade and promised he could compose an appropriate folk song ("A Virgin that's Been Pipelined Ain't a Virgin Anymore." and "Tarry, Tarry Night" were two of his suggestions). He was hurt when Sonia explained to him that what they were organizing was a People's Revolutionary Action Cell and not a world revolution. Marge was in favor of a PLO-type terrorist approach, having found all sorts of security loop-holes suitable to sabotage. Both Marge and Sonia had learned back in Seattle how to make terrorist-type anti-personnel bombs in the style of the Vietcong's Major Zen Lanh, from whom they learned how to pack explosives into bicycles, water tanks, lady's handbags, vegetables, and special bricks. In the movement they had learned to make small bombs from readily obtained materials, like sugar and sodium nitrate and sulfur, powdered aluminum, match heads, toy caps, Coke bottles filled with an assortment of tacks, nuts, bolts and Beebee pellets, as well as gun powder easily purchased from sporting shops for the purpose of allegedly reloading shotgun shells.

They would purchase hundred-pound sacks of fertilizer containing nitrate, then they would take the bag out to some of the deserted gold mine areas north of Fairbanks and spend hours drying it slowly in a makeshift oven. When it was dry they would mix it carefully with diesel fuel and load it into gallon jars. A powder monkey, whom Marge had befriended in Valdez, introduced the pair to detonator timing devices. He also loaned Marge a book—a Government manual—on bombing and the girls had brought several copies of the *Bomber's Handbook* up with them from Seattle. For practice, Marge and Sonia would drive out to the mountains every week or so and blow up rocks and old structures with homemade fuses and detonators. These occasions always excited Marge. "Look, Sonia," she'd say, "We've got the equipment and we've got the know-how. When do we start blowing a few things up and show these motherfuckers a little action?"

"Don't you see," Sonia said to her patiently, "those are terrorist and anti-personnel weapons. They can raise hell, they can kill or maim a few people, but they can't stop the pipeline, and that's what our real goal is.

"The attacks could focus attention on the problem the way the IRA and the PLO have," the more aggressive Marge replied.

"That's okay for them. They have large nationalist groups to fall back on," Sonia explained. "In our case, even the anti-pipeline people, the eco-freaks, the preservationists and the conservationists, would be put off by this approach. Frankly, it would be counter-productive."

The meeting took place during one of the morning talk-ins. Coffee and Cokes were the only beverages served. Pot and booze were strictly *verboten,* but the meetings were informal, and anyone could chime in. In this case, the meeting consisted only of Marge, Sonia, Ernie Mason—the poetic munchkin—and Eli Hurwood—the Brooklyn cowboy.

"Well, when are we going to get into action?" Mason asked. He'd been quiet all this time, and had enjoyed making the money, but now he was getting restless. If they weren't going to do anything, he would like to go out and spend some of it.

"We have to wait," Sonia explained, "until the pipeline is really ready to go. The more work they put into it, the more we can destroy. If we hit it too early, it will just give them more time to put on men and try to patch up the damage."

The group had acquired a small store of automatic weapons—Vietnamese type M-16's, some AK 47's, and a few Thompsons. Occasionally, to keep up the revolutionary spirit, they had driven—in the high-axled International Travelall van which Sonia had acquired out of SHAMAN funds as the official vehicle —to the abandoned gold mines to the north of Fairbanks for instructions in automatic weapons and target practice. But Sonia was not anxious for the group to end up in some flaming shoot-out, like Patty Hearst's SLA mob. Unlike most radical lefters, Sonia was able to concentrate all of her fury and energy on one goal— the destruction of Wilbur Steele's pipeline. At least, that was the way she thought of it—as Wilbur Steele's personal project.

She had been upset at first when she spotted Larry at the big donnybrook in the Rendezvous club. Since then she had tried to stay away from the big dance-hall type places that Larry would probably frequent. At any rate, he was never known to come around the Flame Lounge. But to lessen the possibility of being spotted by him, Sonia had changed to a short black wig in curly ringlets, which in any event most people felt was more becoming to her than the pale Afro.

Even if he *did* find her, she doubted that he would say anything to Wilbur about it. On the other hand, she was also certain that Larry would give no support to the SHAMAN movement. He was much too establishment for that. After all, he had served in Vietnam without protesting, hadn't he? Even though later on he bitched a lot about the war and the uselessness of it. In any event, up to now she was wanted only on some rinky-dink fugitive charge to avoid prosecution in Seattle. Right now, even if she were caught and had to face trial, they probably wouldn't be able to find the witnesses to prosecute. So she felt reasonably safe about Larry. Once in a while she even thought of writing him a letter anonymously and arranging for a drop to get answers from him, but it was too risky.

Several times, members of the group had seen him but it would only be by coincidence that his name was mentioned, since nobody but Marge knew who Sonia really was.

There was only one important logistical need to complete the SHAMAN arsenal and that was plastic explosive material. Conferring with Baronian, who had served in the Korean War, Sonia had become certain that the type of sabotage needed to implement her plan would involve very specifically placed charges. Just lobbing a couple of dynamite sticks into a power house could prove abortive, and either fail to stop the generators or do so little damage that they could be quickly repaired. The generators and the alternate generators—the entire supply of power in the pumping station—would have to be stopped for at least twenty-four hours or longer for the plan to work effectively. This would require precision demolition rather than aimless bombing. It was Baronian too who supplied the clue as to where the plastic explosives could be found.

Although he ranged up and down the pipeline, and into the areas between the camps, in the course of his work, Baronian was based at Denali headquarters, which was located on the leased area of Fort Wainwright, only a mile or so behind Abby Maroon's shop along the Chena River. There was a chain-link fence but not much security between Denali headquarters and the rest of Fort Wainwright. Denali's trucks frequently used the camp itself for auxiliary parking space on an informal arrangement.

Baronian was friendly with some of the National Guardsmen who were pulling their active duty at the

Wainwright camp and he'd acquired a diagram of the camp, which he showed to Marge.

"There's a Quonset hut right here," he said, putting an *X* on the diagram at a point several hundred yards inside the fence that separated the Denali compound from Fort Wainwright.

"That's the munitions dump, where they keep the plastic explosives. You could also get some ammo there if you need it."

Sonia studied the diagram thoughtfully. "No, I don't want to take too much. It would simply be harder to get out. We've picked up plenty of ammo through the years, and we haven't used much of it. We've got enough guns and they're in good shape. We've even got a couple of grenades and some landmines, although I'm not sure what we're going to do with them."

"How much of the explosive will we need?" Marge asked.

Baronian shrugged his shoulders. "Hell, with fifty or a hundred pounds, you could blow up the Polaris Building."

"Good," Sonia said. "That means we could have a team of four and load twenty-five pounds in each knapsack, right?"

Baronian nodded in agreement. "That'd be a good way—then you could have your hands free for your weapons in case there was any trouble. But I don't think there will be. Security is pretty easy on the post now that the war protests have stopped. They just have a couple of those old guard boys, with M-1's, not even automatics. I've watched them with glasses from Denali and in the daytime anyway they don't check by more often than every ten minutes. At night, it might be less, but I haven't had a chance to watch."

"How do we get in?" Sonia asked.

They were discussing this in the middle of the Cushman Street bridge, over the Chena River, watching the swirling muddy waters sweep under the bridge's trusses. It was a spot chosen by Sonia for security reasons. She was reasonably sure that nobody had infiltrated the SHAMAN group, and she didn't think that Maroon's compound was under observance, but so many bugs and taps had been placed in various spots in the past by the FBI that Sonia took no chances.

"Will we have any trouble getting in?"

Baronian shook his head negatively. "There's nothing but the chain link fence between Denali and the Fort. That's even open in the daylight sometimes but there's usually a guard on the gates. You could try to rig up some phony passes, but you'd be better off doing it at night. Just get some bolt-cutters and cut the chain links. There's lots of places that are far enough away from the guards that you could work without being noticed, and if you cut it carefully, even if a guard comes by he won't see that the links have been cut."

"What about the door of the Quonset? How is that secured?"

"As far as I can determine, it's just a big old heavy-duty padlock. You might be able to crack it with a big bolt-cutter or a sledge-hammer, or maybe just a hacksaw. I think a battery-operated electric hacksaw ought to do the job. I saw some up in J.C. Penney's only the other day."

"Who'd you serve your apprenticeship with? Willy Sutton?" Sonia asked, somewhat surprised at the depth of Baronian's technical knowledge.

"I've been around."

It took a while to organize the right team, since it was not always possible to coordinate the R & R of the various members. Sonia tried to assemble a group that would be reliable and not likely to panic. She knew she could depend on Marge. Van Taylor would have been ideal, but had been unable to get away. Finally she settled on Takolik and Ernie Mason as the other members of the attack team.

Ernie Mason was digging containment ditches at Pump Station Eight. He could manage to take a sick day and get in whenever the schedule called for it. Marge had completed a dispatch to Sheep Creek camp. She simply wouldn't go back to the hiring hall until the Wainwright project was finished. So they arranged the assault schedule around Takolik's R & R, which was in the week from July 14 to the 21st. Marge assembled the necessary equipment in advance. Ski masks were no problem, since everybody wore them in the winter. There were half a dozen extra olive green Army surplus masks in the closet that had been acquired from Big Ray's Surplus store on Two street. From Big Ray's Marge also acquired, in the weeks before the operation, several cheap rucksacks, each capable of carrying twenty-five pounds of the plastic, which was extremely stable until a detonator cap was attached. Nothing there to attract attention, since everybody in Fairbanks owned a rucksack or two.

For weapons, Sonia chose to equip all four with the M-16's. They were the lightest for their fire power and there was plenty of ammunition for them. The Russian Kalashnikov, the AK-47's all had limited ammunition supplies.

July 16, 1975—a Wednesday—was picked as "D" day. But then, remembering Pearl Harbor, and the traditional inattention of military guards on Sundays, Sonia switched the date to July 20. It was a little risky, because it was almost the end of Takolik's R & R and by that time, frequently, he was so boozed up that he was useless. But Sonia was sure that she could keep him under control with sex, if no other way.

At that time of year, the sun was out at almost all

hours of the day, but it was decided that the best time to move would be at one a.m. to two a.m.—when there was an hour or so of dusk during which forms in an open field would be hard to make out. Between the fence and the Quonset hut there was not much cover. There was a slight rolling ridge about a hundred yards from the fence that they could make in one dash, out of view of the guard. They could lay there and peer over the top of the ridge until the guard was out of sight, and then make the shelter of the hut in another two-hundred yard dash before he returned.

Sonia had cut a small inconspicous corner of the fence away a week or so before the operation and had checked the timing of the guards and the visibility of the Quonset. They had a good ten minutes to get to the hut, break open the lock, and get inside.

She had watched for several hours and had never seen the guards bother to open the door of the explosives dump. So if they could get inside they would be free to find the plastics, load them into their knapsacks, and time their departure for the next passage of the guard. There was no question that this would be the best time for the raid. In the winter, the tracks in the snow would give them away too easily, and in the early spring there was always mud. But by mid-July, the ground was fairly firm underfoot. Possibly they could have waited until September, but Sonia sensed that the team was getting restless and was anxious for some action. The plastic explosives raid would be a good project to keep them on edge and see how they acted under pressure.

Sonia had the group assemble at ten o'clock. There wasn't that much to go over, but she wanted to have them in control long enough before the mission so that she was certain that none of them were stoned on grass or booze—particularly Ernie or Takolik. She liked grass as well as the next one, but she was convinced that it threw off the timing and gave people a "don't-give-a-fuck" attitude that could be dangerous. Takolik, in fact, had had a few beers and was looking a little woozie. She had made him take a nap until midnight. At midnight she distributed Ritalin to each of the team members. It was a mild upper that would not distort their perceptions. However, she hoped it would keep them just edgy enough to be a bit more efficient.

It was a rag-tag army at best, and any edge would help.

Takolik did not like the M-16. He was used to the heavier Springfield and M-1 rifles, but Sonia explained that at the short distances at which they would probably be operating, the superior fire power and lightness of the M-16 would be preferrable. She distributed a half a dozen of the straight ammunition clips to each member of the team, and in addition, two Army fragmentation grenades each.

Marge strutted, sported and toyed with her weapons like a twelve year old boy playing soldier. Takolik checked everything out in a serious, professional way. Ernie Mason just looked scared and Sonia was afraid he might be the weak link in the team—but he was all she had at the moment. Of course, they could operate with three people and take about thirty-five pounds apiece. But suppose somebody were injured? Running with fifty-pounds of explosives would be a problem, and she wasn't sure what would happen if a bullet hit the plastic.

The uniform of the day was olive drab military surplus light knitted sweaters and green camouflage pants. Sonia knew that in the movies, black was preferred for commando raids, but in the dim half-light of Arctic summer nights, she deemed that the green and broken-up patterns of the camouflage pants would be harder

332

to see. Mosquitoes would be a problem too, once they got out in the field. They were not too bad in the city itself, but in any open field, where there was vegetation, they could be murder—bad enough to create a serious problem. She made each of them spray their wrists, necks and all exposed portions of their bodies with Cutter's mosquito repellent.

"We're really going to sweat in these outfits," Marge said. "It's eighty degrees out there."

"That was earlier," Sonia pointed out. "With the sun down low, it'll probably be sixty-five when we go, so it won't be too hot. As for the mosquitoes, we'll just have to bear up. But whatever you do, don't slap. That's one sound you can hear a mile away on a quiet night."

"Listen, we ought to train a few mosquitoes to fly in there with knapsacks. Those motherfuckers could carry out fifty pounds of explosives without any trouble."

"Yeah," Sonia said, "but we don't know whose *side* they're on."

At one o'clock, the group assembled in the International Travelall. They were tense and keyed up; the Ritalin was taking effect, making them all a bit more talkative than usual.

"This reminds me of 'Guns of the Navarone,' " Ernie Mason said, running his fingers through the eye-holes of the ski mask which he was holding in his hand.

"Takolik, you're playing Tony Quinn."

Sonia, who was at the wheel of the Travelall, turned around irritably. "Shut up you guys. Just think about the job, and for Christ sake, don't think about pulling any movie-type heroics."

"There aren't any Eskimo-type movie heroes anyway," Takolik said.

"Oh, yeah? What about Nanook of the North?" Ernie replied.

"Never heard of him" Takolik said. His face was

grim and concentrated and he was the only one who didn't seem hyped up by the Ritalin, or else he controlled it very well. His black eyes, however, snapped with some inner electricity that was not usually visible in their opaque and troubled depths.

In addition to their weapons, the group carried two battery operated saber-saws with hacksaw blades in their chucks, a heavy and a light bolt-cutter, and small flashlights for work inside the Quonset hut. The bolt-cutters had been stolen by Ernie from the tool room at Pump Station Eight and they had already decided that if they were too loaded down with the explosives, they would leave the cutters behind, since they would be almost impossible to trace. The saber-saws were standard Black and Decker models—very common—and had been bought separately by Abby Maroon and Marge at J.C. Penney's big new store in Fairbanks. It was unlikely that they would be traced either.

Sonia provided each of the team with a pair of brown rubber gloves of the type sold in five and dime stores for dish washing. Ernie Mason had no trouble slipping into them, but Takolik's square hands and thick fingers would not fit. So he substituted a pair of cotton work gloves.

"These things are really awkward," Marge complained. "It's hard to work in them."

"Well, it's mainly a precaution for when we're working in the dump itself. We don't want to leave any fingerprints there. Don't forget—the fingerprints of all of you are on record, with Denali, and the cops have mine."

All of them, except Sonia, had Denali I.D. cards, and Baronian had supplied Sonia with a phony headquarters badge. Sonia drove the Travelall to the rear parking lot of the Traveler's Lodge and parked it. There was a crew-cab yellow Denali pickup truck in the next spot and Sonia indicated that they should all climb into it

334

and put on the yellow hardhats that were on the seat. The key to the truck was, as Baronian had told her it would be, under the rubber floormat.

"What's the idea of changing trucks?" Ernie asked.

"There's a guard at the gate of the Denali parking lot. He doesn't pay much attention, but it's a lot easier to get in in a company truck. Besides somebody might see the Travelall and connect us to it. If we get in trouble, we can always ditch this and run for it."

Takolik looked to Sonia with appreciation. "You've really thought this out, haven't you?"

As the actual moment approached Sonia's eyes also began to glitter with concentration and a deep fanatic gleam, much as Takolik's did.

"Right now, I'm living only for one thing—that's to stop that pipeline. Nothing else counts."

"Mercy was a thing reserved for gentler climes."

—Jack London
Call Of The Wild

Chapter Twenty-nine

The guard at the Denali gate, an Athabascan Indian named Melvin, was known to Takolik from the Savoy Bar. As he saw the truck approaching, Melvin casually hid the can of Colt 45 from which he was drinking behind a pile of reports and stepped out of the guard's booth. Seeing the company truck and the hard hats and perhaps vaguely recognizing Takolik, he waved them lazily into the Denali compound.

Marge, who had been holding her M-16 tensely in her lap, breathed a sigh of relief. "Well, that's step one."

"Take it easy, Marge," Sonia said.

There were a few lights on in the upper offices of Denali—probably cleaning women—but nobody moving around in the parking lot and only a few scattered cars parked there. Sonia drove to the far end of the lot where she'd already cut a small patch in the fence for her reconnaisance. As they drove, the four members of the assault team quickly donned the Army surplus ski masks.

Ernie couldn't resist a giggle at their appearance. "You cats sure look *wild!*"

336

"What do you think you look like, Masked Man," Sonia asked, "the Hooded Rider of the Plains?"

Then turning to the group, she said, "Now simmer down everybody." Her voice came out strangely muffled from behind the knitted mask. Already it was beginning to feel hot and itchy.

"Okay," she said, "this is it. If we play our cards right, we'll get into the hut on the first pass by the guard, load the sacks, wait for him to pass the second time, then make a dash for this fence. Keep low. If you've got anything on you that jingles, leave it behind. Ernie, put that *ankh* of yours in the glove compartment until we get back. Takolik, let me have that identification bracelet."

Reluctantly, the two men handed over their jewelry. Marge, forewarned, had worn none, and Sonia never did.

"If we play this right, we should be back in the truck in twenty minutes, in the Traveler's parking lot and make the switch in five more minutes, and home in a half hour with the stuff. Let's not have any fuck-ups, and everybody stay cool. Takolik, you handle the bolt-cutters, Ernie you pull the fence so he can get at the links."

Wordlessly, Takolik took the lighter of the two bolt-cutters from the back of the truck. Marge took the heavier one and walked behind him. The moment they got out of the truck they were hit by a swarm of brown bombers. Ernie muttered as one apparently found an opening in the thin knitted material and raised a hand to slap it, but Sonia grabbed his arm before he could complete the gesture. She put her mouth close to his ear.

"Cut that out," she whispered, "you can hear a slap a mile away."

337

"Christ! These things are crawling into every open-ing. And there's black flies too," Ernie complained.

"Look, we only have to put up with it for twenty minutes. Did you use the repellent?"

"Shit, they eat that stuff for breakfast."

"Well," she said, "ignore the males. Only the females bite, you know."

She turned from Ernie to the group and signalled to them to get down on the ground. Then again, signalling to them with her hand to stay, she wriggled up to the top of the hummock, from which she could see the guard patrol and the isolated Quonset hut. The guard, a short, stocky figure, came mooning along in about one minute holding his M-1 loosely and looking vacantly at the fiery display of the midnight sun. Every once in a while, he'd slap angrily at one of the mosquitoes or black flies that swarmed around him. There was a square hanger-like garage for heavy machinery about a hundred yards from the Quonset hut. According to the information Baronian had given to Sonia, this was where the guards hung out between tours. The guard made the corner of the garage in about a minute and disappeared. Silently, Sonia signalled to the group and, making only the muffled rustling sound of friction-whipped clothing, they trotted quickly across the bare ground and tufts of grass to the hut.

The lock on the door was a huge brass affair with a shackle that was at least a half inch thick. But the iron loop that held it was only a quarter inch and there was no need to resort to the noisy, motorized hacksaws. The large bolt-cutter, wielded by Marge, snapped it with an alarming "ping" in one stroke.

Quickly, Sonia disengaged the lock from the hasp, opened the door, and motioned the others in. Three silent figures entered, taking their small flashlights from their pockets to illuminate the interior. Sonia entered

338

last, replacing the lock in the hasp so it looked as though it was still fastening the door, and closed the door behind her. Dim light from the fading sun filtered through a few pinholes in the metal Quonset hut exterior. Sonia surveyed the holes and quickly found one from which she could spot an approaching guard. Takolik seemed familiar with the layout and quickly found the row of metal shelves on which the tin boxes of plastic explosives were aligned. They were in five pound units. Sonia, her eye glued to the peephole, felt an especially sharp sting as one of the bigger female mosquitoes drove her blood-sucking proboscis through the tender skin under her eye. Still looking through the hole, she stripped off her right glove so that she could put a finger in and crush the intruder. The mosquito was so busy sucking blood and so confined by the woolen fibers that she was able to find it with her forefinger. As she crushed it she could feel the small load of blood tickling down her cheek.

Takolik slid the boxes of explosives from the shelves, assigning five of the olive drab tins labelled "Danger, Plastic Explosives" to each of the knapsacks. When he was finished he took one of the full knapsacks to Sonia, who was still at the peephole, and exchanged it for her empty knapsack, which he then filled. As predicted, the whole operation had taken no more than five minutes. Sonia, her eyes to the peephole, signaled them all to hunker down and keep quiet. "He's coming back," she whispered. "Stay cool."

She followed the ambling walk of the nonchalant guard as he strolled from the garage, yawning and finishing the remnants of what apparently was a doughnut. The guard walked sleepily to the western side of the chain link fence, about four hundred yards beyond the Quonset hut, took a disinterested look around, and then strolled listlessly back toward the corrugated tin heavy equipment garage.

As he drew abreast of the Quonset hut, he stopped and began to slap at mosquitoes. Then he knelt to tie the laces on his canvas and leather Vietnam-style jump boots. As he did so a small brown field rabbit broke from some unseen hollow in the grasses and hopped off nervously toward the Quonset hut.

The guard was very close. He was an amiable-looking round faced Eskimo—possibly an Aleut. If he had had fur around his head, he would have looked just like the figures that used to sell Eskimo pies. He smiled as he watched the rabbit skitter to safety, and half-whispered to him, "Hop away, you little son of a bitch. I'll get you one of these days."

The rabbit jumped into a burrow hole, somewhere near the shaded entrance of the hut, and Sonia watched nervously as the stocky little figure of the guard shambled in indifferent pursuit.

"Hey, where'd you get to, little fellow?" he called out curiously. By now he was on the other side of the Quonset hut wall, close enough that Sonia could smell his G.I. style insect repellent. He looked at the ground where the rabbit had disappeared, shrugged and turned as if to go, and then idly curious, looked back at the door of the Quonset hut. He was too close for Sonia to whisper to the others. She simply held up her hands in a gesture that she hoped indicated "tension" or at least seemed to communicate it, because the other three now gripped their rifles tightly and assumed taut, expectant postures. The Eskimo guard approached the Quonset hut door, examining the broken hasp and the lock. He pulled gently on the lock and, to Sonia's horror, the door swung open, creaking gently. The guard still did not seem alarmed. He looked into the hut curiously.

"Anybody here? Everything okay?"

Then his eyes, quickly growing accustomed to the not quite complete gloom, spotted the shadowy figures in front of him.

"Hey, what are you guys doing . . ."

There were three, flat, slapping sounds as Marge touched the trigger of the M-16, which was on automatic. The stocky guard fell over backwards, dropping his rifle with a clatter to the hard ground. The noise inside the hut, reverberating from the corrugated metal sides, seemed deafening.

"Shit!" Sonia said. "Now you did it. Okay, let's go! Run, you sons of bitches!!"

The four of them burst from the hut and started on the dead run. The tins of explosives clattered dully behind them in their knapsacks as they headed for the cut-out patch of fence leading to the Denali compound. So far there seemed to be no reaction from the garage, but just as they reached the fence there was a sliver of light as someone opened a rear door in the structure.

"Harold, you all right?"

But there was no sound of alarm.

As soundlessly as possible, the four commando raiders slipped under the fence and headed for the Denali truck. Behind them they could see one of the other guards strolling easily toward the Quonset hut, still apparently unalarmed. Perhaps he had not quite identified the sounds. Sonia had the pick-up truck in gear and moving as the door was closing behind Ernie, the last to toss his knapsack in and close the door. As the truck rolled a short distance toward the entry gate, each of the four removed the olive drab ski masks from their sweating heads, now blotchy with mosquito and black fly bites and shiny with sweat.

"Put the hard-hats on," Sonia whispered, "and keep them pulled down over your eyes. She rolled the truck slowly and smoothly up to the sentry hut and paused for a casual wave at the guard, who was busy filling out forms on the small slanted stand-up desk in the hut. The guard barely looked up, and, recognizing the group from their previous entrance, waved them on.

Sonia was through the gate without having even come to a complete stop. Less than five minutes later they were in the Traveler's Lodge parking lot, transferring the knapsacks to the Travelall.

"God," Ernie said. "That was hairy. Did you have to do that, Marge?"

"What else could I do? In another minute he would have blown the whistle and the whole damn camp would have been down on us."

"I'm not anxious to spend the rest of my life in Leavenworth."

Sonia turned to Takolik. "Was he . . . one of your people?"

Takolik shrugged. He seemed impassive and unmoved, but his face was very quiet and thoughtful. "I think he was an Aleut. Looked like one."

"Listen, I'm sorry about that," Marge said, "but he was a soldier in enemy uniform, right?" For someone who had just killed a man, Marge seemed strangely calm—more so than the others.

"What about the guard? Do you think he recognized you?" Sonia asked.

Takolik shrugged again. "I guess he figured he saw my face somewhere, but with those hard-hats on, I doubt he got a good look at any of us."

"It was dark," Ernie said. "I don't think anyone could have recognized us with those hats pulled down over our faces—except maybe you, Takolik. He looked like he knew you."

"If he did," Takolik said slowly, "he wouldn't tell."

Driving the Travelall through the quiet avenue to-

342

ward Clay street, Sonia began to slap at her fatigue
pants and sweater.

"Shit. I left my glove behind in the hut."

"What's the dif?" Ernie said. "It's only an old five-
and-ten glove. There's no way they can trace that."

"Yeah," Sonia said thoughtfully. "I suppose you're
right. Still I wish I hadn't left it there."

"... Reports from workers and surveillance personnel indicate that when it comes to oil spill reporting there is a tremendous gap between principle and practice. Many pipeline workers tell of spills that were never reported, and there have even been allegations that at some camps those who wish to report spills have been threatened with firing. In many cases spills have been reported with the quantities greatly underestimated. ... If a company that avows thorough oil spill reporting cannot live up to its promise on the small spills, can it be trusted to do any better at preventing a big spill?"

—Richard Fineberg
Pipeline Watch—*All Alaska Weekly*

Chapter Thirty

Larry lay spread-eagled on the queen size bed in his room on the second floor of the Traveler's Lodge. He was sweating lightly in the warm damp atmosphere. Despite the fact that the room cost almost fifty dollars a day, there was no airconditioning. Wally Hickel's planners, when they built the hotel, had probably felt that the period of hot weather in mid-July and August was not long enough to justify the expense of such an installation.

It was now nearly noon and the temperature hovered in the vicinity of eighty degrees. Larry's body was strangely marked by the Alaskan summer sun. The torso itself was the creamy pale color of buttermilk—except where it was laced over by coarse black, curly body hairs. The wrists and forearms were burned dark tan, as was the face and neck, starting from a point high above the collarbone. The tan stopped in a straight line about two inches across the forehead where the hard hat or the tie-band of the welder's mask interrupted the sun's rays.

Except when he was on R & R, Larry had either the hat or the mask on at all times when he was outdoors. On R & R he no longer even wore his beloved Texas Stetson and had given up his pointy boots. There was enough trouble and tension in Alaska without calling attention to his Texas origins.

There was a light rap on the door. Larry covered his groin with one tanned hand, in a cavalier gesture of modesty.

"Who's there?"

"Room service."

"Slide it under the door."

There was the rattling sound of a key in the lock and the door opened.

Deirdre came in, dressed in tight-fitting denims with a gingham shirt open almost to the navel. Her face was flushed with the sun and perhaps the effort of carrying the paper sack. She sat down on the big, firm, hotel bed next to Larry and dumped the sack unceremoniously on the floor. Larry reached over, grabbed her around the waist and pulled her backward, for a playful nibble on the ear. Deirdre turned on her elbow, her face only a few inches from his.

A beam of sun, coming from the window facing west, highlighted the gold threads in her hair and the yellow streaks in her curious green eyes.

"Getting plenty of rest, little man?" Deirdre asked mockingly, but her face was serious and loving.

He leaned forward and kissed her gently on the lips. Her tongue emerged shyly from her open mouth and explored the edge of his lips—at first timidly, and then with hard, deep thrusts. Larry pulled her around onto the bed and they fell into a long embrace, his bare

345

thigh pressed into the harsh fabric of her jeans, her legs clutched around his and her hips grinding in a slow rolling motion. Larry felt himself instantly erect and Deirdre looked down with amused surprise.

"Whoops. So soon? You'll wear it out."

They had eaten at the Seal and Bear, downstairs in the hotel, the previous night, and had returned to the room early for a long tender and passionate night of love-making.

Larry laughed and indicated the paper sack. "E.F. or F.F.?" he said, grinning.

"Let's eat first," Deirdre said. "The grapefruit are chilled and I don't think they'd taste too good warm."

From the sack she extracted two large yellow grapefruits.

"These cost eighty-nine cents apiece," she said. "They'd better be good."

There was also a copy of the Sunday *Anchorage Times* and the *News-Miner* and one of Tom Snapp's *All-Alaska Weekly*. Also, there were two six-packs of Oly.

"Put those papers down. I don't give a damn what's happening out there."

"But I have to care," Deirdre said.

"Well, Goddamn it, we ain't working now. Let's have some breakfast and get to rolling around a little."

He padded over to the chair where his pants hung and took the Buck sheath knife from its holster to cut the grapefruits with. There were also two containers of coffee, some donuts, and four hard-boiled eggs in the sack.

"It ain't exactly what you'd get at Foulard's in Houston, but I guess it's better than getting up and going out," Larry said.

When they had finished the breakfast, Deirdre

stowed the rinds, eggshells, and other leavings in the paper bag and put it out in the hall.

"Why don't you go out to the machine, honey, and get some ice to keep these cans cool," Larry said, opening one of the beers and spreading out a copy of the *All-Alaska*. It was the only paper, as far as Larry was concerned, that gave any real news of what was really going on in the camps.

The headline concerned the shooting earlier in the week of a guard at Fort Wainwright during the looting of a munitions dump on the grounds:

> Wainwright officials are puzzled by the goal of the robbers, who seemed to be Denali employees, since nothing seemed to be missing in the munitions dump. They are, however, taking inventory, to find out what, if anything was stolen. The dead guard, Harold Ivanoff, 19, was a student at Fairbanks University on National Guard active duty for the summer. He is survived by a mother and three sisters on Little Diomede Island.

According to the newspaper story, four men who seemed to be Denali employees, had cut through the fence separating the Denali complex from Fort Wainwright, broken into the post munitions dump, and shot the guard. The Wackenhut gate guard on duty at Denali said that he had not gotten a good look at any of them, although they had shown him their identification cards. Security, the article explained, was never too tight on the grounds of the Denali headquarters, although close surveillance of visitors was exercised in the interior of the building.

Deirdre returned with a plastic bucket of ice as Larry glanced through the article with interest.

"Kind of sad about the Aleut kid," Larry said, as Deirdre placed the cans of Oly in the ice.

347

"Yeah," Deirdre said thoughtfully. "That's really a weird story. I don't follow it. I wonder if those people really *were* Denali employees."

"Well, they had the trucks and the badges."

"Is there anything new in the paper there?" Deirdre asked.

"No, it says they have no idea who the people were, no fingerprints were left, the FBI's on the base because the crime took place on Federal grounds—they got a lot of those FBI guys up here—oh yeah, and the FBI agent says they found one clue. A rubber glove worn by one of the bandits. They've sent it to a special lab to see if they can pick up a print."

"How can they do that?"

"If the material is smooth enough, sometimes they can get a print from the inside of the glove, at least that's what it says here."

"Well, I hope they catch them," Deirdre said, opening a beer for herself, and sitting on the edge of the bed. "There's really been a lot of crime in the camps lately."

"I know, but a lot of it is just picking up trucks and stuff for joy-riding."

"Oh, yeah?" Deirdre said. "How about that guy who snitched a whole D-9 tractor, brand-new? Happened up at Brooks Range a couple of months ago."

"Yeah," Larry said, "that was pretty cool."

"And how about those guys that got caught shipping out Caterpillar parts to reassemble into a tractor in Anchorage? They almost had the damn thing together when they got caught."

"Listen," Larry said, "if you ask me, the biggest rip-off of all is in wages. I haven't seen so many goof-offs in one place since I left the Army. I remember one day our whole crew—eleven men—worked only two

348

hours out of the whole day. Actually, it was two days in a row. One day the fuel truck that took care of the generator ran out of gas and we didn't get any fuel for the rest of the day—just sat around the warmup tent playing black jack. Then, the next day, the light bulbs burned out in the welder's hut and since we couldn't work on the welds, nobody *else* could work. I don't know what the foreman was doing, but he didn't get any bulbs into that shack until the next day, so everybody just sat around there, picking up twenty-five dollars an hour, bullshitting and drinking. At this rate, the pipeline's going to cost more than the Goddamn pyramids. Of course," he continued, "there's been some folks taking shortcuts too. Like those pipeweld x-rays that disappeared. I understand that there's at least six hundred bum welds along that line already, and they're never going to be found unless they dig up the pipe—and you know they're going to find a way to skip that."

"Well," Deirdre said, sighing. "I think we're really doing our best. Dad sent out word that anyone who didn't send out a report on so much as a tea cup of a leak would be terminated without notice."

Larry laughed. "You really think they do that? Why, they lay out those plastic tarps that are supposed to catch the oil—right? But if there's a little rip in it or something, you don't suppose that they send out and tape it up or mend it? Hell, no. The foreman says, hurry up and cover it up with sand before somebody sees it."

"I know, I know," Deirdre said, resignedly. "But we're trying."

"Listen, I hope you're not beginning to believe your own publicity," Larry said laughing. "I mean if you could spill sixty-five thousand gallons up at Galbraith without even *noticing,* and there's not even any damn oil in the pipe yet, just think of what's going to happen when the pipe's full of oil."

"Well," Deirdre said. "I guess we're learning as we go."

"Don't get me wrong," Larry said. "I think it's a lot more important to get that oil coming down through the line than it is to worry about itty-bitty messes in some place a million miles from God knows where. What in the purple, ever-loving hell difference does it make if somebody spills a couple of shot glasses of oil out in the frozen tundra—or even a couple of gallons? The Goddamn Eskimos can't use *all* that land."

"Well, I think it does matter a lot," Deirdre said. "It's just that we're doing the best we can."

Deirdre reached down to the coffee table beside her to pick up the bulky Sunday edition of the *Anchorage Times,* but Larry took it from her hands. He kissed her gently on her neck, just under the ear, and began removing the gingham western blouse. Deirdre held his head close to her as his hands explored the surface of her small, firm, upturned breasts.

"I always said," Larry murmured into her neck, "more than a handful is a waste."

Larry lifted his head to focus his attention on the now bared area of her bosom. Deirdre winced once.

"Sorry," Larry said. "I should have shaved. Does the beard bother you?"

"No," Deirdre said. "I kind of like it. But I hope it doesn't leave marks."

"Why," Larry said. "Who's to see it?"

Deirdre blushed—or was it just the flush of rising passion? As Larry began to suck on her small pink nipples, Deirdre's breaths began to deepen and her hands pressed hard at the short curled hair at the base of his neck.

Larry reached down to unfasten the heavy silver buckle that held up Deirdre's jeans, and she obligingly lifted her hips so that he could pull the tight jeans from her legs after opening her zipper.

"Things were a lot easier," Larry said, "when women wore skirts."

"Who said things had to be easy?"

Now that the dungarees were off, Larry pulled Deirdre's long-legged, smooth-skinned body close to his. He always wondered how it was possible that two figures that looked so ill-assorted standing up and clothed could fit together so neatly lying down and naked. They were kissing deeply and moving their limbs softly against each other. Larry could feel the moistness between her thighs and knew this was going to be one of the best ever. He was amazed that after the night they'd put in, he could still get it up.

In deference to his possible fatigue, Deirdre elected to ride on top this time and they seemed to glide into a slow smooth, dreamily satisfying rhythm. The sliding lubricious movement, up and down, around and around, had a sweet, quiet, flowing quality in the beginning. But then, as the friction mounted, Deirdre began to grind very hard and very close to him and to emit little yelping cries. Finally, as she approached her climax, her small white teeth clenched in the tender skin on the side of Larry's neck and she bit down hard.

"Ouch!" he yelled. "For Christ sake, take it easy. That hurts!"

Deirdre looked contrite and her movements slowed.

"I'm sorry honey," she said, kissing the small bloody spot her teeth had made. "It was just so *good.*"

"It was for me, too, until you bit me like that. Could you take it easy on that stuff?"

"Why? Are you afraid . . ."

Whatever she was going to ask was interrupted by the ringing of the telephone.

"Who the hell can that be?" Larry picked up the telephone. It was Brandon's voice.

"Larry, I want you to get out here to Denali head-quarters as soon as you can. Your father is on his way here now from Houston."

"What's up?"

"The FBI has been here," Brandon said. "I don't want to say too much on the phone but it involves that burglary at Fort Wainwright—you know, the one where the Eskimo was killed?"

"I don't understand," Larry said. "What has this got to do with me?"

"One of the burglars left a glove, remember?"

"Yeah, I saw it in the papers."

"The FBI just got a report on a print that they were able to pick up on the inside of the glove. It belongs to your sister, Penny. Is there anybody with you?"

"Ah, yeah," Larry said, inwardly relieved. However it was that Brandon had located him, he apparently didn't know that Deirdre was there also.

"Well, don't say anything on your end that could be understood. I'll expect you in two hours. Your father should be here by then."

Slowly, Larry hung up the phone.

"What is it, Lar?" Deirdre asked, noticing his concern.

"You'll never believe it when I tell you."

"A Fairbanks resident . . . filed suit against a pipeline contractor, charging that he had been terminated from his job . . . because he disapproved of faked weld x-rays required for the 48-inch pipe.

If allegations . . . are confirmed, it could be the most serious impediment to scheduled completion of the pipeline to date.

—Ray Anderson
All-Alaska Weekly

Chapter Thirty-one

Larry Steele met with his father and Brandon in Wilbur's big suite on the top floor of the Denali headquarters building at Fort Wainwright. The room, like those in the headquarters in Houston and Washington, had steel walls and had been rigorously de-bugged. Brandon was on the phone when Larry arrived and Wilbur, in shirt-sleeves, was perusing a folder of reports. He was gray with fatigue from the long plane trip and looked tired and irritable.

"Goddamn it, Brandon," he said. "You know I can't be up here all the time. Can't you get on top of this stuff? How does all this happen? Labor problems, violence in the camps, big news items in the papers about oil leaks—and now this God-damn business with the welds! I've told you a hundred times, spend the money if you have to, but this pipeline has to get through *on time*!"

He looked up to see Larry standing there, seeming to notice him for the first time.

"Sit down, Larry, for Christ sake. What are we going to do about this mess?"

"I don't know," Larry said. "I just heard about it when Brandon called me this morning."

"Do you know where D.D. is?"

"No. Should I?"

"Well, you've been seeing the Goddamn girl, haven't you?"

"Yeah, but not one hundred percent of the Goddamn time. You're her boss."

Brandon hung up the phone. "I've called all over and I've left word any place she may turn up. We'll probably be hearing from her soon."

Wilbur sighed and pressed his fingers together thoughtfully. He seemed to be battling for control of himself. The two other men remained silent while Wilbur pulled his thoughts together.

"You've always been close to Penny," he said. "Did you know that she was up here all this time?"

"I haven't heard from her. Honestly. But I have thought she could be here."

"Why did she get involved in this thing, with these hare-brained radicals?"

Larry shrugged. "If she is, it started a long time ago."

"How could she get involved in something like this? Doesn't she know it could ruin us? The family, the company, everything."

"It could ruin her too," Larry pointed out.

"I'm sure we can get her off somehow, if only we can find her."

"I don't know," Larry said. "Nowadays I'm not sure that even your money can help her beat the rap if this gets out to the public."

"We don't even know if she's the one who did it."

"If she was on the raid," Larry argued, "she's just as guilty as if she'd pulled the trigger. You know that."

Wilbur sighed again, deeply, and rumpled his carefully groomed hair.

"What are we going to do?"

Larry thought it was the first time Wilbur had ever asked him for advice.

"The FBI man won't talk," Brandon said. "I've been in touch with him. We ought to be able to sit on this for a while."

Wilbur looked up sharply. "I don't know about that. We haven't been able to sit on anything else. Seems like everything we do gets leaked to the press practically before we know about it."

"Well, this won't," Brandon said. "So far, the only ones to know are the FBI and us. They're holding off on a wanted bulletin until we get in touch with them and they've promised that if we can locate her soon enough, they won't put one out at all."

"Can you imagine what kind of headlines this would get, if it ever gets out?" Wilbur said. "And it will."

"Well," Brandon said reasonably. "I don't see how they could tie it to the pipeline."

"You guys seem more worried about holding up the pipeline," Larry said, dropping into one of the chromium and leather Italian chairs scattered around the office, "than you do about Penny. She could get life for this."

"Why did she do this, Larry? Does she hate me? You don't hate me, do you?"

Larry shrugged. "I don't know how she feels. No. I don't hate you. But you haven't been the warmest, ever-loving big daddy that a man ever had."

"Look, I always wanted to spend more time with you. It's just that I never *had* the time. And as far as *you're* concerned—you know I always wanted you to work with me more, but you always seemed to take a different path."

"I'm just learning the business from the ground up—like Grandpa did," Larry said reasonably.

"Well, I think you've had enough on the job training

now. I think it's time you took on more responsibility. After all, there's only Penny and you to take over when I'm gone, and now, Penny . . ." His voice trailed off.

The intercom buzzed and Brandon answered it. It was Susie Wing, Wilbur's executive secretary in the outer office.

"Miss Doheny is here."

"Send her in," Brandon said. He pressed a button, releasing a lock on the door to the inner room. Deirdre came in, looking fresh and feminine in a beige linen suit with a smart-looking brown shirt.

"Well, I'm here," she said. "What's the problem?"

"Where in the hell have you been?" Wilbur asked. "We've had people looking all over for you."

"I was downtown, at the Bookazine, picking up a couple of magazines."

"I told you," Wilbur said, "to always leave word where you were."

Larry was surprised at the harsh tone in which he spoke to Deirdre. He saw her eyes flash in momentary defiance, and then she subsided into timid obsequience, a role in which Larry had never seen her before.

"I'm sorry, Wilbur," she said. "It was only for an hour, though, and I called in for messages."

"We've had some terrible news," Wilbur said. "There was a man killed recently at Fort Wainwright—I suppose you've heard about it."

"Yes I did."

"Well, the FBI has found a piece of evidence that I'm afraid links Penny to the whole mess. Apparently, she's been hiding right here under our noses all this time."

"Penny? I thought she was down in Seattle someplace."

"Well, she's not. She's here and as usual, she's up to her fine high ass in trouble."

Wilbur only reverted to his Texas talk patterns when he was deeply disturbed.

"Can I do anything to help?" Deirdre said. "Where is she?"

Wilbur pounded the desk in frustration. "That's it. Nobody knows. I don't suppose you've heard anything?" he asked suspiciously. "Or you, Larry?"

"I told you," Larry said, "before. I *thought* she might be here. That's all."

"Why didn't you tell me?"

Larry paused. "I dont know. I suppose I just didn't want to stir things up unless I was sure."

"Well, it was just plain damn stupid," Wilbur said. "If you'd told me, we could have possibly been able to find her—before all this happened. I blame you very much for this, Larry."

Larry shrugged. "I don't see how all this is helping Penny."

Wilbur turned to Deirdre. "D.," he said, "I want you to see that this story stays locked up real tight. I don't want any leaks this time. None at all. I'm holding you responsible."

Deirdre looked troubled. "Wilbur, I'll control it as best I can, but I simply am not in charge of all the possible sources of information. It could leak from anywhere."

Brandon intervened. "So far the only ones who know are a couple of FBI agents and us—and the FBI is sitting on it—at least for the present."

Deirdre looked at Brandon with scorn. "The *only* people! What about the teletypists who transmitted the message? The office clerks? You know as well as I do, Brandon, that there's always *somebody* who knows these things. Believe me, it'll be all over town by tomor-

357

row, no matter what you do. With all your security, neither you nor Daddy have been able to sit on any of these things you've tried to hush up—not the oil spills, not the business with the faked x-rays, so what makes you think we can sit on this one?"

"Well, we can *try* to keep it quiet, Goddamn it," Wilbur snapped. "What are you doing about it, Brandon?"

The big, crew cut man shrugged. "I haven't had time to do much. I've had a couple of my trusted people looking around, asking questions. It's a big town, but there aren't too many hippy types around here and I have a feeling that's where she's hanging out. Mostly they're around a few bars on First Street and hanging out in an abandoned building across the Chena River. Of course, she could be living out in the toolies somewhere . . ."

"Or she could have left town entirely," Larry pointed out.

"Yeah," Brandon said in a discouraged tone, "I'd thought of that. But we checked the airports and haven't been able to find anybody who resembled her who left by plane in the last few days. She hasn't had time to get out by road and we put a block on the Alcan highway."

"She could have gotten out by boat," Larry added.

"Yeah," Brandon said, running a hand over his stiff, bristly hair. "But the only way she could make it would be in a private boat—and we're keeping an eye on those too. I'll admit, it's not fool-proof, but it's the best we can do."

"Well, I hope she got out somehow," Larry said.

Wilbur looked up sharply, as though about to contest the remark, and then restrained himself. "Yes, I suppose you're right, but she could be a fugitive for the rest of her life."

Larry shrugged. "She's a fugitive anyway. And you haven't seen her for years."

"I'd almost forgotten about her," Wilbur said softly, as though talking to himself. He swivelled in his chair and looked out the window in silence for a moment. None of them spoke. Then he turned back to Larry.

"Larry, you're all that's left of our family—except for Grandpa Bisset. I know we haven't been close in these years, but I want you to work more closely with me now, on this problem—on the pipeline. Everything. Will you think it over?"

"I will think about it, Dad," Larry said.

"And if she gets in touch with you, will you let us know?"

"I promise I won't do anything without consulting you," Larry said. "But so far, there's no sign she's planning to get in touch with me."

Wilbur got up from his swivel chair, crossed to Larry and took his hand. "I mean it, you know," he said, holding Larry's hand and looking into his eyes.

"I understand," Larry said, and turned to go. He took the handshake to be in the nature of a dismissal.

"Brandon will be in touch," Wilbur said.

"I'm sure I can count on that," Larry said, with a slight note of asperity.

Deirdre started to pick up her bag, as if to leave also.

Wilbur turned to her and said almost in anger, "No! You stay, I still have business with you."

"Yessir," Deirdre said meekly, putting her purse down on the floor next to her.

"Brandon, you get busy on this. I want a full report every day."

"Yessir," Brandon said smartly.

"I'll keep in touch," Larry said, going out the door and exchanging a sympathetic glance with D.D.

359

Brandon was still assembling his notes and papers preparatory to leaving.

"I'll see you first thing in the morning," Wilbur said, "about this x-ray business."

"Yessir," Brandon said, snapping the catches on his dispatch case, and then locking it with a tiny key he took from his watch pocket.

"And, Brandon. I want you to find out who's responsible for all these leaks and take care of the problem. Do you understand?"

"Yessir."

As the door closed behind him, Wilbur turned toward Deirdre, who was still slumped in the office chair, awaiting orders.

"Come with me," he told her.

Deirdre got to her feet obediently. She followed Wilbur through a door on the far side of the room which lead to his private study and lounge.

"I'm very tired, Deirdre," he said. "I want you to mix me a drink."

He laid down on the wide, tufted-leather couch.

"Then I want you to give me a very good and relaxing rubdown."

"Yes, milord," Deirdre said, dropping ice cubes into the tall glass with the W-bar-S monogram.

"(We) wonder why 'the largest single construction project in the history of the world' must force the teamsters to put up with violence, racism and terror, because it can't afford to lose a single day's work but will allow the goons from Big Oil's favorite redneck 'union' to tear up camp kitchens, threaten female employees with rape and molestation, beat Alaskan workers to a pulp and then walk off the job with impunity . . ."

—Edgar Paul Boyko
The Roar Of The Snow Tiger
All-Alaska Weekly

Chapter Thirty-Two

A week passed and nothing was heard concerning Penny from either the FBI or Brandon's private investigators. There were only about 350,000 people in all of Alaska, but there were so many transients, so many indefinite habitations, so much casual moving about, and so many people sailing under false colors that it began to seem that finding this one disguised woman would require time and possibly a tip-off. For a while, the FBI thought of offering a reward, but Brandon was able to talk them out of that, with its resulting publicity. For the moment he argued that secrecy would probably be the best policy. If the girl didn't know she was wanted for conspiracy and felony murder, she might be more relaxed, and likely to reveal herself.

Since he had come that far, Wilbur Steele consented to going on an inspection tour of the North Slope before returning to Houston. He took with him Brandon, Mahlon Doheny, and Deirdre. Doheny ultimately had to be put in the picture regarding the problem with

Penny. He had never been fond of Penny Steele; had resented her rebelliousness and her insouciance.

"That kid's been a trouble-maker since she was ass-high to a tall Indian," Doheny grumbled.

Wilbur Steele looked sour and said nothing, since he had always privately agreed with that opinion himself.

The four traveled north in Wilbur's private Gulf-stream jet, leaving the company leased Lear Jet in Fairbanks. The Gulfstream was larger, faster, more comfortable and five times more expensive. Furthermore, it could fly Wilbur back to Houston without refueling.

The first stop was Alamo's luxurious base at Prudhoe Bay, sometimes referred to as the "Crude Oil Hilton." Since the early days, the central base had been built up into a big two story unit, with surrounding satellite Atcos. Inside the unit were an indoor pool, tennis court, even an artificially lit garden, known as the North Slope National Forest. There was a different movie shown every night, following the TV-news cartridge shipped up from the States one day late; chess, checker, and pool tournaments, and other less formal forms of entertainment were displayed on the bulletin board as they entered the administration building.

Wilbur noticed a crudely done drawing announcing the entries for the "Great North Slope Belching and Farting Contest."

"Do we have to have that?" he asked Doheny. "After all, there are women up here now."

Doheny frowned in resignation. "I can't touch it. The unions would have my ass. We're in a delicate enough position now. We had to practically give up searching the luggage. These guys are bringing booze,

362

dope, cards, and everything on the base. When I make a move to stop them, they go running to their shop stewards. We've had three walk-outs in the last month, and I'm just dreading the day that there's a full-scale walkout. It will cost us millions and plenty of time."

"I suppose you're right," Wilbur said. "The worst thing that could happen to us right now would be a major labor walk-out."

"We need a little grease in the right spots so that the friction doesn't get too great in the upper levels, if you know what I mean," Doheny said winking.

"Do what you have to," Wilbur said, "I don't want to hear the details."

Deirdre suggested that, as a public relations gesture, the group eat in the main mess hall with the Resident Camp Manager, Chuck Avery. Doheny looked unhappy, but finally agreed. Privately, he had been running an investigation of Avery, who had reportedly been taking pay-offs under the table from camp suppliers.

Wilbur's face was known only to a few of the camp executives, mainly original Alamo employees. Contract workers—drillers, and so on—were not familiar with the upper level staff of the oil company. After breakfast, Wilbur retired with Deirdre to the small private suite kept available at all times for him behind the headquarters offices, for some dictation and radio-phoning.

Brandon and Doheny went on for a quick tour of the premises.

After lunch, which consisted of grilled Matsusaka beef, which the RCM had picked up from a Japanese airlines pilot in Fairbanks and kept in a special freezer for surprise VIP visits (the workers were having Swiss steak, asparagus, baked apple and sour cream, so they weren't suffering either) Wilbur suggested that perhaps Deirdre would like to take a stroll and have a chat with her Daddy, as she had not had much time with him during the last few weeks.

Brandon and Wilbur returned to his private office. "Look, Brandon," Wilbur said, "I just got word. They're almost sure to go through with that law requiring double-bottoms on U.S. built tankers, and you know what that'll mean."

"Well, we're already covered by our contingency plan, right?" Brandon said.

"Yes, but this means that the contingency is definite."

The double bottoms law had been a threat to the oil companies for several years and the big spill at Santa Barbara had finally furnished the impetus to push it through Congress. Most tankers—even the big supertankers—had simply a thin skin of iron between them and the sea. This meant that any punctures or leaks would result in oil spilling directly into the sea. Double bottoms were just what the name implied: a second skin around the hull, which provided protection against any rips or tears and also a compartment in which to carry ballast water when the ship was riding empty. This meant that when the ballast water was pumped out, it would not have been in contact with the oil in the tanks, as is now the case. Most of the oil contamination of the seas results not from leaks but from the pumping out of ballast water that's been riding in the oil-coated tanks. While this is illegal, it is always done when authorities are looking the other way. In any case, the penalties—usually five or six thousand dollars—don't make it worthwhile to give up the practice.

"This means we'll have to use different crude supplies for the Puget Sound plant, right?"

"We'll find something to do with it," Wilbur said. "Even with the price of oil quintupled since the embargo, I don't see how we can afford to ship in U.S. bottoms. It'll cost us at least four times as much to ship that way."

"Then we'll go with the Central American plan, right?" Brandon said.

"Exactly. We'll use the big tankers, the one million dead weight tonners that we ordered in Japan." (Wilbur could not have been waiting strictly for the double bottom law to pass, since he ordered the tankers at least a year before. They were to be one thousand six hundred and forty feet long—six hundred and twenty feet longer than the old Queens—and two hundred and seventy-four feet wide. They would draw a hundred feet. You could fit Chartres Cathedral or Notre Dame right inside one of the five major tanks. Loaded there was no port in the world they could enter, or even venture close to, if there was any sort of an off-shore shelf—except Valdez. The old huge tankers have been called VLCC's—very large crude carriers. This applied to ships over two hundred thousand tons. But the bigger the tanker, the cheaper the transport, and the oil companies now were aiming to ship everything in tankers in excess of four hundred thousand tons to be called ULCC's—ultra large crude carriers. The reason Alamo was so interested in the ULCC's was simple enough. One trip from Valdez to any Pacific port by one of the supertankers could represent a profit as high as $20,000,000.00. Even the VLCC's made a profit of $4,000,000.00 on each run. But to use a ship of American registry meant being involved with the Seaman's union and the U.S. Coast Guard regulations. It doubled or tripled the price of shipping oil, therefore most of the oil carriers preferred to register their ships in Liberia or Panama, which had extremely liberal laws regarding safety, construction, and labor conditions. Oil company slang for these ships was Panama bottoms.)

"Are things going all right on the Costa Rican deal?" Wilbur asked in a seeming nonsequitur.

Brandon nodded. The question was not a nonsequitur to him because he knew that the ultimate plan was to send the ULCC's down the Pacific directly to Central America, finally to ship the oil directly across Costa Rica and then transship to refineries in the Virgin Islands, thus making the entire shipment immune to the Jones Act, which dealt with the commerce in domestic oil. At that point, the oil could be processed and sold any place in the world, free of any U.S. price restriction, another important factor in the revised plan.

"A lot of people are going to raise hell when they hear about this," Brandon said.

"Let them raise hell," Wilbur said. "They raised hell at the embargo too, but they soon settled down. After all, we guaranteed that if the pipeline would be put in, the country's energy security would be assured. Well, it's assured, isn't it? I mean, we've got the oil, we've got the pipeline. And if there's ever a war, or if the Arabs cut off the imports, well, we can always make a new arrangement with the Government, and ship the oil into the States—but under our terms. As long as they're going to throw these Goddamn restrictions on us, we'll have to play the game as rough as we always did. Right now, we're lucky, because we've got the only port in the world that'll take one of those huge tankers, though it might be a tight squeeze getting past Middle rock and into Valdez arm."

There was a buzzing on the intercom, and the voice

said, "Mr. Doheny says that we'd better get going if we are going to keep on schedule. He's planning to stop at Happy Valley, Tonsina, and Glenallen."

Wilbur depressed the talk button. "We'll be right out," he said, gathering up his papers.

"We're done here, aren't we Brandon?"

"Yes, I guess so."

As they hurried down the wide corrugated lanes to the parking lot outside the operation center where a deluxe Denali bus waited to take them to the Gulfstream, Wilbur was distracted by what seemed to be loud noises coming from the direction of the mess hall —shouts and crashing sounds.

"What's up in there?" he asked Doheny.

"Nothing, nothing," Doheny muttered, hurrying Wilbur toward the door. "They're having some kind of a celebration. Somebody's birthday or something. The men have to blow off steam somehow, you know."

Wilbur nodded, accepting the report but not quite believing it. It was not his job to get involved in internal disputes. All he was interested in was the question of getting the pipeline done on time.

When it came to boarding the plane, Doheny begged off the return trip, saying he would return in a few hours, after he had finished some business in the camps. Wilbur shook his hand and Deirdre kissed him on the cheek. Brandon favored him with a curt nod. There had been signs in the last few months of increasing tension between the two men.

As soon as the plane had taken off, Doheny jumped back on the bus and raced to the operations center. He cornered Avery, the Resident Camp Manager, in the corridor.

"Haven't you got it under control yet?"

"The guards are trying, but I think we'll just have

to let it simmer down. Most it can cost us is a few thousand in damages. It just isn't going to be worth it to try any rough stuff with those guys."

They were talking about an incident that had taken place just shortly after the Executive group left the mess hall. An assistant cook in the Culinary Union had managed to cut a couple of extra Matsusaka steaks from the executive supply and was eating them for his own dinner in the mess hall when one of the Tulsa welders noticed what was on the tray. The cook, who was black, was slicing into an inch and a half thick chunk of grilled meat. The welder, a tall carrot-topped Oklahoman, stopped in his tracks in simulated astonishment.

He banged on his tray for attention.

"Looky here! Why look what old Sambo is scoffing down over there on that tray—a big, beautiful, grilled steak. The ever-loving pea-brained, cock-bent, sheep-fucking injustice of it all! That black fucker is eating grilled steak and we're eating this Goddamn stewed Salisbury steak. Last week they took away our grill so we couldn't do any grilling out at the warm-up shacks. Are we going to stand for that, men? Fuck no!"

The other pipeliners yelled in a chorus, with some of the Teamsters even joining in: "Give us back our steak," the red-head yelled, and the others took up the chant, slamming their stainless steel trays on the formica surface of the dining tables. Pretty soon the rhythmic chant had spread throughout the mess hall and the noise of the slamming trays was deafening.

Bill Messenger, the camp's chief cook, came out to plead with the group for silence.

"Now, calm down men. I'll try to get you back your grills. You know the thing is in arbitration now."

"Fuck arbitration," a burley Teamster yelled. "We want our steaks. We've waited long enough."

"Yeah, and fuck you too," another Teamster yelled and sent the Gulden's mustard pot sailing past Messenger's head.

This seemed like an inspired move to the rest, who gave up banging their trays and resorted to throwing the only real breakables available in the mess hall in all directions. The bottles of condiments—Worcestershire sauce, ketchup, mustard, horseradish and the rest —were soon flying in all directions, splattering on the walls and the floors. Several of the men upended the big formica dining tables, sending the remaining condiments skidding and splashing onto the floor. But now the fight degenerated as it usually did into a hassle not only between the culinary workers and the pipeliners, but also between the pipeliners and the Teamsters. Chairs started flying—several smashed through the double-insulated windows of the Atco trailer. A Teamster had the bright idea of shoving over the coffee urns and the big orange juice dispensers, so that the brown and yellow fluids sluiced onto the floor in ankle-deep currents. Some of the younger workers got into the pastry division and started throwing pies, muffins and cream puffs indiscriminately.

A rangy, Tulsa pipeliner got into a duel with one of the culinary workers who was wielding a big stainless steel serving fork. The culinary worker, a Hawaiian, managed to impale the right hand of the pipeliner on the tines of the fork. The pipeliner, ignoring the pain and the blood, picked up the small man in his huge tanned paw and sent him sailing across the steam serving table, breaking several of the pipes that heated the food and sending a scalding spray of steam into the air already thick with flying missiles.

369

Doheny looked through the oval window in the mess hall door and then turned away in disgust.

"Can't you get those guys under control?"

Avery shrugged. "I tell you, it's not just the labor conditions. Every once in a while these men get cabin fever up here and they just have to bust loose. It's happened twice already in the last six months, here, and a couple of times down in the terminal, and at Tonsina. You just have to write it off as one of the added costs. The last knock-down bust-up like this cost us about eighteen thousand dollars and a two-day work stoppage. But if we send in the NANA guards and they bust a few heads or make a few arrests, all it's going to do is cause a lot more trouble. And we haven't got enough guards to stop all these guys in any case. We'll just have to hope we can confine the damage to the mess hall. We've got guards outside the doors, and we'll try to cool the men down as they come out."

"Goddamnit," Doheny said as he marched off to pick up a ride on the company Lear jet. "The way things are going these days, I think I might just go back to the wildcatting in East Texas."

"I think having women in the camp is healthy. A person seems to think of his mother and his sister, etcetera. And the type of women we've had here have been the type you could have in a camp, because they haven't been the people who get out of line. . . ."

—Interview with Resident Camp Manager
Pump Station Ten

Chapter Thirty-Three

The fiasco with the Fort Wainwright raid seemed, perversely, to invigorate the little SHAMAN group. The sense of shared danger drew them closer together, although in the first few days after the raid, when the newspapers were full of the story, Hurwood gave signs of bolting for the lower forty-eight. Since the raid had been publicized in the newspapers as being conducted by four people, it was decided in general that it would be a good idea for the group to disperse as much as possible. As far as could be determined, the police were convinced that the raid had been an inside job by Denali employees because of the identification badges and the Denali truck. Sonia felt she would be reasonably safe continuing to work the Flame Lounge or one of the other new go-go places that were springing up outside the town limits on the Steese Highway.

By now, they all had enough experience to be on the "A" list, and, as residents, there was not too much trouble getting job dispatches. Marge elected to go to Pump Station Number Ten on the Delta River, just above Isabel Pass.

Pump Station Ten would be one of those completed for the first phase of the pipeline and was one of the logical sabotage targets when the big day came. Marge's job—for the moment—was to sit tight and make notes on the security situation for future reference and on any personnel who might be included, especially those permanently attached to the station.

Takolik had a job through NANA as a security guard at the main operations center in Prudhoe. This was doubly good, since it gave him a chance to go home almost every week to his village and to keep on top of the situation regarding the Natives, most of whom, to Takolik's disappointment, had readily accepted the pipeline's invasion, and complained only that their share of the work and profits should be higher.

Mason, afraid that routine personnel checks at Denali might uncover his background as a deserter, took off for Valdez, where Van Taylor was able to get him a job as day bartender in the Club Valdez.

After the initial uproar over the Wainwright raid, the papers tended to ignore it. There were already more than a dozen unsolved murders on the books in the Fairbanks area, including the murder of one employee of the Fairbanks *News-Miner,* who burned to death in a suspicious fire at the Chateau Parlor; and the murder of a barmaid named Kitty, who was shot to death in one of the rock dance halls on the outskirts of town before fifty startled witnesses—none of whom could remember anything about the killer the next day.

With most of the group away, it was lonesome. Sonia, who was free most days, tried to maintain a low profile and generally stayed home reading and smoking dope.

Marge, despite her former experience as a warehouseman, found herself reduced in rank back to a bullcook —the only jobs the unions claimed were available. Marge was convinced that she was a victim of discrimination against women, but the job paid nine hundred and sixty dollars a week, took only a few hours a day, and gave her lots of opportunities to poke about the camp, picking up tidbits of vital security information.

The generators, for instance, which would almost surely be the target of any attempt by SHAMAN to immobilize Pump Station Ten, were located right next to one of the security guard gates. Unless the group could place an insider among those assigned to work on generators, it probably would be necessary to in some way distract or immobilize the guards.

Marge was reasonably sure that it would not be necessary to actually eliminate the guard, but to just distract him, possibly by sending one of the women members of the group to the guard shack to claim his attention while someone slipped into the generator building. Once the Pump Stations were built, it was planned that they should operate by remote control and there probably wouldn't be any guard on duty, or only a token guard. The pumps themselves were surrounded only by a chain link fence and there would be facilities for transient technical personnel who might have to work on the pipeline in an emergency. Reporters interviewing one of the pump station camp chiefs helped Marge out by asking the kinds of questions she would have wanted to.

"Wouldn't it be easy for someone to come into one of the pump stations and blow it up and shut down the whole pipeline?" a reporter asked.

"That's not one of the questions I'm prepared to answer," the pump station chief said. "Once we build the pipeline, security is somebody else's job."

Pump Station Ten would be an excellent target, Marge determined, since it was the second largest pumping station, after the one in Prudhoe Bay. "Actually," Marge wrote Sonia, in a hand-carried letter sent via a mutual friend, "our job may be anticipated by nature. This camp is sitting right on top of the Denali fault. This was where, on Good Friday in 1964, there was such a heavy quake that it changed the shape of the terrain as well as the courses of the Tanana and Delta Rivers."

"You'll never guess what happened last week," Marge wrote in another letter. "They held a seven o'clock in the morning meeting—can you believe—to discuss the problem of venereal disease in the camps! The meeting was in the movie hall and it was for women only. Dolly, the only female security guard here, was on the door as we came in. I sat way in the back. There were about twenty-five women there. The camp medic, Ivan Boyoffsky, was the expert (scheduled) to talk. Personally, I think that if there is a V.D. epidemic, he might be the one who started it. Anyway, he got up and told us that there had been ten cases of V.D. reported in the past week. According to the men, there were one or two women in the camp who they suspected of carrying the disease. They didn't name any names, but most of us have an idea who they are. One of the girls, Shandra O'Shinsky, shows up for her job dishing out chow in the mess hall every day so exhausted that you know she must have been up all night working at something else. The other one they call Susie Number One—I never did know why. She's a big, husky black girl, always laughing and grinning, and I understand she has made herself a promise that she's going to fuck every one of the twenty-five thousand employees of the pipeline—men and women included and anything in between.

"Anyway, Boyoffsky requested that all the women in the camp abstain from sexual activity for two or three weeks until the V.D. epidemic could be cleared up. 'I want you to give me your word,' he said. 'It would really be a big help.'

"Now, get this. In the course of this big sex education lecture, he tells us 'we are all human, we all like to make love. It's perfectly natural. But men have a physical, not an emotional need for sex. Women have an emotional need, they don't have a physical need.' At this point I was about ready to walk out, but the security guard said we had to have permission from the medic to leave. 'You gals know whether or not you are the wrong-doers,' he said later. 'I know there are promiscuous women in this camp. Anyone of you who have been with several men ought to come in and get a shot.' 'Oh, yeah,' I said, 'well, what if you've only been with one man? How do you know where he's been dipping his wick?' Jeez, I thought the guy was going to fall off his platform!

"The next thing you know, this guy's deciding maybe everybody ought to get the shots, penicillin, or bicillin or, for those that are allergic, they have something called Trobicin. Now, my question is, if the V.D. is so bad in the camps, how come it's only the women he's talking to? What about those five hundred men who go to town and pick up a dose every week and then come back and spread it around? Some of them are making it with each other too—I wonder if you can get it that way? All I'm saying is that this is just one more example of the prejudice against women in the camps. We always get the crummiest rooms—really badly constructed and much smaller than the ones the men have. And the women who are working out on the line, on the vertical support member pads and all, usually have to hold it in. The men can take a leak anywhere—right on the side of the road—but the women have no place to go without freezing their bare bottoms. Now they say they're going to send Public Health people in, to test the 'women.' How do you like them apples!

"One woman came here from Coldfoot Camp the other day. She says the camp is being run by a bunch of ex-convicts, who have a kind of organized crime ring up there. They bring liquor into the camp, for

375

example, and sell it for fifteen bucks a bottle. When she began to ask a lot of questions about this, she suddenly found herself beat up and they even broke a bottle over her head. When she complained to the foreman, he said, 'Why don't you go home if you don't like it?'

"And then they even had the nerve to try to fire the girl because she'd been in a fight. A NANA security guard saw the whole thing. One of those big Teamsters jumped on her and squashed the piss right out of her and then another guy, who had been trying to screw her for weeks, came in and knocked her on the bed and jumped on her. She kicked out the window and picked up a piece of glass to defend herself. But he grabbed it out of her hand and manged to get a splinter of it in her eye. The next day the camp superintendent told her the reason she was being fired was because she had destroyed Denali property—namely the window in her room. Also she was told that she was being fired for drunkenness. 'If I am, you'll have to fire everybody in this camp,' she said. The guy said he hadn't had any complaints about the others. 'Well, I'm complaining right now,' she said.

"What was the result? Nothing happened to the men and the girl was fired. So she just went back to Fairbanks, joined another union, and now she's here as a bullcook, although she was an operator before.

"Meanwhile the company keeps putting out these bright little newsletters and these announcements of people getting married on the pipeline (some old couple really did this) and acting like it's a real Goddamn paradise. More later.

"Let me know news of the others—

Your Margie.

"P.S. Oh, I almost forgot. Your sibling, Larry S. has been working here for several weeks. A couple of days ago, the big boss man, old Doheny, was up here.

He went right out on the line, called Larry aside, and they had a big long huddle. What can this be about? Do you think Larry has any idea where we are or has spotted you? Would he talk, or is he just becoming one of the establishment? Thought you'd like to know about this. If you ask me, no man can be trusted. Even your own brother.   —M."

"Almost 4,000 welded joints on the oil pipeline under construction in Alaska are suspected of being substandard and may have to be redone, it was reported last week. Poorly welded joints could leak out crude oil, causing thawing, heaving, and subsidence of the tundra and polluting the rivers. Environmentalists had warned of the dangers of leakage. Repairing the joints could cost hundreds of millions of dollars, and delay the pipeline's opening by several months."

—*New York Times*
May 23, 1976

Chapter Thirty-four

It was late September and the termination dust would soon be flying again. Brandon would be happy to get out of Fairbanks before the cold really set in. The trips north always were torture to him, but the great Alaskan pipeline had become something of a runaway stagecoach and at times Al Brandon felt he was the only one who had all the reins in his hand. Wilbur Steele was above it all, dealing in high international finance, but well aware that the failure of the pipeline would probably mean the bankruptcy of Alamo. It would also mean the bankruptcy of Al Brandon personally, or at least a heavy financial loss since, with the first word of the Prudhoe Bay Number One discovery, he had invested heavily in Alamo stock, out of his private finances. These private resources were considerable. Being the bagman for Alamo and making under the table payoffs in Nigeria, Saudi Arabia, Iran, Venezuela, Ecuador, and finally the fiftieth state, had put Brandon in the position of handling hundreds of thousands—sometimes as much as a million—dollars at a time in untraceable cash. Since no receipts were exchanged, and there was nothing on paper (Wilbur wished to keep himself well-estranged from such underhand dealings), it was inevitable that some of this cash would stick to Brandon's fingers. And Brandon never fought the inevitable. In fact, the way Brandon saw his job, it was to see that things *were* inevitable.

In the beginning, he had been certain—and so had Steele—that nothing could stop the pipeline. The successful completion of the embargo deal had insured the profitability of the project, and Fred Steele's expert advice and steering in Washington had enabled Alamo to make an impressive broken-field run through a line of legislative blockers.

Now, with the pipeline half completed, Brandon tried to foresee what obstacles could possibly stand in the way of its completion. The weather they had known would be a problem, but it was worse than they had expected. In the spring of 1975 a huge barge-lift of equipment to the North Slope had been held up when the ice had not broken until it was almost time for the fall freeze-up. The hold-up of the barges would have meant a delay of six months in the completion of the pipeline—a delay that would ultimately cost the oil companies a billion dollars in delayed profits. But strings had been pulled and with the help of the Coast Guard (at a cost of over a million dollars to the U.S. Government) and a late break in the weather, the barges had gotten through and the work went on.

At this point, Brandon could only envision two situations that could seriously delay or block completion of the pipeline: one would be a massive labor walk-out, and certainly there had been signs that this could take place, but here too the right wheels had been greased at upper labor levels and Steele had instructed him to give way on every labor demand possible as long as it would not actually delay completion of the pipeline.

"Remember," Wilbur pointed out, "ultimately the costs will simply be added to the costs of the oil. In the end the State of Alaska will be paying, not us. Just keep those guys working."

Brandon had agreed, but reluctantly. The only labor people he felt at home with were the Tulsa pipeliners, who he thought of as the U.S. Marines of the labor movement.

A second possible source of trouble was the ecological situation. A few more incidents like the big spill at Galbraith Lake could arouse Congress—especially in an election year, like 1976—to a point where serious ecological changes in specifications could be laid down —enough to cause further serious delay. But it was doubtful, Brandon felt, that anyone in Congress would take on the responsibility of completely stopping the pipeline. Not after the billions that had been already invested. If it came to that, the oil companies were prepared to squeeze America's petroleum supplies down to a trickle to emphasize the need of the country for the pipeline, and for that matter the need to develop other domestic sources as soon as the pipeline was finished, such as the Gulf of Alaska, the off-shore areas of New England and New Jersey, and offshore sites in the California coast. It was clear, in any event, that as long as OPEC continued to insure a rising price of Mideastern oil there would be a market for all the Alaskan oil that could be produced. Milton Lipton, one of the chief Congressional Consultants on Petroleum, predicted that OPEC nations would raise crude oil prices to fourteen dollars a barrel by 1980.

For a while in the spring the location of three more huge Saudi Arabian oil fields at Lawhah, Dibah, and Ribyan seemed as though it might be a threat to price stability. They represented perhaps a ten percent increase in the oil reserves of Saudi Arabia, but Brandon had flown out to Riyadh and had spoken to the OPEC bigwigs, who assured him that production would be tightly controlled to prevent a drop in oil prices.

Later there was a meeting at Panama City, Florida, well protected by private guards, where Steele met with Sheikh Ahmed Zaki Yamani, the Saudi Arabian oil minister, along with representatives of Golconda, and some of the other big oil producers. At the end of the meeting the oil executives walked away secure in the knowledge that the elevated price of oil would not be endangered by the new Saudi discoveries. In fact, as far as the Iranians were concerned, the problem wasn't to keep their price from dropping, but to keep them from raising the prices so suddenly as to cause a severe world-wide reaction.

Here Brandon's excellent contacts with Khatami, the Iranian oil minister, served to calm the troubled waters. In the beginning there had been some worry that radical groups, perhaps even Communist or Arab infiltrators, would damage the pipeline by sabotage. But so far there had been little sign of that. There had been a considerable amount of arson in the camps, but this was confined largely to the living facilities and seemed to have been more a result of labor troubles than of any deliberate attempt to destroy the pipeline. In any case, the pipeline was by now too big to destroy by any single act of sabotage, and to date there had been, as far as Brandon could ascertain, no politically motivated attempts to damage the line.

For the last night of his current visit, as was usual, he had scheduled a dinner with Mahlon Doheny at the Bear and Seal dining room downstairs at the Traveler's Lodge, where he had his suite. Doheny had suggested dinner at his home out on the Farmer's Loop road, but Brandon had insisted on being the host. *Fuck him,* he thought. *Let him come to me. I'm not going out in that ass-freezing cold.*

Actually, the temperature was just about freezing—normal for that time of year, and not considered cold by any hardened Alaskans. But Brandon had managed to make more than a dozen trips to Alaska without exposing himself to more than ten or fifteen minutes of intense cold at one time, dashing from plane to heated vehicle to Atco unit to motel.

Brandon and Doheny had three or four drinks in the lounge before going in to dinner, exchanging small talk about the Houston Oilers, developments on their respective ranches back home, (Brandon had a spread out in Sanderson, in West Texas, near the Coahuila border, and Doheny had ten thousand acres in Tatum, New Mexico, just over the line from Brownfield, Texas). Though they had both spent years in the oil business, they had little in common, Brandon's field of expertise being basically administrative and foreign operations, while Doheny's experience was operational and except for the Mexican venture, and now the Alaskan one, he had spent most of his time in the Texas oilfields and in Oklahoma.

At the bar, Doheny drank Crown Royal straight with water back. Brandon ordered a Chivas Regal tall with soda. He had a later appointment and he was trying to conserve himself. For dinner, Brandon had Crab Louis and poached salmon—the only thing he liked about Alaska was the seafood. Doheny, who was beginning to feel he had had enough of all aspects of Alaska, ordered New England little necks and a New York cut steak —well done. Brandon also ordered a twenty-four dollar bottle of Pommard 1964. He pinched the cork, sniffed it appreciatively as Doheny watched him with sardonic reserve, and nodded to the waiter to pour.

"That will go good with your steak," Brandon said

generously, as though he had chosen the wine only to please Doheny, who privately would have preferred a beer.

"Thanks a lot," Doheny had said drily.

Brandon had run out of small talk. The relationship between the two men had never been warm, and even when their interests coincided, they never had the same point of view. If they were taking about professional football, Doheny always favored a running attack, while Brandon opted for the big bomb.

"Were you able to work out anything about those faulty welds?" Brandon asked, picking at the crab.

"They're faulty, all right," Doheny said.

"Well, how do you account for all of those fake welding x-rays going through?"

Doheny shrugged. "You told me we had to put the heat on, and I told the men in the field. I guess they must have figured that the shortest cut is to take one picture of a weld and make it pass for a dozen or so. I certainly had nothing to do with it."

"Look, you know damn well those welds will hold up against almost any situation. Repairing them now is just going to cost time and money—especially time, which we can't afford."

"We can't afford *not* to do it, now that the story's out and the EPA's got ahold of it."

"I know, and that's what bothers me. How does the information get out so fast?"

Doheny swallowed a Little Neck, washed it down with wine, and ignored the question. But Brandon continued to worry at the subject of security.

"I don't understand how every single secret that we want to keep gets out to the papers or the eco-freaks. About the only company secret I can think of that hasn't leaked yet is the one about . . ." he looked around to see if anyone was close enough to overhear ". . . Penny Steele. Anything about that?"

"Not on my end," Doheny said. He wasn't deeply concerned. He didn't give a rat's ass about Penny Steele, one way or the other.

"Look," he said as the steak arrived, charred and overdone the way he liked it, "we are doing a hell of a job here against fantastic odds—political pressure from the lower forty-eight and from the Alaskans, all you Denali clients coming up and criticizing us, weather hang-ups—do you realize we could have been delayed six months when that barge-load of supplies came up here and couldn't get through the ice . . ."

"Yeah, and you would have been, if Washington hadn't sent a bunch of Coast Guard ships to your rescue. You know how much that cost the government? About a million."

Doheny shrugged. "They want the oil, they've got to pay."

"It's funny you couldn't think of a way to get the barges through yourself."

Doheny looked at him quizzically. "How the fuck would *I* do that? *I* don't have a brother in Washington to goose the Coast Guard."

There was a pause and Doheny made a half-hearted attempt to patch the growing rift between the two men. "Look, we're putting out a release tomorrow. I don't know if you've seen the rough—Deirdre has it in her office—but we've already reached the fifty percent mark on completion of the pipeline, which, considering the late start, is not so bad. We've got three hundred and twenty miles of pipe installed and we're three weeks ahead of schedule on that, which is fantastic, considering that we had to change forty miles of the pipeline from below-ground construction to above-ground, most of it just south of here between Fairbanks and

Sourdough. By next month we will have moved twenty-one million cubic yards of gravel and completed eighty percent of the pipeline work pad. We've got at least three hundred and twenty-five miles of ditch excavated for below-ground pipe and about forty-two thousand vertical supports for the above-ground pipe. Half of the pipe has been already welded and we're more than twenty percent complete on the pump station construction and the marine terminal in Valdez, including the ballast water treatment area, and we've started construction on the flotation building and the chemical storage tanks."

"Listen," Brandon said wearily, "that's all public relations bullshit. I don't care about how many percentages you have of this and that. All I want to know is, are we going to be able to open that valve in Valdez in the spring of '77?"

"Tough to say," Doheny said, cutting into the steak. "I'd say we'd be lucky to make it by fall."

"Do you realize how much Alamo has riding on this? We're over-extended as hell and you know it."

Doheny flashed a tight smile at his dining companion. "Yes, but I don't work for Alamo, do I?"

"You Goddamn well do," Brandon said angrily. "Who got you the job?"

"And who double-crossed me on my Mexican oil deal so I had to look for a Goddamn job?" Doheny said. He was flushed from the drinks and wine and little beads of sweat were popping out on an otherwise controlled face.

"I'm beginning to see the light," Brandon said. "I'd been wondering why certain things had been happening around your operation."

"Meaning what?"

"Meaning security leaks, meaning playing footsie with all these eco-freaks and EPA inspectors far beyond the call of duty. Meaning, general foot-dragging."

"Don't bullshit me, Brandon. If it wasn't for me the pipeline wouldn't be nearly as complete as it is. It's you guys with your half-assed engineering and trying to guess what's going to happen up here, without knowing fuck-all about it, that have been causing all the problems. Like that stupid routing of the pipeline through the Atigun Canyon, where any idiot in a helicopter could have told you it was impossible to go. Now we've had to move the whole Goddamn thing and hope the EPA doesn't hear about it before we've finished."

The hostility now was out in the open.

"The way I understand it," Brandon said, carefully separating the backbone from the pink meat of the salmon, "there's a lot of guys up here feathering their nests with money they didn't exactly get on salary from Denali."

"That's really funny," Doheny said. "I didn't hear about that, but I did hear of a lot of bag men traveling around the Middle East and seeing politicians up here and labor bigwigs, who were supposed to have paid off certain amounts of cash, but who didn't exactly turn over the amounts that they were supposed to, if you know what *I* mean . . ."

The two men stared into each other's eyes across the table. It was stud poker and they were down to the last card. Neither had anything showing on the board, neither knew what card the other was holding in the hole, and neither could afford to call, for the moment.

Without waiting for coffee or dessert, Brandon snapped his finger at the waiter for the bill.

"I've got another appointment right now, but I can only tell you one thing, Doheny, and that is, I'm watching you good. So don't try any fancy moves on me."

Doheny remained seated, chewing on the last morsels

386

of the grayish steak. "And I'm telling *you* something, Brandon. Watch your ass."

Brandon walked stiff-legged away from the table, leaving Doheny to drain the last few ounces of the Pommard. In the elevator he looked at his watch and realized he was cutting things close. His next appointment was at ten p.m. Hurriedly he jumped into the shower, washed and shaved, sprayed his arm pits, patted some Brut on his cheeks, and then put a few drops on his abdomen. He slipped on a pair of red silk pajamas and a brocaded Chinese dressing gown he had brought back from Bangkok some years earlier. Room service had brought up ice and soda, as he had instructed them earlier. From his Hunting World carry-on bag he took the last of the three bottles of Chivas he'd brought up for the trip and put it on the sideboard.

At precisely ten-thirty there was a soft knock on the door.

"Come."

The door opened and Susie Wing stood there in a modest black cheong-san with a high slit up the side. Susie had dark snapping eyes and shiny black hair, but she was more Eskimo than Chinese. Her name came from her ex-husband, a Chinese merchant in Anchorage, to whom Susie had been married until it all ended in a "Spenard divorce"—Susie had discovered that her husband was salting away all the profits of his sporting goods store in a private bank account which he was spending on a varied assortment of masseuses, hostesses, harlots, and man-hungry housewives. Susie didn't give a damn about the sex, but she resented the money. So one day, when her husband came home at night, she picked up his Smith and Weston special and put a bullet right through his sternum. "I thought he was a prowler," Susie explained innocently to the court. That year Susie became another Spenard Divorcee.

On one of his early trips, Brandon had met Susie and his investigators soon furnished him with the necessary background details. Brandon got Susie a job with Denali in Doheny's office. If she did her job well and furnished any information that Brandon requested, he explained to her, along with certain other services, she could continue to earn her high-pay Denali salary, plus a small bonus, or even a large one. If she did not, he would reveal to security certain things he knew about her and Susie would be out fifty thousand dollars a year. All in all, she had no arguments with the proposition.

Brandon stood back to look at the striking dark haired girl for a moment, then motioned her in. "Come in, come in," he said. "You'll catch your death of cold out there. Pour us a few drinks."

He took Susie's black diamond mink and hung it in the closet. Susie put the manila envelope on the table and mixed a pair of Chivas and sodas.

Al lay back on the bed crossways, his feet hanging over the edge and accepted the drink lazily. Susie held his head up with one hand as he sipped the drink appreciatively, then took the drink from his hand, put it on the night table, and kissed him lightly.

Expertly her hand found its way under the hem of the dressing gown and into the fly of the red silk pajamas. "My, my," she said. "We're not quite ready, are we?"

"Take care of it, Susie," Brandon said dreamily. "You know what to do."

"Don't worry. Everything will be all right."

Gently she took her hand from behind his head and started to untie the sash of the dressing gown, as Al Brandon fumbled at the buttons of her tight-fitting cheong-san.

388

"VALDEZ (pronounced val-DEEZ) is located 115 air miles east of Anchorage at the east end of Valdez Port, a natural fiord just off Valdez arm . . . Valdez has long been known for its beautiful setting with tall mountains rising on all sides of the town, a picture in any direction you look. A small boat harbor adds the final touch to the dramatic setting beneath the rugged peaks and in any weather the natural beauty here is awe-inspiring.

Climate: The coldest month is January, average temperature is 19.3 degrees. The warmest month is July, average temperature is 53.2 degrees. Valdez has an average of 22 feet of snow a year. The area gets extreme winds of 60 to 100 miles per hour. These occur mostly in the fall of the year and sometimes last for several days . . . Heaviest recorded snowfall was in 1928—517 inches. Greatest depth at one time was 80 inches in 1949."

—*Milepost All-the-North Travel Guide*

Chapter Thirty-five

October 17, 1975

Dear Sonia and Gang:

Whoo, boy. The shit has really hit the fan since my last big report out of here. Population of the town has gone up from about 800 to almost 7000, and all that fancy city planning they did is just out the window. There's trailers and Winnebagos and make-shift shacks all over the place. There's even a little chili joint in the middle of town that's built into the back of an old bus. The phones as you know are even more out of the question than they

are up there, and you've got to stand
in line for everything from gas to
groceries—including pussy, if you don't
have any of your own.

As I've told you, the salmon run has
been so poor the last couple of years
that I just decided to give up the
boats entirely. I couldn't get any
crews anyway, what with them all working on the pipeline. Actually, the
salmon shortage has something to do
with my job over in the terminal. I'm
working in security, you know, but
lately they've had me working with this
guy, Paul Sedlitz. He's a tough old
sour dough from way back—a former
trapper—and they've been using him to
chase bears and fox and so on away
from the camp. Since the salmon shortage there's been a lot more bear
around, trying to get at the garbage
here. Both blackies and browns. Everybody thinks the bears are funny, and
they kind of are if you don't get
too close to them. You'll be working
along the fence or something in broad
daylight, then when it's getting dark,
you'll look around and there'll be a
bear looking at you, just to see what
you're doing, out of curiosity. Usually
you're okay as long as you don't have
any food around; that's what causes
most of the trouble. But they're
peculiar and unpredictable. And they're
really interesting.

Sedlitz told me about a bear up at

Garr Lake that came to the same cabin
every year and knocked out a small
side window, but then didn't enter the
cabin. Finally they put in big strong
shutters and the bear couldn't knock
in the window, or that's what they
thought. But the next spring, looking
at the cabin, they found out from the
footprints that the bear had tried
to bust through the shutter—apparently
for some time—and then he'd walked
around the front of the cabin, smashed
the door, walked into the cabin, broke
the window from the inside, and then
left without touching another thing.
Figure that one out, will you! (I wish
I had him on our side.)

Of course, I'm not the only one that
gave up fishing. There's still a few
stubborn guys who stay in there, but
they're starving to death, what with
kelp, crab, and even halibut selling
off the dock for a dollar fifty a
pound. Why, they'll be lucky if they
make twelve or fifteen thousand dollars a year on a year-round basis—not
much compared to what you can make on
the pipeline, but then you only work a
few months. Some guys are fishing in
season and then working the pipeline.

The thing that gets me is that this
year or next the pipeline will employ
a maximum of about 15,000 people. But
there's more than 25,000 people employed by the fishing business, year
in and year out. And by '77 the pipe-

line will be out of here. Furthermore, the fishermen earn and spend their money right here in Alaska, but most of those Okies on the pipeline take their money out home and don't hardly spend anything here, except maybe in the bars.

Now it's getting to be that every time I open my mouth about the dangers to the fishing, they look at me like I'm an enemy of the state and trying to make everybody in Alaska go broke. You know what you'll have when these oil guys get through, if we can't stop them--a stinking, putrid, harbor with all kinds of garbage and junk and oil floating in it like down in the Lower forty-eight. No fish, no wildlife--probably not even any bears. I'd rather have bears than most of those Texans.

Sedlitz tells funny stories about the bears. He's been up and down all the different camps—Five Mile, Chandalar, and everything—they send for him when they have a problem. For instance, these sack lunches that they take in a truck have been attracting the bears. Lots of times the guys have to go lunchless because the bears have gotten in and gobbled them up, just like Yogi at Yellowstone. At Chandalar, Paul says a grizzly pushed his way into the kitchen and ate the dessert the cooks had prepared for supper. He scoffed down eleven brand new apple pies, just like they were peanuts. The problem

is, everybody keeps thinking the bears
are cute and keeps feeding them. At Five
Mile the bears have broken into the
mess hall five times, and sometimes
they go underneath the pilings of the
buildings and start to rip right through
the floor. Down in the "A" Barracks
here we had an electric fire recently
at the mess hall, and these two electricians crawled underneath to see what
could be done about it. One worker said
to the other, "Boy, you sure got under
here fast," but there wasn't any answer.
It seems the electrician was talking
to a grizzly who was under there, and
had caused the fire in the first place.

One bear here even climbed up in a
crane and made the operator jump for
his life. For a while the bear was
standing right there—I saw him—just
like he was the crane operator! "You'd
better get that guy down from there,"
somebody said. "He don't even have a
union card."

According to Denali rules, we're not
allowed to shoot a bear except in very
special conditions. We have a tranquilizer gun and we've shot a couple
of them that way and taken them as much
as fifty miles away. But they're back
by morning usually. The best thing they
use me for is throwing rocks. If you
hit a bear in a good spot, usually he'll
run away. But first he'll stop to
figure out where the rock came from,
and that's when you have to have a

second rock handy. That's the time I
bust 'em upside the head. But you got
to have pretty good aim and get pretty
close to do it good.

At the distance I've been working,
it's the point of no return, and you
can't out-run those fuckers. The only
gun we have on the premises—and this
may interest you for other reasons—
is one shotgun that belongs to the
Wackenhut, in case of real trouble with
the bears. And even that can only be
signed out under very special conditions. We had one wild incident up here
that occured right outside the camp.
This couple were up there taking a walk
in the woods—necking or something—it
must have been that sexy smell that got
the bear going, because when the man
went into the cabin to get some supplies or whatever he came back and
found her lying there without her head.
A bear apparently slapped her right
across the skull and took her head
clean off. He was a big blondie with
a white blaze, and two weeks later the
same bear showed up in the girl's dormitory. That bear must have been pussy
hungry. Anyway, the only time we were
allowed to shoot one is if he's in a
dormitory or in a mess-hall or if he's
got ahold of someone. That's happened
plenty of times but usually we manage
to shoo them out. This time, though,
Sedlitz figured the best thing would be
to take care of that big old blond

killer bear. So he got the shotgun
loaded with solid pellets. It was a
repeater issued by the Wackenhuts. And
he went in there and killed that grizzly. Later he skinned her out and it
was pretty amazing when you look at the
carcass of a skinned bear. It looked
just like a naked human being, only
bigger.

There's not many freaks around here
of our type, except of course, Mason.
I got him a job at the Valdez Club,
and every night that I see him he looks
more and more wild-eyed. I think Mason
never figures he's going to make it
through to the end of the job. That's
a rough place down there. We were drinking in it the other night and we met
a guy who's working one of the tugs
that come in to the terminus camp. He
said he'd been up here five years and
that he came up after the Venice riots.
I never heard of them, but maybe you
did. He said they were started up at
the Mayall concert. He said when the
cops busted him there they asked what
he did, and he said he was a student.
"Of what?" the cops asked. "Police
science," he said and it was the truth,
but they beat the shit out of him anyway. So he took his bindle roll—about
$40—and hit out for Alaska. The kid's
got a cabin over near Delta Junction,
some dogs and a sled and an old lady
up there. He traps in the winter with
an Athabascan Indian and he says that

the woods up there are full of freaks.
Once, he says, in the middle of the
winter he heard this plane, an Otter,
circling around and they went out to
see what it was. The next thing he
knows, the pilot drops this little package and it's full of dope. There's a
note attached to it. "Can I land?" it
says. So the freaks broke all records
beating it down to the airstrip to pick
him up. And the guy stayed for three
weeks. I didn't get the guy's name,
but he might be useful to you. He
hangs around the Valdez Club anyway
and I know his boat, so I'll get to him.
Don't worry. There are some other good
contacts here too.

They've been trying to crack down on
drugs, gambling, and prostitution here.
But so far they're not having much success. The biggest vice raid in this
town's history took place recently
where they busted a lot of people at
a trailer park and in a couple of bars
and a motel. They got about a half dozen
people at Space Five in Johnson's Trailer Court, and confiscated maybe $6000 in
cash and checks. Hell, we've got poker
games twice as big as that in camp
every night. They also hit the Sheffield House, the Acres Bar, and the
Valdez Club Bar for prostitution. One
of the gals they busted said she was a
virgin and she really might have been.
I remember talking to her in the bar
one day and she told me that she'd

396

taken measurements and figured out that
she'd eaten over nine yards of cock in
one day. "Eat, eat, eat," she said.
"Doesn't anybody around here want
to fuck?"

Anyway, all the places were back in
business the following week and whatever work the whores couldn't do in the
bars, they came out to the camps to do.
If you know the camps, it's easy enough
to lift a badge from some drunk in
town and get in. The walls are porous,
and the fences aren't too secure either
—for your information. I hear that they
are planning to start flowing oil down
here by spring of 1977, but I frankly
don't think they'll ever make it. It'll
be at least another six months—maybe
a year. And then only if they don't
have any big labor trouble. It looks
to me like none of the big union bosses
are interested in a general strike.
Mostly it's been wildcats—just guys
getting pissed off at some little deal
or another. After all, they don't have
much to gripe about—at these wages,
with money, food, and toilet articles,
and entertainment and everything thrown
in—including lodging. But there's always
some who will find a way to grouse.
The way some of these guys act, you
actually begin to feel sorry for the
pipeline bosses—until I think how
they're shafting us with this
whole deal.

They have five generators here and it

may be hard to bust them all out. But
they've got a central message center
that controls almost all the communications. I think that if we hit that it
will do a lot to add to the confusion
on the big day. The way I figure it,
if you get Pump Station Ten immobilized,
then all you have to do is hit Pump
Station Five at the Thompson Pass—that's
the highest point in the pipeline after
it runs down out of the Brooks Range.
If we play it right, we should have
that eight hundred miles of pipeline
hanging there like a big licorice shoe-
string completely solidified.

Burn this letter before reading.

                                    Your friend, Van

P.S. Mason sends love and kisses.

"The myth of oil power. The American people are being duped—there we said it, straight out. Politicians running for office, aware that voters are frustrated and angry about many things, have discovered in the bigness of business—especially oil companies—a convenient explanation for all things wrong with our country. But think about that issue. Where's all that power our critics say we have? It wasn't enough . . . to get price controls removed on oil . . . Oil's power frankly is a myth. But it's no myth that oil companies have become scapegoats. If we sound angry about it, we *are*."

—From a national ad by
Mobil Oil Corporation, 1976

Chapter Thirty-six

In the winter of 1975, Fairbanks experienced one of the worst cold spells in years. Water pipes and sewer lines froze solid. More than fifty percent of the flights to Fairbanks airport were cancelled or diverted due to poor visibility. The entire town was blanketed in a heavy ice fog, a combination of chimney smoke, automobile exhaust, steam from the power plants, and any other noxious gases trapped in the mass of warmer air, which created an atmospheric inversion over the entire city.

For three weeks, the temperature did not rise above forty degrees below zero. Work on the pipeline slowed down to a frozen dawdle, mainly going on only in those areas already enclosed—such as the pump stations, and the administrative units. Grease froze in the fork-lift units so that a traverse of several feet that would normally take a few minutes took an hour.

As a result of all this, nobody was particularly concerned when Brent Heywood did not show up for work. Even the fact that he did not call in was not considered remarkable, considering the state of telephones and other communications in Fairbanks. It was assumed that either he'd had some crisis in his house in the northern suburbs near the University of Alaska, or that he was hung over, or had some minor illness.

Because of Heywood's absence, Deirdre found herself handling much of the paperwork that normally would have fallen his way—coping with press questions about the arson cases in Tonsina (apparently the work of disgruntled pipeline workers), answering requests for information on the new state policy of enforcing the rule for hiring only Native Alaskans, which was arousing considerable hostility from the union executives. To do this work, Deirdre often found it more convenient to sit at Heywood's desk and use his telephone extension. On the third day of Heywood's absence Deirdre put a call through to Al Everhardt to see if he had heard anything, but Everhardt was in Juneau covering a special committee meeting of the State Legislature.

Deirdre got a cup of black coffee from the machine in the corridor and returned to Heywood's desk to handle some of his incoming calls and routine mail. She had hardly settled into his swivel chair when the telephone rang. She accidentally knocked the styrofoam cup of coffee over onto the top of the formica desk as she rolled sideways to pick up the receiver. Distractedly she picked up the phone. It was Everhardt.

"Did you call me?"

"I did, but can you get back to me in just a minute? I just spilled coffee all over the Goddamn desk." She hung up and looked around for some Kleenex or paper towels to sop up the dripping coffee, and finally settled for some back copies of the *Anchorage Times* that were on a radiator in the corner, only hoping that Heywood had not been saving them for some special purpose. The coffee was seeping under Heywood's desk blotter and Deirdre lifted it by the edge to reach under it before the coffee could do anymore damage than it had. There was a two page typewritten memo under the blotter which Deirdre pulled out before the coffee had touched more than just on one corner. In five minutes, she had the desk dry and clean, and had wiped up any remaining drops with Kleenex from her purse. Only the corners of a few documents had been stained by the coffee.

Deirdre lifted the two page memo that had apparently gotten lost under Heywood's blotter, and wiped the remaining coffee from the edge. At first it looked like many of the planning memos they had made in the earlier stages—outlines for presentations on company policy. The page was headed in capitals:

```
FOR THE PURPOSE OF THIS OUTLINE A
SERIES OF AUDIENCE GROUPS WILL BE
IDENTIFIED, THE GOAL THAT WE WISH
THAT GROUP TO ACHIEVE FOR US WILL BE
IDENTIFIED AND THE POSSIBLE MEANS
FOR THAT GOAL OUTLINED. THE AUDIENCES
DO NOT APPEAR HERE IN THE ORDER OF
IMPORTANCE OR IN THE TIME FRAME IN
WHICH THEY WOULD BE APPROACHED.
```

Deirdre scanned the document idly as she picked up the phone waiting for a line to see if she could get back in touch with Everhardt. The first sub-section was headed:

```
"AUDIENCE: COMMUNICATIONS MEDIA,
LOWER FORTY-EIGHT.
GOAL: Allow them to be outraged at
the situation and allow them to pass
that outrage on to the general pub-
lic. Give them news.
```

PROGRAM: Leak information to them
that proves both government and
industry have been lying to them.
That same information will buttress
some of the already stated editorial
beliefs. It is relatively easy to
give them cause to shout scandal,
i.e. falsifying of environmental information, non-public decision to
re-route prior to acceptance of publicly stated route in Atigun Canyon,
specific inadequacies in engineering, etc.

Slowly, Deirdre placed the unanswered phone back
on its hook and straightened up in her chair to read
the document more carefully. It continued:

AUDIENCE: ENVIRONMENTAL GROUPS
GOAL: Give them the information and
ability to create further delays by
supporting their legal and public
efforts. (This may require the dona-
tion of funds for public messages
on their part.)
PROGRAM: Work directly with the
trainees on court cases. Give them
issues, not straw men, for their advertising program. Also, give them
funds to carry out the latter through
newspapers. The earlier stages of
their program will allow them to
reapproach their members and be able
to elicit support, support they have
not been able to get recently because
the issue is considered an old issue.

AUDIENCE: DEPARTMENT OF THE INTERIOR
GOAL: Weaken direct support
PROGRAM: Make public their coercion
in project to date. Make it so embarrassing they must back off. Could
possibly be done privately rather
than publicly. Support of alternative
by many staff people already exists.
Make this public.

AUDIENCE: GOVERNMENT (STATE, LOCAL,
FEDERAL)
GOAL: Continued hearings and delays,
ability to make issue among support-
ers during election year.
PROGRAM: Show them direct economic
benefits from alternative.

AUDIENCE: PRESIDENTIAL CANDIDATES
GOAL: Base support of saving the
planet. Suggest they make public
stink about pipeline issues.
PROGRAM: Democrats in search of issues
may have another Watergate or grain
deal to embarrass Jerry Ford. This is
easiest of all suggestions
contained here.

AUDIENCE: NADER ET AL
GOAL: He pressures Congress into more
hearings or bills so regulating
project that it is no longer feasible.
PROGRAM: Another man here in search
of windmills. He has yet to take a
shot at this one.

Underneath in Heywood's handwriting was "Probably some I forgot. They are around like flies, as are the lies that could be shown to be lies."

Deirdre put the two page memo down on Heywood's desk and twirled thoughtfully in the swivel chair to stare out the window over toward Fort Wainwright. It was true that she and Everhardt and Baronian considered themselves rebels and often joked about the incredible waste and inconsistency and downright treachery of the company. But this memo looked like a fairly serious attempt to outline a program for subverting the entire pipeline operation. For whom had Heywood prepared it?

It might have been just a form of doodling—a mental exercise. But what about the little note on the bottom? To whom was it addressed? And had the document ever been delivered?

The papers still looked fairly fresh, as though it had been done during the past few days prior to Heywood's absence. Deirdre wasn't sure about how she herself felt about it. Certainly she had become disabused and dissatisfied with the operations of Denali since she had been there. What had seemed like a patriotic and important project in the national interest now seemed like a giant capitalistic boondoggle, which in the end would do very little good for the country, but earn untold billions for the oil companies.

Her relationship with Wilbur Steele had deteriorated as her respect for the Denali project had dissipated. The almost hypnotic power he had always had to make her do anything that he wanted her to—a power he had held ever since he took her virginity in the tack room of the stable back in Mitchell Mesa—seemed to be losing its force as she herself was losing her awe of Wilbur and her respect for him. This memo was a serious matter. Treason, one might say. She wondered if she should go with it to her father.

But her affection for Heywood was such that she felt the least she could do was to wait and show it to him when he returned. They could discuss it. Perhaps there was some simple explanation for it all. Maybe it was all just a gag between him — and who? Everhardt? Baronian? But if so, why hadn't they let her in on the joke? Besides, it wasn't worded in a very frivolous manner. In fact, what it did was to present a very potent blueprint for one of the only actions which could halt or delay the completion of the pipeline. It was a program of deadly effective verbal sabotage and political action.

Still unsure of what her plan was, and somewhat distracted, Deirdre again tried to call Heywood at his home. She had been calling three or four times a day —ever since he had failed to show up that Monday. But with the conditions of the phones in Fairbanks, a busy signal meant almost nothing. This time, finally, there was a ringing sound but still no answer. After letting the phone buzz for almost a full minute, Deirdre hung up and called Al Everhardt back at his apartment.

"What's the problem, beautiful one?" Everhardt said.

"Have you seen or spoken to Brent this week?"

Everhardt was puzzled. "No, I was in Juneau the first couple of days this week and I just got back today. I called him but all I got was the Goddamn busy signal. They told me at the office that he hadn't come to work. What's the matter?"

"I don't know if anything's the matter, but this is the third day he hasn't shown up and I'm getting a little worried. I haven't been able to get through on the phone."

Everhardt sounded concerned.

"You want me to go over and check?"

"Yes," Deirdre said. "And I think I'd like to go with you." She wasn't sure why she'd said that. Maybe it had something to do with the paper under the blotter.

"I'll pick you up at lunchtime. Maybe we can have a snack together afterwards," Everhardt said.

"Okay," Deirdre said, and hung up.

Before returning to her office, she made a Xerox copy of Heywood's memo and then flipped the original back under the blotter where it had been. She took the Xerox back to her office, folded it up small, and stuck it in a dead file in the back of one of her cabinets.

CLUBS AND GROUPS
Gay community does exist in Fairbanks.
For further information contact Gay Co-op
Box 81265, Fairbanks.

—A classified ad in the
All-Alaska Weekly

Chapter Thirty-seven

The ride to Heywood's flat, which was located in one of the new housing developments beyond the University of Fairbanks, off College Road, was hair-raising. The ice-fog was so thick that even with the bright yellow fog-piercing lights on Everhardt's Scout, they couldn't travel more than three or four miles an hour.

Heywood's house was a tiny but pleasant A-frame with enough evergreens to keep it looking warm and cozy even in that deadly chill winter. As they pulled into the small parking lot beside the A-frame they could see that Heywood's Volvo wagon was still in the garage with its headbolt heater plugged in. There had been a light snowfall on Sunday night, but there were no tracks leading from the garage or from the house.

"Look's like he's still home," Everhardt said nervously.

Deirdre nodded.

They went up to the cheery door, painted a warm shade of burnt orange. The doorbell was completely coated with ice and ringing it was a hopeless proposition. Everhardt managed to lift the brass door knocker with his clumsy fur mittens and pounded it vigorously. There was no answer from within.

Anxiously, he pounded it again, and then hit the door with his mittened fists.

"Probably drunk," he said, but there was no belief in his voice. Nervously he stripped off the fur mitten, leaving only the thin woolen gloves he wore underneath. He reached into his pocket for his key chain.

"I've got a key to the place," he explained shyly. "Ah—he gave it to me, in case of—ah—emergencies like this. You know, or like if he was away—so I could look after the house."

"Stop explaining," Deirdre said. "Just open the damned door. I'm kind of worried."

After some fumbling with the lock, Everhardt succeeded in pushing the key in and turning it. He pushed the door open.

The entrance hall, which gave onto a white-carpeted, sunken living room, looked as though a regiment of cavalry had galloped through it. Chairs were smashed and the upholstered furniture appeared to have been slashed by a knife—cotton and foam rubber leaked obscenely from the wounds.

"My God, what happened?"

Al Everhardt's face turned white with fear. There are only three other rooms in the small cottage—actually two and a half; a small loft above that Heywood used for his study, a bedroom off the main living room, and a kitchen to the left. On the white wall over the sofa where Heywood had hung his most prized possession, an Ad Reinhardt minimalist black-on black oil painting, there was no painting. And Deirdre saw with shock that the Reinhardt was laying face up, on the caribou rug in front of the couch, slashed just as the sofa had been.

Everhardt now looked genuinely sick. He sat down on one of the ripped easy chairs and put his head between his hands.

"I can't look anymore. Something terrible has happened."

"Well, at least we can be pretty sure that whoever did this left before Sunday. There were no footprints outside the door," Deirdre reasoned. "I wonder if Brent . . ."

Everhardt, his face still in his hands, said, "Call the police, please. I know something terrible has happened."

There was a white Princess phone on the low Parson's table near the couch—one of the few pieces of furniture that had not been broken or ripped. Deirdre picked up the receiver and sat down on the ruined couch. She dialed 118, hoping that for once the call would go through, and by some perverse miracle it did.

The police got there very quickly, considering the weather conditions and the number of emergency calls they had been getting. Possibly all the criminals were off having lunch, as it was noontime.

Ernie Wilderman, the patrolman Deirdre had met a number of times off duty in downtown Fairbanks, showed up first. He was a lanky, hulking young man who only three years before had been playing basketball for the University in Fairbanks. He had been on the force just under a year. With him was Harold Toomey, an old-time Fairbanks patrol officer. He was small and gray-haired and wore steel-rimmed glasses. Behind his back, people called him "Sock-it-Toomey," but to his face they only called him Harold.

"What's the problem?" Toomey asked, looking curiously around the room.

"We haven't heard from Heywood, for several days and then we came in and found this."

"Did you look for him?" Toomey said.

"I'm . . . I'm afraid to. The bedroom is in there."

The door, of smooth, blond, birchwood veneer, was half-ajar. Toomey hauled his notebook from his pocket. "Take a look in there, kid," he said to Wilderman,

409

stepping over the smashed and scattered furniture. The young trooper went to the door and pushed it further open with a big mittened hand. He took one look in and slammed it violently shut.

"He's in there," he said, his ruddy face going stark white. "You can't look. Nobody look. It's terrible!"

Toomey snapped his notebook shut and strode to the door and pushed it open again. He stood for a full minute looking inside, then turned quietly to the two people sitting on the wrecked couches. "Your friend is dead."

Chapter Thirty-eight

The murder of Brent Heywood—a particularly gory
one—shocked even crime-hardened Fairbanksans, at
least for a number of weeks. Heywood had been stab-
bed and sexually mutilated. His body was hung from a
rafter in the bedroom of the A-frame, his abdomen had
been cut and his intestines pulled out and stretched
along the floor like a length of rope. Several glassine
envelopes, which had apparently contained cocaine,
were found in the apartment, as were the murder weapons, a set of Sabatier kitchen knives from Heywood's
own gourmet kitchen.

Newspaper reports hinted delicately at Heywood's
homosexual alliances, his friendship with Al Everhardt,
who had found the body, was expounded to make it
clear—even to the most dense of readers—that the two
men were lovers. In fact, Everhardt was the first choice
as suspect by the police, until they discovered that he
had an iron-clad alibi, having been in Juneau on Sunday
when the murder took place. Police theorized—privately and in print—that the murder was the work of
homosexual drug addicts.

411

Fairbanks was not a place where homosexuals were easily recognized, all of them confining themselves to their respected closets. In a tolerant state, where marijuana was legalized, drugs, gambling, and even murder widely tolerated, homosexuality was looked on with definite disfavor. There were no gay bars or hangouts, and very few gays dared walk the streets in the more extravagant, deviant-type-wardrobes. Any gay activity in Fairbanks was probably confined to rough trade.

Fairbanks' mobile crime lab was called in to try to find fingerprints, fibers, mud or blood, but no clues of any significance were turned up. Because of the unsavory aspects of Brent Heywood's private life, Denali did everything it could to dissociate itself from the picture. But this was impossible.

George Mayberry, an ex-newspaperman who had been doing P.R. work for Golconda, was brought in temporarily to fill the gap left by Heywood's death. Brandon, when he heard about the replacement, was not particularly happy to have another Golconda man on the team.

"I don't see," he argued with Doheny, "why we have to have one of them. Couldn't you get somebody from Alamo, or at least somebody who doesn't have loyalty to one of the clients?"

But Doheny was unimpressed by the argument. "His experience is perfect. He's been preparing all of the big public service ads that Golconda's been running and he's got a good relationship with a lot of the politicians and the ecology people."

"*Too* good, if you ask me."

"What do you mean by that?"

"I mean that ever since we started this damn pipeline, Golconda has been playing patty-cake with Friends of the Earth and all the rest—even contributing money to their funds."

"Well," Doheny said, "that's good public relations, isn't it? Better than having them for your enemies."

"Yeah, maybe," Brandon said bitterly. "Or maybe it's something else."

Al Everhardt, despite the fact that he was no longer a suspect, was grilled over and over by the Fairbanks police in hope of getting clues as to which of Brent Heywood's homosexual companions might have done the job.

"I've told you over and over," Everhardt said. "He didn't fool around that way."

"The wife is always the last one to know," one of the detectives smirked.

Everhardt looked up angrily, but there was little he could do. To be fair, the cops had tried to avoid limp-wrist innuendo, but had not been able to completely stifle their running patter of fag jokes. Two weeks after the murder, after promising that he'd stay in touch and make himself available for any further questioning, Everhardt quit his job and dragged up to the outside, well-aware that since the scandal he had become a liability to his newspaper, and probably would have been asked to leave anyway.

Never having worked for an oil company, or with a contractor associated with the pipeline, the life-savings Al Everhardt took with him when he left Alaska amounted to about seven hundred and fifty dollars and the plane ticket.

Deirdre was in a state of shock and probably would never completely recover from the sense of loss. Brent Heywood had become one of her closest and most reliable friends. And yet, as close as he was, he told her nothing about that memo.

During the second week of the murder investigation, the detectives, desperate for any sort of clue, asked

413

Deirdre's help in going through Heywood's files. Ordinarily, it might have been more suitable to ask Susie Wing, who helped Heywood with some of his secretarial duties, but because Deirdre had been handling much of the work in the days prior to the discovery of Heywood's murder—and to some extent afterwards—it was felt she could best guide the detectives in looking for what they hoped would be clues.

On the day the detectives were expected to arrive, Deirdre went to Heywood's office to retrieve the embarrassing memo from under the desk blotter. When she got there she was surprised to see Baronian there, extracting a file from one of the cabinets.

"What's up, Bobby?"

"Just some personal stuff. Heywood had a file of some of our correspondence and I'd rather keep it myself for reference. If these cops get in here they're liable to seal the whole thing and I'll never be able to get at it again."

Almost defensively he showed her the manila folder which in fact had his name on the tab "BARONIAN." But Deirdre wondered what correspondence had been necessary between the two. Of course, Baronian did take pictures for the P.R. department and probably these letters involved bills for supplies and photo processing and so on. In any event, the cops had not given her the responsibility of guarding the files, and she was reasonably certain that Baronian had had nothing to do with the murder.

Before the police came, Deirdre also decided to look in the file marked "Personal," but the results were disappointing—it was practically empty. There was a little correspondence concerning clothing, arctic gear that Heywood had ordered from Eddie Bauer in Seattle, several receipts from Maroon's Swap Shop and Bookshop, some insurance papers, a clipping describing the raid by the four Denali employees on Fort Wainwright. Deirdre was not surprised to find the clipping there, as it was a subject of logical interest for Heywood, but she wondered why it was in the personal file—perhaps, she thought, it had been misfiled by accident. Also there were copies of several local ecological publications, but again they were located in the personal file. One of the publications was edited by Abby Maroon, one of Baronian's friends, who owned the Swap Shop.

Deirdre remembered meeting him a few times at the Savoy Bar. He was a strange, Mediterranean-looking man with liquid black eyes. Later, she had visited the bookstore attached to the Swap Shop several times. It was the only place that had a good supply of reports put out by the Sierra Club, Friends of the Earth, and other ecological groups. It also carried *Rolling Stone, New Times,* and other publications that Deirdre liked to look through in case the clipping service that supplied them with copies of all articles published concerning the pipeline had missed something, which, in fact, it did—frequently. Maroon obviously remembered her and who she worked for. He had enthusiastically searched through his piles of controversial material and Third World publications for additional subject matter that she might have missed.

"Read it, read it," he urged. "We could use somebody at Denali who can see the light."

"What do you mean we?"

Maroon looked up at her in surprise. "We, I mean, everyone against the pipeline. I mean, me and my friends."

"Does that mean Baronian too?"

"Baronian? Yes, Baronian. Heywood—he helps out. And others . . ."

"And what do you hope to get from me?"

"Nothing." Abby Maroon said. "Sympathy, maybe."

She had dropped the subject at the time.

Halfway through the police check, Deirdre realized with consternation that she had not removed the memo from under the blotter on Heywood's desk. Fortunately, the police check was perfunctory—largely because they were convinced that the murder was the work of "fag dope-fiends." When they had gone, she hastened to check under the tooled leather blotter holder, and was shocked to find that the memo was gone! It was clear to her that only Baronian could have removed it.

In the end, the police were able to find no evidence concerning Heywood's personal life in the office, nor did they find any in the house—his personal address book was missing, taken, it was presumed, by the perpetrator or perpetrators, as the police referred to them.

To some extent, Deirdre felt that her problem of what to do about the anti-pipeline memo she had discovered under Heywood's blotter was solved, or was it? What was Baronian's part in the affair? Had Heywood made up the memo for his own amusement, and then shown it to Baronian? Or were there copies of it around elsewhere? Was it actually being implemented, and if so, did she have any responsibility to do anything about it? Of course, technically she did, since she was taking Denali's money, but in actual fact she was beginning to feel more sympathy, after the things she had seen and heard, for the anti-pipeline faction. It was getting harder and harder for her to square her personal opinions with her daily work. Baronian had left the office on a field trip just after Deirdre saw him in Heywood's office, so it was several days before she was able to get in touch with him. She left a note for him to call her as soon as he got back.

When Baronian finally returned her call, she suggested lunch at the Malamute Saloon in the Cripple Creek resort at Esther, about seven miles south of Fairbanks. It was a tourist place which featured recitations of "The Cremation of Sam McGee" and "The Shooting of Dan McGrew," to the accompaniment of old-time piano playing. But the shows were in the evening and the saloon opened at noon. It was generally empty, except for a few tourists, until later in the afternoon.

Baronian was surprised at her choice of a rendezvous.

"For Christ sake," Baronian said, "nobody goes up there but 'Cheechakos.' "

"Yeah, well there's something up there that . . . ah . . . I thought we'd better check out. It's important, take my word for it," Deirdre said.

Hanging up the phone she wondered if she was growing paranoid. In any event she had chosen the Cripple Creek resort because practically no company executives or employees of Denali ever went there. Now she wondered if she should even have mentioned the place of the rendezvous over the phone, but decided that she *was* being paranoid.

The Malamute Saloon was nearly empty when they entered it. The only other customers were a family of middle-aged tourists with teenager kids, and she saw to it that they sat at a considerable distance from them.

Over sourdough pancakes and beer she brought up the subject that had been bothering her.

"Bobby, I know you took that memo that was under the blotter in Brent's office."

Baronian's deep-set brown eyes stared at her for a full ten seconds before he answered. Carefully he placed his knife and fork back on the plate, although he had only half-finished the pancake.

"What makes you say that?" His voice was dead-serious.

"I know it was there the day before," Deirdre said, "and you were in the office just before the police arrived. I checked when they left, and it was gone."

"So?"

"So, what's the story?"

Baronian sighed and pressed his ham-like palms together and paused as though to compose his thoughts. "I knew we'd get down to it sometime and I guess I would have told you, except for your Dad. Frankly, it was too serious a matter to be trusted to somebody unless I could be absolutely sure of him—or her."

"You knew you could trust me. We've known each other a long time."

"Yes, but there was this personal element. Heywood was afraid."

"Well, what was it about?"

"There are some people that I've been in touch with —sort of ecological people, you might say. They're worried about the pipeline and what it's going to do to this country. And they were looking for help trying to stop it." He paused, still thinking very hard, and then continued. "Those talks we had about the impact on the wildlife, what would happen if there was an oil spill, the earthquake problems, and all the lies and cover-ups the company has been up to. I know we kidded around a lot, but I for one was serious. And so was Heywood, deep down. Were you?"

Now it was Deirdre's turn to pause. "I don't think I really faced up to it. Yes, I suppose I was serious, certainly about what was going on, but I don't know whether I was up to doing anything, like joining a conspiracy."

Baronian laughed, but it was a weak sort of a cackle. "*Conspiracy!* I wouldn't call it a conspiracy. It's just that those people needed some expert advice and Heywood was the man who could give it to them."

"Did Heywood know these people?"

Baronian shook his head. "No, he knew that I was feeding it out to somebody, but he didn't want to know

418

who. He was afraid that he might compromise the group."

"So it was Heywood who was feeding all these leaks out, as it recommends in the memo, right?"

Baronian looked at her curiously. "I certainly think you knew that."

Deirdre shrugged, and said, "I suppose I did. Or I guessed it, anyway."

"And you didn't do anything about it."

"No," Deirdre said, looking down at her plate. "I suppose I wanted somebody to do something, but on account of my connection to my father and Wilbur too, the whole family, I didn't want to be the one."

"And how do you feel now?"

"I feel as though it's too late. I mean the pipeline corridor's been built, most of the ecological damage probably has been done already, so why bother. If someone had been able to stop it at the beginning . . ."

"Is it too late?" Baronian asked. "With all the leaks that have been happening, even before the pipeline oil is running. You think there won't be some tremendous damage, after it gets built? It's not really the pipeline corridor that's going to do the damage, you know, although we've touched on that subject a lot. The caribou will find their way, the Peregrine falcons will find their nest, provided everything is settled down again. But the leaks and the tanker spills. Would you like to see Valdez Bay a pool of oil? And did you ever think what would happen to the Arctic Sea if a leak occurs north of the Brooks Range? And it gets into the Sagavanirktok River? You realize that the pipeline lays right in the bed of the river up through Franklin's Bluff, Happy Valley, all the way up past Galbraith and practically to the Dietrich Pass, except for that funny detour they took at the Atigun River which feeds into the Sag anyway. If they'd ever laid the pipeline in there, there

419

would have been a rupture for sure from all those falling rocks and shifting river beds. And you know what would happen, aside from the food chain, the affect on the wildlife and all that, if it gets out to the Arctic Sea."

"Well, I know about the climate and all that."

"Damn right!" Baronian said emphatically.

Looking at him now for the first time, she thought he was more than a jovial clown: perhaps even a man of some dedication. Why then did she even at that moment doubt his basic sincerity? Still, she knew what he was talking about. The fact was that no one knew exactly what would happen if substantial amounts of oil got onto the Arctic ice, but a lot of meteorologists had suggested that it might have a drastic effect on world-wide weather when the sun hit the dark spots on the ice. The ice would melt more rapidly and the faster the ice melted, the less of it there would be to reflect the sun's energy.

Some weather people said that such an effect could cause the earth's temperature to rise by one or two degrees and eventually produce a serious rise in the level of the world's seas. It was like the nuclear energy problem. Nobody was exactly certain what would happen, but the risks were so enormous that it seemed that it would have to be an equally enormous motivation to take such chances. And by now Deirdre knew that the only motivation was profits for the seven clients of Denali.

Finally Deirdre looked up, past Baronian's hairy fringe, deep into his opaque eyes. Somehow she would feel better if she could see into Baronian's dark pupils, into his brain.

"What do you expect me to do about all this? Do you want me to help?"

"Would you?" Baronian looked at her quizzically.

Deirdre hesitated. "I might."

"Yes, but you paused, didn't you? Because you're too personally involved. That's just the reason that we felt we couldn't bring you into this. There are too many other factors in your life. It wouldn't be fair to you, and it wouldn't be fair to the group."

"And what's this group planning to do?"

Baronian shrugged. "More or less what's in that memo, although those're just guidelines."

"Do they have stateside connections?"

"Listen, Deirdre. What's the point of your knowing all of this? If it gets out, I wouldn't want to think that you were the one who leaked it. I'd rather you didn't know. You understand, don't you?"

Deirdre nodded slowly. "It this all they planned?"

Baronian shrugged again. "Look, I'm not even that tightly connected myself. I'm just a conduit for some of the ideas, a sort of an advisor."

"You realize how serious all this could be?"

"The job? So, I'll get another one. It'll all be over by next year anyway, or the year after. I never had any trouble earning my keep."

"I'm not talking about the job," Deirdre said. "I'm talking about Heywood. Who else knew about that memo?"

Baronian ran his huge hand through his unruly hair. "God knows, I've been trying to think. I suppose Everhardt did. In a way he was one of the parts of the memo. I mean, he probably helped in planning the media aspect."

"He's gone. You know that."

On this subject at any rate, Baronian's concern seemed genuine. "Look," he said. "I've been thinking and thinking. I know damn well that Heywood wasn't hit because he was a fag. I *know* it had something to

421

do with all this. And maybe I'm a little bit scared too. But I figure, if they knew about it, about the memo and all that, they probably knew about the other connections. They can't hit everybody. It must have been that Heywood found out about something else. Something he hadn't yet told anybody else. Something that was just too big and too dangerous . . ."

A waiter in a gingham vest and a sourdough beard brought them deep-dish apple pie, coffee, and a bill.

Baronian grabbed it. "This one's on *my* swindle sheet," he said, but Deirdre didn't answer. She was still trying to think of what it was that Heywood had been able to find out—something that could have brought about such a horrible end.

Baronian slid back in the wooden chair and stood up. "Let's go," he said. "Anybody spots us out in this God-forsaken place, they'd think we were carrying on." He stood waiting for Deirdre to collect her things.

"You're going to go along with this, aren't you? I mean, to the point of not doing anything about the memo?"

"I won't do anything without first consulting you," Deirdre said.

As they climbed into Baronian's yellow Denali Travelall outside the Malamute, Deirdre wondered to herself why she had made that promise, but she didn't say anything.

"What are you thinking about?" Baronian said as he put the four-wheel drive vehicle into gear.

"I was just wondering," Deirdre said, "if we should have come out here in a company car."

When Deirdre returned to her office she found a memo from Mayberry marked simply "FYI." It was attached to a small newspaper clipping from a San Francisco newspaper:

NEWSMAN FOUND DEAD IN HOTEL

Allard Everhardt, a former newsman and columnist, was found dead in his room at the Clift Hotel
last night. Death, according to the coroner, was the
result of an overdose of sleeping pills. An empty
bottle which had contained 100 barbiturates, pre-
scribed for a nervous condition by a San Francisco
doctor, was found on the night table near Everhardt's bed. There was no note, but the manager
and hotel residents said that Everhardt, who last
worked as a columnist for the *All-Alaska Weekly*
in Fairbanks, was despondent over the recent murder of his close friend, Brent Heywood, a Public
Relations man for the Denali Pipeline Company.

Everhardt, according to hotel residents, had
been drinking heavily since he checked into the
Clift several days earlier.

The former newsman was a familiar figure to
many San Franciscans, having started his career
as a copy boy on this paper . . ."

A short obit followed.
Deirdre folded the memo and slipped it into the
top drawer of her desk.
Then she went to the coffee machine in the corridor, drew a cupful of black coffee, and returned to
sit in her office chair staring mindlessly out over the
snow covered frozen landscape.

"Just because somebody's grandfather chased a moose across the land, doesn't mean he owns it . . ."

—Walter Hickel
Governor of Alaska

Chapter Thirty-nine

When Larry Steele arrived back in Fairbanks on R & R it was three weeks after the murder. In the winter there wasn't much to do in Fairbanks except drink and make love through the endless night. But Deirdre was very nervous about being in Larry's room. She had installed a remote-control answering device on her phone so that she was able to check in from time to time, in case there were calls from Wilbur. This irritated Larry enormously.

"Look, he's just your boss. He's not God, you know."

Deirdre shrugged helplessly. "He likes to know where I am at all times."

"Jesus, you'd think you were his slave," Larry said truculently. "You've been weird anyway, since I got up here this trip," he said looking at her curiously. It was the third day of his leave.

"Well, the murder . . . you know . . . it just gets me down. And there are some other things ... "

Deirdre was sitting in her short terry cloth robe removing her makeup with wipe-off pads. Larry lay back nursing a Virginia Gentleman on the rocks. The bottle had been a present from Wilbur on a recent trip from Fairbanks. Since the incident involving Penny, Wilbur had seemed much more solicitous of Larry and more anxious than ever to involve him in the company affairs.

"What other things?" Larry asked quietly, enjoying her movements as she began to brush out her long tawny hair. He wondered when, if ever, they could be together permanently, legally, and he could watch her like this every night if he wanted to. Certainly he had never had a moment's doubt that Deirdre was the one he wanted to marry, although in recent months he had been seeing quite a bit of Ruby, especially when Deirdre was otherwise occupied. She was different from Deirdre, more sensual, more giving, and more grateful for his attentions. But then, of course, she was married. If Deirdre only would stop vacillating and would come to a decision, he wouldn't give Ruby a thought. Not that she wasn't a terrific woman.

"What *is* this other stuff that's bothering you?" Larry asked, cradling the cold glass on his bare chest.

Deirdre put down the brush and went to the large black leather purse that served as her dispatch case and general carryall. From it she extracted the Xerox copy of Heywood's memo, and gave it to Larry to read.

Idly, Larry opened the two sheets of paper and glanced through them. "Hey, what's this?" he said. "Somebody starting a revolution?"

"I'm not sure," Deirdre answered, rubbing skin conditioner into her long tapered legs as they talked. "I found that paper in Heywood's office. I don't know if he was doing anything with it, or who he showed it to, or if any of this work has started. God knows somebody's been playing hardball with us in the last few months. And now, on top of everything, they're talking about breaking up the oil companies entirely . . . Not that that might not be a good idea. Oh, shit, if I had the sense God gave a rubber duck, I'd just keep my nose out of all of this."

"Well, I don't know," Larry said slowly, studying the document. "This sure is one hell of a plan to ruin

Denali and the whole pipeline. Do you think that's such a hot idea?"

Deirdre turned away from him and busied herself replacing things in her makeup kit. "It might be," she muttered.

"What?"

"I said, 'I'm not really sure.' "

"Well, Goddamn it to hell, D.D., I am dumbstruck. I mean, here's you and me been up here all these years —me building it and you defending it—and now you say you're not so sure?"

"Things are changing," Deirdre said slowly. "I'm learning a lot—some of it from you, some of it stuff I've been hearing around the office—from Wilbur, and Brandon, and Daddy. I thought it was a good thing when I first came up. I thought the country needed the oil. I thought we could do it without messing up the country. I didn't really realize how little it takes to mess up this place."

"Shit, that's just plain ridiculous," Larry argued. "The country *does* need the oil. What are we supposed to do, just leave all that beautiful slick stuff laying in the ground for a billion years? And how much of a dent can that little thin line make going through all those millions of acres of toolies? As far as tundra, a little tundra goes a long way with me. I've seen about as much of that damned stuff as I care to see. But I'll say one thing. If you figure you're through with it, I'm willing to cash in my chips, drag up stateside, and get going on something else. I think I've learned about all I want to know about building pipelines, except now I'd kind of like to see it through to the end. Of course, if this bunch gets their way none if us will see it."

He threw the paper down in disgust. "Ah, shit! There isn't anybody that can stop this thing. It's just too big. But I must say, that's a pretty scary plan they've got there. Say, are you going to show this to Wilbur—or your Daddy?"

Deirdre didn't answer for a minute, mainly because she didn't know what she planned to say. "I'd like time to look into it a little more. I wouldn't want to hurt anybody. I have a hunch this might hurt some people that I know and like."

"Well, hell, if they go through with that damn plan it's going to hurt some other people you know and like. Like me and your Daddy and my Daddy. And all of these people here working on the pipeline."

"I'd just like a little more time to think about it," Deirdre said. She got up from the dressing table, slipped out of the short terry cloth robe, and hung it on the chair.

Her skin was rosy and pink and it seemed now to be flushing in anticipation as she walked toward the bed where Larry lay sprawled.

"Anybody ever tell you," Deirdre said, "that you've got darling knees?"

"It's one of my main points of attraction," Larry said, modestly, as she crawled into the bed.

Deirdre was fierce in loving that night and seemed more passionate than Larry could ever remember. It seemed as though she couldn't get enough, and when she had worn him out, she lay with his penis curled in her hand like a child's toy. Laying there in the dark arctic morning Larry Steele found himself in that thoughtful half-wakened state that seems to preceed the ringing of the alarm clock. Deirdre had set it for seven-thirty to give her time to get back to her apartment for a change of clothes before going to the office.

Larry lay back, his hands laced beneath his head, enjoying the warm feel of Deirdre's hand on his groin and the soft stirring of her breath against the side of his chest. The thought that had been worrying him under-

427

neath the surface all through the night suddenly crystal-ized into a clear and disturbing question. Gently, he shook Deirdre's bare shoulder until her eyes opened slowly.

"What is it honey?"

"It's time to get up, Deirdre, but I've been thinking about something."

"What's that?" Deirdre said as she sat up in bed and stretched voluptuously, rubbing her skin where the sheets had left wrinkles.

Larry kissed her tenderly on one of the little red welts.

"I was wondering," he said, with his lips still pressed against her skin, "do you think that dumb memo could have had anything to do with the murder of Brent Heywood?"

"The prospect of traumatic death or injury is the constant companion of heavy construction workers, especially under the severe winter weather conditions and darkness that prevail in Alaska's Arctic and interior. Scarcely a day went by during the past two weeks without an accident resulting in an injury or a narrow brush with death for members of our small crew, numbering around fifteen."

—"Xerxes"
All-Alaska Weekly

Chapter Forty

Larry looked out of the window of the Wien 727 "Wieny-bird" as it dropped out of the dark sky into the ranging clustered lights of Deadhorse. Although he was returning from R & R, presumably well "recreated and rested," he could already feel the fatigue from the seven twelves, or even seven fourteens, in his bones.

Larry had been a journeyman welder now for eighteen months and was drawing near top pay for a working man. But after his weekend with Deirdre, he was beginning to wonder why either of them bothered. It had taken all his persuasive powers to keep Deirdre from dragging up outside following the murder of her friend Heywood. If she had done so, he wouldn't have blamed her. In fact, he would have followed. But some weird compulsion of duty seemed to drive her toward finishing the job. He know how she felt. As tired and fed up as he was, he hated to quit in the middle without staying to see how things turned out.

The Deadhorse hanger was like a corral full of braying, unbranded cattle. Texans, Oklahomans, New Jerseyans, Ohioans, Eskimos, Aleuts, Athabascans, Tlingits, Japs—all wandering around talking at the top of their lungs, slamming each other on the back as they met up with old working buddies, and trying to find the appropriate buses for their barracks. Many of the workers were new; some were long-haired kids from the Northwest, or red-faced Arkansas farm boys. In some cases, the companies that maintained the buses for the camp workers had changed their locations while the workers were away on R & R. Some were old hands in Alaska, but had never worked in Prudhoe Bay before.

"Brown and Root. Brown and Root. Brown and Root. Anybody here for Brown and Root?" a voice yelled.

Another said, "Royal Petroleum Camp. Who's for Royal Petroleum Camp?"

"Alamo Operations here. Alamo Operations."

"Kodiak. Any of you guys from Kodiak?"

A few, not many at that time of year, were transients—equipment salesmen coming up to make deals with the camp managers. Deadhorse was linked to almost all the Prudhoe Bay encampments by gravel berms and snowroads. The Deadhorse Hotel, another Atco unit like the ones in the camp, was being run by the Native NANA corporation, which had bought it for five million dollars. A recently painted sign over the door said, "NANA Services Inc."

According to what Larry had heard, a room in the NANA Hotel ran a hundred dollars a day, but included food. NANA (Northern Alaska Natives Association) had also handled the security for the pipeline construction camps north of the Yukon.

Larry picked up his barracks bag outside where it had been dumped in the snow (there were no baggage facilities at Deadhorse), and climbed in the bus for Denali personnel. A blue-eyed blond kid from Minnesota picked up his bag from alongside Larry. He was shivering and his ears were turning red while his nose

430

was turning white with frostbite, and it was only thirty below.

"Shit, man," he said. "Is it always thirty below?"

"Cold?" Larry laughed. "Why you're in the banana belt here. You ought to be glad youre not working up in Coldfoot or Prospect."

In the bus he was pleased to run into Nick Gordon who had been dispatched to the camp a month or two before. Gordon had gone out to the Deadhorse strip to pick up some parts for his Cat, which had been air-shipped up from Fairbanks.

"How're you goin' Nick baby?" Larry said. "Anything new?"

"Not much. We had two fires last week. One up in Prospect Creek Camp burned out the unit generator, half the camp was freezing their ass in the dark. The other one was over at Happy Valley—burned down a whole warehouse of electrical equipment and radio communications gear. They figure it ran a couple of hundred thousand."

"Well, as long as it wasn't anything serious. How are you doing in the poker game?"

"I'm going easy," Nick said. "I don't want to leave here broke after all this trouble."

"Any new women?"

Nick looked at him wisely. "I don't think you have to worry about that, son. How's your little lady?"

"I don't know," Larry said, "but I think it's getting serious."

"Good. You've been bucking around too long. Its about time somebody put a rope on you."

"What are the welders working?" Larry asked.

"Everything's in high gear," Nick said smiling. "Most of us are getting seven fourteens. Everybody's licking the big lollipop."

"Any good movies?"

431

Nick looked at him with scorn. "You have to be kidding. What've you been doing for fun down there anyhow? You look like you've been rode hard and put away wet."

"This and that," Larry said evasively.

"Anyhow, I've fixed it so's that you stay out of trouble," Nick said. "I told the Crumb Boss to fix you up with an empty spot in my room."

"Great," Larry said, and meant it.

It was a drag coming up from R & R and having to adjust to a new roommate. He was comfortable with Nick. And the older man did tend to keep him out of trouble—namely big stake poker games, many of them run by sharpies who'd managed to get put on in the camp for the purpose of skinning as many of the pipe-liners as they could.

"How many miles you lay in since I left?" Larry asked.

"Not as many as we could. Had some real heavy weather these days and we got blowed out three, four days in a row."

Larry was beginning to feel reasonably at home on the welding job now. He was what they called a "slick," as opposed to a "bronc," or a newcomer. The fact was, he had had plenty of experience with both arc and oxy-actylene welding long before he applied for the apprentice job, and had learned quite a few tricks from Nick before he signed in with the welders, so it hadn't been too hard for him to pass his test.

". . . another reason we didn't get too many miles in," Nick said, "was that we had to go back and redo about a couple of hundred welds—remember, after that big scandal about the x-rays."

"Yeah, I remember," Larry said. "And I didn't think any of those phony welds were mine. I didn't leave any holidays on my welds."

"Yeah, I know," Nick said. "You're a good workman. Fact is, a lot of these guys just don't give a fuck. Some of them are so cabin-happy that they can hardly see straight, anyway. They're just plugging along and if they don't get caught leaving a window in the weld, they just don't give a rat's ass."

Larry checked with the straw boss and found that the shift didn't start until seven a.m. He skipped the day-old TV news capsules and played a few hands of gin with Nick in the room, where he caught up on his mail that had accumulated in his absence.

There was a catalog from Eddie Bauer with some fancy, expensive winter camping gear in it; a short note from Grandpa Bisset who wanted to know when he would take an R & R down at the ranch. Larry wondered if he would be able to coordinate his leave with Deirdre and go down to Mitchell Mesa together. It would be nice. He'd have to write and ask her. There was a plain white envelope postmarked Portland, Oregon, with no return address. Larry opened it up and found a six by nine sheet of paper with a handwritten note. He recognized the handwriting, which said:

Dear Stringbean,
It's nice to be desirable. I understand I am now wanted in fifty states. Please don't worry. I know what I'm doing and I'm all right. I do believe you are the only person on God's green earth who I love. Take care of yourself and don't get hurt. Better yet, go home, and stop supporting the eco-pigs. I'll try to stay in touch, but I am very busy these days.

                    I love you,
                    P

and under that was her favorite monogram, a Lincoln penny that had been rubbed over with a pencil.

Larry looked at the envelope again. He assumed that wherever Penny was she had given it to someone somewhere else to have it mailed; he also knew that he would never turn her in. He wondered if she was in the lower forty-eight by now, or where. And what *did* she mean by saying she was busy?

It had been a shock to him but not a surprise to find that his kid sister was a suspect in a murder. Of course, a check had been made instantly to see if in some way Penny was actually working for Denali under an alias, but it proved fruitless. The fingerprints of every possible suspect were checked and none matched up. This indicated that Penny had evidently been in Fairbanks at least during the time of the raid at Fort Wainwright, and had managed to acquire Denali credentials without actually working for the company. But what had been her motive?

Knowing some of Penny's background, the theft of explosives—or at least the suspicion that explosives were what the group had been after—indicated some sort of terrorist plot. It was the sort of thing that would appeal to Penny. But what and where? There had in fact been no terrorist attempts made since the Wainwright raid, Larry wondered if they actually could make a case against Penny based on the glove and the rather confused identification of the Denali guard.

His feelings for his sister were certainly mixed, or mixed-up. Remembering the tomboy playing around out at the ranch, and even her strange sexual obsession with him in later years, he could only think of her with love. But in the last year or so before her final disappearance, she'd become so flakey and so hostile to the world around her that Larry had found it hard to communicate with her. He could understand Penny disliking her father. Wilbur in the end was a cold ambitious man and not the easiest old Daddy to relate to. But the depths of the hatred Penny had developed for Wilbur Steele shocked and disturbed Larry. There was a quality of madness to it. At times it had seemed to Larry, listening to her bitter rantings, that she somehow was laying the blame for her mother's death on Wilbur, which was patently impossible. Emma Steele had died of natural causes after a long illness. There was some talk that the life-support systems had failed, or been disconnected, at the end, but did that really make a difference? Other than the occasional quivering of the needles and the various devices attached to her emaciated frame, there was no sure indication that she was a living human being, and not just a gelatinous mass of withered and boney tissue.

Larry had occasionally gone into the room in which his mother lay dead or dying—he hardly knew which —and sat waiting and listening for some signal that there was still a mind functioning in that pitiful mass of protoplasm.

Larry's first shift started at seven a.m. Nick was working the same shift so they got up together at a quarter to six so that they could talk for a while at breakfast.

Larry padded in his wooden clogs ten or twenty yards down the narrow corridor of the Atco unit to the communal bath and shower, took a towel from the pile near the door, hung his terry cloth robe on the hook in the wall, slipped the Omega Chronometer that he'd worn since his flying days into the pocket of the robe, and turned on the shower. He lifted his face into the hot steamy water, letting its vapors clear the accumulated mucus from his nostrils and his eyes. One of the hazards of living and working in Alaska is that there was always some sort of a cold or flu hanging

435

around, and it never seemed to be quite gotten rid of, with any amount of vitamin C or whiskey.

After a vigorous soaping then rinse, Larry turned on the cold water briefly to shock himself into alertness. He toweled down and picked up his ditty bag full of toilet articles and went to the row of sinks to complete his morning ritual. It wasn't until he'd finished shaving and was patting some Aqua-Velva on his face that he thought to check the time to make sure he could grab a cup of coffee with Nick and some breakfast before going out on the line. The Omega was no longer in the pocket of the robe.

Slightly irritated, Larry looked around in the other pocket and in the ditty bag, trying to remember if he had definitely worn it into the shower room. But a search of the room indicated the watch was definitely gone.

Nick was slipping into his down-filled insulated underwear when Larry finished going through his drawers and the pockets of his other clothes.

"Nick, have you seen my watch anywhere? What the hell time it it, anyway?"

Nick indicated the alarm clock on the shelf near the bed.

"It's only a little after six. What's the problem?"

"I think some sheep-fucking Okie has gone and pinched my watch."

Nick laughed bitterly. "Sorry about that, kid. I'm not laughing about your loss. It's just that with the pipeline cranking up to full-speed we're getting all these Goddamn Cheechakos coming up—these newcomers—bitching, mean—the whole place's gotten mean. It used to be that you knew everybody and the whole place was like your friends. Now guys just come in, do their shift, make maybe two or three friends, and hate everybody else. Stuff's been missing a lot since you left.

436

It's gotten so much worse—rings, wallets; I lost a pair of bunny boots a couple of weeks ago—remember? They're getting a hundred dollars a pair up here for those things. When I bought them, two years ago, they were seventeen dollars. Parkies—Christ, even this down-filled underwear disappears around here."

"Yeah," Larry said bitterly, "I hear they even took one of those D-8 tractors."

"We've been losing tools and fittings, valves, torches, hoses—everything—out on the line. Did you hear that somebody got a 750-kilowatt diesel generator? And took it away down from Happy Valley!"

"How in the hell did they get it out, you suppose?"

"I don't know," Nick said. "Probably made a deal with one of the guys flying those Hercs. They caught a guy dragging up to the States the other day and he had a half a side of beef—must have weighed forty pounds—in his duffle bag."

"Used to be they only searched you coming in," Larry said.

"Well, they don't like to search you either way, unless they got a good tip. Too much trouble with the unions."

Larry's warm-up shack was located on the pipeline itself about fifteen miles south of Prudhoe where the first big block valve was located on the Sag River. The warm up shacks were set up about every eighty feet for about a kilometer along the pipeline. It was one of the stretches where the faked x-rays had been used to verify welds that might have been faulty. Fortunately, this stretch of the pipeline was on vertical support members so it would be easy to inspect the welds—except for the part of the pipe where the weld itself was resting on the support member.

Scattered along the pipeline were several side-lift cranes that could raise the huge forty-eight inch pipe high enough so that a welder could get underneath for a good look at the repair job if necessary. Trailing along behind were the yellow mobile x-ray trucks. To repair the welds they had cut an opening in one of the pipes in order to insert one of the pigs, or go-devils, to run through the pipe and clean it prior to the welding.

In addition to the go-devil, which cleaned the inside of the pipe, it was also necessary to introduce a futuristic robot called "The Crawler." The Crawler was a device that had to be set up directly behind each weld before it could be x-rayed. It was controlled by radio signal beeps that made it go forward or backward, except when it went backward when it was supposed to go forward or vice versa, or when it wouldn't move at all, or when it would take off on its own momentum inside the pipe. Once, the Crawler got loose, careened out of control down a steep hill, and nearly creamed a woman welder (the first one to work on the pipeline) who was working inside the end of the pipe. There were people who wondered just how accidental that near-disaster was.

The warm-up shack Larry had been assigned to was about fifth down the line. On the outside there were a few bits of graffiti such as the men had taken to painting on the fiberglass walls to give them some sort of individuality. Larry's was adorned with a rough map of Texas and the motto "The South shall rise again!" Up in the corner somebody had written "Fuck the IRS, plead the Fifth."

Inside the shack, already inspecting the welds, was "Curly" Bob Shelden, a fellow Texan Larry had worked with before in various camps from Coldfoot down to Glennallen.

"Well, Curley Bob, good buddy," Larry said, slapping his gloves against those of the stocky Texan in an approximation of a handshake. "What have we got here?"

"We've got a weld with more windows and widows in it than an old folks home. I don't know how this one ever got through," Curly Bob said. "Looks like it must have been done by one of these young broncos, still wet behind the ears. I think the best bet is, we get on either side of this motherfucker and downhand weld the ass off it—just do the job all over again."

"Whatever you say, buddy boy."

It was one of those days not quite cold enough to call off work, which they usually did when it was sixty below or colder. But at forty-five below the cold was penetrating, even without much of a breeze. Larry gave a big wheezing, hacking cough, and spit out a gob of rust-colored phlegm.

"It's a bitch, ain't it?" Curly Bob said. "Never seem to be able to get rid of those colds and coughs up here. I remember when I was working the pipeline down in Salty Arabia, I thought that was really shit, but I'd give a day's pay right now for some of that A-rab sunshine."

"Yeah, but you weren't making a day's pay like this down there."

"That's for dang sure, buddy boy. A big ten four on that," Curly Bob said.

"Well, let's get going," Larry said, vainly dabbing at his streaming nose with the bulky glove hoping to get some of the mucus off before it froze. "We'd better get one of them side-boom cranes in here. This fucking weld is sitting right on a VSM. Have to lift her up a little so's we can get a look see under there."

Larry poked his head out of the shelter and gestured to a long-haired blond kid sitting on the side-boom D-8. "Hey kid," he said. "Bring that over here. We need a little boost."

"Right-o," the kid said.

Larry remembered having seen him around before. He was a drop-out from Gonzaga University in Washington State, a little hippy looking, but a good worker once he got the hang of things. He'd only recently transferred from the Laborer's Union to the heavy equipment operator's union.

There was a grinding sound from the D-8 and then a silence.

"Shit!" the kid said. "I think the clutch is frozen."

"You didn't turn it off, did you? You dumb-ass," Larry yelled.

"No, of course not. I didn't turn it off. But there's something in the transmission looks like it froze up while it was idling there. I'll get it fixed in a minute."

The kid climbed down from the side-loader and rummaged around on the back platform of the machine for a propane torch.

"Well," Larry said, ducking back into the shelter. "I guess we might as well take a little break while that kid gets the clutch thawed or whatever."

Curly Bob reached into wooden box where he'd stowed some extra equipment and a Thermos jug. After some trouble, he managed to get the jug open without taking off his glove, only to bang it down in disgust.

"Fuckin' coffee's frozen already. Even put a little vodka in there for anti-freeze. Just too damn cold here today. Unless you'd like a coffee-sickle."

"Nah. Forget it," Larry said. "He'll probably have that thawed out in a few minutes. You ought to keep that vodka inside your parkie . . ."

Larry's remark was interrupted by a great roaring whooshing sound and a piercing scream. Quickly Larry bounded out of the warm-up shack, in time to see a great tongue of orange-red flame sweeping from the hose of the propane heater, which apparently had split

440

in the forty-five degree cold and was now shooting great clouds of flaming propane gas all over the landscape. The flames suddenly roared out and grabbed the Gonzaga student in a hot embrace. In what seemed a split second he was a flaming human torch. The blond kid ran back and forth in front of the D-8 slapping at the flames with his hands and arms in a futile effort to extinguish the blaze. But this only succeeded in fanning the flames to a greater intensity.

Curly Bob, who had popped out of the other side of the warm-up shack, stood frozen in horror. Larry, realizing what had happened, sprinted the ten yards that separated him from the Gonzaga kid, tackled him, throwing him down on the snow covered ground, and started rolling him in the hard-packed snow.

Curly Bob finally realized what was happening and came running over to throw himself on the group to help smother the flames. But it seemed that each time they managed to get one licking tongue of flame extinguished another would spurt up in its place.

The three men rolled on the ground, dabbing frantically with their gloves at the patches of flame that sprung up one after another almost as soon as they were doused. Larry could feel the searing heat of the flames singeing his eyebrows and moustache, giving off the pungent rotting egg smell of burned hair—or was it the fur on the edge of his parka that was catching fire?

Desperately the men rolled over and over, trying to get off the hard-packed snow of the work pad and into the softer more enveloping drifts at the edge. Finally, gratefully, they rolled into a drift about three feet deep and were able to extinguish the last of the flames. Wheezing and gasping, his eyes watering furiously, his face stinging where the cold contacted the sudden moisture on his eyelashes and cheeks, Larry stood up. He felt sick and weak, and his lungs felt as if he had inhaled the entire propane fire into them.

'Jesus," he said. "I thought we . . ."

His voice trailed off. His lips felt thick and blistered; he staggered a few feet, suddenly unable to keep his balance.

"Look out!" Curly Bob shouted. It was too late.

Larry, half-blinded by smoke and tears, had staggered to the edge of the abandoned ditch where the pipe had lain buried until elevated on the VSM's. In the haste to get the VSM's constructed, the work crew had not come through to re-fill the ditch, which was about ten feet deep and six feet wide.

Later, Larry could only remember a soft falling sensation and a cracking thump as he hit the permafrost at the bottom of the ditch. He was conscious of an excruciating stab of pain in his right leg and then the lights went out, except for a dim pilot light. Vaguely, through the stupor, he could hear muffled voices calling.

"You all right Lar? You okay?"

"Get help, somebody!"

"For Christsake, a guy's hurt!"

And then the lights went out entirely. Larry had no way of knowing for how long. It seemed like days.

He was laying back now in a narrow canoe, the sides rising up on both sides of his shoulders, somewhere in one of those little streams that fed into the Terlinqa River below Goat Mountain on the Mesa. But he didn't know where the canoe was going. It just kept bucking up and down in the fast waters and he couldn't seem to move his hands or find his paddle. He was strapped in the bottom of the canoe, floating, tossing and turning in every direction. There seemed to be others around, and he heard voices.

"Take it easy. He's got a bad break there. You'd

442

better put that leg in a traction split. Otherwise we're going to have bones coming through all over the place. Looks like a bad spiral to me."

The voice had a Spanish accent and Larry thought for a minute it was one of the Mexican hands from the ranch. There were more voices, and Larry felt that the canoe had somehow been attached to a giant balloon, as he felt himself lifted up, up, up.

The wire, mummy-type stretcher into which Larry had been strapped was being slowly elevated in the sling of one of the side-boom cranes to the edge of the ditch where a white emergency medical truck waited with its doors open and its light flashing. There was a stab of searing pain that went through Larry's groin as one of the men bumped a corner of the stretcher against the loading platform of the truck. It was only a slight nudge, but the sudden jarring pressure set the boney splinters in Larry's smashed leg lancing into the sensitive exposed nerve. He screamed once. A loud, long, agonized wail, and his eyes popped open.

"Take it easy, buddy," a voice said. "We'll have you in a chopper in no time."

The four men around the stretcher lifted and slid it gently into the truck. As they did so, Larry's eyes, sharpened by the pain, opened again for a moment and he caught a glimpse of a hairy, exposed wrist as one of the stretcher bearers extended his arm to slide the stretcher the final few inches into the truck. There was a bright silver gleam of metal and the yellow-white glare of the work light, which had been turned on to help with the loading in the rapidly fading daylight.

"My watch," Larry screamed, his lips still stiff with pain. "You've got my watch, motherfucker!"

"What did he say?" one of the stretcher bearers asked, his face muffled in a ski mask.

"I guess he said to watch out. Couldn't hear what he said. Anyway, he's out now."

The two men shoved the stretcher all the way in, and closed the door bearing the red cross. The ambulance roared off toward the helicopter pad, where a chopper was already landing to evacuate Larry to the hospital in Fairbanks.

"They talk about turning the most desolate and forbidding place on earth into one of the most sought after places. Sought after by who, I'd like to know, except the oil companies? Certainly not by the polar bears any more. They run out onto the ice and then headed north as fast as they could. And as for being the most desolate place—the Eskimos didn't think so, and neither did the ducks and the geese and the caribou."

—Harmon Helmericks
Alaskan Bush Pilot

Chapter Forty-one

January, 1976

To: Sonia, at Swap Shop, Fairbanks

By Hand

Dear Sonia:

I will tell you something funny. My people have been living up here for maybe five, ten, twelve thousand years —who knows how long?—and now working up here in this Goddamn Prudhoe Bay Camp, suddenly I feel like I am the outsider and all these Goddamn white men, Okies, Texans, Californians, or whatever, are the ones that belong here.

Nothing I can see here in any direc-

tion except pipes and derricks and
machinery—and one Goddamn Atco barracks after another. I've worked in a
half dozen camps and they are all the
same. There are hardly any Natives
in any of them and most of _them_ are
from inland or the south. Those
Texans do not exactly spit on us,
but I would not say that they are your
friendliest people. And sometimes
they are downright rotten.

When I look around me, I can see
one thing: the pipeline is going
through no matter what—weather, snow,
ice, nothing is going to hold it back.
And nothing is going to hold me back
either if I decide to go back to the
village. The time to stop the pipeline
was long ago. Now everybody is interested in making it go through.
When I go back to the village they
all look at me like I'm some kind
of wild man from the tundra. They're
making good money and they're not
thinking of what they will do when the
pipeline is done and they have to go
back from making $50,000 a year to mak-
ing $1,000 or $2,000!

The Teamsters are not going to stop
the pipeline. Jessie Carr has admitted that the company is paying them
$500,000 every single day. I guess
that's what you call good will. You can
be damn sure there will not be any
strike as long as that money is rolling

in. And as long as those unions are
in control there is not going to be
a lot of Natives hired either. Even
NANA, which runs my outfit, is hiring
more whites than Natives.

Also, I'm getting very horny up
here. So far they have only hired about
two Native girls. One is a bullcook
and one is an apprentice welder, but
there are always men buzzing around
them like flies around a moose nugget
in summer. Last week I thought I was
getting lucky. I came back to my room
and there was a big long-haired blond
sleeping naked in there. But it turned
out he was just one of the surveyors
assigned temporary to my room. He had
been out three days and didn't have
any sleep. I guess that's why he
passed out without any clothes. Usually
they put a colored man in with me.
That's because most of those pipeliners don't like to be in the same
room with an Indian or an Eskimo.

Did you find out how many people in
the villages in Alaska voted for the
Republicans? It's about time they wake
up and straight vote Democratic
tickets right down the line. Even
though those Democrats are in the oil
business just as much as anybody else.
I am more of a citizen than I ever was
since I am giving four or five hundred dollars a week to Uncle Sam but

don't seem to have a damn thing to
say about it.

Another thing. I'm on my seventh
week of this Goddamn dispatch and am
getting tired of getting white man's
grub. They say it's so great, but I
would rather have muktuk. Yesterday
I threw away half of my steak. I saw
a white fox and a cross fox outside
the mess hall the other day and I
bet they are eating damn better than
I am.

One good thing. We are near the
village and I go back a lot, but like
I said, they all treat me like I was
some weirdo. Meanwhile, I notice more
and more drunks in the village laying in the snow, freezing sometimes.
And prices are sky-high in the stores.
It disgusts me and I'm trying to stay
sober as much as I can. But it's not
easy up here.

Everybody you talk to is from someplace else. Not only Texas and California, but Africa and Puerto Rico
and Europe and all those places.
There is none of them you can talk
to—some of them don't even speak
English. I don't know how they got
the jobs while good Native help is
still looking. Anyway, I'm looking
forward to some good seal oil, moose,
king salmon, and all that. I don't
think I will come to Fairbanks on

my leave although I miss you
know what.

I don't know what in the hell I
want. Maybe nothing. Sometimes I think
I want to die. I like to remember
when I was hunting polar bear and
seal. That was man's work—an Eskimo's
work. Now I sit with a Goddamn notebook and pencil in a little hut and
just sign people in and out. I thought
a security guard was maybe some kind
of a man's job, but it's just bullshit. We don't have any guns. We
just sit in a little hut and check
people's badges and make sure they
don't take too much booze into the
camp or too much company property out
of the camp. Sometimes they call us
in to break up a fight in the mess
hall, but all we do is close the doors
and let them settle it. I'm not going
to get a busted head getting in between a Teamster and a pipeliner.

Last week a man in my village shot
a cop by accident when he came to
break up a fight in a bar. They say
he'll get ninety-nine years, but when
people murder somebody in Fairbanks
they just walk away on probation.
Last week my own uncle got a 584
dollar fine and 88 days in jail for
nothing—just getting drunk in the
Savoy bar, believe it or not.

But sometimes I think all the
Indians are turning white with all

this pipeline work. They all listen
to Merle Haggard or R.W. McCall singing all this country-western with an
Okie accent. You haven't heard anything funny until you've heard an
Eskimo trying to talk like one of
these Okies. And they're dressing
like them too, in jeans and cowboy
boots and funny hats. I just remember
how the white man has used people in
every part of the world—not just
Eskimos. They take them and give them
wage employment and carry them thousands of miles from their homes and
families to a land that's not theirs,
and they have them work damn hard as
laborers with somebody else taking
the profit—even taking them away to
high school to make them learn white
man's way, but not teaching them
about the Eskimo way.

So now they hire Natives first, and
they take them away from villages
and give them huge salaries. What do
they think will happen to these
people? How can they ever go back to
their own villages? Their whole life
style is broken now and the only way
they can live is by leaving their
home and family and land and working
twelve hours a day at some job that
has no meaning at all.

And this is happening to me too.

The villages are all going to hell.
Not only is everything sky-high ex-

pensive, but nobody will work. The
fellows that used to take care of the
sewage plant and water supply are
not going to work for any Goddamn $250
or $300 a month when they can make
ten times as much per month working
on the pipeline. So nothing is maintained in the villages anymore. And
supplies that used to come in slow
before are even worse now because
the airplanes are all working for the
pipeline camp. Even the mail doesn't
come in on time.

I could have told them all this.
I saw it coming long ago. But nobody
would listen to me. They all wanted
the money from the pipeline jobs.
And now that they're getting dividends
from the regional corporation out of
the land settlement, they think they're
really rich. What can they do with
$200 or $300 a year, or even more,
especially with prices being
what the are?

Another thing. I don't like to write
much on paper, even though I am not
sending this through the mail. Certainly there is not much in the way
of security up here, except at the
camp gates. Once you are in the camp,
everybody can go anywhere pretty much
as they please. Especially if they
are like me, in security. The place
we have to keep an eye on mainly
is Pump Station Number One, which is

the origin station. There is a serious
problem because, in addition to the
three alternate generators in this
camp, they could probably move emergency generators from Royal American
or other plants if they had to. It
would be a very big job to stop the
pumps.

There is a gas line that goes near
the pump building and maybe something
can be done with that. Also, there
are some big block valves out past
Deadhorse airfield. Maybe we can stop
the oil flow at that point.

I wish I had somebody up here with
some engineering knowledge to talk
to about this, but there is nobody you
can trust. Sometimes I wish I could
just fly off to the moon or walk off
onto the floe ice and not come back
anymore. It is too sad, what is happening. And if I never come back to
Fairbanks, I wouldn't be unhappy
either, except I would like to see
you, even though you are a white
woman. You are the only one who has
been decent.

Last night, a nightshift mechanic
from Ketchikan came across a wolf on
the haul road between Happy Horse
and base operations camp. He ran that
wolf and ran it and finally ran it
down and killed it, hitting it hard
over and over with the snowmobile.
Later he told security that he hit
the wolf by accident when it jumped

his snowmobile. But I saw the tracks
and I know different. That's the kind
of people who are working here.
    I hope The Day comes soon. I can't
stand it here any more.

Your Friend
Takolik

"Americans should try to look on Texas in the light of its history . . . See a people, conquerers and conquered, never entirely leaving their soil with an almost sacred sense of that soil . . . see a population that remembers where grand-parents are buried and that has changed only superficially from horse to auto over a hundred years. Then perhaps things fall into place: the pride, the politics, the patriotism —for land and people and symbolic nation . . . the deep if unarticulated sense of territoriality or peoplehood, the eternal feeling for time and place, and above all, for place and people without regard to time."

—T. R. Fehrenbach
"Seven Keys to Understanding Texas,"
Atlantic Magazine

Chapter Forty-two

Larry Steele sat in his wheelchair, cradling a tumbler of Virginia Gentleman on his belly, and squinting at the sun setting over Bisset Mountain. It was satisfying being back somewhere where it was daylight all day and then, after a flaming finish, darkness all night, until the great golden glow in the east started the whole pro-cess all over again.

He turned to the erect old man in the elaborate wheelchair next to him.

"Nice, ain't it," he said, sweeping his hand toward the red-gold rimmed mountains.

"Like a picture on the wall," the old man said. "That's something you don't see on your color TV."

The two men lapsed into silence again. It had taken Larry Steele a long time to get used to the rhythm of leisure after the frenetic alternation of seven fourteens and drink-and-sex-filled R & Rs. At the Medical Center

454

Hospital in Houston they had told him that the spiral break would take at least six months to heal to the point where the cast could be removed, and then he would need at least another six months to build the leg up to normal use. Larry could live with that, but what brought on a lot of heavy thinking was what they told him about his lungs.

At first the doctors had been deeply concerned by the shadow on the chest x-ray, until they discovered it was largely iron oxide—which he had inhaled during the long hours of pipe welding.

Lying in the stretcher on the plane returning to Texas, tranquilized to the eyeballs, Larry had been aware even through the muffling blanket of drugs of sharp pains in his chest and an aching, feverish headache that wouldn't go away. In Houston they diagnosed it as pneumonia.

"Your lungs are so full of fluid you could hold a water polo game in there," Dr. Blumenfeld told him, as he scanned the large x-ray plates. "You sure you had plenty of ventilation when you did all that welding?"

"Hell," Larry said, "You don't *want* too much ventilation when you got sixty-three degrees below zero temperature. I guess we plugged up the drafts as best we could."

"Well, there's your problem," Blumenfeld said. "Did you have any respiratory complaints out there? Eye watering, catarrh, sore throats, coughs, breathing difficulty?"

"All of them."

"Well, there hasn't been much work done on welders problems, but just the same, that's what you've got. Chronic bronchitis, emphysema, and now pneumonia. If you hadn't busted your leg, you might have drowned in your own lung fluid before you got finished up there. And that's what left you wide open for the pneumonia. I wouldn't do anymore welding if I were you. You got some other way of making a living?"

"Two or three. I ain't all that much in love with welding anyhow, but it pays like a busted slot machine."

"Well, I would suggest you find something else. And while you're looking around, I wouldn't get involved with anything too strenuous. I don't know if those lungs of yours are ever going to be back in good shape. You've been through a lot. Better give them at least a couple of years rest. Just take it easy and find something to do that isn't too strenuous. Can't your father find a place for you somewhere?"

"I reckon he can," Larry said, dispiritedly.

At the Medical Center, Larry had had lots of time to think about what he would do next. Wilbur had flown to the hospital a day or two after the accident and had shown touching concern for Larry's condition. It was not a role that he played easily—the concerned father. Larry wondered if old Daddy might be getting soft and sentimental in his old age.

"You just start breathing that good Texas air again. That will get your lungs back in good shape. And then we can have some talks about what you're going to do next, son."

Usually that take-charge tone of voice would send the adrenalin racing through Larry's system, setting up deep currents of psychological resistance. Whether it was fatigue or creeping maturity, Larry was not sure —he just lay there and listened with little reaction. Maybe it was the tranquilizers.

"If you want my lungs to start healing," Larry had croaked, "you'd better get me back to Mitchell Mesa. The air in Houston is like breathing shit."

456

Larry returned to Mitchell Mesa in March in time to see the buds begin to pop out on the branches, then the blossoms in the apple orchard and on the cherry trees flash through their brief cycles. From a corner of the ranch terrace, he could look into the meadow beyond the big barn and see the new longhorn calves wobbling uncertainly to their mothers' sides in the distance. Things were being born again and the memories of twenty-two hour nights, cold-numbed fingers, aching lungs, and freezing cheeks were receding rapidly.

Deirdre took off two weeks to come down and comfort him during the early part of his convalescence, bringing him news and gossip from the camps and Denali. The pipeline was getting closer to completion, and if there were no major delays it looked as though oil would be flowing no more than six months after the target date, about the fall of 1977.

"Well," Larry said. "That makes me feel warm all over."

"I know what you mean," Deirdre said. "But it *does* make me feel good. I don't know if its because the job will be over or out of some cockeyed sense of accomplishment . . ."

"Accomplishment! I thought you felt the whole thing was a cancer on the face of the earth."

"Well, that's the other part of me," Deirdre said, without too much logic. "The working part. It makes me want to get the job done and done right."

"And the other part?"

Deirdre sat on the wall overlooking the canyons and the mountains to the west. "The other part I worry about, but there isn't much I can do about it. I think about oil getting into the Yukon, and finishing the fish, or getting up in the Bering Sea down the Sag River and melting the ice. I think about what Valdez will

457

look like in a few years, even what it looks like now, and I'm not exactly proud."

"You can always quit," Larry said reasonably.

"I should have a long time ago, but now it's like putting down a book before you finish it, or leaving a movie before the end. I feel like I've got to see it through."

Despite her convoluted reasoning, Larry understood what she meant. He too felt a sense of regret at having left before seeing the end of all that work.

"I guess I'll try to make it up there when they pull the chain—"

"—and suck Valdez Harbor dry," Deirdre finished the sentence for him, smiling.

"Don't make me laugh too much," Larry said. "It hurts my lungs."

"Oh, Larry," Deirdre said, "I'm sorry. I really shouldn't have gotten you riled up like that."

"Honey, you're better than a million units of penicillin. Don't let it worry you—it was just a twinge. You couldn't climb up on this wheelchair, could you, and give me some kind of comfort before you go?" he asked. But it was an empty plea. His balls were as hollow and dry as a pair of old walnuts, and even the gland stirring sights and sounds of the new spring had worked no erotic miracles.

Deirdre laid a warm tanned hand on his arm. "We'll be together soon," she said. "This is just something we'll have to go through."

"The greening of Larry Steele," he said, smiling feebly.

"Something like that," Deirdre said. "But you're not the only one going through some changes."

"Meaning?"

"Nothing we have to talk about now."

458

When she had gone back, Larry wondered often what kind of changes she was going through.

In the beginning, Larry was too tired from pain and illness to be bored. Mainly what he wanted was to sleep a lot. He would read a little, then doze off into an exhausted dream-like sleep. Often it seemed that even the interruption of meals, brought by the nurse Wilbur had imported from El Paso, was a chore. It seemed like too much work to move his jaws up and down and stay awake long enough to get the bland food down.

Nurse Rodrigues was Mexican-German-Irish, with the dark golden skin of the south and the blue-green-yellow-flecked eyes of her European ancestors. She had the short, strong, competent fingers of a sculptor or a craftsman and a slender, full-bosomed figure that almost succeeded in stirring Larry's sluggish sexual appetite. Nurse Rodrigues was all business and spent a lot of time dropping hints about her "old man" back in El Paso, and how they were saving up to get married as soon as he got his certificate as a para-medic.

Toward April and May, when Larry felt better, he would sit in his wheelchair side-by-side with Grandpa Bisset, swapping yarns about the pipeline and the early oil days, along with macho tales about fights and women and gambling. In a strange way, now that Larry was also in a wheelchair, he felt that they had suddenly become contemporaries.

"Now, that thing that happened to you," Grandpa Bisset said, "the kid catching fire and all, puts me to mind something happened to me when I was working for Midwest Oil in the Salt Creek field up in Casper, Wyoming. I remember we were boarding out at the Lewis Camp and I was sitting with one of the tool-dressers, getting ready to work.

" 'Boy,' he says. 'I sure hate to go out tonight, because there's a job there I don't hanker to do at all.'

"What's that? I says.

" 'I gotta go and change a control head.'

"This guy's name was Lester, and he was a real nice guy. So I says, Lester, I don't blame you one bit. I would hate to do that job myself.

"About this time Nigger Jim comes in—he wasn't really a nigger, we just called him that 'cause he was kinda dark—and he says, 'I'm going to eat me a big breakfast, because I think this's going to be my last meal on earth.'

"Well, I says, if I felt that way, you couldn't hire me to go out on that well tonight.

" 'Well,' he says, 'somebody's got to do it. Because it's leaking real bad.'

"Well, about that time a couple of drillers spoke up and said they didn't feel too good about it either because the well was really a wild one and they were scared of it too. This was about midnight. And since I was on the morning tower I just laughed it off. Anyway, around daylight a tool-pusher comes out and he tells us we better shut down our rig and put out the fire because the crew on the next well's going to change their control head. And that we'd better make sure our boiler was cool so we wouldn't set anything on fire. That was a big well there that time. I guess it was making about four thousand barrels a day. So we pull our tools out of the hole and shut down the boiler—we were firing with natural gas—and me and my tool dresser, we go out and we sit on the edge of the derrick floor and we were watching the other fellows, because they were only about one location away—maybe about three hundred feet.

"I was just saying to my driller that I didn't envy

460

that job changing the control head and I was looking over at that derrick—it was about an eighty foot rig—when all of a sudden the whole thing busted out in flames. Of course, the two of us jumped up and started running over there. But it was so damn hot we had to turn back.

"Just about that time I see that crew, first one and then the other, come running and jumping off the derrick floor. And the whole rig was a mass of flames. Altogether there were six men on that crew, counting the boss himself. Lester, he'd been sitting out on the walking beam trying to stab the control head with a joint of pipe screwed in on the casing. He didn't have a chance. He burned up, right there! Because they were all soaked through with crude oil. And then three of the other fellows, they just kept running, and as they run they was setting the grass on fire behind them. It was the most horrible thing we ever saw in our lives, and we couldn't do nothing about it—not a damn thing. First one, and then another dropped dead, and we could hardly stand it, watching them.

"In fact, I got real sick to my stomach and threw up, right off the derrick floor. It's hard to realize what a terrible thing this was unless you really saw it. Those men were just balls of flames. When it was all over I turned to my tool dresser and I said, Well, I'm going back to camp.

" 'What are you going to do?' he says.

"I have worked my last oil rig, I says. I quit.

" 'You ain't serious,' he says.

"Well, I says, if you don't believe me, you just watch me."

"And what happened," Larry asked.

"Well, I did quit. I sold my car and everything. Cut out, went to the city for a while. That was down at

461

Casper. Got me a job in the Agway selling feed and all that, but it just didn't seem to have all that much excitement. Then I went trapping up in Canada and I come back down to Texas, worked in Monkey Ward selling tractors, and pretty soon a fellow wants to give me a share on a lease he had out there in East Texas and I was thinking I might as well get a job and watch my money working. Well, before you know it, there I am back in the damn oil business. I guess it just gets in your blood."

"Yeah, maybe," Larry said, without enthusiasm.

"Oh, I ain't trying to make any high-flying beautiful, poetic thing out of that there, it's just a business, a way of making money. But it sure beats the shit out of walking behind a plow, or working in Monkey Ward, for that matter."

There was a long silence.

"You going to stay with it—the oil business?" Grandpa Bisset asked, seemingly without curiosity.

"Right now," Larry said, "I can think of about a skillion other things that I'd rather do."

"Yeah, but *are* you?"

"I'm still thinking," Larry said, spinning in his wheelchair and heading back into the ranch house for his afternoon nap.

The old man never asked that question again, and Larry was not sure why he asked it in the first place. They had a lot of time to talk that spring. And eventually the talk got around to Penny.

"That kid always had a crazy mean streak in her—like one of those broncos that never gets trained to the saddle. I like her, but somehow I could never get a handle on her. I'd surely like to see her again sometime, before . . ."

462

"Well, I'm sure you will, Gramps. You got a lot of mileage on you yet. I reckon she'll turn up."

"And then what?" Grandpa Bisset said. "A murder trial? I don't see how she can show her face again, wherever she is."

"I had a letter from her," Larry said. "She didn't say where she was. She was all right, she said, but she was busy."

"Busy making mischief, I'll bet," Grandpa Bisset commented bitterly.

"You say you like her, Gramps, but you *don't* really, do you?"

"I used to—when she was a kid. But she started turning bitter about the time your Ma got sick. And when Emma died it just seemed she went mean and started hating everything—especially your father. You were about the only one she'd still talk to. I got the feeling that even those crazy college kids she'd bring home with her every once in a while—she didn't like them hardly any better than she liked anybody else. You know, she got a bug in her head about somebody pulling the plug on your Ma, and she blamed Wilbur for that."

"But Wilbur wasn't even here when it happened. And I was in the Orient."

"Yeah," Grandpa Bisset said, "but Brandon was here."

"Oh. You think he did it?"

Grandpa Bisset shrugged, and drained the last of the bourbon from his glass. "Don't matter much, does it? I only hope that when I'm in that shape someone'll pull the plug on *me*."

He turned the wheelchair at a slight angle so that he could look directly into Larry's face. "You know I'm not joking about that, don't you, Larry? I don't want

463

to lay there wasting and shrinking away and curl up like an old dry leaf—puny and naked and mindless. I'd like to keep a little dignity and still look like a man when they stretch me out. Remember that Larry, if it ever happens to me like to your Mama."

The old man's eyes, still bright and keen, bored into Larry's with unusual intensity. Larry felt that he was extracting a promise.

"I'll remember."

They both turned and wheeled their chairs back to the house for supper.

"SPOKANE, Washington (AP)—A rich copper deposit has been discovered during preliminary exploration in northwest Alaska, two major mining companies say. But . . . more exploration and testing are needed to determine whether it is feasible to mine the ore . . . in the Brooks Range north of the Arctic Circle.

"The two companies said that one drill hole recovered ore containing nearly 6.8 percent copper . . . By contrast, Anaconda [Company] commercially mines much lower grade copper from its huge Berkeley open pit in Butte, Montana. The ore contains an average of .5 percent copper . . . Consulting geologists in Spokane said the high copper value indicated 'a possible bonanza discovery.' "

Chapter Forty-three

The Bicentennial year was a good one for Denali and the pipeline. Ecological critics had quieted down, and now that the line was more than three-quarters constructed, even political opponents had little to say, except for a continuing battle over the attempts by some Alaskan politicians to increase the State's share of the surplus profit tax. This effort, however, was successfully beaten back with the help of all the Alaskan newspapers and most of the elected politicians.

Having opened its arms to the oil industry, Alaska was in no mood to discourage it. By now the state could almost taste the $1,000,200,000.00 per year profit they expected to make once the oil started flowing in 1977. It began to look as though the target date would be missed by at least three months and that oil, instead of flowing in the spring of 1977, would more likely flow in the summer or fall.

Even newspapers like the *All-Alaska Weekly* had given up their truculent attitude and were now soft peddling bad news about the pipeline and playing up more positive aspects. The unions, which had several times threatened to give trouble via wildcat strikes, had largely stayed in control in spite of intense bickering and, often, rioting in the camps.

With the optimism reigning on all fronts, the stock of oil companies in the Denali consortium rose proportionately. And Wilbur, the crap-shooter that he was, decided the time had come to double up on his bets. He instructed his operatives on Wall Street to make an offer for control of Atalanta Copper, the world's largest copper refining company.

Brandon had been puzzled when the move was first suggested to him, over pressed duck *bigarade* in the Tour d'Argent in Paris. Brandon was back from another trip to the Middle East to see that the interests of Alamo were well cared for. Now that the oil was close to flowing, it had seemed a good idea to Wilbur to encourage the Iranians to press for another price raise, thereby reminding the Americans how dependent they were on Alaskan oil. This Wilbur hoped would ultimately open up the way to completely break the FEA price controls on domestic oil.

"How did things look to you in Teheran?" Wilbur asked looking through the big picture windows at the view of night-lighted Notre Dame.

"I think they'll go our way. They'd better," Brandon said. "But what is it with this copper deal? Aren't you stretching us a bit?"

"Do you realize how much copper there is up there in Alaska? We've been quietly buying up a lot of mineral leases. There's a lot of other stuff too—uranium, things like that. We already have some uranium companies though, so that's not going to be a problem. And it looks as though congress may put through Jerry Ford's idea of turning uranium production over to private industry. That should send those stocks jumping also."

"I suppose you're right, but it's a big gamble."

"That's where the fun is," Wilbur said, with a tight smile. "Gambling. Besides, if we get prices up where we want them and get to use the big new Globtik Alamo, the million tonner, I figure we stand to clear in excess of a billion a year for our share, and thats on the oil alone. There are other plans in the works, of course, some of which you know of—the railroad idea, you've acquainted yourself with that . . ."

"You mean to run a railroad from Fairbanks across Alaska down to Chicago?"

"That's right. When that goes through it's going to shoot the price of our mineral investments up enormously. And make maintenance costs on the pipeline itself go down. And I'm not even counting the profits on our share of the gas pipeline that will parallel the oil line. Now that we've got the whole state stirred up we can start developing the Gulf of Alaska, PET 4 and all of those good oil spots we've got picked south of the Brooks Range. We're just starting this ball game. The main question is to keep anybody from knowing how much Goddamn oil there is up there. Anybody out of the business, anyway. My guess is that there's nearly a hundred billion barrels up there. Of course, a lot of this will probably not even be accomplished in my lifetime, but it's a good feeling to leave a solid structure behind."

"By the way," Brandon asked, "how's the kid?"

"Larry's coming along good. They're taking off the cast next week—he'll probably have to walk with a cane for another four or five months. They say the leg will be shrunken up a bit. It'll take plenty of exercise to get it back, but he'll be okay. Of course, with his lungs in the shape they're in, I don't think he's going to want to go back to working in the field. We've been having some talks back home and I think he's almost on the verge of coming in with me."

"Well," Brandon said, "I don't think you should push him. I mean a man has to be dedicated to be in this kind of thing. He really has to want it. If he's going to go about it in a half-assed way . . ." He paused to masticate a piece of tender, crisp-coated duck meat, and to wash it down with a mouthful of Chateau Latour. "He's got to be hungry—the way you were. Maybe, the way you still are. It's no business for people who don't have their heart in it."

"Well, you're hungry enough for two," Wilbur said with a mirthless smile, "and you'll still be around, won't you?"

"I'm not going anyplace," Brandon said firmly. "But if the kid's coming in, I think we should have a long talk."

"There'll be time for that," Wilbur said, waving the question aside.

Brandon stared at him for a few minutes, his knife and fork still poised for another slice of the duck. He could see that Wilbur had closed off discussion on the subject.

"Have you got any word on the condition of the tanker?"

"Well, she's on the ways at the Mitsubishi place in Koyagi. It's going to be a beauty of a ship, automated all the way through."

"SBT?" Wilbur asked.

"Of course. We had to do that. It would have cost a fortune to go double-bottomed. On the other hand, it is a little easier to navigate with the double-bottom, because you can shift the ballast around between the two hulls. But I figure those Japs know what they're doing.

They've made some pretty good ships and there hasn't been a serious loss in some time. Of course, with the automation, we'll be able to operate the thing with a very small crew and the cost per barrel should go down accordingly." He turned his attention to the road.

"I wish we could get a restaurant like this in Houston," Wilbur said, chewing the fine pressed duck meat slowly, and savoring the hot juices.

"Keep going the way you are," Brandon said, "and you'll be able to lift the whole Tour d' Argent up with a helicopter and fly it to the top of the Denali building."

"That would be something, wouldn't it?" Wilbur said. The way his eyes glittered it seemed he was giving serious thought to the idea.

"One million tons of oil. It would be the biggest shipment ever made."

"That's right,' Wilbur said. "And we'll get a lot of attention on it. Better make sure it's handled right. Has Deirdre got contingency plans for all of this? Is she working on the inaugural speeches, the publicity—we must have all this ready well in advance. Especially, we've got to be ready with a lot of information about how we're going to handle leaks when they come up—and spills. There's going to be plenty of questions about that."

"Haven't *you* seen her?" Brandon asked, with some surprise.

"Actually, no. We, ah, haven't seen much of each other in the last year or so. She's been taking a lot of long leaves down at the ranch. She's given Larry a lot of moral support—which I appreciate. The kid was pretty depressed at first when they told him about his lungs."

"Reckon they'll get married?"

Wilbur shrugged. "They haven't said anything yet, but I don't see how anything else could happen. Speak-

469

ing of the family, have you heard anything new on Penny?"

Brandon shook his head morosely. "Not a tip. We don't even know if she's still in Alaska. For all we know she way have had plastic surgery done on her face or her finger tips, changed her prints—they can do damn near anything these days. Hell, they've even got a plastic surgeon in Fairbanks and he advertises too."

Wilbur looked up curiously.

"No, no. We checked him. If she did that, she didn't go to him."

"The girl's disturbed," Wilbur said. "That much is clear. I think with all the time that's elapsed, they don't have much of a case against her. If we could find her I think we could get away with a plea of insanity."

"Others have failed," Brandon pointed out.

"Yes, but they don't have much on her in the first place. These cases tend to fall apart in time. Anyway, keep up the effort. I'm surprised you've been able to keep this all from leaking so far."

"It's cost plenty."

"I noticed, by the way, that since that Heywood fellow died, there haven't been that many leaks, and the press has been much kinder. You don't suppose he had anything to do with all that?"

Brandon shrugged. "Doesn't make much difference now. As long as the leaks have stopped, everything has worked out to our advantage. And it's certainly helped the progress on the pipeline."

"Yes," Wilbur said. "I suppose God moves in mysterious ways."

Brandon looked up and stared at his boss for a moment, wondering how he was expected to take that remark. But Wilbur's face was as bland as a *blancmange*.

"As the Pipeline Goes Rolling Along
(sung to the tune of "The Caissons Go Rolling Along")

> Over hill, over dale
> We will make a dusty trail
> As the pipeline goes rolling along.
>
> Through the mud or the ice
> We keep raising up the price
> As the pipeline keeps rolling along.

> —Charles G. Cameron,
> Fort Wainwright in
> *Camp Follower*
> —pipeline newspaper

Chapter Forty-four

By April of 1977, basic construction of the first phase of the pipeline was completed. Pump stations One, Three, Four, Eight, and Ten were completed as planned in the first phase. When the pipeline was turned on in this phase, it would have a capacity of six hundred thousand barrels a day. In the second phase, three pump stations would be added—Six, Nine, and Twelve—and the capacity would be doubled. The final phase was not expected to be completed until seven years after initial start-up, when stations Two, Five, Seven, and Eleven would be brought on the line and the system would reach its final capacity of two million barrels a day.

As work neared completion, the labor force dropped from fifteen thousand to about nine thousand men. The impact on the welfare and unemployment offices was noticeable, although many of the laborers were out-of-staters who returned home to enjoy their Alaskan-gotten gains. The approval of the new gas pipeline to parallel the oil pipeline was an encouraging sign that there would continue to be work provided by Denali for at least another ten years. And it appeared very likely that the Fairbanks to Chicago rail link would ultimately be approved. In general, feelings were high and optimistic in the Fiftieth State. But there was much work to be done before oil could actually begin to flow through the pipes.

First, there had to be a complicated series of tests of all the individual components, such as pipes, valves, pumps, turbines, telecommunications, and instruments, and corrections made of any faults. Then the main line pipe and the connecting fitting were to be subjected to special dimensional checks—non-destructive testing, and hydrostatic field tests. This involved pressurizing the pipeline in sections of about fifteen miles each. Each section was to be sealed off and filled with a test liquid (basically Alaskan water treated with anti-freeze chemicals) and the pressure raised to a hundred and twenty-five percent of the predicted maximum operating pressure for that part of the line. This pressure would be held for a twenty-four hour period in each section without additional pumping. If leaks were indicated by a current of unexplainable pressure changes, they would be located, repaired and the entire test repeated.

After the completion of these pressure hydrostatic tests, the tested sections would be linked with short sections of pipe, which themselves would be separately pretested. Then it would all be tied in together and the welds radiographically tested. In addition, the major pumps—main pumps, suction booster pumps, and injection pumps for Station Five, crude oil transfer pumps for the terminal, and the fire water pumps for the terminal—would have to be tested and subjected to the same sort of hydrostatic pressure tests as the pipeline system. Then there would have to be field tests of the electrical generators, of the circuits, power distribution centers, instruments, supervisory control systems, meters, topping units (these were small refineries used to supply fuel for operation of the various stations), the ballast treating system, oil and gas piping, heating systems, and fire protection systems.

The consortium had agreed that the oil tankers, which previously had been accused of adding to the pollution by blowing out their ballast tanks at sea, would unload their ballast water into special holding tanks where it would be treated and returned in a purified state to Valdez Bay.

Once the whole system was set up, the plans called for running it for seven days on chemically treated water to make sure that there were no problem areas. All the storage tanks too, including the oil tanks, ballast water tanks, and fuel tanks, were also to be hydrostatically tested. The microwave and electrical generating equipment of the telecommunications system were also due for separate tests. The goal was to be sure that there was no outage of power or communications that would exceed forty-three minutes during a thirty-day continuous operating period.

After much negotiating, backing and filling, red-faced argument, and subtle behind-the-scenes pressures, Wilbur was able to gain the consent of other client members of Denali for Alamo to ship the first tanker of oil passed through to new pipeline.

The publicity gained through the use of the new Globtik Alamo, he argued, would be a good thing for all of them. And, in addition, he agreed that Alamo would absorb all the expenses for the start-up and inaugural ceremonies, although the saving of a few hundred thousand dollars was hardly likely to influence the other companies. The fact was privately many of the others had felt it was just as well to assume a low profile and let Wilbur Steele be the target of any critical blasts that would coincide with the opening of the pipeline. Those with large gas station affiliates also felt that the publicity might arouse a certain amount of hostility that could be reflected adversely in retail sales.

In the camps and pumping stations along the way, the SHAMAN team had also managed to hold and consolidate its position. Since they all had several years of seniority, they were not easily displaced, even in the initial discharge of workers following completion of the main phases of the pipeline.

That winter, further announcements from OPEC of a unilateral decision to decrease production and increase oil prices, caused another wave of excitement about the opening of the pipeline. An elaborate chain of memos was prepared to answer press questions about why the Globtik Alamo would not put into an American port. The question was easy to answer since there was no port on the West Coast equipped to handle it.

The oil, it was explained, was to be piped across Central America and delivered to U.S. refineries in the Virgin Islands. What was not explained was that by this process the provisions of the Jones Act had been evaded and the oil would now be subject to free market conditions—without any control—and might in fact never actually reach a single American gas tank.

There was a good chance that there would be a new chorus of criticism when this information was more closely examined and appraised. But the oil consortium was ready with its arsenal of millions—if necessary—to counteract any storms of protest. After having overcome the initial attack on the pipeline itself, it seemed unlikely that anything could stop progress now that the pipeline was finished and the oil was ready to flow.

Chapter Forty-five

In the spring of 1977, six months before the opening of the pipeline, two groups were setting up their equipment, testing their resources, and focusing their attention on the target day, October 22, 1977. O-day they were calling it, for the oil that would then flow. The Denali team was busy with its hydrostatic tests, patching up leaks in the pipes where welds had given way, testing and re-testing the remote control valves, the power lines, and the communications systems.

Meanwhile, the members of the SHAMAN team were also studying, practicing, and testing. They took small batches of explosives out into remote fields and tried their technique with detonators.

They tried to set up cells of sympathizers in each camp without betraying the structure of the organization. At Prudhoe, John Takolik made a friend of Simon Orloff, an Aleut from Kashega on Unalaska Island. Orloff was convinced that oil pollution from Valdez would ultimately completely engulf his tiny island and kill all the seals and whales upon which his people depended. He was a gentle little man—boy, actually. He was only twenty-two, and had been to college at the University of Alaska where he spent a lot of time studying ecological problems. Orloff was a strange combination of sophistication and naivete—he had never, until he went to Fairbanks to study, been more than a hundred miles from home. And now, at Prudhoe, he was farther from home than he'd ever been.

When Simon was on duty in the guard shack, he spent a lot of time trying to write down and recall the myths he'd heard from his grandparents and great-grandparents about the days before the Russians came, the great wars with the Eskimos and Kodiak Islanders, the days when the men of Unalaska took slaves in warfare, the great hunting stories, and the spirit tales about the birds and sea mammals on whom his people depended.

Simon claimed that he could remember having been dipped into the sea to give him strength, according to the old traditions of his people, even before he was baptized by the Orthodox Church of Unalaska. And then the stories they told about when the Russians came and killed nine-tenths of the Aleuts in what was said to be a series of "misunderstandings." And the stories of how the Aleut hunters were eventually enslaved by the Russians to hunt for the dwindling sea otter herds, and how his people were taken away to south-eastern Alaska and even to California.

"Then why did you come to work here?" Takolik asked, puzzled.

Simon looked at him with his great soft, black eyes.

"The same as you, to find out their magic, so I could defeat them some day."

Simon was a dreamer, even Takolik could see that.

476

But he encouraged the poetic young Aleut and felt he was the only one who could be trusted.

Sonia gave up her job at the Flame Lounge and migrated to Valdez where she found work as a barmaid at the Pipeline Club. It was a good spot for getting information and for making friends with important people such as security guards out at the terminal.

The big problem would be coordination. With communications so bad, the group would just have to set a time a day or so in advance, and perhaps send a code message.

Marge at her Pump Station had also succeeded in recruiting a potential saboteur or two. Basically, they were bullcooks and other women workers (she once suggested wiping out the camp with an overdose of LSD in the food, but the suggestion was vetoed as nonproductive and ineffective. The only ones who would be hurt were the workers, who could easily be replaced.)

From Baronian, and others close to the oil company, they knew that a few of the clients of Denali—particularly Alamo, which depended on the North Slope oil more than the others for its economic existence—could go broke if the pipeline were closed down for a couple of years, as it would be by their planned sabotage. Of course, others, like Golconda, could survive anything, as could Royal American. But Royal American had complicated deals with other American oil companies and much of its success depended on the early flow of the oil.

If SHAMAN succeeded only in destroying Alamo, Sonia would feel that the project was a total success.

Deirdre too had new responsibilities. She had been placed in charge of making arrangements for the publicity and ceremonies to attend the inaugural oil shipment. There was to be a great junket with hundreds of TV news men from the lower forty-eight and foreign countries. Accommodations had to be booked at least six months ahead of time, transportation arranged, and an entertainment program provided. Brochures giving all the facts and figures of the pipeline history had to be prepared, scientists had to be found to assemble the information to answer the latest questions concerning possible results of spills and pollution, and, in Japan, sea tests had to be run for the Globtik Alamo, chartered for its first two years exclusively to Alamo and expected to earn for that company as much as fifty million dollars per trip.

Ever since the pipeline had hit its final phase, Wilbur Steele had spent little time in Alaska. Much of his efforts had been taken up with juggling the assets of Alamo in an effort to keep it solvent and to give an illusion of financial health until the oil started flowing from the north. This involved dropping plans for developing a Canadian market completely, giving up an ambitious scheme to develop oil from midwestern shale, selling off hundreds of gas stations, and also selling a certain number of pipeline systems, an East Coast refinery, a few producing properties, and some real estate in Canada, and concentrating marketing efforts on the two coasts.

With the North Slope oil, Alamo could easily become one of the biggest, if not the biggest, and most prosperous oil company in the world. Without it, they would probably go broke.

Late one night, in the summer of 1977, Deirdre was working overtime at Denali Headquarters near Fort Wainwright, when she was startled by the ringing of the phone. She was surprised to see that it was the direct line to Wilbur's office and it was in fact Wilbur on the phone. Deirdre had not seen him in almost a year. He had only been to Alaska once or twice in that period, and when he had invited her—or rather commanded

478

her — to join him in New York, or Houston, or at Mitchell Mesa, she had found reasons to refuse. When she did visit the ranch to see Larry, she was always careful to be sure that Wilbur was in some different part of the country or overseas.

"Close up," Wilbur said, without any preamble to his conversation. "I want to see you now."

"Wilbur, I'm way behind and this is important work. You know how close we are to target day."

"Look, I'm tired of all this crap you've been handing me. I want to see you *now*."

She could hear Wilbur struggling to control his anger.

"Never mind the Goddamn work! It can wait. Now you come on down here. Do you hear me?"

That commanding, cold, hard tone brought up childhood memories—the pain and humiliation that she had somehow been made to feel she enjoyed.

"I am not . . . I won't . . . I won't come, Wilbur. I'm not starting that over again. It's finished. I don't *feel* like that anymore."

Wilbur's voice was low and cold, and trembled from contained anger. "You Goddamn little bitch! Who do you think you are? You get down here this Goddamn minute."

Deirdre bit her lower lip, trying to choke back the cry of anguish that she could feel welling up like bile from her stomach, and dabbed with her knuckle at the sudden hot stream of tears that ran down her cheeks.

Without answering, she hung the phone up and began to throw papers wildly into a manila folder which she jammed into her leather dispatch case. She was slipping into the light suede jacket that she'd taken as protection against the evening chill when Wilbur burst through the door. His face was flushed with anger and the thick vein down the middle of his forehead that always stood out so vividly when he was excited was bulging there now like a small pink snake.

Deirdre darted behind the desk, putting its wide expanse between her and the angry Texan.

"What in hell is the meaning of this, Missy?" Wilbur demanded.

Deirdre was frightened of Wilbur when he was like this, but his anger showed his vulnerability and somehow made her more sure that she could cope.

"I'm not doing that anymore, Will I've changed, I've out-grown it. It's very bad for me."

Wilbur Steele said nothing, but stared at her, with eyes like knife blades.

"Please don't mess my mind, Will. You don't need me. I'm nothing in your life, and that's what I want to be. You can find a hundred women right here in Fairbanks who will do what you want."

Wilbur let out a hot rasping breath, like a sigh of fury. He reached across the desk so quickly that Deirdre wasn't able to move and grabbed her by the collar of her denim workshirt. "You do what I say, damnit!" he said. "This is the time I need you."

"Let go, Will," Deirdre said desperately. "Let go—" Her hand scrabbled desperately over the nearly bare surface of her desk and finally closed on the slab of stained oil-test core which she used as a paper weight. "Let go, Will, Goddamnit. I just don't want to play anymore."

Wilbur shook her until she felt as though she could actually feel her brain sloshing in her skull.

"Let go!" she said again, even more desperately, and almost without thinking swept up the heavy paper weight and crashed it into Wilbur's bulging brow. Wilbur's eyes went blank and unfocused from the pain of the blow and his hand loosened on her neck as he clutched for support on the desk. His eyes clouded with

480

agony. Before he could recover his senses, Deirdre grabbed her jacket and ran from the room, barely able to find her way through the empty office because of the blurry veil of tears that obscured her vision.

Outside she jumped into her yellow company Mustang and headed down Gaffney Road to the airport highway as fast as she could drive.

"For the moment, however, a million-ton tanker is enough for almost anybody's imagination, not to speak of peace of mind . . . Such a ship would have a length of 1,640 feet . . . a breadth of 274 feet, and a draft of 100 feet. The prospect of such a ship, helplessly adrift *anywhere* while waiting for tugs doesn't bear thinking about, least of all if it were full of oil and close to some coast."

—Noël Mostert
Supership

Chapter Forty-six

Captain Willy Coutts was the manager of the Globtik Alamo (his title of Captain derived from his service aboard tankers plying from Aruba to Maracaibo during World War Two). He stopped his cup of black coffee, laced with Alfonso Primero brandy, just before it danced off the edge of the chart room table. The vibrations were worse than ever and Coutts decided to take on an added fifty thousand tons of sea water as ballast and to reduce the speed from sixteen to fourteen knots. This would throw the Alamo oil program off schedule, and even a half day's loss would mean hundreds of thousands of dollars. But Coutts was placed in the position of manager because of his experience. It was quite an honor to be in command of the largest vessel ever floated by man. In fact, Coutts had only accepted the job from Togo Marine (which had chartered the Liberian registered ship to Alamo on a three year lease

482

agreement) because of the chance to top off his long career by managing this greatest ship of all time.

Even at the rate at which tankers were growing, this one—a quarter of a mile long and almost the length of a football field across—had double the capacity of the nearest record-holder (it was six hundred and twenty feet longer than either of the old Queens). It drew a hundred feet, a far-cry from the little sixteen thousand six hundred ton T-2 tankers that Coutts had commanded during the war. The vibration that had irritated Coutts was due to the fact that the ship was traveling empty, with only a quarter of the tanks loaded with salt water ballast. On this trip at least, since the tanks had not yet contained any oil, the sea water could be discharged without treatment into the ocean when the Globtik Alamo was finally loaded at Valdez.

They were now ten days out of Tokyo, wallowing through the North Pacific, parallel to the Aleutian Islands, but far enough at sea to avoid any shoal waters. Generally speaking the waters of southern Alaska were comfortable for the huge ship. Aside from the somewhat chancy narrowness of the entrance to Valdez Arm, Coutts anticipated little trouble despite the unwieldiness of the vessel.

Togo had been kind enough to provide him with twin screws instead of the single screws which had been deemed adequate for the other huge supertankers up to this point. This gave him added control, provided he could keep his speed up above the three or four knots that were needed for steerage. Even riding empty, the Globtik Alamo drew forty-two feet, eight feet more than the Queen Mary when it was fully loaded. The bridge of the Globtik Alamo, as in all recent tankers, was located at the stern end of the ship and towered a hundred feet over the sea. Through the windows,

483

Coutts could survey a vast acreage of red-painted steel decks with occasional raised catwalks lacing across the bare expanse.

Coutts was a big lantern jawed man with a pronounced underbite that gave his chin an appearance something like an Arctic ice-breaker. His jutting chin, along with the imposing sweep of his beak-like nose, and his six foot four inch height, gave him a physical authority that no one would question. It was hard to picture Coutts as anything but the commanding officer.

With him on the bridge at the moment were four men. The first officer, Tom Wallace, had commanded a mine-sweeper off Cape Cod during the war and was a veteran tanker officer since the days just after the Suez War when supertankers became the wave of the future. An Indonesian, general-purpose-rating First Class, named Abdul Hatta, was at the wheel (although this was only a precaution as the ship had been set on automatic pilot and running that way for days in the open sea). There were also two Japanese, Eisako Kato, the Electronics Officer, and an Electronics Cadet named Mori Arakawa. The Electronics Officer was a member of the governing committee of the ship and carried a masters rank, as did Coutts. This committee of almost-equals consisted of the Navigational, Engineering, and Electrical Officers. They met together once a day just like a corporate committee to discuss various problems involved in the running of the ship.

The advantages of making these tankers larger every year were obvious. The crew of the Globtik Alamo was only a few men larger than the Globtik Tokyo, which carried a third of the cargo. The bigger the ship, the less the crew costs, dockage, and energy needed to propel the cargo.

Coutts looked sourly at the men assembled around

him in the huge sweeping bridge and excused himself to retire to his cabin on the deck below. He had never gotten used to the idea that almost all of his tanker crews consisted of what he thought of as Wogs and Chinks; Wogs being anybody except a north-European or an American, and Chinks being anybody of remotely Asiatic extraction. But since the ships that he sailed were almost always flying flags of convenience (Liberian or Panamanian), the crews tended to be a very mixed group, both in terms of nationality and experience. And Coutts felt that the standards of professionalism were far beneath those even on those wretched wartime T-2s. Fortunately, the ships were almost completely automated and the function of the officers was largely to see that none of the machinery went awry.

Most of all, ship's manager Coutts disliked young Arakawa, the Electronic Officer's Assistant. Arakawa had long, greasy, black hair to his shoulders, which looked incongruous under his peaked petty officer's cap. He was short and wiry and always seemed to glide or dance across the deck rather than to walk or roll like a proper seaman. Coutts privately believed that the man was some sort of a poof—ships were getting filled with them these days. Nothing wrong, of course, with a little buggery on a long voyage, but these men were downright *deviants*.

Coutts had no way of knowing it, but young Mori Arakawa thought little more of him. As to being queer, Coutts' suspicion was only partly right. Mori thought of himself as being pan-sexual, willing to accommodate any person of any sex, or any agreeable animal, that came his way. But Arakawa's mission aboard the Globtik Alamo was not hedonistic pleasure.

As a student, Arakawa had been an ardent follower of Yukio Mishima. When that right-wing ideologue committed suicide in 1970, Arakawa shifted his sympathies to the Japanese Red Army Party, which had aroused his admiration for its part in the Lod Airport massacre in Israel and the 1972 Olympic massacres in Munich. Arakawa burned with ambition to achieve similar dramatic prominence and the time came when, through one of the revolutionary groups' contacts at Togo, Arakawa was hired away from his job in electronic development, at Hitachi Electric Company, to serve as Second Electronics Officer on the Globtik Alamo. The mission assigned to him by the Red Army group would satisfy his deepest ambitions for a dramatic gesture and at the same time would strike a blow for the Arabs, and against the Americans.

When Coutts slipped from the bridge, Arakawa took down the thick volume of charts and diagrams covering the thousands of electronic circuits for the giant supership. Electronics Officer Kato was pleased to see the diligence of his assistant.

"Excellent, Arakawa-san," he said. "I am pleased to see you are applying yourself to study of the ship's electronic system."

The senior officer looked over the shoulder of the long-haired young man. "Very good. I see you are studying the generator system—most important. If the generator systems should fail, that is the most disastrous thing that could happen to the ship. If we lose power, we are helpless in the sea. That is one of the reasons our job is the most important one on the ship, even though the tall *gaijen* may think that *his* is."

Kato, a pudgy little man of about thirty-five built like a Buddha, stood beside the younger man as he poured over the generator diagrams, put his hand lightly on Arakawa's shoulder, and said:

"For whom has my heart,
  Like the passion-flower patterns
  of Michinoku
  Been thrown into disarray?
  All on account of you."

Arakawa frowned and shook the hand off. "Really. I told you I am not interested. Besides, Narihira is so corny. It's for old men."

"You hate him because you're a Communist."

Arakawa turned to the older man and looked into his eyes. "Communism is not love," he said. "Communism is a hammer which we use to crush the enemy."

"And who is that?" Kato asked peevishly.

"Mao Tse Tung," the long-haired young man said.

"Indignation over the rape of the environment is an avocation of many people who are paid to do other things. Making money is the full time occupation of the oil drillers. They can be patient, they can ride out the storm. Sooner or later emotional fatigue overcomes the viewers with alarm. Even the worst news ultimately becomes a bore. Apathy and anomie set in and the drillers take over . . ."

—Garret Harden
Professor of Biology
University of California,
Santa Barbara

Chapter Forty-seven

Deirdre Doheny never stopped running until she got back to Mitchell Mesa. From the Seattle airport she sent a telegram to Mahlon Doheny explaining that she had been called away on personal business, and would discuss it all later on the phone. There was no home left for her now in Texas except Mitchell Mesa. When Mahlon Doheny went broke on his Mexican oil venture he had been forced to sell their comfortable house in Riveroaks near Houston, most of the oil leases in East Texas, and hundreds of sections of ranchland in the western part of the state. Of course, by returning to Mitchell Mesa she took the chance of running into Wilbur Steele all over again, but she felt that the presence of Grandpa Bisset and Larry would keep matters under control.

Larry was overjoyed to see her since she was not due for R & R for another four weeks, and had indicated that she might not even be able to take that particular leave because of the pressure of preparing for the inauguration of the pipeline.

"What brings you home so early?" Larry said. He

was walking now, shakily, with the help of an aluminum cane that partially braced his arm. The heavy cast had come off the week before and been replaced with a lighter cast with a steel brace on which he could rest his weight lightly.

Deirdre looked off into the hills, avoiding a direct confrontation with his eyes. "I had a fight with Will . . . your father."

"Well, I wouldn't get too riled up about those things. I know you've been bothered by some of the problems with the pipeline, but, hell, it's done now. They might as well get the oil going."

"It wasn't about that," Deirdre said. "It was more personal."

Larry hobbled around to face her and took her shoulder in his free hand. "What do you mean? Did he try to . . . to do anything?"

Deirdre faced him with sad eyes, and thought a long time before she answered.

"Well, Goddamnit," Larry said impatiently, shaking her shoulder, "what did that son of a bitch do to you?"

Deirdre was thinking. Could Larry handle the whole, unwholesome story? If she told him what her relation with Wilbur had been since she was a teenager, how could he face his father again, or live with him? And was it fair to make this a part of Larry's problem? More than that she worried about that inbred Texas machismo, which might lead Larry to take violent action against Wilbur.

"Goddamnit, D.D.," Larry said impatiently, still holding her shoulder in a paralyzing grip, "are you going to tell me or not?"

Deirdre made her painful decision. "It was just something he wanted me to do. I didn't like his tone of voice. He's so bossy sometimes. I guess we've been rubbing each other the wrong way. It may be because I'm unhappy about the work."

Larry held her eyes suspiciously. She had never lied to him—that he knew of—but her words had a very hollow sound.

"You're not telling me the whole story."

"Oh, Larry," she said. "It's too complicated, but everything's okay now. Let's go talk to Grandpa."

Later the three of them had a Tex-Mex dinner at a table set up on the terrace. Washing down the highly seasoned chili and bean mixture with cold draughts of Pearl beer, Grandpa Bisset said, "I knew you couldn't stand that son of a bitch. Nobody can work for him. That man may be a great oil man, but when it comes to human beings, he's as dumb as a fencepost. You sure you didn't run out just to hare-lip him?"

"Maybe that was a bit of it," Deirdre said, looking down into her plate.

"Well, hell!" Grandpa Bisset said as he wiped the chili gravy from his moustache with one of the red bandanas Miguel had laid out in lieu of napkins. "He's always mule-cating about something. But it's a stack of yellows to a white chip that he's just a little tight-ass over gettin' this damn pipeline finished and on stream. He's been spreading his bets a little thin, liquidating a lot of company assets to copper his bets. If that oil don't get flowing by next fall he's going to have to go back to lease-brokering in East Texas and work his way up all over again."

"We were talking about that the last time he was down here," Larry said, mopping up the remains of the gravy with a tortilla. "For the first time, maybe, I began to see what he was all about. It isn't all the fancy clothes and the trips east and the fancy restaurants, and all this—" he swept the tortilla around to

490

indicate the broad sweep of the ranch and the hills beyond. "It's that he likes the game of it. I swear, he likes to make money, swing deals, the way some people like to ride horses, paint pictures or sing songs. I think if he lost the whole spread, quarter horses, cattle, ranch, leases, house and all, that son of a bitch would be back on top in five years."

"Yeah," Grandpa Bisset said, "and he wouldn't care who he tromped on to get there, either. That man's got a smile like a Texas river—a mile wide and an inch deep."

"Your Dad, too," Larry said, turning to Deirdre. "Of course, they're cut out of the same mold."

"The difference being," Grandpa Bisset said, "that Mahlon Doheny is a straight arrow, as oil men go, and your Daddy's got more curves and wiggles than a diamond-back rattler."

Miguel Carreras shuffled out onto the terrace carrying the sand-colored princess phone on a long extension. sion.

"*Telefono* for Senorita Doheny. It's from Alaska."

Hesitantly, Deirdre took the telephone from him. It was Susie Wing's voice. "Miss Doheny? Your father would like to talk to you."

Deirdre heaved a high of relief. She did not feel she could have faced talking to Wilbur, especially with the other two present.

"Yes, Daddy," she said. "How are you?"

"D.D.? What in the purple-ever-lovin' hell got into you running off like that without giving us no warning. I'd've given you a couple of days off if you'd wanted it. But you just split out like a streak of blue lightning, without saying nothing to nobody. Wilbur was cussin' everybody in the place up and down as if the whole operation depended on you. He says for you to get

491

your fine high ass up here and finish off your job. Right now he's gonna need you, especially since he's not going to be back until the inaugural."

"You mean he's gone?"

"Shucks, he left right after you did. Next morning. Went down to Washington to see Fred. They got to get some of those Washington lobbyists to explain the fact that there just ain't any room on the West Coast for all that oil we're gonna be shipping down. Seems they haven't got it clear in their heads that this stuff is going either to Japan or the Virgin Islands. Well, if it ain't one damn thing it's another. Oh, yeah, he said to give you another thousand dollars a month just to cool you off. What on earth happened between you two? Not that I blame you . . ."

"I don't know, Daddy," Deirdre said. "I guess the strain was getting to me. But I'll be all right after a few day's rest."

"Is Larry there? Put him on."

Deirdre handed the phone to Larry.

"Yeah, Uncle Mahlon. How's things going up there?"

"They're going lousy, son. All the shit is hitting the fan at once. The closer we get to finishing, the more there seems to be to look after. I need a right-hand man, real bad. And your Daddy and me both think that you're the man who can handle the job."

"What's the matter with Brandon?"

"Brandon is a big high-falutin' executive, spends his time in Washington and Paris. I need a *field* man, somebody who knows what it's like out there, so's we don't get into that farunctious mess we got into with those phony weld x-rays; somebody who can deal with the men if there's a union problem, someone who can figure out where all the damn equipment's going that's being stolen right and left. Just a good old boy that

492

knows the territory. There isn't a son of a bitch up here that I'd trust as far as I could throw an oil rig. You on your feet yet, anyway?"

"Yeah," Larry said, slowly. "I'm walking with a cane."

"Hell, that's good enough. You only need one foot to kick somebody's ass."

"Uncle Mahlon," Larry said. "Is this some kind of a shuck you and my Dad cooked up—some kind of cooked-up-on-the-job-occupational therapy?"

Doheny's voice was dead serious. "I swear to Christ, son. It's true your Pappy put the idea in my head, but once he did I couldn't think of any better man. All these candy-ass executives up here never had a callous on their hands—they don't know a welding torch from a Dunhill lighter, let alone anything about the oil business. And the main thing is, they don't know how to deal with the men."

"What kind of money are we talking about." Larry asked cautiously.

"Seventy-five grand."

"Shit!" Larry said. "I was making almost as much as that welding."

"Yeah," Doheny said, "but here you don't have to freeze your ass and fall in ditches and all that kind of shit."

"Make it a hundred, just so I'll feel it's worth packing for."

"A hundred grand," Doheny sputtered, "Goddamn that's near as much as *I* get—for a busted-up oil hand, with only one good leg."

"I'm one hell of a hopper, though," Larry said. "And I bet if I wrap some of that long green around my leg, that ankle's going to heal up real fast."

"Okay you old horse-trader," Doheny said. "I can

see you got more of your pappy in you than I ever thought. Throw some stuff in your duffle bag and get your ass up here. And bring that uppity oil princess along with you. We'll be looking for you."

Larry hung up the phone and looked around him. He wasn't sure how either of his two dinner companions would take his decision, but he didn't think he could hang around Mitchell Mesa another day watching television and reading dog-eared mysteries and paperback Westerns.

"Well, shit, folks," he said. "A man's gotta do *something* right? I can't do much stompin' around with this gimpy leg and these shot-down lungs."

Grandpa Bisset held up his mangled, two-fingered hand in protest. "Son, I wasn't saying nothing. You'd be a damn fool if you didn't go into it. Better'n starting some fart-ass rinky-dink flying circus, like you were planning. You got a *future* with this. Besides, the oil business, it's in your blood, in your veins—seein' as how you're a third generation man, and that's about all the oil business this country's got to talk about. You're a pioneer. Just like your great-grand Daddy that fought with Sam Houston."

"Grandpa, will you cut the bullshit?" Larry said. "You told me yourself, you never had any use for the Goddamn business. Clothes smellin' of oil all the time, high-flyin' trash-mouth, power-hungry, money-grubbing, la-di-da phonies!"

Grandpa Bisset leaned back in the fancy wheel chair and looked at him with amusement. "You don't believe all that horse doodle, do you son? Everybody talks like that. Me? I wouldn'ta had it no other way. It's time you got out there anyway and started swinging your weight, instead of playing around with them toys out in the field. That's a kid's game. Anybody stays at that after the age of thirty-five ain't got the brains of a fundamentalist preacher.

Grandpa Bisset leaned across the table, holding onto it with his mangled hand for balance. "You got some good blood sportin' around in your veins, son. The Bissets were one hell of a family. And your old man, he didn't get where he was with shit for brains. I never could believe that you'd be so lame that you'd keep lolligagging around like some illiterate roughneck for the rest of your life. Underneath that dumb Steele face I always figured you had a mind like a bear trap. A man's got equipment like that, he better use it somewhere."

He pulled himself closer to the table and stared closely into Larry's eyes. "You get in there and in five years, I'll guarantee you, you'll shove your old man right out of the business. Same as he did to me."

"Well, I wouldn't say I was so all-mighty ambitious as that," Larry said, smiling. "But I might welcome a challenge at that."

He turned to Deirdre, who was pouring a round of Fundador to go with the black coffee Miguel had brought to the table.

"I'd give a solid gold tooth to see you try it, Larry," she said.

Larry laughed and tossed off the brandy and held out his glass for another. When he caught Deirdre's eyes he could see that she wasn't laughing. The expression on her face was dead serious.

"We face the removal of Prince William Sound from human use, except for transportation of oil and other commodities."

—Donald Cornelius, Biologist
quoted in *Anchorage Daily News*

Chapter Forty-eight

In the weeks before the opening of the pipeline, Valdez was like the eye of a storm. Of the four thousand or so workers who had been completing the terminal, three thousand had been laid off when the work was finished, and more than half of the remaining thousand would soon be discharged.

There was a brief breathing spell and a beautiful Indian Summer in September. Deirdre had come up from Texas shortly after the phone call from her father. Larry, after giving his leg another month to strengthen, had followed. Both his leg and his lungs had improved considerably, and, except for an occasional chest pain and a cough and a wheeze, he was not aware of any excess fluid in his lungs. His right leg, however, was atrophied from disuse and Larry was still forced to limp along with the aid of a cane. The one he found, in a curio shop in Anchorage, was made from a walrus penis.

Target date for the completion of the terminal was October 18, Alaska Day, but it soon became clear that that date would be missed by a least a month. Larry was kept busy flying up and down the line— sometimes piloting his own Cessna—stopping in at all of the camps where trouble threatened delays. There had been more than the expected breakdown of welds during the hydrostatic tests and this was one of the things that caused delays, for once the welds had been repaired, more tests were required. There was also a flurry of environmental protest about releasing the test water, which contained anti-refrigerants. But the protesters were not able to show any specific damage done by the release of the water, which, at that time of the year, required only minute quantities of anti-refrigerant chemicals to prevent it from freezing.

With the schedule he was on, Larry was lucky if he spent one weekend out of two with Deirdre. As for marriage, there was a tacit understanding that it was something that would be talked of when the project was completed. Termination dust fell in Valdez late that year. There was no snow until October 20th. The fact that the first oil shipment would not go out until mid-November presented no special problems except for the fact that from the beginning of October strong winds began occasionally to blow across Prince William Sound, sometimes reaching eighty and a hundred miles per hour. This fact had been minimized in all Denali propaganda, which claimed that the average wind was "below seven miles an hour, ninety percent of the time."

It was determined that the official opening of the pipeline—as far as the public was concerned—would start with the loading of the Globtik Alama. Six of the five-hundred-and-ten-thousand-barrel storage tanks were ready and two more would be by the time the huge ship arrived. This would be more than enough to fill its tanks and would make possible a fast turn-around. The oil itself, at seven miles an hour, took four and a half days to make the trip from Prudhoe to Valdez, pushing the scraper before it to separate it from the test water in the pipes.

In the final months, the main thrust of publicity at

Denali was to explain that the situation had changed since the pipeline had started and that there was no longer a need for the Alaskan oil on the West Coast nor was there a place to store it. Ultimately it was suggested that a pipeline could be built from the West Coast to Texas and from there to the East, but that would take at least two years and several billion dollars. In the meantime, the cheapest way to get the oil to the East Coast, where it was most needed, would be via the Central American crossing, and the Virgin Island refineries. By now Congress was so close to taking controls off domestic oil that it hardly mattered that this method circumvented the Jones Act.

Deirdre was busy constructing a program of events, entertainment, speakers, etc., and directing a newly hired group of employees—mostly female—who were to supervise billeting of the thousands of expected guests.

In anticipation, several of the now empty dormitories at the terminal were set aside for invited guests of Denali and the press, which was expected to come from all over the world, but particularly from the British Isles (the English, with their North Sea oil, were particularly interested in petroleum developments), Japan (which would be receiving some of the oil and had built the Globtik Alamo), the Middle East (obviously), and Western Europe (which would very likely receive its share of the oil from the Virgin Island refineries.)

Weeks ahead of time, tourists had claimed spots on the causeway outside of the gates of the terminal at Jackson Point, just across the port from the new city of Valdez.

The Valdez Glacier Wayside Campgrounds had also been filled for weeks, its hundred spaces overflowing, and hundreds of unauthorized campsites were set up on the roads outside of the town in honor of the occasion. The over-taxed police did not bother to chase off the trespassers.

The Village Motel was managing to fit ten guests into a six room vacation cottage. Sheffield House added several stunning additional mobile homes, divided in four, to serve as "annexes" to the hotel. The rooms went for fifty-five dollars a night.

The town began to fill with whores, gamblers, and drifters, who rapidly took the place of the welders, pipe-fitters, mechanics, heavy construction equipment operators, and laborers who had been discharged at the completion of basic work on the terminal. Big time poker players, in ostrich skin cowboy boots with chamois trimming on their stockman's jackets, flashed bigger wads of cash than even the pipeliners. A roll of hundreds, wrapped in a lone single, was their trademark. The really heavy hitters had a second rubber band running crosswise. Inside the rolls were little hand scrawled notes of debts and credits and who they were going to finance to a game or be financed by. The real pros smoked smuggled Havana cigars and drank mineral water and coffee from glasses wrapped in paper napkins. They never drank.

Table stakes games of a hundred thousand dollars or more were not unusual. The influx of the visitors and the decrease of actual pipeline workers changed the quality of life in the town. There was less big brawling and more boasting. But in many ways the newcomers were twice as rough as the pipeliners had been, and just as greedy. Bordellos set up in trailers on the outskirts of town and on the road to the airport thrived, with lines of men stamping their feet in the thin early snow, impatiently waiting their turns, and piles of condoms a foot high forming behind the Winnebago units. A week before "O" day, the Club Valdez, the Pipeline Club, the Glacier Club, and the Totem Lodge were all packed every night with raucous singing, dancing, and brawling men and women. At night—by now the sun was setting at four p.m.—the terminal across the water looked like a glittering imperial city, with colored lights on the completed storage tanks, the communications tower, the loading booms, and the remaining buildings stretching for a thousand acres into the blasted-away hills beyond Point Jackson. Denali tugs were busily puffing up and down the harbor, in and out of Valdez Arm, placing buoys, confirming depths, and checking communications facilities.

A new six and a half million dollar vessel communications center had been erected by the Coast Guard in Sitka to monitor movements of the tankers in and out of Valdez.

Sitting at the bar of the Club Valdez in the afternoon, looking past the masts of the anchored fishing fleet toward the mountains tinted pink with the setting sun and glimmering with the vast complex of terminal lights, one would have thought for a moment that Valdez was one of the great beauty spots on earth. But in the daytime, with the dust rising from the unpaved dirt roads, the harsh, new-painted steel construction, the silver-sided tanks, and the gawky loading cranes, it was like a view of Carteret, New Jersey, on a bad day. Of course, there were always the mountains above, but in October, more days than not, they were shrouded in heavy fog.

The final date was set at November 18. The Governors of California, Washington and sixteen other states promised to attend, as well as an equal number of senators, the Secretary of the Interior, the head of the Bureau of Land Management, and the head of the Bureau of Indian Affairs, representatives of the Tanana Chiefs' Council, and other Native groups. Tlingit, Haida, Aleut, and Athabascan dance groups were scheduled and a blanket tossing contest was planned by the Natives of Point Barrow.

Arranging the festivities represented a considerable logistical problem. There was much discussion at late night meetings in the Wainwright offices of Denali as to whether the ceremony should properly be when the oil was on stream or when the Globtik Alamo was finally loaded a week later. In view of the dramatic value of the shipping out of the world's largest tanker, with the world's largest oil cargo ever, it was finally decided that the ceremony should center around the send-off of the Globtik Alamo. This decision came fairly late and involved a lot of schedule rearranging by Sonia's small-but-growing group of saboteurs.

The pipeline was controlled by a set of huge block valves on either side of every pump station. It was now decided that in addition to knocking out the generators, the group would also decide to short circuit the remote control system which operated at least one of the gates, close them down, and then blow up the valve control system so they could not be opened from the main control station in Valdez. That station theoretically could control the entire pipeline remotely via a complicated network of electronic satellite communications and computers at the twelve remote stations. The master control at Valdez would continuously scan data from all remote stations. Approximately two hundred data signals and fourteen hundred status and alarm signals would be reviewed cyclically every ten seconds, twenty-four hours a day. The terminal operator's desk would be manned around the clock, and there would be a telecommunicator's desk also which would not be manned fulltime but which would be instrumented to permit constant surveillance by the dispatching group.

The terminal dispatchers in the control group would be controlling the flow of pipeline oil from the ten big storage tanks to the various tankers, directing the flow of oil through loading lines and manifold valves to the desired tanker berths. Four separate automatic alarm systems were provided by the computer to detect any leaks in the system and the computer would constantly monitor the system for any pressure deviations, flow deviations, or variations of flow from point to point in the line.

An alarm would be sounded whenever there was a change in the pressure or flow of more than one percent. If a leak was indicated, the data display would enable the dispatcher to determine just where the leak was located. The dispatcher could then take immediate action to shut down the pump stations and isolate sections of the line, initiating repair and recovery operations. The average section of pipe between pumping stations contained some fifty thousand barrels of oil, so that this would theoretically be the maximum leakage probable in case of severe damage of any section of the pipeline. Reserve tanks existed at all stations to pump off any extra oil flow that could be salvaged. The pump stations could be closed down by remote control in six minutes while other remote control valves could be closed in four minutes more. Contingency plans called for aircraft or ground patrols to pinpoint the leak or problem. Maintenance teams then would repair the leak, contain the spill to the smallest possible area, and begin recovery and repair operations.

One of the first steps taken by the crews as they

arrived at the spill would be to create dikes, pits, and other containment structures for the leaking oil. Oil that could not be picked up would be recovered by absorbent materials, and in some cases residual, unrecoverable oil might be burned, but only with the prior approval of appropriate government authorities.

The harbor itself seemed ideal for the terminal operation, which was why it had been chosen. It was long and narrow, with sheer cliffs and steep rocky beaches. The average water depth in the harbor was in excess of seven hundred and fifty feet, more than seven times what the Globtik Alamo required, even loaded. The velocity of water currents off Jackson Point was estimated to be less than half a knot, and in Valdez Narrow and Valdez Arm it was reported to be only one knot or less. Generally, wave action in the protected harbor was not more than one foot in height, but in storms, waves of two or three feet had been observed. This seemed to be within safe limits.

Special seismic detectors distributed along the pipeline would shut it down in case of any sudden earth tremors and would also detect the gradual movement of the earth which might indicate an impending quake.

Denali did not send out information, or invite the press for the first test of the opening of the oil line. It simply declared that they were continuing with the testing, and in a sense it was a test. Wilbur Steele and Mahlon Doheny both agreed that there was no point in calling public attention to the first flow of oil, in case there should be some mishap, such as a spill or a leak, so that by the time the information that oil was already flowing reached Sonia's group and could be coordinated, the tanks already had enough of the oil to fill the first Alamo ship. Still, Sonia argued, one ship more or less (even at a million barrels) didn't really matter as long as the SHAMAN group fulfilled their goal of stopping the entire line. The problem was to get messages to the members of the team without using public telephones or the mails. A phone code system was set up for the second date and "D", for Destruction Hour, was set for 1 p.m. on November 18th when presumably security personnel or supervisory people on duty would be at lunch.

As the pipeline neared completion, sabotage incidents had decreased and security had become casual and relaxed. Sonia and her group did not anticipate any problems except with their plan to destroy the multi-million dollar electronics and computer center at Valdez. Sonia had made the acquaintance of Red Holman, the supervising Wackenhut guard in that sector of the camp, and was reasonably sure that she could gain entrance for herself and at least one associate. Holman had several times in the past taken her in to show her the wonderful array of lights, alarms, and signals in the huge central unit. The plan for Valdez was to have Van Taylor sabotage the generator units so that the lights would fail at the same time that Sonia had succeeded in gaining entrance to the central control unit, where she would do as much damage as she could to the control system with plastic explosives carried in her camera bag.

Talking with Van Taylor at the Club Valdez, she tried to answer his objections.

"Honey, I'm no military genius," Van complained, "but this plan is just too complicated. There's no *way* it'll work." He was making small nervous rings with a wet glass on the bar.

"I've known all along it was a Goddamn fool plan," he said morosely.

"Then why have you stuck with it so long?" Sonia asked. Her voice was gentle, almost sympathetic.

"You, I guess."

Sonia looked surprised. "Really?"

"Well, you know . . . I don't know. Maybe it *will* work."

"Look, Van, the point is that it doesn't have to *all* work. If we get a couple of those valves blocked— even just one or two—that could do it, especially up north. And if we can fuck up the communications system—even a little bit, those things are delicate—it'll take them days to straighten it out. By that time the oil in that pipe will be as solid as asphalt."

"Listen. What's the difference to me? This harbor'll be fucking useless once they start shipping that oil anyway. I'd just have to clear out and go someplace else. I've really had it good here. I liked salmon fishing, kelp, and all that."

"Okay, then you're with it, right?"

Van looked up with a worried expression on his face. "Sure, sure. I'm with it."

Sonia lifted her glass of Oly high and toasted him. "To destruction."

"To destruction," Van echoed, forlornly.

"HOW TO BLOW UP AN OIL WELL

Pipelines are the most vulnerable, but the least effective points of sabotage. Not only are they easily patrolled . . . you can see for ten miles from a helicopter I am told—they are also no cinch to blow up. 'The pipe they've got there . . . is an inch or more thick. A roving band of eight or ten guerillas with a couple of hand grenades— they would have a hell of a time blowing it up. It takes someone who knows what he's doing,' one engineer told me. Moreover, if the right men and equipment are on hand, it can be mended in a matter of a day or two.

'If you really wanted to shut a country down,' I was told, 'you would go after the wells and the pump stations. But to really wreck a pump station you have to have some technical expertise, and an awful lot of dynamite, because the equipment is heavy and it doesn't blow apart easily.' Still, to a saboteur it would be worth the effort because one well blown pump station can shut a pipeline down for six months or more."

> —Andrew Tobias
> "War, the Ultimate
> Anti-Trust Action,"
> *New York Magazine*

Chapter Forty-nine

Sonia was living in a half-wrecked Winnebago with a makeshift addition made up of beaver-board and plywood sheathing tacked on indiscriminately and patched with sheet aluminum. The motor, tires, and wheels of the camper had long since been sold or cannibalized. Sonia had purchased it with SHAMAN funds from a subcontractor who was closing up his business after the completion of several residential units in the "Black Gold" grid of middle income houses beyond Egan Drive.

She shared the quarters with Ernie Mason (although he was not her lover) and Van Taylor (who occasionally was) and any other drifters who needed temporary flopping privileges. That October, Ernie Mason had to grudgingly make room or find other quarters on those nights when Red Holman was staying with Sonia.

"Admit it!" Ernie said argumentatively. "You *like* the guy."

Sonia shrugged. "So what? The point is, we need him, and if this is the way to get him, why not enjoy it at the same time? As a matter of fact, he's not such a great screw, but at least he isn't a nag, the way *you* are."

Ernie told her to go fuck herself and went into the small built-on addition that served as a study and second bedroom to write a sonnet about a king salmon who couldn't find his way home to spawn because of oily pollution. About a half an hour later Sonia rousted him out.

"Do that somewhere else, Ernie. I've got some figuring to do."

She sat down at the desk before a big yellow pad to outline the deployment of the SHAMAN team:

1. Pump Station One, origin station. Personnel: John Takolik, Simon Orloff, others? Targets: Sag River Block valves and main generators.

2. Pump Station Four, Galbraith Lake Camp. Personnel: Marge and friend (who?). Targets: Main power station.

3. Pump Station Ten. Personnel: Eli Hurwood (anyone else?) Target: Main generators.

4. Main Terminal. Personnel: Van

Taylor, me, Ernie Mason, Red Holman. Note: Baronian and Maroon
will be on hand to give what
assistance they can, particularly
Baronian for last minute information. (Why didn't Baronian let
us know when the oil started flowing?) Target: Generators and control center. Control center:
me, Red Holman and Ernie Mason.
Generators: Van Taylor.

Sonia checked over the various points of her memorandum. It was a shame to use three people on the
control building, but she had not wanted to risk letting
Red Holman in on the scheme. His end of the job was
to supply phony I.D. badges for herself and Ernie.
While in Valdez, Sonia had taken to wearing a long
blond wig and huge sun glasses so that, generally
speaking, even people who had known her from Fairbanks would not have recognized her.

" 'Supertankers can't avoid collisions,' former White House Science adviser Ed Wenck told Washington pipeline hearing, 'since it takes one seventeen miles to stop and five miles to turn 360°. Consider the prospect of a spill from a 250,000 ton supertanker carrying two million barrels of oil. The slick would be fifty miles long and five miles wide.' Wenck further stunned his audience by reciting some statistics he had compiled: assuming that only a hundredth of one percent of the oil carried is spilled—the current world wide spillage rate—when the line is in full use an average of thirty tons of oil will pour into the harbors every day."

—*Newsweek* Feature Service

Chapter Fifty

By Armistice Day, the Globtik Alamo was cruising into the Gulf of Alaska with the huge peaks of the Kenai Mountains towering in the northwest. East of Middleton Island, Ship's Manager Coutts directed the wheel man to alter course to enter Prince William Sound between Montague and Hinchinbrook Islands. The islands were separated by five miles of deep water and presented no problems of passage. But as the Globtik Alamo entered Prince William Sound a heavy low-lying fog rolled in from the mountains, necessitating operation on Loran and constant touch with communication facilities at the Terminal and the Coast Guard Station in Sitka.

The Globtik Alamo, like all tankers destined to use the Valdez harbor, in addition to standard navigational equipment for celestial and terrestrial navigation, was equipped with fathometer, radio direction finder, ONC, two independent radar systems (ultra high frequency and very high frequency), and single side band and radio telegraph. In addition, navigation was assisted by strategically placed fixed navigational aides and radio buoys, situated by the Coast Guard.

Just west of Bligh Island, Coutts ordered the ship's speed reduced to six knots, the slowest the ship could operate and still maintain steerage with safety, while waiting for the rendezvous with the helicopter scheduled to land aboard the tanker with the pilot from Valdez. Gusts of heavy wind forced him to turn the ship's automatic controls over to manual and supervise the operation himself. The ship, ballasted to only a quarter of its capacity, was riding ninety feet out of the water and presented a huge freeboard to the gusty winds. But the bay was wide and deep and Coutts anticipated no problems. Still, the job required all his concentration.

To his right, he was irritated to see Arakawa pouring over the book of electronic diagrams for the ship's systems.

"Are you on duty on this bridge?" Coutts asked irritably.

"No sir."

"Well, then, clear out."

The Japanese bowed and started to move off with the huge ring-bound book of diagrams.

"Leave the Goddamned book here on the bridge. There isn't any electronic problem, is there?"

"No sir," Arakawa said submissively. "I was just studying."

"Do your studying on your own time," Coutts said. "Get out. We're trying to run a ship here, not a Goddamn pachinko machine."

Arakawa bowed slightly, returned the electronics diagrams to their slot to the right of the compass binnacle, and retreated from the bridge, backing out like one leaving the presence of royalty, punctuating his departure with a tight bow every ten feet or so.

Because of the wind there was a delay of several hours before the helicopter with the pilot could land. But the Globtik Alamo was still thirty or forty miles from Valdez Arm and was able to cruise along slowly awaiting the pilot pickup without anticipating any problem. The pilot was finally landed from a small, two-passenger Bell Alouette chopper in one of the helicopter pads near the aft end of the deck. He was a wiry, slim blond young man with sun-bleached hair and long, pale lashes. He didn't look over twenty-five.

"You the pilot?" Coutts asked incredulously.

"Ivan Johannsen, sir."

"You know these waters?"

"The Coast Guard says so, and I've been fishing in them for ten years." He looked around the ship with interest, but some distaste. "That is, until you fellows come along."

"Any problems?" Coutts asked.

"Nothing we can't handle, sir, what with the communications and equipment you have here. There's a little fog but it's not actually down to water level. We've been getting some stiff winds, and you have to watch out for icebergs along here in that heavy wind—if it's blowing eastward—because it brings 'em right out into the channel."

"But there's no pack ice up here," Coutts said.

"No, sir. It's from the glaciers." He pointed over to the west. "Over there is Columbia Glacier. They take passengers over there to watch the big bergs drop off. The ship lets off a big blast of its fog whistles and the vibrations make a chunk of ice four hundred feet high fall into the sea. But generally we have a west wind, so that shouldn't cause us any problems. There's an-

511

other Glacier inside Valdez Arm called the Shoup Glacier, but that one doesn't calve as much and the bergs almost never get into the channel."

He looked around the ship admiringly. "This sure is a big fucker, isn't it?"

"The biggest man-made object ever put afloat."

The pilot whistled appreciatively. "I read about it. A million tons, eh? That's one hell of a lot of oil. Well, now that there's not going to be much fishing around here, I suppose I'd better be glad to have this job."

Coutts introduced the blond pilot to Tom Wallace and left the two of them to bring the ship into the harbor while he went to the deck below for tea and brandy in his quarters.

The two men hovered over their charts as the ship glided past Potato Point, then Entrance Point, and into the Valdez Narrows.

"You can see you have better than a mile of deep water here," Johannsen pointed out. "The only tricky spot is right up there." He pointed to a place on the chart about two miles ahead. "Middle Rock there. I suppose you've looked these charts over before?"

Wallace nodded.

"Well, the channel there is deep, plenty deep, so you shouldn't have any problem there either. After that we just hug the middle of the channel past Anderson Bay past Jackson Point where you'll tie up at Berth Five, a floating dock near Saw Island, unless they radio instructions otherwise."

"Got it," Wallace said. "Coffee?"

Why not?" the pilot said.

Wallace filled two styrofoam cups from the ten gallon urn on one side of the bridge. "You nervous?" he asked as he brought the coffee to the young pilot.

"Naw, it's just a job."

"Kind of an historic occasion, though," Wallace observed mildly. He had narrow blue eyes and a long horsey face that made his head sit strangely on his five foot seven body.

"Yah," Johannsen said, with a note of bitterness. "It's fucking historic, all right." His eyes scanned the base of the mountains visible below the blanket of hovering fog. "I don't suppose the place will ever be the same again."

"Continued rising prices for Mideast oil will guarantee a market for all the oil Alaska can produce," Milton Lipton, the legislature's chief consultant on oil and gas policy said.

Lipton's statements bode well for oil companies but not for oil consumers, particularly as price controls on domestic oil are gradually eliminated. He predicted the OPEC nations would raise crude oil prices to fourteen dollars per barrel by 1980, which will generate more domestic exploration and demand for oil.

Lipton said Arctic areas of Alaska and Canada would be of 'tremendous importance' in the nation's future energy picture."

—*The All-Alaska Weekly*

Chapter Fifty-one

On November 14, the key personnel of Denali were moved to temporary headquarters in the Operations building at the terminal at Jackson Point in Valdez Harbor. Mahlon Doheny, Deirdre, Larry Steele, and the rest from Fairbanks established semipermanent quarters on the base. Larry was still flying up and down the line checking tests of new welds, conferring with the communications chief about the operation of the microwave and satellite stations, checking and rechecking remote valve controls, and contingency plans in case, despite all these precautions, a leak or a spill should occur. The most complicated, and expensive, contingency equipment was located at the terminal at Valdez.

Each of the huge, cone-topped, five hundred and ten

thousand barrel storage tanks was surrounded by a dike which would contain one hundred and ten percent of the content of the tank in case a rupture in the tank wall occurred. Also, ten thousand feet of floating booms were available to surround any oil slicks from a ruptured tanker. Oil skimmer boats and barges were available to remove slicks or other oil that might escape from the containment booms in case of a rough sea. Hundreds of tons of straw and special absorbent polyurethane, both in liquid and solid forms, were available for soaking up spilled oil. There were even devices for repelling sea birds so they wouldn't be contaminated in case of a spill.

One large storage warehouse on the harbor contained pumps, hoses, vacuum trucks, fire trucks with high pressure pumps, water pumping systems that could be operated from shore, truck, or boat deck, bulldozers, a front-end loader, tugs and mooring launches, and high intensity lights that would permit recovery of oil in the darkness—all were on standby, along with personnel who had been specially trained in oil recovery techniques, some of them veterans of the massive Santa Barbara blow-out.

The contingency plan called for sea-going tugs to deliver necessary equipment from the Port Valdez base in case of a spill and a special fleet of planes on standby to airdrop major equipment from other sources at the spill site.

"Okay," Doheny said to Larry, as they poured over the plans again. "Explain to me what happens if there's some kind of leak in that big sea-going elephant."

"Right. Now, if we have a fairly calm sea—say no more than two-three foot waves—and that's the way it is most of the time—we put a big circular boom completely around the tanker, wherever it's leaking, and that's held in position by three or four boats—whatever we need. Heavy duty floating skimmers will be deployed to recover as much oil as is feasible. Okay so far?"

"Right," Doheny said. "And what happens if the seas are higher than that?"

"I'll get to that later," Larry said. "Meanwhile, if we can hold the leak inside the booms, we'll pump out the oil and transfer it to available storage equipment on barges or other tankers. And also we have those collapsible, floating, blimp-kind of tanks. If the weather isn't too rough, we'll have skimming barges there at the spill site fitted with sweeping booms and the sweeping operation can be conducted as long as necessary to remove the floating oil from the surface of the water."

"What about keeping it off the beaches?" Doheny asked. "You know how much hell they raised about that—not just in Santa Barbara but in Wood's Hole."

"Well, there probably wouldn't be as much heat about the beaches here." Larry pointed out, "since they're not essentially recreational beaches as they were in those other two places. Anyway, we can run a line of booms down along the beach, which would tend to keep much of the stuff in the center until we can skim it off. We've got planes on charter, and some that we own, deployed all over the damn place that we can use to find and track any floating slicks. If the oil stays on the surface of the water long enough to get tarry, and lumped up, then we can use rakes and shovels and scoops, and send in the skimming barges again to scoop up anything that's left. Of course, if it's cold, the oil may sink . . ."

"What about detergents?" Doheny asked.

"We've got them on hand, but there's been a lot of stink. Some people say detergents kill more life than the oil does. The way I understand it, if we ever have such a spill, we're going to have a hell of a big problem up here, because the oil just doesn't degrade in these cold waters the way it does down south."

"Well, the good Lord must have loved crap shooters," Doheny said, "because he made so many of them, and your Daddy's the biggest crap shooter of them all. You know what the insurance premium on that fucking big tanker is? Just for one year? Pretty near five million dollars."

"Well, at least he's got that bet covered, right?"

"If you ask me," Mahlon said, "he's rushing the whole thing and I think that these ULCC's — these ultra-big tankers—are a mistake."

"Well, they cut the cost of oil shipping in half," Larry pointed out. "And anyway, we didn't buy them, we just leased them, so if there's a change in the marketing situation, we can just dump them after a couple of years."

Deirdre came through the door of the huge pre-fab Operations Building, her face flushed and pink with the wind.

"Boy, there's a brisk blow out there," Deirdre said. "Must be twenty-five, thirty miles an hour, sometimes."

Doheny and Larry exchanged glances.

"I sure hope it dies down by the time we start loading that big oilberg," Larry said.

"Hell," Doheny said. "Sometimes it doesn't blow for a week at a time. It's this fog that bothers me."

"The fog isn't really a problem," Larry pointed out. "With all the electronic gear they've got they can fly blind without any trouble at all. These fishermen run in here and out again all the time in the fog and it doesn't bother them. Besides, it generally doesn't come down to water level. It just hangs there a hundred feet or so above the Bay."

Doheny turned to Deirdre. "What have you been up

to, girlie?" he said. "You got all these muckymucks stowed away and stuffed with propaganda?"

"Well," Deirdre said doubtfully, "I think we found quarters for most of the invited guests here at the Terminal. And I've been trying to arrange places in private homes and make dormitory arrangements in some of the churches, but it's really going to be pandemonium."

"When's Wilbur coming?"

"He'll be flying in to take part in the ceremonies on the day the Globtik Alamo leaves. He'll go out with the ship itself and go off with the pilot."

"Just coming down when all the work is done to get in on the gravy, huh?" Doheny said bitterly.

"Well," Deirdre said, "I think there's quite a bit that had to be handled in Washington and New York to make the thing go off right."

"Did you get invitations to all the Denali owners?" Doheny asked.

Deirdre looked at him scornfully. "Of course, Daddy, ages ago. But I don't think many of them are coming. They figure it's Wilbur's show and they'll get aboard when they have their own oil to ship."

"Yeah," Larry said. "Maybe they're trying to keep their hands clean in case anything goes wrong."

"Well," Deirdre said, "they won't get the blame if anything goes wrong, but then they won't get the glory. And in the end, I suppose, it really *was* Wilbur's project. He was the one that broke the agreement and went ahead and found oil on the Slope and forced the whole issue of the pipeline."

"Yeah," Larry said with grudging admiration, "I guess the old man shot the well that was heard around the world. You know," he said, "I've heard that the pipeline is the only man-made object that can be seen from the moon."

"The President coming?" Doheny asked.

"Of what?" Deirdre said.

"Of the U-nited States."

"Oh, him. He's sending a message. But the Secretary of the Interior, a crew from the Energy Commission, and the new Commissioner of the EPA will be here. We'll be geting terrific coverage of course. All this week there's going to be specials on all the networks—TV and radio — and a feature in the *Times* magazine, *People, Newsweek, Time*—I understand we have the cover on both *Time* and *Newsweek*. And I've arranged for an eighteen hour continuous showing of a selection of our films—'Alaska the Great Land," "The Alaskan Eskimo," "City of God," "The High Road to Alaska" —although, God knows, with all the boozing, whoring, and gambling going on in this town and the general fooforah, I don't know how many people are going to have time to sit through a batch of propaganda films. Anyway, I've arranged to loan prints out to most of the public broadcasting stations that want them and to the schools, and to some of the smaller, independent stations. They've been showing them all week. It can't do any harm."

"What are you going to do once this is all finished, Uncle Mahlon?" Larry asked.

"What are *you* going to do?" Doheny countered.

Larry scratched his head. "I don't know. Probably go back and work with Alamo out of Houston. Maybe take *your* job when they start building the gas pipeline. Unless you're planning to do that."

"No," Doheny said. "One eight hundred mile pipeline in a lifetime is enough for me."

"You retiring then?"

"Not exactly," Doheny said. And it seemed to Larry that the older man had trouble meeting his eyes.

"Then, *what?*" he persisted.

"Oh, I've got plans," Doheny said. "You'll find out in due time. Meanwhile let's get off our asses and see what we can do to get this show on the road. Okay, kids?"

"A trip to the Columbia glacier is often the most memorable experience on a trip to Alaska. . . . the seaward face of the Columbia glacier sheers upward from the greenish water in a crevassed and pinacled blue-white ice cliff, from one hundred to four hundred feet high, and with a front of nearly three miles wide. As it slowly 'flows' at a rate of less than three feet per day, massive bergs topple in slow motion into the sea, churning up leaping fountains of spray and foam.

"Many sea birds have their rookeries in the cliffs in this area. Harbor seals are often in view in great numbers in the water or on the floating ice near the glacier. Whales and porpoises are common sights on the trips to and from the glacier face."

—Milepost
All-the-North Travel Guide

Chapter Fifty-two

When O-Day finally arrived, the tiny town of Valdez was booming and bursting at the seams. Sue-Anne Dalton, mixing up a Long Slow Screw, said to a blond hooker with artificial fingernails two inches long, "This here ain't no boom. It's a boom-erang. Look at all these dudes."

The Club Valdez was, as it had been for the entire previous week, packed to the walls as early as nine a.m. of the big day. The Globtik Alamo, according to the schedule of activities listed in a program by Denali, was supposed to cast off from the loading dock at two-thirty that afternoon, accompanied by tooting tugs shooting sprays from firehoses, and a massive show by an Air Force acrobatic team from Eielson Air Force Base. A Coast Guard Band would be on the dock serenading the ship's departure and hundreds of cases of California champagne had been ordered for invited guests who would see the ship off from a giant, specially constructed glass-enclosed viewing stand on the site of the old Jackson Point salmon cannery.

In addition, each of the Denali owner-clients had set up hospitality huts scattered around the terminal base and also in the town itself. Press planes and helicopters would be made available for television cameramen to overfly the departure of the giant ship through the Valdez Narrows and into Prince William Sound. Red, white, and blue bunting dripped from every building, public and private, and rows of colored lights strung across the pot-holed, muddy, and pitted streets of Valdez glowed through the seventeen hour night.

The scene in Valdez was a combination of the Fourth of July, New Years Eve, the State Fair, and a political convention. Drunken pipeliners, Eskimos, Indians, politicians, tourists, and hippies were picked like berries from the sidewalk by the over-taxed six man police force, sobered up, and sent back into the streets to get drunk again (fifty local Valdez men had been sworn in as special constables for the occasion).

Pick-up campers, Winnebagos, and camping trailers rocked and vibrated from the cavorting of impromptu launch parties assembled inside. Happy drunks wandered through ankle-deep snow and mud (it was still only about a degree or so above freezing, so cold was not a problem in Valdez), barging in through the open doors of trailers or motel rooms as eager but uninvited guests at any party that would have them.

Hookers were operating not only in the bigger campers but in the back of cars, station wagons, Volkswagen vans, and even out in the bushes of the Glacierside Camp Site.

On the night before the launching, the Governor had ordered an all-night fireworks display, which would have kept those few people who had planned to sleep awake in any event. An ex-fisherman-turned-Denali-bullcook viewed the scene sourly.

"I suppose this was what it was like in Skagway during the big gold rush."

"Only bigger and better," a horse-faced tourist in a white cowboy hat said. He was wearing a four inch celluloid button that said "Oil shall make you free" and another that read "We drove the Alaska Marine Hiway."

"I been to the moon launching in Canaveral, the opening of the Verrazano Narrows Bridge, and the Indianapolis 500 and I'm telling you, boy, this is the biggest and best yet."

Sue-Anne looked at him sourly and served him another "Black Gold," which was going for four dollars a shot (Guiness and cheap champagne, half and half—invented for the occasion.)

"Yeah," she said. "But you don't have to clean up when it's over." She wore a button that said, defiantly, "Alaska for Alaskans."

"What are you complaining about?" the tourist said. He was from Florida, it turned out, and had driven all the way from Ocala in three weeks. "You folks are going to get rich out of this."

"That's what they tell us," Sue-Anne said, moving down the bar to attend to another customer.

"People rant and wave their arms about the billions needed to get this thing going. But it's nothing if the oil is there. We used to say, 100,000 barrels a day hides all the mistakes. If you can get 1,000,000 barrels a day in Alaska, nothing you could do would hurt this thing."

—Robert O. Anderson
Chairman of the Board
Atlanta Richfield Oil Company

Chapter Fifty-three

SHAMAN—Prudhoe Bay—11/18/77; 12:30 p.m.

John Takolik and Simon Orloff met for jelly doughnuts in the mess hall of Alamo operations base for one last check before taking off on their assigned tasks.

"You got everything?" Takolik asked the young Aleut.

"In my parka," Simon said. "Plastic detonators, wire."

"Okay and what do you do?"

"I turn on the power control, drop the gate on the block valve and then blow up the controls. Right?"

"Right."

Simon's eyes glittered with delight. Takolik scowled at him.

"Remember, Simon, this isn't just a game — some damned high school stunt. This is the biggest thing *you* ever did."

"Right," Simon said, straightening his wide smile. "What about you?" he asked the northern Eskimo.

"I stowed a bunch of plastic in the bottom of the emergency first aid kit yesterday. I just told the guy on duty it was part of my job on security to check the kits."

"What if somebody gets hurt and has to use them?"

"No sweat. It's all in flat sheets, packed on the bottom. Nobody would notice it anyway. I got the detonators in my pocket, plus a Smith and Wesson .38."

"I thought no guns were allowed on the base."

Takolik looked at him scornfully. *"Officially,* no guns. But, hell, half the guards have their own—and half the pipeliners, too, if you ask me."

"I haven't got a piece," Simon complained. "What if there's a guard on the valve?"

Takolik looked at him impatiently. "There're no guards on the valve. What the fuck would they have a guard on the valve for? They ain't afraid anybody's going to steal that."

Takolik stuffed the last of his jelly doughnut into his round cheeks, wiped the granules of sugar off with a napkin, took a last swallow of coffee, and shook Simon Orloff's hand.

"Good luck, brother," he said.

Simon held Takolik's hand in both of his, looked into his eyes and said, "Remember Angoon."

It was a funny thing to say, Takolik thought as he slipped into his parka, checking the pockets to make sure the detonators were there. Angoon was an atrocity inflicted by the Russians on the Tlingit. Simon was an Aleut. Maybe what he meant to say was that all the Native Peoples were brothers now against the whites.

Simon checked the small Denali pick-up out of the motor pool, telling the dispatcher he had left some equipment out on the line. The big block valve that was Simon Orloff's target was located about twelve miles out of camp via the haul road on the Sag River. Simon drove out past the Royal American Camp, the Crazyhorse Camp, and the Deadhorse Airfield. The haul road here diverged widely from the pipeline, which was elevated most of the way to Franklin Bluffs on vertical support members.

By now the work force at Prudhoe had been reduced to a basic maintenance crew of only seven hundred and fifty people. There was only last minute touch up work being done on the line; painting, repairs, repairing insulation, and minor mechanical adjustments. Security was employed mainly at the entrance to the camp buildings. Occasionally a guard was left when equipment sat in the field, but now it was lunch hour. Almost the entire force was in the mess hall. In any event the only security on the pipeline itself would be an occasion pass by a Denali chopper. If one should fly overhead it would be doubtful if they would find anything wrong with a Denali truck being parked near the block valve and a man in a Denali hard hat working on the valve. By the time the chopper spotted the damage, it would be too late.

The access road to the block valve was clear and unobstructed. By one p.m. Simon Orloff had climbed the twelve foot support member and was packing explosives around the stem of the huge block valve. This one could be closed by a remote control gas driven engine, and also a huge, gasoline-powered wheel. At exactly one-fifteen, Simon was to close the wheel of the block valve, shutting off the flow of the oil, so that the remaining oil in the pipeline, without the flow pressure, would slow down in the cold air, cool, and eventually solidify.

After he had packed the plastic around the stem of the block valve and planted the detonators, Simon checked his watch. At exactly one-fifteen he pushed the gate control button to set the gasoline engine in motion and close the gate of the Sag River block valve.

The natural gas pipeline, which was designed to parallel the oil pipeline for the first hundred and twenty miles or so and supply the power for the pumping stations north of the Brooks Range, ran alongside Pump Station One's interior oil lines, which went to the various wells in the field, and passed through a metering building where computers could calculate the amount of oil being passed through for any given company. The field fuel-gas building, from which all the gas pipelines ran, was located several hundred feet behind Alamo's discovery well, in the northern part of the camp, west of Prudhoe Bay.

Takolik checked out one of the huge balloon-tired Rolagon units. He filled its fifty gallon gas tank and loaded on six five gallon spare jerry cans of gasoline. Outside he had the Ski-Doo snowmobile he used in patrolling the camp perimeter. To this, Takolik attached a trailer-sled, which he had previously loaded with dehydrated foods, pemican, his Springfield Rifle (which he had smuggled into the camp weeks earlier), ammunition, an Arctic shelter tent, and heavy-duty Erwin Bauer down sleeping bag—all the equipment needed, in fact, for a lengthy, self-sufficient, cross-Arctic trek, even in that cold month of November.

Takolik leaned skids against the back of the huge Rolagon and drove the Ski-Doo onto its deck. He had started the Rolagon earlier that morning—just after breakfast—to make sure it was warmed and ready to go. He explained to the motor pool clerk that it was needed for a check of reported trespassers on the outer perimeter of the camp and produced a forged NANA buck slip as authorization.

All this was not too difficult, as the camp bureaucracy was so complicated and the changes of personnel so frequent that nobody knew—or cared much—who was doing what, with which, and to whom.

At one p.m. Takolik was at the field fuel-gas station. Usually there was at least a maintenance mechanic on duty in the gas building, but with the camp personnel now cut to a basic minimum, it was not considered necessary to have a guard on duty during the lunch hour. Takolik was relieved. Many of the personnel on maintenance duty now were Native friends from Barrow or Point Hope. Takolik would not have liked to pull a gun on one of his own.

The building had been locked, but the lock snapped easily under pressure from Takolik's three foot bolt cutters. Inside, the building was a puzzling mass of intertwined pipes, meters, and valves, but it was not hard for Takolik to pick out the main intake pipe leading from the gas supply at Alamo Discovery Well Number One. Any explosion, he reasoned, that would rupture the pipe would cause enough damage to halt the pumps for at least a couple of days and probably more, if the gas fire spread.

Carefully, Takolik climbed the small metal ladder to the main intake valve and packed plastic explosives around the end leading from the gas well. Attaching his detonator, he set the timer for one-fifteen—it was now one-oh-five—climbed down, and left the central compressor plant. Once the pipe was ruptured, the gas would come roaring out of the well at anywhere from six hundred to twelve hundred pounds per square inch of pressure. What would happen to the rest of the buildings and the installations nearby once that gas was ignited, God only knew. Takolik was anxious to put as much space as possible between himself and the compressor building before the blow-up.

But before Takolik could reach the Rolagon, he was intercepted by Kubek, the gas plant engineer, a big, roly-poly Polack who had formerly worked for the Fairbanks Power Company. He knew Takolik from the bars on Two Street as well as from the camps, and he was not noted for his tolerance of Natives.

"Hey, blubber snapper. Where you going? What were you doing in my shack?" he shouted, as Takolik hastened to board the Rolagon.

Kubek was sucking on a toothpick, still savoring the shreds of Salisbury steak left between his yellowing teeth.

Takolik didn't waste time drawing his pistol. Almost without thinking, he leaped up with both feet, Eskimo style, and landed with both heels against Kubek's puffy middle. Takolik's snow bunny mukluks sank almost a foot into the chubby engineer's midsection and the undigested remains of Kubek's recent lunch spewed out onto the gravel berm.

The surprised man rolled onto all fours and kneeled heaving and drooling into the snow. Without looking back, Takolik ran to the Rolagon, its engine still idling, climbed aboard and headed due west—toward the pack ice of Prudhoe Bay and away from all operations of Origin Station Number One.

Pump Station Three—11/18/77; 12:45 p.m.

At a quarter to one, Margie and Sydne Harris, a short-haired girl from Puyallup, Washington who had been Margie's roommate for the last six months, left the mess hall.

Margie had not explained the entire mission to Sydne, simply that she was going to pull a stunt that would fuck up the oil company. That was all Sydne had to hear. Her job would be finished in a few weeks anyway, and she would be dragging up to the States. The worst that could happen, as Sydne saw it, was that fucking up the pump station might give her further work, if they had to send a repair crew in. She worked for culinary services in the main mess hall of Pump Station Three.

Margie and Sydne had spent several weeks buttering up the assistant chief electrician, who was mainly on duty in the generator shack, and Margie had had a good chance to study the three five-hundred-kilowatt Siemens generators. She wasn't exactly sure where their vulnerable point was, and had been unable to get the information from Eddie Dugan, the engineer—even after a chilly and distasteful sexual encounter on the tool bench in the rear of the generator shed. It wasn't so much that he didn't want to tell her as that Marge didn't understand the technical jargon and couldn't ask her questions specifically. In any event, Marge decided to place her charges at the shafts on which the three generators turned. She was reasonably sure that this would stop the generators from moving and would blast loose enough wires to incapacitate the huge electrical units.

At a quarter to one, leaving Sydne outside to intercept Dugan should he come back early, or at least give a warning signal, Marge was climbing about among the huge cast iron frames of the 500-KW Siemens Generators. It took her almost twenty minutes to pack the unwieldly explosives around the shafts and set the three separate timing detonators she had picked up at the Swap Shop on her last R & R in Fairbanks.

At precisely five minutes after one Marge managed to complete the job and get out of the shack.

"Come on, Sydne," she said. "We'd better get out of here before the thing goes off!"

"What thing? What's happening, anyway?"

"You'll find out," Marge said grimly, hurrying the girl along the path.

About fifty yards away from the generator shack,

toward the recreation hall, the two girls ran into Dugan, a good-looking New York Irishman with a chronic case of acne.

"Eddie," Marge said. "Back so soon?"

"What do you mean, 'Back so soon,'" Eddie said. "I'm ten minutes late!"

Looking back at the building, Marge had a twinge of conscience. "Listen, Eddie. Nobody's going to know when you get back to work, right?"

"I suppose," Eddie said slowly. "What have you got in mind?"

"Come on, let's go back to our room for a while and fool around."

Eddie looked at his watch doubtfully, shrugged, and then, grinning widely, he put his arms around both girls.

"Sure, what the hell! You only live once."

Pump Station Ten—11/18/77; 1:04 p.m.

In the first place, Eli Hurwood was late getting out to the generator plant. He had been caught in a conversation in the mess hall and had not been able to think of a way to get out of it. The explosive and detonator had been packed in his guitar case, the only place Hurwood could think of where they would not be conspicuous. Hurwood carried the guitar case wherever he went, and entertained his fellow pipeliners with varying degrees of success.

Pump Station Ten was located on the Delta River at the foot of the Castner Glacier, and almost astride the Denali fault. Hurwood had been pleased to be assigned there, since that camp, along with Galbraith and Isabel Pass, was rated one of the most beautiful along the pipeline. It was a few minutes after one when Hurwood reached the generator house. He would barely have time to get the plastic installed and wired before the agreed-on hour. But, in a big deal like this, what was ten or fifteen minutes more or less?

Hurwood had checked the personnel situation at the generator shack and knew that Buck Connor, the assistant electrician, always shot at least one game of pool after lunch before returning to duty. As work on the pump station had been completed, the monitoring of off-and-on duty hours had become more and more slack. And besides, Connor was shop steward for the International Brotherhood of Electric Workers.

During his two month stay at Pump Station Number Ten, Hurwood had made few friends, certainly none he could trust, so he had been unable to arrange for a look-out for the job. He just had to depend on Connor's regular irregularity.

Inside the pump station he felt in his side pocket for the three detonators and nervously began to unsnap the hasps on his tooled leather guitar case. He had just gotten the case opened when there was a rattling at the metal door of the shack, and Connor walked in, wiping his mouth with the back of his hand and belching.

"Hey, Jew-boy," he said. "What you doing in here? Fixing to serenade the generators?"

"Errr, no," Hurwood said. "I was just fixing to do some practicing."

Connor looked around him in mock awe. "Funny place to practice. This ain't no concert hall."

Now that Connor was closer, Hurwood could see his blood-shot eyes and knew that it hadn't been Kool-ade that Connor had been drinking at lunch. Even when working seven twelves, Connor never forgot when it was Friday. Friday was the day to get drunk back home, and Connor made no exception just because he was working a seven day week. Besides, you didn't have to be sober just to sit on your lard ass and watch a bunch of dials all day.

"I thought you were shooting pool."

"One rule," Connor mumbled. "Never shoot pool when you're drunk—never for money, anyway." His reticulated eyeballs fell on the guitar case.

"Hey Jew-boy, play us a song. Play that 'I'm Dreaming of a Fat Paycheck.' That's a sumbitch!"

Wildly, Hurwood looked around for a weapon. If he could find a pipe wrench or a hammer or something, maybe he could stretch Connor out and get on with the job. But the electrician was a big fucker, and besides, he was wearing his hard-hat. How was Hurwood going to knock him out when the big man had a hard-hat on? By the time he could do any damage, the man would be all over him, probably beating his brains out.

"Play the fucking song."

"Okay, okay . . ." Nervously, Hurwood fumbled at the catch of the guitar case, trying to shield the rest of the contents of the case from Connor's bleary eyes.

"Hey, what you get in there?" Connor asked. His eyes took on a sly look. "You boosting stuff too? Naughty, naughty."

"Just some stuff . . . I was working on," Hurwood mumbled, closing the case as he quickly removed the guitar.

"My goodness," Connor said. "I thought you were a regular Boy Scout, but I see maybe you got the makings of being one of the boys. Now play the Goddamn song." Connor leaned back spraddle-legged in the plastic chair he had appropriated from the mess hall and Hurwood mounted the high steel stool beside the tool bench and began playing nervously, without

533

stopping to tune his instrument, to the melody of "I'm Dreaming of a White Christmas."

> "I'm dreaming of a fat paycheck,
>   Just like the ones the Teamsters get;
>   Cash for pure indulgence,
>   and sly investments,
>   For my mother at the Home . . .
>
> I'm yearning for those high wages,
>   Just like the ones the welders get;
>   Each deposit receipt
>   Will look so neat
>   to see those figures in a row . . ."

Valdez—11/18/77

Van Taylor was not such a big drinker, certainly not an alcoholic, but the occasion itself was intoxicating. Rules at the Terminal Station in Valdez seemed to have evaporated in the excitement of the occasion. Impromptu parties were being held in the rooms of many of the invited guests and some of the workmen. Bottles of wine and vodka were produced openly in the mess hall and the Wakenhut guards pretended they saw nothing. Van took a twelve ounce Screwdriver in a styrofoam cup from the mess hall at breakfast time. He had a big job to do that afternoon and he felt that a couple of shots would relax him.

Every once in a while he laughed as he looked around at the bunting and Japanese lanterns adorning the grim facades of the terminal building.

Boy, he said to himself as he picked his way to his station at the duty shack at the end of the Terminal Approach road, *we're going to give these guys something to celebrate before the day's over.*

Taylor's duty partner was Gilbert Kinegak. Kinegak was a half-Eskimo from Kotzebue. His father had been a Catholic priest who converted to Orthodox when Gilbert was conceived because Orthodox were allowed to marry and have children. Nobody in Kotzebue commented about Gilbert's seemingly short gestation period.

"How's she going, Van?" Gilbert said cheerily as Taylor entered the shack and put down his orange-colored drink. "Having a little extra breakfast?"

"It's the day for it," Van said, echoing his cheerful demeanor.

Kinegak crooked a finger at the Valdez fisherman, and pulled the Valdez phonebook from its pocket on the side of the check-in desk and pointed inside. "A pint of ninety proof, Everclear alcohol. It's equal to a quart of vodka, more compact, easier to hide." Underneath the desk was a cardboard six-pack of Diet Pepsi. Gilbert patted his bulging beltline. "Getting too fat on this camp food. But alcohol has no calories. If you don't drink any sugar with it."

He took his cardboard cup from the desk and offered a toast to Taylor. "Here's to O Day."

Taylor picked up his styrofoam cup and they managed a clumsy toast without cracking either of the containers.

"To O Day," Van said, taking a great draught of the vodka and orange juice mix.

"Goin' to any parties afterwards?" Gilbert Kinegak asked him.

"Oh, maybe a few," Van said evasively. "How about you?"

"I'm gonna dance with my baby tonight," Kinegak sang to the old tune. "Hey, what did you do in civilian life—I mean, before the job."

535

They had met only a few times and had never shared shack duty together.

"Fisherman. Salmon. Right here in Valdez."

"Oh, yeah," Kinegak said. "Salmon. I had plenty to do with those sonsabitches." He refilled his cup from the flat bottle of clear liquid, pouring in about a quarter cup of alcohol and filling the rest with Pepsi. "Got to watch this stuff, you know. It's a hundred *percent* alcohol, not a hundred *proof*."

"Right," Van said.

"Top you up?" He offered the bottle.

"Well, maybe just this much," Van said, holding up a pair of closely measured fingers.

They drank another toast.

"To the fucking salmon," Gilbert Kinegak said.

Van wondered how many Gil had had already. Or was it true that Eskimos got drunk faster? It certainly seemed to be.

"I tell you. You know what I did with salmon?" Gilbert Kinegak said. "I used to work in the slime house—you know what that is? It's where we take all the guts out of the salmon, up in Kotzebue. Used to work for the coop, loading Japanese ships with salmon when I was a kid. Put in fifty hours a week, right up until I got this job, in 1972. I'll tell ya, after an hour of cleaning and cutting salmon, everything's covered with blood. The floor, the tables, the workers—every Goddamn thing."

"It was different for me," Van said, sipping at the screwdriver. I just worked out of my boat, had other people handle the cleaning. We worked shares."

"I make it sound terrible," Gilbert Kinegak said, "but it wasn't so bad. I got three-fifty an hour, built up my muscles."

"Yeah, it'll do that," Van said, pouring himself

another snort from Kinegak's bottle and topping it off with some of the diet cola.

"Yeah, I remember after a long bloody night, I'd walk home, feel that morning breeze, nice and cool, watch the seagulls, looking and fighting for food—all those fish guts out there. The town empty and quiet. A few dogs barking. Maybe a couple of birds chirping somewhere. Go home to a nice hot sponge bath, a good bed. I didn't mind it."

Time went quickly for Van when he could talk about salmon and fishing and the minutes were lubricated by the smooth tasting Pepsi-Everclear mixture. There were so many people going in and out of the gates that Van had neither the time nor the inclination to check their badges thoroughly. Most of them were visitors with special guest badges anyway. There would be no way to check those out properly, although he had a list of invited guests on his desk.

Pipeline workers were bringing their girlfriends in from town for a birdseye view of the send-off of the Globtik Alamo, and invited guests were bringing in girls and other friends they'd met in town. Shit, nobody'd expect a man to check on all that.

By eleven-thirty Taylor's mind was as cloudy as the fog hanging over Valdez Bay. "It seemed like there was something important I had to do this afternoon," he said.

"Oh, yeah? What was that?"

"Oh, well. It's just something that I have to attend to. Remind me if you get a chance, will you? About one o'clock."

"Sure, sure," Gilbert Kinegak said. "I'll try to remember. It's a hell of a day, hey?" he said. "A day to remember."

"That's right," Taylor said. "A day to remember."

Sonia, Red Holman, and Ernie Mason breezed by the check-in desk without anybody even glancing at their badges. Sonia hung back a few steps from Holman, who had promised to show them the complexities of the control shack prior to the opening day ceremonies. Ernie was carrying an Army surplus musette bag over his shoulder. It had a few cameras on top, and the rest of the gear needed for the afternoon's work underneath.

"Did you notice Van Taylor?" Sonia said to him out of the corner of her mouth. "He didn't even give us a look."

"I guess he didn't want to let on he knew us," Ernie said reasonably enough.

"Yeah, I suppose so," Sonia said, "but he sure looked funny."

Holman looked back at the lagging pair. "Hey, Sonia, Ernie, come on if you're going to look. That place is going to fill up with visitors pretty soon, when we get near the ceremony time. You're just going to have time for a fast look. I'm not supposed to let anybody in there. Just take a look around, grab your shots, and then go. I don't know why you want to see it anyway. It's just a dumb bunch of lights and buzzers. I couldn't get you in at all except Andy Schultheiss, the control, is a friend of mine. So just take a look. Right?"

"Right," Sonia said.

She was pleased to see that Schultheiss was alone in the control shack, which was a large building filled with a complicated set of flashing lights, meters, and digital readouts. Shultheiss was reading some charts and sipping coffee when the three came in.

"Oh, hello, Red."

"These are the friends I asked you about," Red

said. "They just want to take a fast look around, right?"

Schultheiss looked doubtful. "Okay, but make it fast, right? All the big bosses are around now, and they don't like anybody in here. You know, you can run the whole Goddamn pipeline clear up to Prudhoe from right in this room," he said, proudly sweeping his arm around. "Remote controls up and down the line, run the loading dock, everything goes through here."

Sonia threw a fast, appraising look around the room. She had had no previous information as to the inner layout, and could only guess as to which were the important lines, but, with such a complicated system, she was pretty sure that a good sized blast would throw a serious monkey wrench into the operation, especially with the generators going out at the same time.

Cautiously, she reached into the deep pocket of her blue down parka and clutched the twenty-two caliber Beretta she had bought at the souvenir shop of the Sheffield Hotel two weeks earlier. All that was needed to buy the pistol was proof of residence and that she had forged long ago. No license or registration were required.

"Okay," said Holman, "take a few pictures if you like and then let's get out of here before I get in trouble."

Nervously, Ernie began to fumble at the straps of the musette bag. Sonia backed into a corner of the room, her hands now clammy with nervous sweat as she grasped the butt of the pistol in her pocket, and pulled it out.

"All right, Red, you—what's your name? Get your hands up! This is serious. I mean it!"

Holman looked astonished. "Come on, quit kidding. What is this?"

"I'm not kidding, Red. This is a real gun with real bullets. And if you want to find out, just make a move."

The red-haired guard stared at her for a moment and then his face suffused with rage. "Why you bitch! What the hell is this all about?"

"Get to work, Ernie," she said, ignoring the question.

"Sonia," the little man said nervously, "should we really do this? I can't . . . I don't want to go through with it."

"Get going you little fuck," she said. I'd just as soon shoot you as look at you, you fucking creep!" Menacingly she waved the gun between Ernie and the other two men.

With nervous fingers, Ernie Mason finished opening the musette bag and took out the three fist-shaped lumps of plastic, the last of the cache that they had stolen from Fort Wainwright.

"We're going to blow this shack to pieces. Where's the best place to put this stuff?" she said to Schultheiss.

He shrugged, his lips frozen in horror.

"Oh, fuck it," she said. "Put it anywhere. Put it behind that big board there, put it all behind that panel there."

Woodenly, Ernie Mason did as he was told.

"Okay, now put in the detonator and the timer."

Mason went back into the bag, took out the small detonator, and the clock-like timer.

Is it wound?"

"Yeah, it's wound."

"Okay. Hook it up and let's get going." She waved her pistol at the two men who were still standing with their hands in the air. "You guys too. Don't worry. I'm not going to leave you in here."

Without waiting for further orders, the little poet slithered out the door like an Arctic weasel.

"Okay, now you two guys."

Sonia stood by the door, herding the two men out. Red Holman, his hands still in the air, measured the distance between them, as he approached the door. When he was within five feet of her he suddenly lashed downward with his hand, catching Sonia's gun-arm at the wrist, and sending the little Beretta clattering to the floor. Sonia looked at him in shocked pain for a moment as the red-headed guard dived for the pistol, and then, seeing that she had no chance to recover her piece, she bolted for the door before Schultheiss could make a move to grab her.

Holman snatched up the pistol and ran through the door in pursuit. He dropped to one knee as the parka-clad figure of the girl ran down the gravel path.

"Stop, or I'll shoot!" he yelled and simultaneously pulled the trigger. There was a dull click. The stupid girl had forgotten to put a shell in the chamber. Quickly, Holman slid the receiver back, rammed a shell into the chamber and pulled the trigger again. Sonia by now was almost fifty yards away. The bullet apparently caught her somewhere in the lower back. She stumbled a few steps further, then went sprawling into the trampled snow of the path. Almost immediately a scarlet stain started spreading from the point of impact.

"... a temperature rise [in the Arctic] of only a few degrees would melt all the polar ice within a decade or less, with certainly distressing and perhaps disastrous consequences for modern man. One way to raise the temperature is to darken the surface of the ice and so capture the energy that is now reflected back to the sky. The most effective darkener would be a substance that would float on water and consequently would spread quickly and widely."

—John Lear
"Northwest Passage to What?"
Saturday Review,
June 25, 1969

Chapter Fifty-four

The blast at Valdez Control Center raised all sorts of hell. In the first place, an automatic alarm system alerted the central fire station, and within three minutes the two diesel powered, four-wheel drive pumper trucks arrived with klaxons screaming from their stations near the loading dock, equipped with seven hundred and fifty gallon foam supply systems. The blast had started an electrical fire in one of the control panels and the Denali fire fighters were forced to combat the noxious fumes emerging from the control building with self-contained breathing apparatus and masks.

Meanwhile, the breakdown at Pump Station One and Three, caused by Takolik's sabotage of the natural gas line and Marge's destruction of the generator station, as well as the drop in pressure occasioned by the sealing off of the Sag River Block valve, resulted in an automatic shutdown of the entire pipeline.

Despite the blast, most of the automatic equipment in the Control Shack was operating—lights were flashing, and alarms sounding all over the board. Part of the contingency plan in the construction of the control panel had been to create a complete parallel "redundant" system, which could take over when any other part of the system was incapacitated. The system was also rigged that any drop in pressure on the line would result in an automatic shut-down.

Within a few minutes, a panic call was in to the operations center where Larry was conferring with Deirdre Doheny on last minute plans for O-Day. The Globtik Alamo, which had been loading all week, was now almost full, riding low in the water at the loading dock, and waiting only for the ceremonial last drops before casting off. Larry picked up the urgently ringing phone, listened for a few minutes to the agitated voice of the Terminal Fire Chief and hung up.

"There's been a blast at the Control Center," Larry said to Deirdre. "Where's your father?"

"I haven't seen him in an hour or so."

"Well, find him. We've got big trouble!"

Larry raced outside and jumped into the yellow Denali Nova that he used around the Terminal, while Deirdre began phoning around the camp trying to locate her father. At the control center, the fire was already extinguished when Larry arrived. The emergency team had acted so quickly that the flames had hardly had a chance to start, but the multi-million dollar room was a shambles, with slippery foam all over the walls and floor, the cathode ray tube display boards, and the computer panels. Schultheiss was standing behind Fire Chief Orlando wringing his hands.

"It all happened so fast, there was no way I could stop it."

"What happened?" Larry demanded.

"Some girl and a kid came in with . . . one of the

guards . . . a fellow named Red Holman. She pulled a gun on him and me and the two of them blew up my panel—plastic explosives, I think." This in Schultheiss's mind seemed to make it worse.

"What happened to them?"

"I don't know what happened to the kid—he ran away somewhere—but Holman shot the girl. She's over in the medical ward now. He's got her under arrest, and I guess he'll question her when she comes to. She lost quite a bit of blood."

"Who is she?"

Schultheiss shrugged, hopelessly. "I never saw her before. Maybe she's one of the bargirls from town. I think I might have seen her in the Club Valdez one time. Anyway, I'm certain she didn't work here. But she had an I.D. badge. Might have been one of the guests."

"Okay. I guess she's not going anywhere for the time being," Larry said impatiently. "What's the damage?"

"Well," Schultheiss licked his lips nervously, "Panel Number One is down completely. There's been quite a bit of damage to Panel Number Two. We'll be automated on some of those circuits, but on others we'll have to go to manual. The communications panel is intact."

Another yellow Nova raced up to the parking lot beside the control room and skidded to a stop. Deirdre raced out, breathless.

"Larry, there's more trouble! It looks as though there's been some kind of sabotage conspiracy. Just after you left we got two phone calls from Pump Stations One and Three. One of the Eskimo guards set off a bomb or something in the gas compression station at Pump Station One. And there's been some kind

544

of an accident at the block valve on the Sag River. It's closed and the controls seem to be out of order. They sent a team out to inspect it now. The whole pipeline's shut down! That's not all—two women have completely wrecked the generators at Pump Station Three—with explosives too. They caught one of them, but she says she doesn't know anything about it. And she won't tell who her friend is."

"Holy shit!" Larry said. "Have you been able to reach your old man?"

Deirdre shook her head. "I made a few calls, but there's no sign of him so far. I'll try to find him. Can you handle things here?"

"Not much choice, is there?" Larry said. He could feel an exhilerating charge of adrenalin running through his veins now. The very magnitude of the disaster seemed to excite him. He turned to Schultheiss.

"You say the communications network it still intact —microwave and all?"

"That's right."

"Okay. Have them pump some clean air into this place—get rid of the fumes—and then get in there and see what damage there is. Call in your chief and get in any control maintenance men you can find who aren't drunk yet."

"What about the boat?" Deirdre asked.

"*Ship,*" Larry corrected her automatically. "Float it out as soon as possible. I don't see any reason why it shouldn't go. In fact, we don't know what's going on here. There might be a sabotage attempt on that too. I think we should get it out of here as soon as we can."

"Well, it's scheduled to go in about an hour."

"Let's get it out on time. And, Deirdre, try not to

545

release any news on this until you have to. If you get any questions, stall."

"I don't know if I can do that, Larry. The news is bound to get out and there'll be all sorts of rumors."

"What's doing with the press and the guests?"

"The TV and radio people want to come up an hour early and get set up."

"Hold them at the gate," Larry said. "Don't let anybody in until we clear away some of this smoke and emergency equipment. You think your staff can handle that?"

"They can," Deirdre said. "I'll get right on it."

"Okay, and let's at least see if we can locate your old man. He's the one to put out any statements. If necessary, we'll work up something together to tell the press. In the meanwhile, I'm going back to the operations shack to see what we can get in order."

The offices in the operations shack were almost empty. Larry managed to corral two or three of the secretaries and got them busy on various phones. Fortunately, phone and radio connections within the Denali complex were extremely efficient in comparison to the Alaskan public telephone system.

"Sally," he said, "I want you to call the RCM of each operating pumping station and tell them to drain down the oil into stand-by storage tanks. Sheryl," he said to another rosy-faced secretary, a Valdez native, "you get me Pump Station One and find out if they've got the fire under control—and get me the RCM.

"Gloria, you've got the most experience. I'm going to give you a responsible job. I want you to get a full report on the damage to the generators at Pump Station Three. Find out if any of them can be made operable and get back to me right away—or as soon as you know."

The telephone on the desk rang. It was Willens, the RCM at Pump Station One. Larry listened as Willens gave him a condensed rundown.

"The gas fire is still burning out of control, but we've succeeded in turning off the main valve at the well and expect the flames to die down soon of their own accord. The fire team has kept the compressor building from going up in flames by dousing it with water and foam. But it's impossible yet to estimate the amount of damage here."

"Okay," Larry said. "The generators can operate on liquid fuel as well as gas, right? Switch them over to liquid fuel. Use your motor fuel reserves and if you run out, run on pure crude. I think it will handle it. At least we can try it. Meanwhile, try to get some Hercs or tanker trucks down to the other stations and get all the fuel they can spare, especially from the camps with topping plants—or get it from Fairbanks. I don't care how you do it. Can you handle that?"

"Right," Willens said.

"Now, what's the condition of that block valve?"

"It's closed down and the controls have been blasted away and there's a pretty bad leak running down into the Sag River."

"Shit!" Larry said. "That's liable to cause us more trouble than anything. If somebody hears about that— how much do you think got out?"

"Well, it's ten miles to the next check valve above the block valve. About half way to Franklin Bluffs."

Larry whistled. "That's a hundred and ten thousand barrels. How fast is it flowing?"

"I haven't been out there yet," Willens said, "but they say that whatever that guy used to blow that valve blew a big hole where the pipe joins the casing."

547

"Okay. Try to get some packing or absorbent material into it. How near is it to the water?"

"It's right near the edge."

"Get some dozers in and put a dike around it—as big as you can, as fast as you can. And get a tarp on the dike to keep it from seeping through. That ought to slow it up a bit anyway. What's the temperature up there?"

"Twenty below."

Larry thought for a minute. "I'll tell you what—get some hoses and put up some dike enclosures as far from the river as you can put them. And then see if you can pump whatever's leaking out into the dikes, it'll freeze solid there and we can salvage it later. Now, send somebody up the line and cut a couple of small holes, just big enough for the hose, and start pumping it out every mile before it solidifies. Dump it on the ground if you have to but try to dike it. Think you can handle that?"

Willens sounded doubtful. "I'll try."

"Well you'd better, or that stuff's going to gum up solid in twenty-four hours and we'll have to lay ten miles of new pipe. Can you cut a hole in below the check valve and send a go-pig down to keep the line clean?"

"Will do," Willens said.

"I'll be back in touch. Let me know when you get the fire under control."

"Right," Willens said.

Larry hung up, his forehead wrinkled in concentration. The leak at the block valve was bad. It meant tens of thousands of barrels—at least—going down to the Arctic Ocean. The papers would raise hell when they got hold of that one. And yet, could they blame Denali? For sabotage? It was one of the last things anybody would have suspected. There had been no sign of serious organized opposition since the ecological groups had thrown up their hands in despair several years earlier.

Gloria signalled him as soon as he hung up the phone on Willens. "I've got Vogel at Pump Station Three."

Larry picked up the phone. "What's up?"

"Two of the generators are completely wrecked. Generator Number Three can probably be fixed but it will take a couple of days."

"Is that all the damage?"

"Well, the generator buildings kind of fucked up but we can operate on one generator if we have to. There aren't many people left in the camp and we can close down a number of the barracks, move everybody together, and cut down on our camp usage. Get by with the one generator."

"I'll tell you what," Larry said. "Pump Station Four is not on stream yet?"

"Right."

"Call the RCM there and tell him to start dismantling one of his generators and get a Herc to fly it in. Use that to replace one of your dead generators and get busy fixing the one that's repairable. You can cannibalize one of the other generators—or all of them for that matter—at Pump Station Four if you need parts. We're not going to need those for another year yet, anyway."

As he was talking, Larry suddenly remembered something else. He hung up and dialled a direct number for the RCM at Pump Station One, making rapid notes on the pad before him as he waited for the connection to go through. Then Willens' voice was on the line again.

"Willens, remember when that block valve—the first one we installed—cracked because we didn't have the proper refrigeration coils around it? What happened to that?"

"Jesus, I don't know," Willens said. "I think it's in a warehouse somewhere."

"Well, check it out, because I think it's around there someplace and you can cannibalize it to fix the block valve on the Sag."

"Good idea," Willens said. "Will do."

They broke off the connection.

Larry dialled Deirdre's office, which was at the other end of the operations building.

"Any luck finding your father, yet?"

"He's not on the base," Deirdre said. "One of the guards says that he saw him heading off toward town."

"Well, call town, or better yet, run down and get him. Do you think you can find him?"

"Well," Deirdre said, "the town's not too big. But it's awful crowded right now."

"Check the big Sheffield Bar and Restaurant. He's probably either there or at the Pipeline Club. I don't think he'd be in any of the other joints—certainly not in the Club Valdez."

"Yeah," Deirdre said, "but he might be with one of the guests in a room."

"Well, we only put guests in the Sheffield and the Totem Lodge—right? I mean, the big shots. And in a couple of mobile units. Can you check all those?"

"I will," Deirdre said, "and I'll have some of the girls in town get busy looking around too."

"Okay, get back in touch," Larry said. He looked at his watch as he hung up. It was only two-fifteen. Deirdre had apparently, on her own, had her crew of assistants handling press relations as the guests began to filter in.

At two-thirty—an hour and fifteen minutes after the accident—the external evidence of the disaster at the control unit had been eliminated, the fire trucks driven away, and only the clean-up squads left. Larry could

550

only hope that attention would be focused on the huge ship, now receiving its last couple of thousand barrels of oil from the five steel loading arms pouring into its bays. The loading arms, fortunately, could still be operated and supervised from the damaged control shack. Actually, the story of the sabotage could have the result of gaining public support for Denali. But he was not in charge of the operation and it was not his job to make public relations decisions or to be spokesman for the company. That was Doheny's job. It did seem strange that he was not on the base at a time so close to ribbon-cutting.

Wilbur Steele was in Anchorage somewhere, or probably had already left by helicopter to land aboard the Globtik Alamo, where a T.V. crew would be waiting. The plan was for Wilbur to be greeted by a small contingent of invited VIPs aboard the Globtik itself—the Secretary of the Interior, the Director of the Federal Energy Agency, Governor J. Hammond, Mike Bradner, the Speaker of the House of Alaska, ex-Governor and former Interior Secretary Wally Hickel, both Senators, various Congressmen, Joe Beck, the "Bard of Alaska", who would read a poem for the occasion, Eben Hopson, Isaac Samuelson, Charles Edwardsen, and other Native leaders, and Alaska's 1977 Snow Queen, Shirley Panieff, a tall, black-haired, Russian-Athabascan. The ceremonies were none of Larry's affair—that was up to Deirdre and her department. But he'd planned to be aboard the Globtik Alamo for the ceremonies, if only to say hello to Wilbur, whom he had not seen for more than six months.

After the ribbon cutting, the plan was for the dignitaries to depart and for Wilbur to accompany his ship through the Valdez Narrows, into Prince William Sound, and to return with the pilot to join in the final festivities. Larry was half-inclined to call Wilbur and ask his advice

551

in this situation. But Wilbur would have been of little or no use as far as the pipeline operation itself. Larry was sure he had done as much as could be done to cover the situation. In any event, Wilbur was not what one would call a technical man. There had been no mention of Brandon, but Larry assumed that his father's right-hand man would accompany him.

In Valdez, Deirdre had searched frantically in all possible spots—the Totem Lodge, the Sheffield House, Denali Headquarters, and even the small Municipal airport, where Doheny might perhaps be meeting one of the guests. Frustrated and worried, she decided to drive the four or five miles back to the terminal.

At Mile Marker 3.5, passing Old Valdez, the site of the town that had been wiped out in the 1964 Good Friday earthquake, and which had been subsequently used as a pipe storage yard, Deirdre slowed down. There were now only a few stacks of pipes stored there for emergency and repair purposes and these soon would be moved to the main terminal. What caught her eye was a familiar-looking International Travelall van. She pulled off the road and drove across the wide, flat, empty field, which looked east across the harbor toward the terminal, where the huge bulk of the Globtik Alamo could be seen clearly lying low in the water at its loading dock. As she drew closer, Deirdre could see that the Travelall was almost surely the one her father habitually used in his runs between the terminal and town. As she pulled alongside it, she could see that there were three men inside it. They were so absorbed in their talk that they seemed not to notice the small Nova as it pulled alongside.

Deirdre leaped from the car. The three men looked up in surprise. All three were familiar to her: one was of course her father; the other two were Bobby Baronian and Abby Maroon.

"Laboratory experiments in Britain and Canada have shown that the rate of natural decomposition of oil in sea water also depends on the temperature. It is much faster in warm water, and falls virtually to zero at five degrees centigrade . . . Canadian scientists . . . found themselves so ignorant of the effects of cold weather on oil that they resorted to the simplest of all experiments: a mixture of oil and water was shaken in a jar, and put in the freezing section of a domestic refrigerator to see what would happen. (The oil separated out before freezing occurred and formed a layer on top of the ice)."

—Noël Mostert
Supership

Chapter Fifty-five

In Deirdre's absence, Larry took the responsibility of announcing that the ceremonies would be delayed "due to technical adjustments." The television crews, which had been late getting in anyway, were pleased by the delay since, in any event, they would be taping for later broadcasts. Besides, due to the time zone differences, they would have plenty of time to make the six o'clock news coast to coast. At three o'clock, the dignitaries who had been given champagne and sandwiches to keep them from grumbling, were paraded out to the mammoth tanker, which was hung with flags and bunting, as was the three hundred and ninety foot long floating dock to which it was moored. Bleachers had been placed along the shore on both sides of the bay for the spectators and they were soon filled with a beer drinking, flag waving crowd.

Several small launches crisscrossed the bay with signs, "Keep oil out!", "Denali Go Home!", and "Kiss Prince William Sound Goodbye!" A few pickets with similar signs paraded around outside the gates, but the protest movement was minimal by this time. Larry postponed going out to the dock until the last minute, taking phone calls on the progress of containing the oil leaks caused by the sabotage at Prudhoe, and seeing to it that the restoration of the damaged equipment was well-started.

At ten minutes after three, Wilbur, who had been apprized of the delay at Anchorage, arrived as the Coast Guard Band, in flashy whites, played "The Stars and Stripes Forever." He stepped under the still-twirling blades of the helicopter followed by Al Brandon, to respectful applause from the assembled VIPs. Wilbur joined the group gathered on the broad deck of the Globtik Alamo, seated on metal folding chairs, and hastily greeted the invited dignitaries.

"Hello, Jay, Harry, good to see you. Wally, Mike, Ted, glad you could make it. It's an honor."

Deirdre had returned at two-forty-five. Accompanied by her father. Both of them looked subdued.

"You're kind of down at the mouth, Uncle Mahlon," Larry said.

"Well, hell, I guess it's all over for me. The job's done." He swept his arms toward the sprawling complex behind him. "The oil's running. Time to move on."

"Well, nothing to be sad about, right?"

"I guess not," Doheny said glumly. "By the way, Larry, thanks for taking care of things while I was gone. I hear you did a terrific job. What do you think caused it all?"

"From the way it was coordinated it had to be some kind of a plot, right? But I can't imagine who it could be. Probably one of those radical underground groups."

"Maybe some disgruntled labor elements. They've been doing a lot of sabotage throughout the whole job," Doheny said.

Larry shook his head doubtfully. "I can't see the

point in that. Not now, when it's all over. And besides, it's too organized for a wildcat sabotage."

"Well, I guess we'll get to the bottom of it—someday," Doheny said, turning now to greet Wilbur and other friends on the dais.

Larry had contacted Ship's Manager Coutts as soon as he had had a moment free and requested that the crew of the Globtik Alamo look for any further signs of sabotage. Coutts had the members of the crew each check their respective areas and no problems were encountered.

"Not to worry," Coutts told Larry on ship-to-shore radio-phone. "My men know this ship from top to bottom, and nobody's been aboard it except the pilot and Coast Guard officials since we left Japan."

"Well," Larry said, "I'm glad of that. In any event, it's your concern. My responsibility stops at the dock."

At three-fifteen a small flotilla of fireboats arranged themselves out in the bay displaying wreaths of water spray. Wilbur ducked into the Captain's cabin and emerged in a white boiler suit, to the delight of the television crews. Now the symbolic red, white, and blue ribbons were cut, the dock master signalled that the last drops of oil had flowed into the tanks from the steel loading arms, and got an okay from the control room to raise the arms, disconnecting them from the ship. The band played the dignitaries to shore, where they were to watch the departure of the ship from the enclosed reviewing stand, and then marched down the gangplank after them. Unnoticed in the crowd, a small long-haired Japanese crew member slipped ashore with the departing guests.

Larry and Deirdre were the last to go ashore with the exception of one TV pool cameraman who was allowed to stay aboard, while others covered from following helicopters.

Wilbur's face was bright with excitement and Larry thought he looked ten years younger in the white jump suit with the Alamo emblem.

"Well, kids, this is it," he said, taking them each by the hand. "It's the proudest moment of my life. And I want to say sincerely that I'm proud of both of you. You've done a terrific job. Larry, I heard how you took hold in the crisis out there, and I'm pleased to call you my son."

It was the warmest thing Wilbur had said to Larry since he'd shot his first double on a dove hunt when he was nine years old.

"You'd better get ashore now. We're behind schedule as it is." He shoved them both toward the gangplank and as Larry started down it, he gave Deirdre a playful but painful pinch on the rump. Deirdre turned angrily but was disarmed by Wilbur's cheerful and innocent smile.

"Friends?"

She paused for a moment and then said, "Friends," but her tone was low and truculent.

The huge ship, its whistles shrieking in farewell, was edged away from the floating dock by the four Denali tugs, also suitably bedecked for the occasion. The crowds on both shores cheered as the last line was thrown off and the biggest man-made object ever to float on the seas drifted out into the middle of the channel. When she was well placed in the deepest part, Port Valdez, between Anderson and Shoup Bays, four miles east of Jackson Point, the tugs gave the huge vessel a final shove and tooted their farewell. Slowly, and majestically, with Ivan Johanssen at the helm the ship wallowed out toward Valdez Narrows, making the minimum six knots necessary to maintain steerage. Ship's Manager Coutts gazed with satisfaction at the towering mountains above him. A brisk breeze had sprung up, quartering from the north and the east, and caused the banners and flags strung from the radar masts and superstructure to the deck to flap pleasantly in the crisp air.

Coutts supervised the young pilot himself, with Wallace and several other assistants standing by for the occasion. Johanssen made an adjustment for the wind. But there was no response. He moved the lever forward to increase the speed on the starboard engines which would turn them a bit to the east to counter the wind's force, but there was still no response.

All of a sudden, lights began to flicker and go out all over the bridge. At four o'clock the dusk had set in and the bridge was in almost complete darkness. Emergency battery lights were turned on and Coutts called frantically below to chief electrician Kato.

"Kato, what's happened? We've lost all power!"

"I don't know sir," Kato said. "There's some kind of fire in the control boards and in the main generators.'

"Well, sound the Goddamn alarms. What's happening? We're losing control!"

"I'll try to get you alternate battery power, Sir," Kato said. Alarm Klaxons and bells began to sound all over the bridge.

"That won't do any good," Coutts shouted over the noise. "That's not going to control the Goddamn ship! Let's get this vessel going! Wallace! Radio for the tugs. We're going to need them to hold our position."

He pushed levers on the console in front of him frantically, as Johanssen stood by puzzled and helpless.

"Both engines are completely out now. We're just laying dead in the water, and the Goddamn wind is coming up worse than ever. It looks like a forty, fifty knot gale there. She's pushing the ship over toward the shore." Coutts voice was taut with worry.

The Globtik Alamo was now gliding forward, still at four or five knots, under the momentum of the last kicks of the twin engines. Coutts watched with trans-fixed horror, his hands still frantically fumbling at the dead controls. He didn't believe this could be happening. The biggest ship afloat, with a million tons of Alaskan crude aboard—floating and drifting helplessly in the Valdez Narrows and now entering the three thousand foot channel that bottled the harbor, being blown inex-orably toward Middle Rock, the huge jutting stone tooth that divided the channel in two. It was all hap-pening so fast that there was no time for the tugs, which were three or four miles away, back in the main part of the port, to get there and lend any assistance, although Wallace assured him that the message had already gone out.

Standing in the harsh glare of the battery-powered lights, Coutts peered anxiously through the darkness, waiting for the inevitable crunching, ripping noise, a sound he'd never heard in his thirty-five years on oil ships, except in his dreams. The first contact with Middle Rock was so slight that it seemed only a glanc-ing blow and Coutts began to hope wildly that the ship under its forward momentum might slip through with only a few scrapes on its bottom. But now a sudden gust of northeast wind caught the broadside of the huge ship and he could hear the submerged tearing, rumbling sound—so far away, five hundred feet or more, that it transmitted only minor vibrations to the bridge.

"We've hit the rock," he said to Wallace. His voice was surprisingly calm and controlled.

"I know," the younger man said. His voice was quiet too. It was as though someone had died. "What's that smell?"

It was an acrid odor and there were noxious fumes now, coming from below decks—brown billows coming out. Kato reappeared on the bridge, his face blackened with smoke and tears, coughing, and wiping his eyes.

"Big electric fire below decks. The insulation is making bad smoke. Automatic fire control is out too. We're trying to foam it out with hand held extinguishers but the flames seem to be very hard to control."

Coutts could hear the bleating horns of the tugs, which were already arriving at the scene, with the fire boats not far behind. He picked up a bullhorn from a rack underneath the bridge and ran to the starboard side to look over. The rock itself—or the part that projected out of the water—was some seventy-five yards from the ship, which apparently had snagged on an underwater rock projection some hundred feet down. The ship had assumed a three degree tilt to the starboard and it was impossible to see what was happening below. From the duration of the sounds from below, Coutts was sure that at least three or four of the starboard wing tanks had been ripped.

Wilbur Steele, who had retired to the cabin to shave, freshen up, and to make several phone calls, came rushing up from below decks. "What's happened, Captain?" he asked. "The lights went out in the owner's cabin, and then there was this crunching, grinding noise . . ." A look at Coutts' fish belly pallor and air of barely controlled hysteria was all that Wilbur needed to understand the situation. "My God, no! It can't be!"

"If the salvage crew works fast," Coutts said, "we may be able to save most of the cargo, and the ship will probably be okay too. It takes more than a hole in the bottom to sink something this size."

"Well, what are you doing?"

"We've alerted the tugs and the terminal shore units as well as the Coast Guard. Talked to your people at the base—they're putting their contingency plans into operation. Now we're waiting for help."

"What's the damage?"

Coutts shrugged. "I can't see from here."

"Well get a chopper in. We can hover over the side and get a good look."

"Pretty dangerous with this blow on," Coutts said, indicating the wind which was now shredding the bits of flags and buntings hanging from lines stretched to the big deck.

"You don't know our pilots," Wilbur said. "They've operated in worse weather than this. Send for a chopper."

"I'll send for it, Sir," Coutts said. It'll be up to the pilots whether or not they want to go out. I know the Coast Guard will not go out in a blow like this."

"The hell with the Coast Guard," Wilbur said. "We've got our own men."

Once the ship was out of sight around the bend, the crowd at the base ashore had largely dispersed after a farewell round of drinks, into the rec hall or the more rowdy attractions of town. Larry Steele was exhausted and decided to have a drink at a party for terminal workers in the operations building before retiring to his bunk for a long solid sleep.

It would be five hours before Wilbur was due to return with the pilot.

The call from the Coast Guard station hit him like a fifty pound medicine ball. All the Coast Guard knew at that point was that the ship seemed to be aground on Middle Rock and without power.

"How did it happen?" Larry asked. "Was anybody hurt? Is my Dad okay?"

"Sorry, Sir. We don't have any information on that yet. We're sending relief vessels to the area from Sitka but it's still too windy to send up any choppers. Will you get your people busy on contingency plan A?"

"Will do," Larry said wearily, as he hung up and pushed the button for another extension. He dialed the harbor master's number. Budd Kowalski, harbor master for Denali, had already heard the news, monitoring the calls on radio.

"I know," he said, before Larry had a chance to say anything. "I've got boats going out with booms to seal off the narrows. If there's any spill we can contain it within the harbor and I've got a couple of other boats running absorbent booms around the ship."

"Do you know how bad it is yet?"

"Nah, it's too dark to see much. But there's oil coming out of there. You can already see the slick a half a mile away from the rock. We'll have to wait a bit for the winds to die down before we can do much. The ships can't operate too well out there in the heavy winds, although the sea isn't too rough."

"I thought they had maximum seven knot winds here," Larry said. "At least that's what they said in the specifications."

"Yeah, well, the little men who make the winds don't read the specs. I told them we always get heavy winds this time of year here—in the fall. Christ this is nothing—fifty, sixty knots. We get seventy, eighty sometimes. Sure—it doesn't happen that often, but when it does there isn't much you can do about it."

"Are you getting skimmers and the other stuff ready?"

"I've got the Union Husky skimmer and the oil recovery barge—they'll get out there as soon as the wind dies down. Also we've got six small skimmers and a large skimmer like the *Medusa*."

As they talked there was a sudden rush of air and a slight vibration. The whole operations building shook, as thought it was a minor earthquake.

"What the hell was that?" Larry asked Kowalski.

"Can you see it from where you are?" Kowalski's office overlooked the whole harbor.

"Shit, yeah, it looks like she's blown or something. There's a big glow from down there. That was one hell of an explosion."

"My god," Larry said. "My father's on that boat."

"Yeah," Kowalski said. "So are a lot of other people."

"Who can visualize the consequences of a . . . firestorm rising from a broken million-tonner . . . It would of course require some extraordinary circumstance to break the entire frame of such a vessel, but it is not unreasonable to suppose that at least one of its two giant tank-sections could be torn open and set ablaze in a collision. God knows the fireball created by just one of them is more than the mind can grasp."

—Noël Mostert
Supership

Chapter Fifty-six

By the time the tugs, fireboats, and workboats had arrived—less than a half hour after the huge Globtik Alamo struck Middle Rock—more than fifty thousand tons of oil had escaped from starboard holds three, four and five, all of them badly ripped as the huge ship scraped along the rocky bottom. The boats, battling stiff gale winds and an increasingly choppy sea, tried to keep their work lights trained on both the damaged and the offshore side of the huge tanker. Since all of the damage was below the waterline, all that could be seen was massive bubbling, black gouts of oil rising to the surface of the choppy waters.

Inside starboard hold number four, which was at a slightly higher angle than the others and therefore emptying faster, the sudden drop in the oil level had left a huge empty space with the volume of a small apartment house, filled with highly volatile hydrocarbon gases. The hundred foot hold was so vast that the action of the waves, blasting bits of spray through the ruptured side plates, began to generate enough static electricity to create a small thunderstorm within the hold itself. Thirty-five minutes after the Globtik Alamo ran ashore, hold number four exploded with shattering violence, causing the huge ship to develop a crack along the midship seam, and begin leaking oil now from two of the tanks on the starboard side. Altogether the ruptured tanks held at least two hundred and fifty thousand tons of Prudhoe crude.

On the bridge, after a brief consultation with Chief Engineer Harold Schiffman, Coutts ordered a general abandon ship alarm, the same one they had rehearsed so many times in the long boring trip across the Pacific. The ship was equipped with four fifty foot fiberglass lifeboats on gravity davits, each of which held fifty men—a total of ten more than the entire ship's crew. The boats were driven by diesel engines and had fireproof asbestos canopies to protect them from flaming oil or debris falling down from above.

The Globtik Alamo, with its full cargo aboard, had only about thirty feet of freeboard, so it wasn't a great distance to lower the lifecraft into the sea.

Now with the alarm klaxon sounding over the ship, crewmen abandoned their posts and rushed for their lifeboat stations. Due to the fire the two lifeboats on the starboard side were considered unsafe, and the entire crew began to load into the two port side boats. As the officers began to leave the bridge, Chief Engineer Schiffman said to Wilbur:

"We might as well leave too sir, and as quick as possible. There's not much that we can do about this. The fire and work boats will have to take over."

"I suppose a few insurance companies may go broke over this," he said grimly as they headed down the

564

ladders to the main deck, where Coutts was supervising the loading of the lifeboats.

The ship was now groaning and squealing alarmingly as steel plates snapped loose and rubbed against each other in the rough seas. With some of the holds empty and some full, the strain on the long, thin hull of the tanker was becoming unbearable, and there was a more than small possibility that the entire ship would break into two or three pieces. The two lifeboats were already bobbing in the sea beside the Globtik Alamo when Schiffman, Coutts, and Wilbur finally made it over the side to climb down the long steel ladders to join the rest of the crew. Coutts chose the forward ladder and Wilbur and Schiffman the aft one.

The wind, which had been shifting erratically, quartered to the west and increased in force. The two men held on with difficulty to the swaying ladders as they descended the ten yards or so down the side. Wilbur, still agile and fit, had almost reached the bottom rung of the swaying steel ladder and had one foot aboard the boat, with helping hands reaching up, when a sudden wind-driven swell threw the lifeboat against the canted side of the ship, causing Wilbur to lose his balance and bang his head heavily against the ship's side. Before the two crewmen who had started to grab the oil man's legs to help him get aboard could get a firm grip, Wilbur, stunned, fell into the space that had rapidly opened between the lifeboat and the ship. One of the seamen managed to catch onto Wilbur around the knee, but before he could pull him aboard the heavy hull of the lifeboat crushed Wilbur Steele painfully, twice against the side of the Globtik Alamo. At the second blow a gush of blood-colored vomit burst from Wilbur's throat and his eyes rolled back, revealing nothing but whites.

Two seamen scrambled to pull the unconscious man

aboard, while two others cast off the lines and quickly gunned the diesel motor to drive the lifeboat away from the dangerous side of the foundered ship. Wilbur lay between the legs of a confused and frightened young Pakistani sailor, bleeding heavily from his mouth, nose, and ears. One look told everybody in the boat that the battered man on the floorboards was beyond the help of any first aid kit. Chief Engineer Schiffman, who was in command of Lifeboat Two, came over to inspect Wilbur Steele's eyeballs and to check for a pulse. He shook his head doubtfully as the boat drove at full speed back toward Valdez harbor, through water already coated and gummy from spilling oil.

"Get this boat out of here fast," Schiffman said, "before that oil catches fire, or the whole bunch of us are going to be fried."

"Yessir!" said Petty Officer Wallace, who was at the helm of the lifeboat, as he advanced the throttle, so that the lifeboat was now slamming through the choppy two and three foot high waves at over twenty knots.

"What about him, Sir?" Wallace asked with concern.

Schiffman shook his head hopelessly. "He's still alive, but that's just about it," he said. "Anyway, let's get him and ourselves in as fast as we can."

Lifeboat Number One was also making back for the harbor at top speed—about seventy-five yards ahead of the boat carrying Wilbur Steele.

Schiffman, staring back at the tanker heaving and groaning, and breaking its back on the hard rock shelf, was surprised to see a small figure emerge from a below decks hatch onto the main deck. He grabbed a pair of binoculars from their case beside the wheel and trained them on the figure on deck.

"For Christ sake!" he said. "It's what's-his-name, the Jap. The electrician. Kato. I didn't know he was still on board."

566

"There's no way we can still get him now, Sir. That fire's really going. The deck plates are probably almost too hot to stand on right now. And anytime one of those other holds is liable to go."

"The small smoke-blackened figure walked slowly toward the forepeak of the Globtik Alamo, looking down at the steel plates below his feet as though searching for something. Schiffman kept his glasses trained as well as he could on the figure as the boat bounced through the choppy sea. He was surprised to see that Kato was not wearing a lifebelt.

"That idiot. If he's going to jump, he'd better get a lifebelt on. Although God knows he won't last two minutes in this cold water."

The figure of the Japanese electrician was growing smaller and smaller in his glasses as the lifeboat bumped across one of the containment booms into the slightly less oil coated waters of the inner harbor. The rest of the crew too kept their eyes glued to the tiny figure in the soiled white boiler suit, and watched as Kato, disappearing for a moment into the forepeak, finally emerged at the very prow of the Globtik Alamo, paused dramatically for an instant, and then leaped, stiff-legged, over the side, into the cold churning waters.

"That . . . that dumb slant-eyed son of a bitch," Schiffman screamed. "He's committing suicide."

But nobody heard the words because, just as he uttered them, there was an enormous shattering roar as two more of the rapidly emptying holds exploded. A solid column of boiling red and black flame clouds shot up into the air five hundred feet, like a giant propane weed-burner. The impact of the blast was almost enough to capsize the two lifeboats, which were now already some twelve hundred yards away from the burning ship. The men looked back in horror and awe as the whole surface of the sea took flame and the roaring, sucking action of the fire began to create hurricane force winds of its own. In the glaring light of the flame, the retreating seamen could see huge black clouds lifted by the self-created firestorm billowing high into the air, carrying tons of oil in fine droplets out of sight into the dark sky.

"... a one degree temperature change would mean that a greater portion of the icecap would melt. There would then be less ice to reflect heat back into the atmosphere (known as the Albedo effect) and more water to absorb the sun's warming rays. This in turn would lead to an accelerating temperature rise for the whole region, causing an ever-faster melting rate, according to the Wilcox theory."

—*The New York Times*
December 22, 1975
citing Dr. Howard A. Wilcox,
author of *Hothouse Earth*

Chapter Fifty-seven

Chief Engineer Schiffman had called ahead on the lifeboat's radio and the terminal ambulance was waiting at the boat pier below Jackson Point when Lifeboat Number Two pulled in. Huge crowds had gathered, some of them using the bleachers erected for the Globtik Alamo's maiden voyage, to watch the dramatic mounting column of flame, which climbed the sky and then blew westward over the Shoup and Columbia glaciers, along the towering peaks of the Chugach Mountains.

On the dock, Larry waited with Deirdre, Mahlon Doheny, Brandon, and Herb Carpenter, the base medic. The wind was still too heavy for a helicopter, or even an airplane, at the moment.

"With any luck," Carpenter said, nervously, as the lifeboat pulled into the boat landing dock, "we'll have your father out to Providence Hospital in Anchorage in an hour or so." (Valdez was less than two hundred air miles from Anchorage.)

The lifeboat threw a line to one of the assistant dock masters waiting at the pier. The dockmaster snubbed the line to a cleat and hurried to help the four seamen who were lifting Wilbur Steele's stretcher to the white-painted canvas-covered dock. Two television crews had arrived as the boat pulled in and pushed forward to film the arrival of the survivors. Lifeboat Number One had arrived five minutes before and one of the Indonesian messboys, who had suffered a broken leg during the transfer to the boat, was already splinted and waiting in the ambulance.

Larry rushed forward as the four crewmen, aided by the dock master, placed the stretcher gently on the deck. Carpenter, the medic, and D.D. were close behind him. He knelt down, peering closely at the drained, waxy, and blood-stained flesh of Wilbur Steele's face. The crew had wrapped Wilbur's body in blankets and strapped him into the steel mesh stretcher so that all that projected above the navy blue Globtik Alamo blanket was Wilbur's ruined patrician head. The medic gently pushed Larry aside, unfastened the strap around Wilbur's shoulders, pulled the blanket down and put a stethoscope to his chest. He listened closely for a few minutes, moving the bell to different positions on the chest, then folded the stethoscope and put it in his pocket.

"Too late," he said. "He's dead."

"What do you mean dead?" Larry asked. "He's not *dead*. Look at him." Larry peered closely at Wilbur's blood-caked and bruised face. It appeared to him for a moment that there was a twitch in the left eyebrow, and a quivering in the cold blue lips, as though to bestow some final instructions. "His eye, his lips—they're moving! He's alive, I tell you!"

The medic shrugged, and said regretfully, "Just reflex. Take my word for it. There're probably a couple of doctors in town today and we can get them here quickly, but you can believe me. I've seen a lot of dead men since I began working on this pipeline, and this man is gone."

Larry crouched down on his knees beside the stretcher and took Wilbur's lifeless right hand in his. Deirdre Doheny and Brandon stood close around him in a protective phalanx as the two television cameramen and several still photographers from the wire services and the West Coast papers crowded in trying to get a shot of the dead man and his grieving son.

"For Christ sake!" Doheny said angrily, "Can't you guys leave him alone? The man is dead."

"Sorry sir, just one shot, just one more . . ."

The cameramen and photographers all apologized but none of them stopped shooting. Larry replaced his father's lifeless hand on the blanket and stood up slowly, his eyes dull with shock.

Slowly pushing their way through the gradually growing crowd, Carpenter and his ambulance attendants carried the stretcher to the waiting ambulance. The medic put one hand on Larry's grief huddled shoulder.

"We're taking him down to the clinic. You can come along later if you like. Just to be sure, I'll try to get a doctor here as soon as I can."

Larry nodded wordlessly and Deirdre moved close to him, putting her arm around his shoulder as he walked off with his eyes on the ground followed by a still-busy queue of newspeople.

"Do you have any idea about what you are going

to do now, Mister Steele?" A reporter from the *Seattle Times* asked.

Larry looked up angrily. "Will you leave me the fuck alone?" he said. Then he paused and stood with his hands in his pockets, and Deirdre's arm still around his shoulder. He looked at his feet for a moment, as though for counsel from the ground. He took a deep breath, straightened his slumping shoulders, and looked at the waiting gallery of newsmen and curiosity seekers.

"You don't have to tell them anything, Larry," Brandon said. "Tell the bastards to get lost."

Larry threw Brandon a hard cautionary look.

"Listen, people," he said, "I've had a terrible personal blow and there's a major disaster still happening out there in the Bay. As soon as I can get myself together and get all the information organized in one place, I'll have a statement to make. Miss Doheny will let you know when that will be."

"Just one question," the man from A.P. said. "Are you taking over Alamo? Do you inherit the company?"

Larry looked at the man coldly. "I'll answer all questions at the proper time." He walked off toward the operations building, trailed by Brandon and Doheny. The two antagonists walked along in silence for a moment.

"You didn't have anything to do with this, did you Doheny?" Brandon said quietly.

Doheny looked up in surprise. "With what? What do you mean?"

"With that," Brandon said, pointing to the tall tower of flame and smoke still visible five miles away at Middle Rock.

Doheny stopped in his tracks and looked at the bigger man. "Say that again, you son of a bitch!"

"Look, I know Goddamn well you're mixed up in all

this stuff that's been happening. Now I just want to know if you're involved in . . ."

Doheny's arm drew back, as though to launch a roundhouse uppercut, and then froze in madair as the overwrought oil man brought himself under control.

"I hope we're getting a little too grown up for that kind of thing," Brandon said bitterly. "You know Goddamn well I could drive you right into the ground."

"Just watch your mouth," Doheny said. "A man died here tonight."

The two men trudged on in silence to the operations building where a growing crowd of newsmen were clustered outside, waiting for the promised announcement.

"How about it, Mr. Doheny?" they said as the stocky Texan approached. "You have any statements to make at this time? How is that oil spill going to affect Valdez Bay? Can you salvage the ship? How much oil has been spilled? How long will it burn?"

"You'll get your answers in due time, gentlemen, just be patient. We have to assemble our information," Doheny said as he retreated into the big pre-fabricated building. Susie Wing was inside, waiting for his return, her eyes tearful.

"I heard . . . I heard . . ." She started to say, but then broke down in tears and deep racking sobs. Mahlon Doheny put a clumsy arm around her shoulder and pulled her head against his parka.

"Pull yourself together, Susie," he said. "You're going to have a lot of things to do—things just have to go on."

"I know," Susie sobbed, "but it's just so terrible."

He stood back from her and held her by the shoulders. The black mascera with which she emphasized the slight Oriental cast to her eyes was running in ugly streaks down her cheeks.

573

"Clean yourself up," he said, "and then go outside and tell those newsmen to go over to the mess hall and get some coffee. See if you can find some drinks for them somewhere, too. Tell them that I'll be out there with Mr. Steele and, ah, Mr. Brandon just as soon as we find out what's happening. Tell them nothing will be held back."

"Yuh, yuh, yessir," Susie said, tottering off to the ladies room.

The four old acquaintances met in Mahlon Doheny's big birch-panelled office. He opened the bar in the wall, from which he took a bottle of Crown Royal, and poured four straight drinks.

"I think this will help a bit," he said, as he handed them the drinks. They accepted them wordlessly and sank into the chairs.

"Well," Doheny said, "what are we going to do? We have to handle this somehow. We can't stall those guys for long. Deirdre, what do you suggest?"

"Well," Deirdre said slowly, "I think, since this was really an Alamo affair, the senior executive should make some kind of statement. As soon as we can get some information, we're going to have to have answers about the insurance, the leakage, and I'll try to get some people together to answer questions about ecology—which they are bound to start throwing at us. Some of that can wait until tomorrow, when we'll have more information."

"Well, I guess as Senior Executive of Alamo here," Brandon said, "I ought to . . ."

"I'll do it," Larry said. His voice was flat and uncompromising. He retained only a little of the huskiness of grief.

"Well," Brandon said, "I don't think that this is the time to get into that . . . It's just that, I mean, I am

574

number two man in the organization—number one, now, I guess . . ."

"In the first place," Larry said, "you're not. There's still a chairman of the board and a few guys over you."

"I meant here in Valdez . . ." Brandon explained, finding himself off-balance and not entirely sure of the man was he was dealing with now, although he had known him since he was five.

"Brandon," Larry said, "Alamo is a family company. It always has been. The Bissets and the Steeles have always had the controlling stock. I know you've bought in quite a bit in the last few years and I don't begrudge it to you—not much anyway. But you know Goddamn well that my father's will leaves his stock to me and my sister—wherever she might be. And to a family-held foundation. Other than that, the only other major outstanding block of voting stock is held by my grandfather, Whitney S. Bisset. I reckon I'll have to admit that you've been my father's right-hand man for a long time, and I doubt there's been anybody who knows more about the financial operations of Alamo than you do today. If you can work with me, I'm going to need you. This company's in big trouble right now. I know that Dad was stretching himself and Alamo to their limits to make this pipeline go, and we ran into a lot of unexpected trouble—even before today.

"But I'm going to tell you one thing, I'm not going to stand around and see the company my family built up—my grandfather, and my Dad, and my mother too I guess—I'm not going to see it all go down the hole.

"I think you've got a pretty big stake in all this yourself, Al. If we go down, you go down. Now, as of today, *this is my company*. And when I want you to do the talking for it, I'll let you know. Don't forget it."

Brandon leaned back in the canvas directors chair he had chosen. Larry's speech, especially at a time like that, so soon after Wilbur's death, took him by surprise but did not entirely shock him. Since Larry's accident, Brandon had sensed a maturity and a hardening of purpose in the younger man. It was as though the physical strength he had lost was being siphoned off into other channels. There was a tense silence in the room. Deirdre looked at Larry with respect and a greater pride than she had ever felt. Her father's face was a blank mask; he sat studying the two men as though he were a spectator at a stage play—a cold-faced critic, not given to betray his bias. It was the face of a man in a poker game sitting between two wild raisers, and knowing that he himself held the winning hand.

Brandon stood up and went to the bar where he poured himself another bourbon. "I guess we can work something out," he said, his voice tight and controlled, but nonetheless sounding of deep regret.

"All right," Doheny said. "For the minute we're in the Denali terminal. You can take care of your Alamo business when the time comes. We'll set up a conference," he looked at his watch, "in about an hour. Deirdre, you round up any of those eco-freak friends of yours, get hold of Baronian—I know he's around here somewhere—"

Deirdre looked at him sharply.

"—and be ready to answer some tough questions. Larry, you've been handling the operational end of it. I'll leave it up to you what you want to tell them about that sabotage plot. See if they've identified any of the people yet. It seems like a Goddamn Commie plot to me, although I don't know what they'd have to gain. Maybe the A-rabs were behind it."

Deirdre could no longer control her impatience.

"I think after today, Daddy, we all *know* who was behind it."

Brandon looked at her with interest. He had his own ideas on the subject. Larry on the other hand seemed genuinely surprised.

"What do you mean?"

"Don't get in over your depth, Deirdre," Mahlon Doheny said, his voice edged with menace. "Just don't forget where your own interests lie."

"I know where my interests lie, all right," Deirdre flashed. "They lie with Larry and Alamo. I know you were bitter when Wilbur double-crossed you on that Mexican deal, but I never thought you'd go as far as you did to get even."

"What's this about?" Larry said, deeply interested.

"The gal's over-wrought," Doheny said. "It's been a horrible day and I think that she's just over-strained, aren't you honey?"

"I'm not over-strained," Deirdre said, in a level voice. "And I know who I saw you with and what you were doing with them." She turned to Larry. "Remember I told you long ago that I knew Baronian was hanging around with a strange group—and maybe I was a little bit too, I guess. Anyway, when you sent me to find Daddy, I found him with Baronian and a man named Abby Maroon from Fairbanks."

"I don't think I know him."

"No, you don't. But I know him. He was the leader of a group of crank radicals in Fairbanks. I knew something about them, but I didn't think it was anything serious. They'd put out leaflets and were complaining long after the Sierra Club and all those people shut up . . ."

"Are you sure you want to get into all this? Doheny protested.

"Yes, I do," she insisted, "but it probably will never get out of this room. And even if it did, there wouldn't

577

be any way to prove it. Anyway, I'm not about to try my own Daddy on a sabotage conspiracy charge."

"What?" Larry said.

Brandon seemed not at all surprised and kept his silence.

"As far as I can put it together," Deirdre said, "Daddy's been working for one client in Denali all the time he's been here, and that's Golconda. You remember, Golconda's had plenty of crude all along, and they were the last ones who wanted to get this thing on stream. They were always bringing up objections and were the first to concede any point that would result in a delay of the pipeline. I think Rawhide Robertson and Daddy got together. Daddy's going to need a good job when this is all over. And Golconda's the one that can do it. Maybe set him up on his own in some little side corporation. This job was never big enough for Daddy. He doesn't see himself as a hired hand. Right, Pops?"

Doheny was leaning back in the swivel chair behind his desk now with what was almost an amused glint in his eyes. "Go ahead. I'd like to hear your theories," he said. "They're very interesting."

"Rawhide Robertson provided the money, and Baronian was the bagman. He distributed it all to these radicals in Fairbanks—a scruffy bunch of hangers on and their friends. Basically all just living around Maroon's Swap Shop on Clay Street. I think when you check out the identities of the people who've been involved in this you're going to find that they're all involved in some way with Abby Maroon. They said it was an Eskimo guard who fired up the natural gas station in Prudhoe. And I know that one of them was an Eskimo from Barrow or Point Hope or someplace like that. I met him once. And as I understand it, the kid that got caught down in the control room this morning gave that Clay Street address in Fairbanks as his home base. When we find out who blew up the generators, I think you'll see connections. The same connections."

Doheny's weathered face now actually cracked into a rueful grin. "Well, it's a good theory and maybe you can make it fit the facts, as far as that one radical is concerned. But I don't see how you connect me to it."

"I don't see what else you could have been doing with Baronian and a guy like Abby Maroon, parked in an empty pipe yard."

"There could be lots of reasons for that," Doheny said, grinning broadly. The game was up and he knew it, but what difference did it actually make? He had succeeded in his goal and Deirdre was not wrong in assuming that he had a very lucrative offer to work with Golconda as an affiliated independent. But there was no reason to show his hand at this point.

Larry sat there for a moment trying to digest the information and Doheny, anticipating the train of his thoughts, hastened to interrupt them.

"Wait a minute, Larry. I'm not admitting anything. Right? What happened, happened. There's one thing I want you to know. I don't know what happened to that big ship out there, but I'll swear on my daughter's head, my mother's grave, or whatever you want, that I have absolutely nothing, nothing at all to do with the wreck of the Globtik Alamo. I don't know if *anybody* did. That was a heavy wind they had out there today."

"They lost all electrical power before they went on the rocks," Larry said. "It makes sense that if there was sabotage in the rest of the places, there was sabotage there. Are you sure you had a complete rein on all these maniacs you were subsidizing?"

Doheny held his hand out. "Wait a minute. I never said I was subsidizing anybody. But I'll stick to what I said. Neither I nor anybody that I know had anything to do with whatever went wrong on the Globtik Alamo."

Larry stood up, crossed the office and leaned on the desk in front of Doheny. "Look," he said. "I know the oil game is a cutthroat business. You guys didn't get where you were by playing nice-nice with each other. But I will personally guarantee one thing to you. If I find out you *did* have anything to do with the sabotaging of the Globtik Alamo, and the death of my father, I will kill you. And I don't mean that figuratively." His eyes were hard, and cold, and deadly. And his tone was chillingly convincing.

Doheny held his gaze evenly for a moment. "If you find out that I had anything to do with this," he said leverly, "I'll personally load the gun and put it in your hand."

The tension between the two men was snapped by the abrupt jangling signal of the telephone.

"I thought you told them to hold all calls," Larry said to Doheny.

"Except top priority. We're still in an emergency situation here, right?" He picked up the receiver and listened for a moment then handed it to Larry.

"It's Susy Wing. She says it's urgent."

Larry listened for a moment, acknowledged Susy's message with grunts, and hung up.

He turned to the group with a grim expression on his face.

"The saboteur at the control center—the woman who was shot—has just been identified. It's Penny."

There was a moment's shocked silence.

"My God!" Doheny said.

"I can't believe it." Deirdre seemed stunned with the news.

Larry looked concerned, but not surprised.

Brandon sat, stolid and unexpressive, as though the news was another personal defeat.

"For the moment, I'd like this news kept strictly confidential—until I can work something out . . ."

"Larry, the press is bound to find out," Deirdre said.

Larry slumped into a chair. He seemed suddenly to have aged five years.

"I know they'll find out," he said finally. "We'll announce something as soon as we can. I just want an hour or so to think things through."

> "Oil pollution is eons old, mainly on land although also in the sea; but it has required man and his oil tankers to make it an issue involving the survival of the living tissue of much of this planet."
>
> —Noël Mostert
> "The Age of the Oil Berg"
> *Audubon Magazine*

Chapter Fifty-eight

INTEROFFICE MEMORANDUM

Denali Pipeline
Service Co.

SUBJECT: Report and transcript sum-
ray general press conference,
November 18.

TO: Lawrence B. Steele, Mahlon Doheny,
A. G. Vaughn, Albert O. Brandon,
Distribution A

DATE: November 20
The press conference subsequent to
the sabotage attempts and accidental
explosion of Globtik Alamo on November 18 was attended by the following
people for Denali: Lawrence B.
Steele, Mahlon Doheny, Albert Brandon, Augustus Vaughn, Budd Kowalski,
Robert Baronian, Susie Wing, and
Sheryl Cook (stenographer).
 Press attendance was large-approx-

imately seventy-two correspondents and reporters attended. This included representatives of AP, UPI, Reuters, North American Newspaper Alliance, NBC, CBS, ABC, Westinghouse network, all local papers and radio stations and many of the larger city newspapers including reporters from all three New York City papers, the Washington Post, the Washington Star, the L.A. Times, the San Francisco Examiner, the Seattle Times, Time, Newsweek, U.S. News and World Report, Forbes, plus representatives of various public interest groups, i.e. the Sierra Club, Friends of the Earth, etc.

Also present was a considerable contingent of foreign press, including the London Times, Telegraph, Mirror, Mail, and Express, the Asahi Shinbun and other Tokyo papers, TASS, and the Arab News service. For quick study I have attached a summary transcript of the most significant questions. A full transcript is available for those who wish to examine it.

SUMMARY

FRED VINTON, CBS: "Can you give us a summary of the situation to date on the Globtik Alamo, Mr. Doheny?"

DOHENY: "Well, I've been talking to Budd Kowalski, the harbor master, and some of our other salvage people. The damage has been confined to starboard side wing tanks four, five, six, seven and eight, and portside tanks five and six. We have put booms across the entrance to Valdez Harbor and are attempting to confine the spreading of the slick to the inner harbor. High seas yesterday caused some spillage over the booms, but generally speaking the oil has been contained. Estimated spillage is two hundred and fifty thousand tons. A fleet of twenty-one recovery and clean up vessels is on the scene and tank barges are standing by to drain any remaining oil in the ruptured tanks when the fire has been brought under control. The ship has split into three pieces with the aft end believed in some danger of sinking into deeper water—which is approximately seven hundred and fifty feet at this point. If the aft end should sink it will not be a hazard to navigation as there will be at least five hundred feet of water over it. The midsection and bow seem to be well supported by the underwater ledge structure of Middle Rock. The cargo was fully insured by Alamo and the ship itself by its owners, Togo Tanker Service.

The fire is believed to be burning

itself out and we believe that as
the fuel is consumed we will be able
to smother the remaining flames
within several days. Of course, the
more loose oil that burns on the
surface of the water, the less there
is to clean up. So, to some extent
it is not bad that the fire is burning. We do not believe that it will
damage any structures or civilian
habitations in the area, as the land
on both sides of the Valdez Narrows
is largely uninhabited.

DICK STERN, NEW YORK TIMES: We understand that the firestorm effect has
raised clouds carrying tons of oil
into the air being dispersed at
levels above five thousand feet.

DOHENY: Yes. Our ecologist, Gus
Vaughn, tells me that this is the
natural effect when such a huge fireball is generated. But whatever oil
is swept up in the firestorm of
course will not remain to pollute
the Valdez area.

STERN: We have received reports
already of oil raining down from the
sky twenty-five miles away. Won't
this cause enormous ecological
damage?

DOHENY: It would be more appropriate
if Mr. Vaughn answered that.

VAUGHN: Of course, any spillage or deposits of oil are to be deplored. But we believe that the high winds and the minute size of the oil particles will result in an even and not harmful distribution. The areas in the Chugach Mountains west of here are largely uninhabited. We do not anticipate that the animal life will be significantly affected.

GROVER, SIERRA CLUB: In 1970, the black rain from the Norwegian tanker, Polycommander, killed hundreds of cattle who died from eating oil-covered grass. And that was only a sixteen thousand ton spillage. I don't see how you can say that the ecology will not be drastically affected. There are extensive moose ranges and caribou feeding areas in the Chugach. Besides, we have no idea where these oil clouds will finally leave their deposits, since they were last seen blowing over the Chugach toward the Bering Sea.

VAUGHN: I agree that there have been insufficient studies on the effects of this type of pollution. However, we are dealing with a much larger and less inhabited area here than was involved in the Spanish situation. And most of the forage is now covered with snow. We hope that by

the spring, the oil that has fallen
on the snow-covered ground will be
drained off into rivers and streams
and be sufficiently diluted so as
to cause no harm to the ecosystem.

NOTE: At this point there was a long
discussion between Grover, of the
Sierra Club, and Vaughn concerning the
effects of the Woods Hole and Santa
Barbara spills on the ecosystem. Vaughn
suggested that this was not a suitable
time to discuss other spills.

HIDEKI, TOKYO, ASAHI SHINBUN: Will
any of this airborn oil reach the
shores of Japan or Japanese waters?

VANGHN: That is very doubtful--at
least not by air.
(laughter)

GORDIAN, TASS: It is expected that
some of this oil may be deposited in
Chukchi Peninsula and parts of
Siberia. Is this not true?

VAUGHN: It is impossible to predict,
at this point, but it is rare for
airborne substances to be carried
such great distances. Almost surely
most of it will be dispersed and
will rain down on the sea.

STERN: Charles Rodney Weir, of the
Coast Guard Oceanographic unit in

Washington, reported in the <u>New York Times</u> that a test on polar ice of the effects of crude Prudhoe Bay oil indicated that such a spill would have a severe effect on the heat energy budget of the Arctic. According to Weir, Arctic ice usually reflects from ten to thirty percent of the sunshine that falls on it. But ice treated with Prudhoe Bay oil absorbed ninety-three percent of this energy. In a test he ran, oil soaked ice disintegrated and sank within five days, while adjacent ice did not melt at all.

VAUGHN: As you may have noted in that report, if you read further, no firm conclusions were reached as to the global effect of this melting tendency. We are still in a new area here and must have further data. However, we have had some cases of Arctic oil spills and they are still not growing palm trees in Anchorage. (<u>laughter</u>)

In any event, Weir's test was conducted with oil-saturated ice. In the present case, if any of the oil reaches Arctic ice in cloud form—and this is a big if—it will probably be so dispersed as to have no effect.

STERN: Won't the effect on the heat budget be the same? If oil is scattered in low percentages over a larger area?

VAUGHN: We have no data on that as yet. But it is not necessarily true.

STERN: Wier's experimenters tried scraping and cleaning the ice and said that it still melted at a much faster rate.

VAUGHN: You must recall also that according to Weir's report--and he was dealing with the possibility of a hypothetical barge spill, with highly concentrated oil contamination--that all of the contaminated ice in such a hypothetical spill would disappear within two years.

STERN: Yeah, but that's because it would all be melted.
(laughter)
But in the interval, what will happen to the water level and the salinity of the ocean?

VAUGHN: I don't think anybody is ready to answer that question as yet. But remember, it's a very big ocean.

BESS FOREMAN, AP: What will be the effect on the river systems if the oil comes down inland?

VAUGHN: Again, we haven't exact data,

but we believe the oil will be so
widely dispersed that the effect
will be minimal.

FOREMAN: A million barrels is a
lot of oil.

VAUGHN: Yes, but only a small percentage of it became airborne. And
remember that Alaska has almost six
hundred million square miles and it
has three million lakes of more than
twenty acros, and ten thousand rivers
and streams. It would take one hell
of a lot of oil to pollute all
that water.

FOREMAN: Well, you've certainly made
a good start on it.
(laughter)

ERIC SEWARD, ABC: We have reports
that a column of smoke from your
burning tanker can be seen as far as
seventy-five miles at sea. Will
you confirm?

VAUGHN: You'll have to ask whoever it
was that saw it. However, in previous wrecks columns of smoke have been
seen at a considerable distance.

EMIL SCHENBERG, FORBES: I'd like to
ask Mr. Steele what the plans are for
Alamo, and how this wreck affects the
financial structure. Is it true that

Alamo is over-extended and in a
dangerous cash flow position?

STEELE: Alamo's net worth is measured
in the billions. While it is true
that we have closed some of our
retail operations, and refineries,
Alamo's interests in the North Slope
oil fields and leases in the Gulf of
Alaska, the Brooks Range, and elsewhere promise a substantial flow of
oil and cash. Alamo is solid and will
continue in the family tradition of
service to the public, and to its
stock holders.

SCHENBERG: Will there be any difference in Alamo's position in ecological matters? Would you ship again in
a single bottom tanker? Isn't it true
that a double bottom might have
survived the impact on Middle Rock?

STEELE: I'll leave that up to the
engineers, but we will certainly
examine the situation. Obviously,
the contract with Togo Tanker company is inoperative for the next
couple of years, so we will find
other ways of shipping our North
Slope oil. I would hope we could find
ways of doing it in American tankers
with double bottoms, but this will
have to be worked out with our technical people and the Board of
Directors.

591

ALWYN REID, <u>ALL-ALASKA WEEKLY</u>: Since
Denali started operations in Alaska,
prior to this disaster, there were
seventy-five spills totalling over
one million gallons and this was
before the pipeline was even on
stream. Do you seriously expect that
this unacceptable level of spillage
will not continue?

DOHENY: None of those spills were
crude oil--basically they were motor
fuel in temporary installations and
the spills tended to be scattered
accidents in a major program which
covered many years. The recent incidents of course were due to exterior
factors: sabotage by a group of
radical fanatics, and security measures will be taken to see that it
will not happen again. I would like
to point out that existing security
measures and design elements resulted
in a relatively minimal damage to the
ecology and the pipeline in spite
of the efforts of this group of
crazies.

IAN WILLIAMS, <u>LONDON MIRROR</u>: Have you
identified any of the perpetrators
of this sabotage? Are they in any
way connected with the PLO or any
of the Arab extremist groups?

DOHENY: There were two saboteurs in
the Prudhoe Bay Camp, one of whom is

still unidentified and, as yet, we have no lead on him. The other was a NANA guard named John Takolik who had been working on the pipeline for some years. So far there are indications that John Takolik was associated with a group of people based in Fairbanks. Several of them are believed to have lived in quarters behind a place called the Swap Shop on Clay Street. A girl arrested at Pump Station Three is an accomplice in the destruction of the generators —she has not given us any information as yet. We cannot find any tie between her and the Takolik group. There is believed to be another perpetrator, a female, who was the leader of that particular cell. Witnesses are being questioned and we expect to have more information on that soon.

WILLIAMS: What about the group arrested here at the Terminal?

DOHENY: There are two suspects—one of whom was wounded by Guard Arthur Holman while trying to escape. That perpetrator is presently under police guard at Anchorage Community Hospital. The second perpetrator, Mr. Ernest Mason, has engaged an attorney and so far has not given us any further information. He is being questioned by the Alaskan State troopers and the Denali security people.

ALAN FISHER, UPI: What about that other saboteur--the one that was shot --can you give us any information about that?

DOHENY: That is a security matter. It is still an open case. No comment.

FISHER: Is it true that it was a woman?

DOHENY: No comment.

FISHER: Is it true the F.B.I. is conducting an investigation about the possible link between these saboteurs and a foreign group?

DOHENY: The FBI is not involved. This is purely a state matter. We are cooperating with the State Troopers in keeping this information embargoed until further investigation.

IVOR LANG, LONDON DAILY EXPRESS: Mr. Steele, is it true that there is evidence that the Globtik Alamo was sabotaged? There have been reports that a Mr. Kato, the Chief Electrician, committed suicide, rather than be rescued.

STEELE: The report as I got it from

594

the survivors--and I was one of the
first to speak to them--was that
Kato was trapped and tried to escape
by running to the forepeak. Unfortunately, he drowned while trying
to escape the ship.

LANG: I've talked to some of the
survivors also, and they report that
he wasn't wearing a life jacket when
he went off the ship. How do you
account for that?

STEELE: There is no accounting for
human actions during a panic situation like that.

SAMUEL PICK, LONDON DAILY MAIL: We
heard that the whole thing happened
because of a fire that started in
the electrical control systems. Kato
was Chief Electrician. How do you
account for that?

STEELE: If Kato had committed suicide it could have been over his
shame at the fact that the failure
occured in his department. So far we
have no evidence of sabotage.

ARNOLD GAYLE, NATIONAL ENQUIRER:
I've been informed that Kato's assistant is also missing. Do you have
any information on him?

STEELE: A Mr. Arakawa, the Second

Electrical Officer, is still missing
and can be presumed dead. No trace
of him was found following the
explosion.

ELLIE MORGAN, NBC: Mr. Steele, I
would like to extend my sympathy to
you in the death of your father and
ask if it's true that the oil on the
Globtik Alamo was not destined for
the United States.

STEELE: That is not true. It has
been established that there was a
surplus of oil on the West Coast of
the United States and further that
there was no harbor that could
accommodate the Globtik Alamo, which
as you know, was the largest ship
afloat. The oil was destined for
American refineries on the Virgin
Islands. It is a one hundred percent
U.S. operation from well-head
to refinery.

STERN: But isn't it true that the
oil will be coming into America, if
at all, at uncontrolled foreign oil
prices?

STEELE: The energy shortage will be
substantially alleviated by Alaskan
oil which is American oil and American controlled. It is in the interest of our national security. As
for the price, naturally we will

demand only rates to which we are
legally entitled.

SAMUEL RINEHART, FRIENDS OF THE
EARTH: Mr. Doheny, will you now admit
that the Alaskan pipeline has been
an ecological disaster for Alaska
and possibly for the whole world?

DOHENY: The Alaskan Pipeline represents the American way--the development of a necessary American resource
to suit American needs. It was the
most carefully researched and most
ecologically secure project ever
undertaken. It was also the greatest
privately financed engineering project undertaken ever. I think we can
be proud of our record. No enter-
prise of this size could exist without some occasional accident. On
balance I think we have a record to
be proud of. The tundra will survive, and the caribou will survive.
The seas will absorb the minimum
spillage we anticipate. And technology will improve as time goes on.
We believe that in addition to the
present oil fields, there will be
developments in the near future in
the Gulf of Alaska and in the Brooks
Range as well as Bristol Bay. Certain
mineral rights are also being looked
into. This should be a boon to the
State of Alaska and the American
people and the economy in general.

STERN: Is it true you will resign
once the pipeline is on stream and
go to work for Golconda oil company?

DOHENY: No comment.

NOTE: The above transcripts give an
idea of the questioning. Much of it
was hostile, but I think we got a
reasonably good break from the press,
and so far, because of the outside
influence-sabotage aspect, nobody is
screaming to break up the oil companies or deactivate the pipeline.
Despite the magnitude of this disaster,
it seems to me that by keeping an open
line to the press, giving them as
much accurate information as we can,
we can avoid a strong anti-oil reaction by the general public.

"We are all ready to be savage in some cause. The difference between a good man and a bad one is the choice of the cause."

—William James

Chapter Fifty-nine

The bullet that had entered Penny Steele's back was not a large one, but it caused extensive internal bleeding and severe damage to her liver and kidney. When the news reached Larry that the female saboteur injured at the Terminal pump station was his sister Penny he was not entirely surprised. Having learned that she had participated in the munitions raid on Fort Wainright had stirred suspicions in his mind that his sister might have been involved in the sabotage.

It was late in the afternoon of November 19, the day after the wreck of the Globtik Alamo, that Larry was informed. Brandon had gotten the news first, through his FBI contacts, the minute the identification bureau confirmed that the prints of the girl in the hospital were those of Penny Steele. Brandon took the liberty of putting a tight seal on the information as he had after Penny's identification following the Wainright situation. For the moment the Troopers and the FBI were willing to go along. They had their prisoner and the surge of publicity which would follow the revelation of

Penny's identity might wreck any chance for tracking down the other members of the sabotage gang.

Her face was sallow and the skin in her cheeks sunken from the loss of blood. Tubes of plasma, glucose, and other fluids dripped through needles taped onto her arms, and one tube ran into her nostril. In what seemed to be a sentimental mood for the occasion, Larry had worn his Stetson hat and pointy boots as the uniform of the day for his visit to Penny.

Because of the publicity about "radical terrorists" two Alaskan troopers had been assigned to guard the door to Penny's room. Larry showed the pass that had been obtained for him through the commandant of troopers by Al Brandon.

"Hello, paleface," he said with a grin as he entered the room. "You look like a raw tortilla."

"Nothing that a bottle of Pearl's and a plate of pinto beans wouldn't fix up."

He pulled the room's one metal chair up beside her bed. There were no flowers, cards, foil-wrapped potted plants, or other morbidly cheery artifacts to dress up the room. Larry sat down on the chair and stared into the hatband of his Stetson. Finally he said: "We'll stand behind you, of course. Me and Grandpa. That's all that's left."

There was a long pause and Penny said, "Thanks," in a weak voice.

"How in Hell did it ever happen, Penny? I don't see how you got to this."

"It was there all along," Penny said. "Even back in college days. It wasn't ever any different since I was a kid."

"Since Ma died."

Penny inclined her head slightly in assent.

"It wasn't just the oil and the ecology and all that was it?"

"Mainly," Penny said.

"But there were other things. I know you hated Dad."

"I had reasons."

"You think he was somehow responsible for mother dying, but he wasn't even there."

"He sent Brandon to pull the plug. I know it. I saw him go in there. He came out and then later people found out that she was dead and the respirator wasn't plugged in."

"It may have been for the best."

"Maybe," Penny said. "But I didn't want him deciding. It was just his whole way of using people and then throwing them away. She wasn't any good to him anymore, hadn't been for years. All shriveled up, probably brain damaged—I guess he figured it was useless to have the old hulk around."

There was a long pause. Larry got up and walked to the window and looked out at the tower of the Westward Hotel, the tallest building in Alaska.

"I wish you had been able to work it out some other way. This is really going to be a pisser. Not the sabotage thing, because we can square that all right. Not press charges or something. But there's bound to be a real blast of publicity when the news of your identity comes out, and that should be pretty soon."

"I wouldn't blame you for anything," Penny said. "That's what you have to do now."

"No, no. I won't have anything to do with pressing charges. But if the State steps in, who knows? It's the other thing. The Wainright thing. A man was killed. We'll have to get a top lawyer, maybe someone like Percy Foreman. In any event it'll probably be expensive."

"I don't care," Penny said. "I'd just as soon defend

601

myself. We didn't mean for that boy to get killed. You know that."

"Hell, honey," when you point guns at people, and they're loaded, there's a pretty good chance that somebody's going to get killed."

"It was a fuck up." Penny said, apologetically. "I wish it had never happened. Especially him being a Native and all."

"I can't see any way out except maybe going the insanity route. Is there anybody around that will testify against you?"

"A couple of people. But I think they're loyal, if not too intelligent."

Again there was an uncomfortable smile.

"So you're number one, now," Penny said, smiling. "The big range boss."

"Isn't it a bitch? Can you see me sitting behind a desk in a Savile Row suit dealing with those big muckamucks?"

"You wouldn't let Brandon take over?"

Larry grinned self-consciously. "That might have been part of it. Maybe I don't feel too differently from the way you do on that."

She reached a feeble hand over and touched him on the shoulder. "Larry, we were really close, weren't we? You're the only person on earth I really love, you know that."

"Well, thank God for small favors," Larry said with a tone of bitterness. "That will be nice when I come to see you in the booby hatch on visiting days."

"Larry, I want to defend myself. I want to take my punishment. They don't have capital punishment up here. I'll probably get sprung in ten years or so . . ."

"If they don't throw you out of jail for being an agitator. No, I can't let you do that. With the right lawyer

602

we'll get you off—or, at worst, you may have to put in a year or so in some hospital."

"It's phony, Larry. I don't like it."

"I don't think it's phony. I suppose you think you're sane? I've known you were goofy for years. I just didn't know you were a terminal crazy."

His hand was lying lightly on the coverlet beside her. She picked it up and examined his fingers curiously.

"Still got some callouses I see. These will all be white and manicured in a few years. Just like Dad's."

Larry shrugged. "I guess I'll put in a lick of work from time to time. As soon as these old lungs clear up."

He looked at his watch. "They're holding a plane for me out at International Airport. The fire's still burning and I guess they need me to coordinate some of that equipment they're getting in there, and answer questions."

"So it's starting in already," Penny said, smiling. "Pretty soon you'll have colitis, ulcers, high blood pressure, frown lines running off your nose, and gray hair."

"We're all different people, Penny. I'm not Wilbur Steele. He did things his way, I'll do 'em mine, and I'll still be me. Although, I guess I'll change a little. Having control of all that dough's gotta go to my head some way. But don't go thinking that I'm going to turn into him. I'm me.

He got up to go. "I'll be back to see you as soon as we get the fire under control, and we'll talk about your defense. There's no way I'm going to let you defend yourself. If you're going to have an idiot for your counsel, I'll pick him. When you're better."

He took her by both shoulders and leaned down awkwardly to try to fit his lips under the tube snaking over her shoulder and into her nostril. He finally managed a little peck. "Can you understand what I did— why I did it?" Penny said, holding desperately to him.

"I will never understand you. But you're family. I'll stick with you."

He picked up his Stetson and went out past the troopers.

One of them, a young earnest freckle-faced kid said, I'm sorry for your troubles, Mr. Steele."

"I'm afraid," Larry said, "They're just starting.'

"Anthropologists and others who have lived in the Arctic for only brief periods have written that the Eskimos see spirits in all things—in weather, rocks, animals, and so on. This, as far as I can determine, is not true. Rather, the Eskimo observes taboos connected with natural events, such as childbirth or death so as to avoid invoking the wrath of spirits. If a man knowingly or unknowingly breaks such a taboo—and there are countless such—then the hunting may be bad or the weather turn against the people."

—Duncan Pryde, *Nunaga*

Chapter Sixty

By the time the Rolagon ran out of gasoline Takolik had traversed the entire Wildlife Range and was at a point some two hundred and fifty miles east of Prudhoe. He had at first gone out from the land across the sea ice and it was not long before the wind drifted over his tracks. He crossed some invisible line—it meant nothing to Takolik—where the white man had said the United States ends and the Dominion of Canada starts. The Inupiat—the Real People—were not bound by white man's rules. They lived in the Soviet Union, they lived in Canada, they lived in Alaska. Only in Alaska had the Inupiat welcomed the oil barbarians. In Canada they had fought them off and they were still independent and free of the derricks and the trucks and the haul roads and the pipeline—for the present.

Takolik rolled the snowmobile off the Rolagon. When the wind died down a little he erected an Arctic survival tent—the snow was the wrong kind for an igloo. Inside the tent he disassembled the carburetor, dried the parts, put starting fluid on the distributor points, and after an hour or so got the motor going.

In late November it was cold—not as cold as it gets, but cold. Takolik had been driving for more than a day without sleep but he was not tired. Sometimes he had fallen asleep at the wheel of the Rolagon, but it would hardly matter, especially when he was on the great open sweeps of sea ice. There were no other Rolagons to hit, no trucks, no cars, not even any dog sleds.

It was dark most of the time, except for a few hours. Sometimes Takolik would see signs of animals that survived even in that cold white expanse the white man thought of as barren. There were ptarmigan, and occasionally polar bear tracks. November was good for polar bear. And there were signs of white fox and wolf. Takolik knew that in the mountains all winter— the mountains to the south — lived the ravens, the snowy owls, the gyrfalcons, and even jays and crossbills. Dall sheep wandered the North Slope where wind kept the snow cover light and the ridges bare. Far off, on the south side of the mountain, caribou browsed even now, hidden in the darkness.

Takolik slid the Ski-doo out of the tent and crawled into his Erwin Bauer sleeping bag and slept for four hours. When he woke up it was still dark. He took the trailer sled from the Rolagon with the supplies and extra gas tanks strapped to it. The rifle and a box of shells he took up onto the Ski-doo to ride beside him. He had gas enough for nearly a thousand miles, he had his gun, he had his knowledge of the Arctic.

He climbed astride the gently vibrating snowmobile and headed east into the Arctic provinces of Canada toward Inuvik, Tuktoyatuk, and the land the Canadians called the "Barren Grounds" stretching up to the Beaufort Sea and Amundsen Gulf. He crossed another invisible white man's line that separated the Yukon Territory from the Northwest Territory, then turned south, following the surface of the McKenzie River toward Port Good Hope. He had never been in this place, although he had met other Inupiat from the villages. And they were the same as he was. He felt comfortable, happy, light-headed, as if he could lift the steering wheel of the whining, bouncing Ski-doo, point it toward the moon, and fly off the earth.

Wind swept up the valley of the McKenzie and threw the thin snow cover into whirling clouds. Takolik steered the iron sled by sight when he could—by instinct when he couldn't. Soon the snow blew high and the air turned white—completely white. Takolik could see nothing ahead of him or behind him. Even the sky was a canopy of pure luminous white. As the Ski-doo raced through the white-out it seemed to leave no tracks on the shadowless ground.

Soon the image of the Eskimo disappeared into the drifts.

Sniffing the ground where the snowmobile had vanished, blending with the whiteness to the point of invisibility, was a small white Arctic fox.